Penguin Books
A Winter in the Hills

John Wain was born and bred in the Potteries, and still
finds the Midlands the most congenial area of England.
After graduating from Oxford he spent the next eight
years as a university teacher of English literature, but
decided in 1955 that this was not compatible with an
author's life, and gave up his post, since when he has
devoted himself entirely to writing. He has published
novels, short stories, poetry, a book on Shakespeare and
critical essays. He has more fiction and poetry in progress,
and finds to his dismay that the more books he writes
the more ideas he gets for more books, so that he has to
write faster and faster. He has not yet hit on a solution to
this problem.

Once a considerable traveller, Mr Wain nowadays prefers
to stay quietly at his home in Oxford with his wife and
three sons; his chief recreation is to go canoeing on the
small, slow rivers in which Oxfordshire is particularly
rich. In 1973 he was elected Professor of Poetry at Oxford.

John Wain's books *Hurry on Down*, *The Contenders*,
The Smaller Sky, *Strike the Father Dead*, *Nuncle and
Other Stories*, *The Young Visitors*, *Death of the Hind
Legs and Other Stories*, and *A Travelling Woman* have
been published as Penguins.

John Wain

A Winter in the Hills

Penguin Books

Penguin Books Ltd, Harmondsworth,
Middlesex, England
Penguin Books Australia Ltd, Ringwood,
Victoria, Australia
Penguin Books Canada Ltd,
41 Steelcase Road West,
Markham, Ontario, Canada
Penguin Books (N.Z.) Ltd,
182-190 Wairau Road,
Auckland 10, New Zealand

First published by Macmillan 1970
Published in Penguin Books 1974
Reprinted 1974
Copyright © John Wain, 1970

Made and printed in Great Britain by
C. Nicholls & Company Ltd,
The Philips Park Press, Manchester
Set in Linotype Pilgrim

To the Tŷ Gwyn mob

He had much industry at setting forth,
Much boisterous courage, before loneliness
Had driven him crazed.

W. B. Yeats

The solid Mountains were as bright as clouds.

Wordsworth

Part One

The man with the spade bent down and shovelled some earth on to Geoffrey's coffin. He seemed to be in a hurry to get the grave filled in and move on to the next. People were dying all the time; you couldn't hang about.

Roger looked down at the shiny coffin. Another spadeful of earth landed on it with a loud drumming sound. If Geoffrey had been alive inside that box with the brass handles, the noise would have given an unpleasant shock to his ear-drums.

It was time to go away. If only he could wake up from this dream-like state of unreality. He realized, now, that he had not heard a word of the burial service. It had been read by the cemetery chaplain or whoever he was, a nondescript parson with a beaky nose. This man, he saw, was hovering beside him.

'No other mourners, Mr Furnivall? Are you alone?'

'Yes, I'm alone.'

'Was the departed your only brother?'

'Apart from a couple of remote aunts in the West Country somewhere, he was my only surviving relative. Our parents were killed in the war.'

'How sad,' said the clergyman in a hushed, professional voice. His long nose looked as if, in cold weather, it would have a permanent dew-drop on it.

The man with the spade had almost covered the coffin now. Only one corner was showing, and part of a shiny brass handle. Good-bye, Geoffrey. Lie in the London earth.

'This is your second death, my poor brother,' said Roger into the grave. He ignored the clergyman and the grave digger and spoke the words aloud. 'At least it was more merciful than your first one. Good luck, Geoff. If you want to come back as a ghost, come and see me. I shan't mind. I'll always be glad to talk to you.'

The man with the spade chucked another load of earth and pebbles down, and this time the coffin disappeared altogether.

'Can I give you a lift anywhere?' Roger asked the silently watching clergyman.

'No, thank you. I have more duties to attend to here.'

'Got to bury some more people, I suppose.'

'We all go out through the same gate,' said the clergyman gravely. 'It's what we find on the other side that matters.'

'I wish I could believe that.'

'You heard the burial service. In sure and certain hope of the Resurrection to eternal life.'

'It's the hope that's sure and certain,' said Roger. 'Not the resurrection.' He held out his hand. 'I don't want to disparage your faith, believe me. And thank you for officiating.'

'I hope you'll get a rest now,' said the clergyman. 'This must have been a trying time. You cared for your brother deeply, I can see that.'

'I shan't get a rest,' said Roger. 'But I shall get a change. I'm going to North Wales for the winter. On professional business.'

They parted courteously, at the cemetery gate.

'I don't know your name,' she said. 'Here am I yacking away to you for hours on end and I don't know your name.'

'Roger Furnivall.'

'You don't seem to want to know mine,' she said, and gave him that smile again, half lazy, half mischievous. He could not quite read her smile. She seemed so relaxed, an indolent long-legged doll: was she sensual, her guard completely down, a push-over already? Or was she merely unconcerned?

'I do want to know it,' he said, giving her his full attention.

Her lovely mouth stopped grinning long enough to frame, 'Beverley Knockholt', or some such surname: Beverley, any-way, that was all he need remember. Anyway, if things went as he hoped they would, she might just as well have a number.

'I'm glad to know you, Beverley.' *Not as glad as I intend to be, when I've done a bit more work on you.*

'My privilege, sir,' she said half mockingly.

'Your glass is empty,' he said, rising.

'It should stay that way, really,' she said without much conviction. 'I'm very unused to drinking.'

Of course you are. Too young to need it. Your kicks come from elsewhere.

'Oh, well, just a thimbleful,' he said. 'To keep me company.'

Taking her glass and his own, Roger went over to the bar. God, this was a bit of luck. The Palace Hotel, Caerfenai. End of season. The last few tourists hanging about like dying flies. Waiters pretending to be busy. He had taken one look and re-signed himself to a slow death from boredom. And then, on his very first evening, this vision had blown in Or rather, popped in on her funny motor-scooter, all chrome, with a flag. California, rich, nineteen years old or perhaps as much as twenty. Touring, looking for fun and adventure, wide open to what came along.

'Well,' Roger said to himself, 'it was time for a change of luck.'

There was a discreetly tinted long mirror behind the bar and as he said this he saw his lips move and realized that he was talking to himself, actually uttering the words out loud.

The barman, a slick Liverpool boy in a short white jacket, came briskly along to where Roger stood. He was being very attentive to the customers in the hope of keeping his job through the winter. Roger got fresh drinks and went back to Beverley.

'This'll make me talk all the more,' she said, leaning back on the cushions and lifting her arms behind her head. The ges-ture brought her breasts into relief under the careless check shirt, and Roger, loosening his collar with a quick hand, prayed inwardly that it would not be long before he managed to shake her loose.

'I like you to talk,' he said, looking away from her breasts.

'At this rate, you'll know all about me and I won't know a thing about you,' Beverley said, but not as if she cared much. Perhaps, he thought, she didn't care much about anything. All that California sun, that impermanence, that tear-it-down-and-build-another attitude to everything. And her old man's money, always in the background – the foreground, indeed. There seemed to be nothing behind her eyes. Probably she couldn't even imagine a deep experience. Well, that was all right. She could leave the deep experience to him, as long as she delivered the right goods.

'There's nothing to know about me,' he said, drinking.

'There must be *something*. What do you do?'

I suffer. That's my profession. I walk the earth's crust aching all over with misery. 'I don't do anything,' he said.

'That makes two of us,' she smiled, all indolence again.

'But tomorrow,' he said with mock sternness, 'I intend to do something. I shall spend a busy day.'

'Oh? Doing what?'

'Showing you the mountains.'

She registered a flicker of interest. 'The mountains? The Welsh mountains? Are they near here?'

'The Snowdon range. We're on the edge of them.'

'I saw some sharp little hills. But mostly it was flat when I was coming here.'

'You came across the Denbigh moors. We've already settled that. And you didn't see the mountains because they were hiding themselves in mist.'

She stirred among the cushions. Her jeans, he noticed, seemed to have been applied with a spray-gun. 'You know the country well, Roger?'

'Not at all. This is my first visit.'

'Really? But you know where the mountains are?'

'On my way here in the train, from London,' he said, 'I unfolded a map of North Wales and studied it for an hour and more. As a result, I know where everything is.' His eyes flickered across her *balcon*. 'And it will be my pleasure to show you.' *I'll show you something you won't forget in a hurry.*

'But,' she demurred idly, 'you don't have a car. You said you rode the train from London.'

'Precisely,' said Roger crisply. 'We shall go on your scooter.'

She laughed at that. 'What a joke. You trust me?'

He nodded. 'Implicitly.'

Soon afterwards, they parted for the night. Roger put out a tentative feeler or two, but he had no serious hopes of getting the show on the road straight away. She had ridden her pop-popper a good many miles that day, stopping only for scratch meals. ('I got some fish and French fries and ate them right on the street.') She needed sleep. He would make the big *putsch* tomorrow.

The next morning, Roger was up early. He shaved carefully and paid attention to his dress and appearance generally. Standing before the mirror for a last inspection, he noticed the book that lay open on the dressing-table. Dr Conroy's *Beginner's Steps in Welsh Grammar*, printed at Pontypool in 1904. According to his original schedule, Roger would have been starting work on Dr Conroy this morning. He was glad to be departing from his original schedule.

Not that he intended to be idle. He had come here to learn Welsh. Philology was his profession, and a professional man ought to be constantly broadening his cope. Roger also wished to broaden the scope of his sexual activities. He had discovered that the University of Uppsala had a large department of Celtic studies, and he had reason to believe that if he added Welsh and possibly Irish to his scholarly armoury, and made a few contributions to Celtic philology, he would land a job at Uppsala. His motive for going there was that he liked tall, blonde girls with perfect teeth and knew that in Uppsala there were a lot of them about.

By studying Dr Conroy, and by staying for a month or two in an area where most people spoke Welsh, Roger hoped to increase his professional potency and set his sights definitively on Uppsala. On the other hand, that was a long-term plan, and his needs were short-term. Roger had often wished that a merciful creator had arranged the whole question of reproduction differently. Say a period of sexual activity every three years and the rest of the time in peace. *Homo sapiens* seemed to him an over-sexed animal. Still, this was the situation and he was in it like everybody else. A quick look round the hotel, on his arrival the previous afternoon, had disclosed no likely quarry. The girl behind the reception desk was a classic Welsh beauty, but that was the trouble : being so beautiful, and being on her own home ground, she would be booked up solid. Roger was realistic in these matters. At forty, he was no longer young; he was not rich; he had never been more than ordinarily good-looking. Such successes as he enjoyed were won by persistence and by never missing a chance.

Fired with this spirit, he went down to an early breakfast, then set to work. There was no sign of Beverley – she was the kind of girl who would sleep late, probably without realizing that there was anyone in the world who didn't. He wheedled a packed lunch out of the hotel kitchen, went along the street to a wine-merchant and got two bottles of hock, and stowed the whole lot in a neat shoulder-bag. Then he fetched his raincoat down from his room, and, folding it tidily on the seat beside him, sat down in the hotel lobby and watched the lift doors. Beverley was going to be caught when she came down to breakfast, and reminded firmly of their arrangement for the day. No wandering off, in a fit of absent-mindedness or change of mood, and giving him the slip. The dark beauty behind the reception desk threw him a cool and, he thought, slightly satirical glance as he settled down to watch his mousehole, but Roger was too hardened to care. His dealings with women had been like this since he could remember. Hit and run : grab what was going and move on.

Towards ten o'clock she came down. He had to remind her all over again that they were going for a ride in the mountains, but once he had made it clear that he was going to hold her to the arrangement, she acquiesced in that easy, unconcerned way of hers, as if to argue against anyone else's ideas was just too much trouble and she might as well be doing one thing as another. Under his watchful eye, she breakfasted, went up to her room, came down, and then, suddenly, all systems were go. Without delay she led him into the yard, pulled her motor-scooter off its stand, started the fussy little engine, swung into the saddle and motioned him to the pillion.

'Which way?' she called above the pop-popping.

'To the left,' he answered. And they were out, swerving among the traffic. The houses thinned, the road began to climb, Roger's theoretical knowledge of the terrain began to pay off, and their day, their wonderful day, had begun.

Even the weather was with them. The sun came out and dried the heavy mist; the sky turned from white to hazy grey, then to dim blue, finally to bright blue. Bees lurched among the heather. That day was the hinge, where the last of summer met the first of a full, golden autumn. The air, full of the salt of the sea and the wild fragrance of the mountains, delighted Roger's lungs. They climbed and climbed, with the fat little tyres gripping the steep, curving road. Roger kept his hands decorously on his knees, but every so often, when they heeled over on a turn, his body would brush against Beverley's, and the electricity ran through his blood vessels till he could have shouted aloud.

He still found time to look at the mountains, and to feel surprised. He had not expected such wildness and loneliness. The sprawl of cities was only just over the horizon, and the map would show some trivial height above sea-level, yet his eyes and nose told him that these were real mountains: hard, old and obstinate. Sheep clattered away indignantly as they puttered round steep shoulders of scree; torrents streaked the valleys; fat crows walked on the thin grass. Or were they ravens? And were there really still eagles up here?

The sun was hot and vertical. Time for rest, food and pleasure. Roger's eye began searching for a suitable place, an outdoor bedroom screened from prying eyes. Aha, there it was, above them. A cup of heather guarded by tall boulders.

'We'll stop here.'

'All right.'

She was all docility, as if she had left her own will behind when they set out. They dismounted, she swung the scooter on to its stand, and he led the way up a stony path.

'This'll do,' he said, dropping the shoulder-bag. 'A pity there isn't a stream to cool the wine. But one can't have everything.'

'Oh, but we have got everything,' she cooed. 'Sunshine, and vacation, and these marvellous views all round.'

Not quite everything, darling. That comes a little later.

Beverley's perfect teeth closed on everything he gave her; the wine gurgled down her creamy throat. Then, sticky with orange-juice and heavy with wine, she lay back on Roger's raincoat, which he had spread on the springy heather to make the simulacrum of a mattress. Her shirt pulled away from the top of her jeans, revealing a stretch of lightly tanned belly, an innocent navel. Every line of her relaxed body conveyed readiness for pleasure, and nothing beyond that readiness.

Roger drank down the last of his wine and tossed the paper cup aside. Then he was beside her on the raincoat, his lips on her lips, his warm hand on her naked midriff. The whole universe had suddenly resolved itself into a simplicity of male and female, and he was the male half and she was the female, and together they made up the whole of creation.

But she was twisting her face away from him, rolling on to her side, pulling the female half of the universe away from the male half. Not fiercely, not in fright, but in a kind of lazy refusal that hurt by its casualness.

'No, really.'

He waited. Two words? No more?

She sat up. But she still did not tuck her shirt in; her movements were still lazy; he might have been a fly she had brushed away.

'Why no?' he asked.

She shrugged. 'Does there have to be a reason?'

He was still lying down; the heather was springy under his shoulder-blades. 'It seemed too good a chance to miss.'

She looked down at him with cool amusement. 'Nobody grabs *every* chance.'

'But,' he struggled, 'what harm could it do?'

'No harm. I just don't want to, that's all.'

'You can hardly blame me if I –'

'Did I say I blamed you? You're just doing your thing. But I just – don't want to. I don't feel in tune with it, that's all.'

As she sat beside him, her breasts were so near. Her thighs were long and easy and knowledgeable. What right had she to bring it all so close, lay it out so enticingly, and then at the last minute douse his male eagerness with such casual, such trivial denial?

He said bitterly, 'Don't tell me you care all that much. One man more or less, in a lifetime of men.'

'I didn't say I cared much. I just said, I don't want to.'

He saw that he had made a mistake. He should never have appealed to her on the ground that the experience was too trivial to matter. He had reduced himself to the level of a male house-fly. Well, wasn't that the level she usually inhabited? Anger blazed in his veins, and he got abruptly to his feet. Beverley remained sitting casually on the raincoat, not looking at him. The sun had gone behind a small, thick cloud.

Roger's lust had turned to hate: he felt black inside, vindictive, ready for violence and cruelty. Some saving instinct made him turn on his heel and stride away. Leave her to sit there and think about it for a bit. He needed to be alone, to move his limbs, to let the pounding of his pulse die down in that sweet, silent air. Oh, gender, what a gift and what an agony:

the thought filled his mind like a sackful of sharp gravel. He walked quickly away, following the long ridge that crested the hill.

For half an hour, for forty minutes, he walked, gradually regaining control of himself. As he went, he talked himself back into reasonableness. Sexual adventures on mountainsides with girls like Beverley were the kind of things that happened to other people. It would be different at Uppsala, where he would be able to set the whole business up more carefully and proceed step by step. Now, he was cool. Suddenly, as a gust of fresh wind swept along the crest of the hill, he realized that this was true in a literal sense. An hour ago, it had been inconceivable that the day could be anything but blue and gold and hot; now, while he was preoccupied with his thoughts, the sun had been screened off by clouds, a breeze was mounting, and there was a distinct threat of rain. His raincoat – but Beverley had been lying on it, and no doubt she still was. He shivered slightly. On these unsheltered slopes, a rainstorm would be very trying.

Then he grinned. Ah, well. He had been forced to give up on the girl: no sense in giving up on the raincoat as well. Humour and realism, these came to a man's aid at such a time, and always hand in hand. He started to walk back to where he had left Beverley. After all, it would be a kind of victory, to go back to her in a smiling, genial, tolerant mood, a man of mature philosophy. He would even take her back to Caerfenai (he depended on her for transport, anyway) and stand her a dinner somewhere. That would show that his way of 'doing his thing', as she put it in the woefully impoverished idiom of her generation, would include generosity and humour.

His mind rinsed by these thoughts, his body hardening itself against the chill wind, Roger strode back along the ridge to the hollow where he had left Beverley. She had gone, and so had the raincoat. His leather shoulder-bag was there, the paper cups and plates were still on the grass and so were the two empty hock-bottles. That was her way: to take what she happened to want and leave the rest for the crows.

He climbed on to a rock and looked round. The world had changed colour since he last stood here. Opposite him, across the valley, stood a great dome of a hill, grass-covered to the top, which his eye had registered, then, as emerald green beneath the empty blue of the sky. Now the grass was sombre, its green lowered almost to grey; it seemed to draw light into itself and hold it, draining from the sky what little colour still seeped round the raw edges of the clouds. At the far end of the valley, where the higher mountains began, the grey stone slopes and densely heaped screes were suddenly menacing. Below him, the river wound rapidly through the valley as if hurrying to merge itself in the sheltering sea, that sea which now, as he turned slowly in a circle, his eye searching for Beverley, he saw spread out before him on the western horizon like a sheet of lead. Everything was battening down, rejecting light and warmth. It was lonely, cold and anti-human, so high up. Quickly, he stuffed the débris of that hopeful lunch into his bag, slung it across his shoulder, and began to walk. He could not see Beverley, but if he made for where they had left the scooter, it was a safe assumption that they would link up along the way.

Down, down he plunged, till the highest of the scattered small-holdings proffered the welcome shelter of its stone walls. He looked over at the cottage; no smoke, no light, yet the place was not dilapidated. Somebody's holiday base, alive at week-ends with erupting children, family cars drawn up outside, bearing Liverpool or Manchester number-plates; the rest of the time, dead. Well, the wall was useful. He stood flattened against it as the first wave of rain came whipping across, driving in from the sea. This was no joke. The scooter must be found, and they must scud before the gale back to warmth, light, a bath and a change of clothes. Nothing else mattered. His sexual emotions were as dead as if they had never been. The wind dropped for a moment, and he moved on quickly until, crossing a level shelf in the hillside, he came in sight of the road that wound down, on the seaward side, towards the slate roofs of a village and ultimately to the main coast road. There were transport, telephone boxes, pubs, garages, restaurants, all these things thickening as the road drew nearer to Caerfenai. At the highest point of this mountain road, just before it curved down to join the river-valley, they had left the scooter: and now he saw it, waiting on its stand in an attitude of patience, its front wheel off the ground, its soaked pennant drooping, its chromium plate gleaming as dully as water under the heavy sky.

The scooter was his first objective. He moved downward even faster, following the narrow path marked out by the feet of sheep and farmers. But the second objective, the scooter's owner, was still nowhere to be seen. And the scooter, he remembered with dismay, was secured by a thief-proof device which held the front wheel at full lock and could be released only by a key. Beverley had not only the moral right to the scooter, but also the physical means of getting it into action. Where the holy hell had the stupid girl got to?

Another rain-bearing gust, and now for the first time he felt the chill clasp of water against his skin. His jacket, his trousers, were wet through. And his hair was a soaking mop; really he must give up this affectation of never wearing a hat. He hurried, squelching now in an implacable wall of rain.

Here was the scooter. Yes, yes, he could easily turn the petrol tap on, easily tickle the carburettor, kick-start, get it going, but the damned thief-proof device was unyielding. The front wheel was locked almost at right angles. Rain poured over him like a sea-wave as he bent to examine it, tugging and shaking the machine in his irritation. *Where was Beverley?* He straightened up and searched the rain-blurred horizon. Had some dire accident overtaken her? Was she lying broken-backed in a gully, moaning to the incurious sheep? Somehow, he did not believe it. She wasn't the kind of girl to whom dreadful things happened; she was one of those people who can wave a wand and make life move their way.

As he grew wetter and colder, Roger ceased to speculate. Only one question remained: whether to stay here, or to start walking down the mountain. The coast road could not be more than two or three miles down, and before that there was the village, which might or might not have a pub. (Though nonconformist local authorities, he knew, had been able to see to it that vast areas of North Wales were publess. And if there were one, it would not be open for hours yet.) At one point he even started walking, but after a few paces a cold blast sent him crouching in the shelter of the wall. It was unthinkable. Surely she must be here soon?

How long he waited beside the scooter, Roger never knew.

He avoided consulting his watch – that way madness lay – and simply concentrated his mind on keeping warm. He could not get up and swing his arms about, being unwilling to forfeit the twenty per cent shelter afforded by the low wall. He decided, therefore, to tense his muscles, area by area: first his stomach wall, then his arms and shoulders, then his thighs, then his calves, feet and ankles, then back to the stomach wall again. It did not help much, but by concentrating on the effort he managed to keep himself from despair. Crouching, the rain sluicing over him as the wind veered and blew now from this side, now from that, and now appeared to be blowing vertically downwards on to him, he contracted his muscles so violently that his face screwed up with the effort.

'You look funny.'

Beverley, wearing his raincoat, had come up to him unheard, because of the drumming and roaring weather, and unseen, because of his eyelid-squeezing concentration.

'Oh,' He jumped up. 'What have you been doing?'

'Walking on the mountains in the rain. It was fun.'

'My raincoat fit you all right?'

'Yes, thanks.'

'I'm glad of that. Now shall we get going?'

She moved quickly to the scooter, unlocked it, turned on the fuel supply, kicked smartly at the starter, and suddenly she was in the saddle and bumping forward over the sodden roadside grass. As he went towards her with a 'Hey, wait for –' he saw, suddenly, that the face she turned towards him was full of cold spite. Little fool, she *was* angry, she *was* affronted, just like any Victorian miss, that he had taken her for 'that sort'. Through the beat of the rain he heard her voice: 'It'll do you good to walk.'

'To *walk*?'

'It'll cool you off,' she said. The motor surged, and she was gone.

Hugging the wet slopes, slapped by a wind from the dark sea, the village of Llancrwys prepared for another stormy night. Sunset still flamed along the rim of the Irish sea and over the vast stranded whale of Anglesey, but darkness had come already to this drenched hillside. Llancrwys was a village thrown up hastily during the Victorian heyday of the slate industry, to provide a habitation for the quarrymen who must, in those days, have given the place some sort of cohesion by all working at the same trade and sharing the same trials and dangers. Now, the great quarries on the mountain above the village were almost worked out; a few men still pottered about there, a few wagon-loads of slate rolled out every week, but Llancrwys had lost its *raison d'être* and, like all such places, it was sad and disjointed. Its barn-like chapel had probably not seemed like a barn in the days when it was the centre of life for the quarrymen and the families from the scattered farms on the hillside; now that it was never crowded, never flooded with joyously loud singing, it was like an old actor endlessly repeating a star role in an empty theatre. The village had no inn; its two grocery shops were both controlled by distant chain-businesses run by men who had never been to Llancrwys and would take care never to go there; it had no assembly rooms or library or market-place; the older citizens spent each evening staring at their television sets, and the adolescents took the bus down to Caerfenai or, if they lacked funds for this, stood about in the oblong patch of wet light thrown by the window of the fish-and-chip shop. So much for its social life. From an aesthetic point of view, the best one could have said for Llancrwys was that the uncompromising plainness of its terraces seemed to answer the bareness of the mountains and the uncluttered sweep of the bay. In the twentieth century, it had grown a tumour of red-brick council houses that did nothing to make it seem more modern.

Aesthetic and social considerations were entirely absent from the mind of the newcomer who now came sloshing his way down the gusty street. It had taken Roger nearly an hour's walking to get this far from the point where Beverley had stranded him, and his anger and gloom had increased with every soaking step. Nothing was going right, nothing. When he first came over the ridge and saw below him a few pinpoints of light in the dusk, his spirits had risen slightly at the thought of getting to a village. But now that he had reached the village he realized that this had been an illusion. There was nothing here. He might as well be marching furiously down the bare mountainside.

It was now almost entirely dark, and Llancrwys had very little street lighting. There were some concrete lamp standards in the crescent of council houses, and half-a-dozen old-fashioned lamps, with iron posts, in the main street where the chapel, Post Office and fish-and-chip shop were situated. This street lay horizontally along the hillside, so that Roger, walking rapidly downhill in the teeth of the rain-driving wind, entered it from above, at the crossroads which was evidently the centre of the village, insofar as it had a centre. He looked rapidly to right and left. Each street-lamp stood in a rainy pool of light. The window of the chip-shop gave out a yellow gleam, within which the loitering figures of three or four boys and girls bore witness that the place was not entirely depopulated. Otherwise it might have been a village struck by bacteriological warfare. Everybody was home from work, champing away at the evening meal or watching television. In many of the houses, Roger had no doubt, they were doing both at once, with the aid of frozen TV dinners and specially designed TV furniture. They were not gossiping in one another's parlours. They were not standing about in the street. They were not bawling hymns or arguing politics in the village institute, because there was no village institute. They were not drinking beer in the public house, because there was no public house. This was what nineteenth-century puritanism, the refusal to countenance anything more entertaining than a Chapel sermon, had led to. Not to piety, not to theological study, not even to poker-work and tatting, but to frozen dinners and commercial television.

Roger's teeth chattered. He moved a step or two in the direction of the fish-and-chip shop, the one blessed amenity left in a wilderness of closed doors and rain. Then, suddenly, his feet halted of their own accord. He was revolted by the idea of fish and chips. In the same instant he remembered why. Beverley's young, unconcerned voice; 'I got some fish and French fries and ate them right on the street.' Roger was cold, hungry, and liked fish and chips. But he could not, because of the bitterness he had still not been able to cast out of his bones, the bitterness of sexual disappointment and privation, bring himself to buy some and walk along the road eating them. He could not, for the moment at any rate, do anything that Beverley had done. Evidently he hated her. Or, at least, hated what she stood for: the release and fulfilment that were at present unattainable and looked like staying unattainable for a long time.

He began to walk downhill, leaving the main street behind him. Llancrwys had nothing to offer him. Perhaps this was no more than an emblem, perhaps the whole world had nothing to offer him. An outcast in cold, wet clothes, his hair plastered to the sides of his head, Roger felt his bones aching with pure grief. *I need happiness* he wanted to shout, suddenly, into the gusts of rain. *I can't go on like this! Make room for me somewhere, let me live!* The words came so strongly to his mind that he could not be sure he had not howled them aloud. What matter if he had? There was no one to hear him in this Gehenna. Nothing but slate and rock and rain and thin, impoverished grass, rooting itself stubbornly in soil that lay only a few inches deep on the unyielding rock, and had all the mineral richness washed out of it by the unceasing downpour. Nothing, nothing. Except rubbish, of course. Old buckets, bicycle frames, broken bottles, tipped into every gully. And even in the middle of the village! Why, here, right in front of him, not ten yards from the village crossroads, someone had dumped a derelict bus. Just pulled it off the road and left it, there on the verge, when it got too worn out to . . .

No, it was not a derelict bus. Roger saw, suddenly, that it was intact, and even that its paint was quite fresh, gleaming primrose-yellow in the deep dusk. He walked round it. The destination was written up in front: CAERFENAI. Somebody ran this bus. The tyres were inflated, the glass intact. It might even be going, fairly soon, to Caerfenai. (A hot bath, food, whisky.) No, no, his luck couldn't be that good. But he could get into it and shelter for a moment. If anyone challenged him, he was simply a prospective passenger, waiting to go to Caerfenai.

Shivering again, he reached up to the door-handle. It slid open. He went up the steps into the bus and slid the door shut behind him. At once the noise of the rain and wind subsided. He could think calmly and constructively, not give way to hysterical self-pity. The buffeting of the cold rain had begun to unhinge his reason. Poor naked wretches, wheresoe'er you are,

That bide the pelting of this pitiless storm. He saw what the man meant. It was quiet in the bus, and dry. The seats were of genuine leather; it must be an old bus. It smelt of leather and tobacco and oil, the smell of humble usefulness. He liked it. He liked his bus, his shelter, the friend that had loomed unexpectedly out of this night of wet disappointment. Perhaps things would start looking up.

Roger sat on one of the front seats. After a moment, he got up, leaving a wet mark, and moved to another seat. If he sat down in each seat in turn, some of the water would be squeezed from his clothes. Not very fair to the other passengers. What other passengers? Perhaps the bus had made its last run for the day. Perhaps it was here for the night. But did buses ever do that? Didn't they get put away in garages for the night? Usually, yes, but not in a place like this. Here, everything would be primitive, stark, unequipped. Roger began to sink back in dismay. It was dry in here, yes, but not very warm. He would get rheumatic fever or something, if he simply sat here for hours, waiting for someone to come and drive the thing to Caerfenai. Well, better get out and walk. A splatter of rain hit the windows, and he shuddered. Was there nothing he could do? Perhaps the bus had a heater. He went and sat in the driving-seat. It was a small bus, seating about thirty-six, and the driver was not partitioned off. The driving-seat was on one side of the engine cowling and there was a passenger seat on the other side; then the usual rows behind, with a central aisle. Roger fiddled with switches. The first one he found was the interior lighting. The whole bus was suddenly lit up like a ship on a dark sea. His spirits rose at once. Being in a lighted place made you feel warmer. And, of course, an electric light bulb does give off a certain amount of heat. He stabbed again at the row of switches, and this time the headlights came on, two hard fingers of light stabbing out into the rain, illuminating the swirling drops. Man fighting back against the elements. Roger felt quite buoyant now. But still there was no heater to be found. Well, in any case the heater would not work unless the engine were running. And that was out of the question. He could see where the ignition key would fit, but of course it was missing.

He sat in the driving seat, his hands resting loosely on the big steering-wheel. It was quite a comfortable position; well-designed, by somebody years ago. The bus was a real antique. He wouldn't be surprised to learn that it was pre-war, or at any rate about 1940. No, surely. And yet those rivets looked old-fashioned, like rivets on a tug-boat. And the real leather in the seats, terribly worn as it was, must have dated from the original building of the bus, so it must have been before the era of universal *Ersatz*. How interesting. Perhaps a museum ought to buy it. The controls, too, seemed large and well-made, as if they might have genuine brass in them or something. Roger cautiously moved the hand-brake forward on its ratchet. The bus shivered slightly. It was moving! No. Yes. It was perceptibly moving. Must be in neutral. Put the brake back on.

Roger did not put the brake back on. The front wheels of the bus rolled on to the tarmac of the road. He eased the steering over and the back wheels followed, each making a slight bump as it left the grass verge. Rain flowed across the windscreen; if he could have switched on the engine, the windscreen wipers could have been started, but as it was he had to look between the long streaks of rain. It was not too difficult, and in any case there was no traffic on a mountain road at this time of night.

The lighted yellow oblong began to slide faster through the darkness. Roger had the intoxicating sense of being embarked on an utterly improbable adventure. He pumped the brake-pedal a few times and found, to his relief, that the brakes worked well. There would be no trouble about holding the bus, even on a road as steep, and as wet, as this. He gripped the wheel confidently. He was driving! How about that, Beverley? He wished she could have seen him. *It'll do you good to walk. Cool you off.* Well, rusé old Roger knew a trick worth two of that. He just found himself a bus and rode down to the main road. Because he knew, now, that he was definitely going to do it. It was illegal, it was anti-social, but he was going to do it.

Roger sat back in the driving seat and kept the bus moving at a steady speed. No need to take it too fast. There was enough gradient to see to it that they wouldn't stop moving, and that was all that mattered. He concentrated on the job in hand. Good, well done. He was using only his correct side of the road, and yet the long bulk of the bus was moving quite briskly. Another village loomed up, one long downward street this time, with the inevitable dark bulk of the chapel to one side, and what looked like the equally inevitable bunch of council houses on the other. Hello, good-bye. Would he ever know the name of that village? Well, he must have gone past the bus-stop, but no one had tried to flag him down. But of course not, they knew their time-table.

The tyres swished on the wet road; walls and trees flowed by. All too soon, Roger felt the momentum slacking, and ahead he could already see the headlights of cars on the coast road. The escapade was almost over. From here, he could melt into the night and nobody would ever be able to prove that he had been near the bus. The perfect crime. And harmless. A little inconvenience would be caused, a little annoyance, but what about the inconvenience and annoyance to him of having to walk all that way down the mountain without a rain-coat? He felt no compunction. So long, that is, as he did not damage the bus. Careful now. Ease her off the road.

There was a broad grass verge close to the junction with the main road. Roger had to make up his mind quickly. He peered through the rainy windscreen at the grass as it came towards him. Was there a ditch hidden there? It didn't look like it. Must take the risk. He swung on the wheel. The bus moved obediently on to the grass, nearside wheels first, offside wheels smoothly a second or two later. Roger braked. For an instant he braced himself, in case the wheels should run into a hidden ditch and the bus settle over on to its side, but nothing happened. The earth under them was firm. He halted the bus. The wall beside him stopped moving and the stones looked in impassively through the window. The adventure was over.

Quickly, Roger switched off all lights, opened the door, got out, and shut the door behind him. The bus was just as he had first seen it. Its yellow paint still had the same pale gleam, the rain drummed in exactly the same way on its roof. He felt sorry, suddenly, that the brief and rewarding association between them was to end so abruptly and so finally. 'Good-bye,' he said to it, standing for a moment in the steady downpour, 'and thanks for the help. I needed it.' Then he walked rapidly away.

Here was the main road. Now what? The nearest bus stop? No, he was too cold to stand and wait. Let the next bus catch him up. And besides – he peered down the road in the direction he was to go – there it was at last. An illuminated sign. The Something-or-other Arms. The local at last. He would get a drink right away, and the rest could follow. Wet, cold, tired, but with the feeling that he was winning, Roger walked fast towards the pub.

In the Bar Parlour, a bright fire was burning. This took Roger's attention so quickly and completely that he had hardly a glance to spare for the customers who were already sitting about the room. Pausing only to ask the landlord for a double whisky, he made his way over to the mass of glowing coals and bent over it, letting the heat strike upwards on to his body. Steam rose in a large cloud from his clothes. For the first time for hours his skin felt warm, warm.

'Here it is, sir. Nasty night out,' said the landlord, setting down the small glass of golden liquid. 'Five shillings,' he added before taking his hand away from the glass. Roger, realizing that his appearance must give the impression of a tramp or perhaps an escaped lunatic, entered into the spirit of this last remark and paid up without a murmur, before picking up his glass and tossing the whisky down his throat. It splashed with a crackle of blue lightning into the frozen nerves of his stomach, and at once the blood started moving again.

'Aaaaaaaah,' he said quietly, and smiled at the landlord. 'Now I'll have a pint of bitter to chase that with.'

The landlord smiled tidily. He was a small, very contained man with rimless glasses that made him look more like a bank teller than a publican. He drew Roger's pint skilfully, put it before him, and said, 'Two shillings, please.' The 'please' was because Roger had established his claim to politeness by paying up like a gentleman before gulping his whisky.

Roger moved over to the fire, carrying his beer. He intended to stay in the warmth until it had dried him completely. Now and only now did he take in the fact that counting the landlord there were four persons present, all male. On the other side of the fire sat a small, skimpy man with a lined and weathered face, wearing a cap slightly too large for him and a pair of boots very much too large for him. Midway between him and the door sat a very young man with dark hair and a shy, unformed face. Only his eyes showed any character and these were full of watchfulness and care. Opposite where Roger was sitting now, just inside the door and under the lee of the bar, sat another young man, immensely thick-set and with a bruiser's mug. He had deep-set eyes, curly hair as wiry as heather on the mountain, and huge knuckles which he seemed to be examining attentively in the lamplight.

At the moment Roger entered, this quartet had been engaged in general conversation, in Welsh. It now entered Roger's consciousness that he had caught the last phrase or two of this conversation, before it died out into the silence naturally produced by the entry of a newcomer. This silence now continued for a moment, while those present waited to see if Roger intended to make any conversational overture, or perhaps to offer any explanation of how he came to be walking about hatless and coatless on a wild autumn night in North Wales.

To satisfy them briefly on this point he turned to the man in the boots and said, 'Changeable weather you get round here.'

'Well,' said the man, appearing to consider the question deeply, 'it is if you don't know the signs.'

'It caught me by surprise,' said Roger. 'When I had lunch up on the top' – he gestured vaguely towards the mountain – 'I wouldn't have said there was any possibility of rain. A perfect day. And an hour or so later, the heavens opened.'

'Ah, yes,' said the man in the boots. 'That's with not knowing the signs. It didn't surprise me because I do know them. I suppose every man understands his own trade.'

'Yes,' said Roger.

'It comes up quick in the mountains,' said the shy youth quietly, as if to himself.

'When you've got three hundred sheep to look after,' said the little skimpy man, stirring his great boots in the firelight, 'and they might be anywhere in ten miles of mountain, you learn to know your weather.'

'Yes,' said Roger again. He wanted to encourage them to take no notice of him. In a moment or two, he would become simply part of the furniture of the pub. Just another fool of a visitor who should never have left the big city. Not enough sense to take proper clothes when walking in the mountains. He was content for them to think that, to think anything, so long as they left him alone.

Now that he had explained himself, they turned back to their own conversation. Roger sat in the beautiful warmth of the fire, relaxing and enjoying the sound of their voices. The old shepherd did most of the talking. His voice was hard and resonant; like his boots and his cap, it seemed to belong to somebody much bigger. The shy youth said very little, and the boxer type only grunted as he studied his knuckles, perhaps trying to detect a minute fracture in one of them. The landlord carried the other end of the conversation; his voice was quiet and sounded ironic. Both he and the shepherd spoke North Wales Welsh, full of gutturals. Roger knew enough to recognize that fact, but as far as meaning was concerned he found their speech entirely opaque. It did not sound like a language any outsider could ever learn. Listening carefully, he tried to detect one word, or one combination of syllables, that he remembered hearing in any other language. Except that *ia* appeared to mean Yes, he had no success. Well, Dr Conroy (Pontypool 1904) would set his feet on the right road tomorrow, and meanwhile the fire was warm and the beer was well brewed, and his legs . . . his legs . . .

Roger drifted into a doze, a trance of comfort. How long he sat in this happy state he did not know, but he was jerked back to alertness when the door was thrust open, admitting a swirl of rain and, close behind it, three bulky and mackintoshed figures.

The first one to enter, a woman, was saying in a ringing Lancashire voice as she pushed the door open, 'It's only common sense to have something to drive the wet out of our bones. There's nothing for it but pneumonia else.'

'You're quite right, Mrs Arkwright,' said the man who followed her in. 'To say nothing of the fatigue. Good evening, Mr Parry.'

'Good evening, Mr Jones,' said the landlord composedly.

'Mrs Arkwright will take a little whisky,' said the man, 'and I don't think we could do better than follow her example, eh, my dear?'

The third newcomer, obviously his wife, nodded and said, 'Yes, Cledwyn, for this once.'

'Three whiskies then it is, Mr Parry.'

Mr Parry poured out the whiskies. The Lancashire woman, Mrs Arkwright, drank hers off in a way that revealed her as no stranger to hard liquor, and at once launched into an echoing recital of the ordeal they had just been through.

'Hubert always warned me,' she said dramatically, handing her glass over to Mr Parry, who wordlessly refilled it. 'My Hubert, when he was alive. If I go before you, Nell, he said, you'll be better off going back to Bolton. Be among the people you're used to. A widow's too helpless to fight her own battles. No, Hubert, I used to say. I'll live on in the home we've made here. And I do, for his sake. Because he loved it so much. But there's times, oh, there's times when I think I ought to get straight on a train and go back to Bolton.'

'And this must be one of the times, I'm sure,' said Mr Cledwyn Jones promptingly. He had an iron-grey quiff that gave his face an inquiring look, but his glasses flashed with certainty, as if he had settled all the queries that could ever arise.

'Well, I ask you. I appeal to your common sense,' said Mrs Arkwright, rounding on the shepherd and Roger. 'I decide to go down to Caerfenai, to have a cup of tea with a friend for old time's sake. I have no car. Hubert always did the driving, and of course he left me with enough to have bought myself a car any time I needed it, but I reckoned I was too old to learn to drive now. It's the bus for me. So I go and stand at the stop, in the pouring rain. I find Mr Cledwyn Jones and Mrs Jones there. Going to the meeting. A very important occasion.'

'Cledwyn's the secretary,' said Mrs Cledwyn Jones. 'He keeps the minutes. They'd never get on without him.'

Mr Cledwyn Jones modestly indicated a large and well-worn black book he was carrying in his hand. All present looked at it, and at him, with respect. Roger never knew, then or subsequently, of what association, club or body this was a meeting, but it evidently enjoyed high local standing.

'It's raining,' said Mrs Arkwright. Roger enjoyed both her vivid use of the dramatic present and the wonderful vehemence with which she flattened the first syllable of 'raining'. 'It's raining. We wait for Gareth. He's supposed to bring the bus down. He doesn't bring it down. The rain's running down our necks by this time and speaking for myself, I'm not dressed for it. I'm dressed for an evening in town.' She indicated her light, urban overcoat.

'Very open to saturation,' said the shepherd, shaking his head.

'After about a quarter of an hour,' Mrs Arkwright continued, 'we see somebody walking down through the darkness towards us and naturally we think it's another passenger. Another would-be passenger, I should say. But no, it's *Gareth*.'

'Walking?' said the landlord intently.

'Walking,' said Mrs Arkwright. She finished her second whisky.

'Bus out of order, then?' said the shy young man in his barely audible voice.

Mrs Arkwright shook her head. 'Not out of order,' she said. '*Missing*.'

A wave of disturbance ran through the assembly. Mr Cledwyn Jones opened his mouth to say something, but Mrs Arkwright continued. Roger felt grateful to her for one thing: if she had not been present, they would obviously have been discussing the matter in Welsh, and he would have been sitting there helplessly, trying to guess what they were all getting excited about. And this, after all, concerned him. He had been responsible for it, he had caused Mr and Mrs Cledwyn Jones and Mrs Arkwright to be late in getting to Caerfenai and also to get soaking wet. He had also caused humiliation and inconvenience to this Gareth, whoever he was.

'It's this kind of thing,' Mrs Arkwright declared, holding the floor, 'that makes me think the place'll beat me in the end and I'll have to take my old bones back to Bolton.'

'Well, Gareth has his troubles,' said the shepherd judiciously.

'I know Gareth has his troubles,' said Mrs Arkwright. 'But if Gareth's troubles are going to get too much for him and stop him from running a decent bus service, it's time Gareth let somebody else take the service over. There's people that need to get where they're going.'

The boxer-like young man stirred on his bench and said hoarsely, 'It's worser for Gareth than what it is for them.'

'I don't deny that,' said Mrs Arkwright. 'But when people

live four miles from the town they've got to have a bus service. Your own common sense'll tell you.'

There was a short silence and then Mr Cledwyn Jones said, 'The meeting will be half over.'

'But what about the bus?' said the landlord. 'Any idea who's taken it?'

'No one's taken it,' said Mr Cledwyn Jones, speaking quickly before Mrs Arkwright could open up. 'We all walked down the hill together and there it was at the bottom.'

'At the bottom?'

'On the grass at the side of the road.'

'Was it damaged at all?' said the landlord keenly.

'Gareth was just checking on that,' said Mr Cledwyn Jones. 'We left him looking at the engine and that. He said if it wasn't damaged he'd take us to Caerfenai. There were some other people there, the Idris Joneses and young Gwenlyn and George Roberts's cousin. But they were too fed up. They didn't accept Gareth's offer. They went straight across to the stop and waited for a General.'

There was another short silence. Roger imagined that downhill walk through the sloshing rain: this Gareth, mad with worry about his bus, surrounded by a platoon of wet, angry non-passengers. Had they scolded him? Or merely been sullen? Had no one taken his part? Who, in any case, was Gareth? Was he the driver of the bus, or its owner as well? And did he own a number of buses, or just one, the one Roger had put him in such an awkward situation by borrowing?

'It'll be all General soon,' said the shepherd. He got up deliberately and, his boots thudding on the linoleum, took his glass over to the bar to be refilled.

'It'd have been all General a year and more ago,' said the landlord, 'but for Gareth.'

'So it should have been,' said Mrs Arkwright. 'A big company's more efficient.'

'The fares'd go up for sure,' said the shy young man.

'Better that than have to walk through a rainstorm,' said Mrs Arkwright. 'You should have heard my Hubert on one-man businesses. I've seen 'em come and I've seen 'em go, he used to say.'

The door opened and this time a hunchback came in. He

wore an old leather jerkin, dark with rain, and a torn tweed jacket and navy-blue trousers. He was hatless, and his thin red-dish hair was pasted by the rain on to his great dome of a head. The face under it was clenched into a series of straight lines. It was a face that, even in relaxation, would look as if it had been blasted out of rock. The upper part of his body was as broad as a bull's, but his legs in their soaked trousers were short and frail. Roger felt a stab of remorse at the thought of those thin legs carrying that heavy body down the hill from Llancrwys. For this, as he knew at once, was Gareth.

'We've just been talking about you,' Mrs Arkwright opened up. Roger did not know whether to admire her blunt insensi-tive fearlessness or to be ashamed that an Englishwoman, among these intensely alien Welsh, could show such utter crassness. As if Gareth could possibly doubt that they had been talking about him!

'Is the bus all right, Gareth?' said Mr Cledwyn Jones. He spoke quietly and gently, perhaps to try to cover up Mrs Ark-wright's lack of these qualities.

In silence, the hunchback walked over to the bar. He took half-a-crown from his pocket and put it down on the polished wood. The landlord took a pint mug and a bottle of stout, opened the bottle and poured the stout into the mug, topped it up with draught beer from the pump, and handed it to him.

With the mug in his huge, calloused hand, the hunchback swivelled his head slowly round, as if taking in every detail of the room. But his eyes in their deep caverns were unseeing. They looked as unfocussed as the eyes of a blind man.

'As God sees me,' he said at last, 'this time I'll kill him.'

'Now, Gareth, now, Gareth,' said the landlord.

'I want everybody to hear me say it, man,' Gareth cried. His voice was deep, almost volcanic; like thunder from a cav-ern. 'I'll kill him before I'll let him take the bread out of my mouth.'

He lifted the stout-and-beer to his mouth, and lapped slowly, without setting down the mug, until it had all disappeared into that great tun of a torso. Then, putting the glass down dismiss-ively, he turned to the room at large.

'I got the bus outside,' he said. 'I'll take anybody in to Caer-fenai that wants to go. You going, Mr Jones?'

'They'll have moved on from the minutes, by now,' said Mr Cledwyn Jones, 'but I might as well show up and get them initialled.'

'Hardly worth going in, by this time,' said Mrs Arkwright, shooting an aggrieved look at Gareth.

'Well, take it or leave it,' said Gareth. 'I shall be coming out at ten o'clock as usual, and on that run the regular fares will apply, but I'll take anybody in now for nothing.'

He nodded to the landlord and walked out. Rain blew in on the wind as he opened the door.

'Might as well go,' said Mr Cledwyn Jones. He and Mrs Cledwyn Jones hurried out, followed by the intermittently grumbling Mrs Arkwright.

Into the silence the shepherd said. 'We haven't seen the end of this business. There'll be trouble before we do.'

'There's trouble already,' said the landlord.

'I mean real bad trouble,' said the shepherd.

Suddenly Roger was on his feet. He could not have said why, but he wanted to get back into Gareth's bus and go into town with him. A prudent person would have sat still and been thankful that the storm-centre, which had passed so close without touching him, was now moving away. But something had happened to Roger on the mountain. He was no longer a prudent person.

'I think I'll go into town,' he said.

'Well, it's free,' the landlord nodded.

With a quick 'Goodnight,' Roger was outside. He was just in time. The bus was still where he had left it, but Gareth was in the driving seat, the lights were on, and Mr and Mrs Cledwyn Jones were settling into their places. He ran, waving, just as the motor coughed and began to turn over.

Gareth leaned over and opened the door, turning to him for an instant with an indifferent glance of recognition. Then he slid the door shut with one powerful, practised movement, and the bus moved out into the main road, turning and accelerating. The empty seats vibrated, the transmission whined and drummed under the floor-boards, and Roger had the uncanny sense that he and the bus were sharing a guilty secret, as if together they had deceived Gareth and flung him into despair. But what was it all about? Who was it that Gareth was going to kill 'this time', for trying to take the bread out of his mouth?

The bus rattled into Caerfenai, and pulled up alongside a number of other buses in the wide square. Mr and Mrs Jones clambered out and hurried away, Mr Jones carefully shielding the society's minute-book under his coat against the still pouring rain. That left Roger and Gareth. In an unthinking reflex of meaningless courtesy, Roger stood back to let Gareth get off the bus ahead of him, but Gareth simply stood beside the driving-seat and waited. Naturally, as captain of the vehicle, he must get out last. Roger went quickly down the steps, feeling himself diminished, even shamed, by this squat figure with its motionless suggestion of strength and endurance. Gareth was obviously immersed in his own sombre thoughts, and saw Roger simply as a faceless passenger, someone who had happened to be present in the pub at the foot of the mountain and, hearing him say that anyone could ride into Caerfenai for nothing, had thriftily accepted the offer. He did not understand that Roger had impinged, briefly but sharply, upon his life and his dark, mysterious sufferings.

So the ride was over. Roger was standing on the cobbles of the square. Behind him was a statue of some frock-coated local worthy in an attitude of boundless, confident benevolence. Over at the end of the square, the dark bulk of the castle reared itself against the moon-streaked sky. On either side stood buses, some with people waiting in them, others dark and silent. Most of them, Roger now saw, had the word 'General' in large letters on their sides. He remembered the voices in the bar parlour. 'It'll be all General soon.' 'A year and more ago. But for Gareth.'

The rain had stopped, but he was still wet and chilled. The hotel was five minutes away. A bath, a change of clothes, a drink in the lounge bar before they closed? A polite nod at Beverley, if she were there, over the rim of his glass? It was tempting, in a way, but boring. Real life was not there. If Beverley had gone along with his plans, she would have been real life, but having refused him she had become meaningless, a paper cut-out. In any case, the hotel with its middle-class comfort, its pretentious, tasteless cooking, its clutter and paraphernalia, was trivial. Gareth and his bus were real; they held potentialities of tragedy.

35

Gareth had switched off the lights of the bus and was walking without haste across the square, pausing to let the thin traffic go by, making for a narrow street that disappeared into the medieval shadow of the town wall. Roger followed, as automatically as he had started to his feet in the pub. He had no choice: Life was beckoning. Dodging the cars, he crossed the square and trod rapidly over the blurred patches of light thrown by shop-windows on the wet pavement. He turned into the side street just in time to see Gareth, some eighty yards ahead, go into a pub. He followed, then stood outside the door, irresolute. He did not want to force himself on Gareth's notice. One the other hand, the situation pulled him too strongly to allow of drawing back now; he must go in, at least. But still he hung back, unable to nerve himself to open the door and follow Gareth inside. The solution was obvious. All pubs had at least two bars. Gareth had gone into the public bar; Roger would go into the saloon bar. Then he could take an unobtrusive look at Gareth from time to time. Why? He had no clear idea. To hear if Gareth was airing his grievance, collecting a knot of cronies, repeating to them his threats against the unknown adversary, or just sitting in bitter isolation. To eavesdrop, for whatever reason, on Gareth.

Roger entered the saloon bar. The pub was horrible. Perhaps Gareth had chosen it for its dismalness, matching his black mood. The air was stale, coloured a dim blue by tobacco smoke and laden with a faint but persistent tang of carbolic. The walls were decorated, if that was the word, with last year's advertisements for soft drinks and cigarettes. The bar was covered with formica, the furniture sticky with varnish. But the place had one advantage. The bar ran down the middle, so that the two rooms were on opposite sides, and the landlord served the saloon customers through a large hatch. This hatch could therefore be used for observation. From where he stood, Roger could see Gareth, who had evidently just got himself a drink and sat down with it. Gareth was alone. He was staring ahead of him as he had done in Mr Parry's pub. His sparse red hair caught the light and made his head, between those huge shoulders, look more than ever like a hornless bull's. A minotaur, robbed of his maze, facing his Theseus in a closed alley.

Roger unobtrusively bought himself a drink and sat down

where Gareth could not see him if he chanced to look across. He feared Gareth, yet he felt other things for him beside fear. What other things? He sipped and pondered. Awe. Pity: not the protective pity one might feel for a small trapped thing, but the tragic pity aroused by the sight of some mighty protagonist going down in a titanic struggle. Behind these feelings, he had to admit, was a layer of pure curiosity. He wanted to know what chain of events had brought Gareth to this pass. The hunchback's threat, uttered in that bar at the foot of the mountain, was no idle form of words. Something, someone, had driven him to desperation; it was written in his face, in those eyes which seemed to stare from wounded sockets, in that thin straight line of a mouth under the beak of a nose.

Approaching the bar to get his glass refilled, Roger took a cautious look through the hatch. Gareth was sitting as motionless as a rock. On either side of him, men in caps talked quietly over their pints of bitter. The clientele seemed almost entirely middle-aged. If young people in Caerfenai went to public houses, they went to other ones than this. The general impression was one of a solid, settled melancholy into which neither high spirits nor total despair would ever intrude. Gareth sat in the middle of this quiet assembly not as a stranger, but as one to whom the place and its inhabitants were too familiar to be noticed. He evidently had nothing to say to anyone, did not heed any stray remark that came his way. His whole attention was focussed on his problems, whatever they might be. Suddenly Roger felt a great wave of guilt. One thing was clear enough: Gareth's desperation was linked to the episode of the bus.

So there it was, the naked moral fact. He, Roger Furnivall, had injured Gareth. His mood of black recklessness, aroused by sexual frustration and indulged in one freak of anarchic action, had come to Gareth as the last in a long series of blows that threatened to beat him to the ground. What was to be done? Only one thing. He must have a few more drinks, get grogged up sufficiently to muster some courage, and then go to Gareth and own that it was he who had tampered with the bus.

Roger shrank away from this conclusion, but then he had realized all along that he would shrink from it and that he would nevertheless come to it. He was not a coward, and since he wished to be able to live with himself during what remained of his time on earth, he could not face the prospect of turning into a coward at this stage. Drink would be needed; well, drink was here. Going up to the bar, careless now as to whether Gareth spotted him or not, he ordered a large brandy, drank it, then took a bottle of beer as a chaser. The beer was a mistake. He had already had quite enough. But it was down his throat before he understood clearly just how much of a mistake it was. Confound it, he was drunk now. Sitting down, he looked carefully at the floor; yes, the damned thing was sliding about like bilge water on the deck of a ship. Well, there was no help for it. If Gareth dismissed his story as drunken babble, he would make it circumstantial enough to compel belief. All that mattered was not to leave the man under his delusion.

Firmly, treading down the waves, Roger went to the door and out to the urinal. Emptying, he breathed deeply and tried to steady his vision, without much success. Still, he felt more comfortable now. Forcing himself to move briskly, he went straight to the public bar entrance. It was simple: he would walk in, sit down next to Gareth, and in a few words tell him: 'I was the one that moved your bus. Not whoever it is, the man you want to kill. This time, it's nothing more sinister than –' As the words gathered themselves in his head, he took hold of the door handle. But it turned without his help, opened, and Gareth was facing him, filling up the doorway with his twisted bull's body on its shrivelled pins.

Roger was stunned by the sudden confrontation. Gareth, still taking no more notice of him than he had in the bus, moved mechanically to one side, his unseeing eyes brushing past Roger's face. This was terrible, he must stop it, but oh God, he was drunk, really drunk. He laid his hand on Gareth's sleeve. The great head swerved sharply to look at him.

'Just a minute could I –'

Gareth put Roger's hand away, quite gently yet with one firm, unambiguous movement. Roger felt a jolt of utterly unplumbed, metaphysical despair. Did he not exist? Could he impinge on nothing and nobody? Beverley had driven the motor-scooter past him in just that way. He must not sink out of life, become a ghost before his time, damn it, they must take account of him, he was a human being, not dead like Geoffrey, even if he was drunk, and what was so bloody wrong with being drunk . . .? He swayed, put his hand on the wall; Gareth had already moved several paces away, not looking back. Roger hurried after him and planted himself in his path.

'I want to speak to you f'ramoment.'

'Well, speak,' said Gareth.

'Your bus. You found it gone. Up there? You know?'

Gareth's head came sharply back as he looked into Roger's eyes. Into them? Through them, to the depths of his brain.

'What about my bus?'

'I moved it.'

Gareth put out an enormous hand and drew Roger close, holding him by the front of his jacket. 'How much did he give you?'

'Y' don't un'stand. Nobody gave me anyth –'

'Don't fool with me, mister. Dick Sharp put you up to it.'

'Wrong. I do' know anyone called Dick Sharp, and if I did –'

As he spoke, Roger suddenly saw that Gareth was going to hit him. He saw this as clearly as if he were sitting in a cinema watching a slow-motion film. But he was in the same film and he could not move any faster. Gareth was still holding Roger's jacket with his left hand, and with his right he delivered a single crushing blow to the solar plexus. Roger's face swung down to knee-level. There was a red mist before his eyes; his belly was a hard bunch of agony; he felt that he would never breathe again. From a long way off, he heard Gareth's voice saying something about Dick Sharp, but it did not matter any more. This breathless shock filled the universe. Had his heart stopped? Was he dying? Gareth's voice was joined by another, and above his head the two of them exchanged a meaningless jumble of sounds. Still nothing mattered. Then he felt a hand on his shoulder. He tried to shrink into himself, to disappear into the earth before Gareth could hit him again. But the blow did not come. Instead, the hand drew him slowly upright. 'You can come along too,' the new voice was saying. The red mist slowly cleared; he was looking at a policeman.

'You can come along too, to the station,' the policeman was telling him. Gareth stood by quietly, his eyes hidden in pools of shadow. 'I saw him assault you. We'll take your statement.'

Roger slowly put a hand on his belly. It was incredibly pain-ful to touch, but he felt, for the first time, that it would one day heal and allow him to hold himself normally. His abdomi-nal wall was not, he thought, actually *burst*. 'I don't want to make a statement,' he said.

'It's not a question of whether you want to or not,' said the constable. 'Let's get moving, now. Come along, Gareth Jones, unless you want the handcuffs on you.'

'I got to take the ten o'clock up,' said Gareth.

'You'll take no ten o'clock,' said the constable shortly. 'The night in the cells, that's what you'll take.'

'It's all a mistake, officer, said Roger suddenly. 'There's no need to go to the station.' He was sober now. 'He didn't as-sault me.'

'Didn't assault you? I saw him fetch you one in the belly. I'll have you in too, for obstruction, if you – ?'

'Officer, I refuse to make a charge. If you take me into court and say that Gar– that Mr Jones assaulted me, I shall deny it and the case will be dismissed.'

'No it won't. There's my evidence too. You're drunk and the test will show it.'

'Breathalyser tests are applicable only to motorists. I'm a pedestrian.'

'Been reading law books, have you? Come along and don't waste any more of my time.'

The constable seemed about to lay impatient hands on him and drag him away. Roger spoke quickly. 'Mr Jones and I were sharing a joke and he gave me a friendly dig in the ribs. That's what you saw.'

'If that was a friendly dig in the ribs,' said the policeman, 'I'd like to know your idea of a blasted good punch in the stomach.' He turned and looked for a long time at Gareth, who could not be said to give the impression that he had been shar-ing a joke with anyone. 'A joke, eh? Are you trying to make a fool of me?'

'Officer,' said Roger gently, 'why not let's forget the whole little episode? It's very right of you to be so watchful and alert, but anyone's vision could be tricked by the bad light.'

'The smell that comes off you,' said the policeman with cold dislike, 'is more likely to trick anyone's vision than the worst street lighting in the world. I'd advise you to go to wherever you're staying and sleep it off.'

He stood back, surveyed the two of them for a moment, then walked majestically away. Disapproval radiated from his back. He had probably been in the force about two years.

All this time, Gareth had been standing still, with that tremendous immobility of his, more emphatic than any motion, which Roger was beginning to recognize. Behind him, the twelfth-century stones of the town wall stood as motionless as he did. Now he moved his head to look directly at Roger, and it seemed in the faint light that his features had softened slightly, becoming less of a granite mask.

'Well?' he said.

'Well, what?'

'It seems to be your place to tell me that, mister,' said Gareth. 'What.' As he uttered the word again, a silent storm of laughter blew up somewhere in the great cauldron of his chest. He made no sound, but his mouth stretched apart and his whole frame shook, then steadied itself into grave watchfulness again. He jerked his head to indicate that Roger should accompany him, and together they set off towards the square.

Gareth said nothing more until they reached the bus. Then he slid the door open and said, 'We can talk in here.' Once inside the bus, he shut the door and sat down in one of the front seats, facing Roger. He did not switch on the lights; they saw each other clearly enough by the headlights of passing cars and the dim silver of the moon.

Abruptly, Gareth opened the questioning. 'You still say you don't know Dick Sharp?'

'Never heard of him.'

'Usually,' said the hunchback softly, looking out of the window at the square, 'when people tamper with my bus it's because of Dick Sharp.'

'I'll tell you how I came to tamper with it. I was walking down from the mountain in the pouring rain. I'd been with someone who'd – behaved in a pretty irritating way and capped it all by going off with my raincoat and leaving me stranded, miles up there. I walked down and by the time I got to that village – I don't know its name?'

'Llancrwys.'

'– Llancrwys, I was pretty fed up with everything and every-body Not to put too fine a point upon it, I was feeling savage and in no mood to care about other people's rights or their feelings. I saw the bus and got into it to shelter and rest for a bit. Then it struck me that I could coast down the hill and save myself a bit of walking. So without more ado I took the hand-brake off, put it in neutral, and coasted down.'

Gareth considered this. 'Ever driven a bus before?'

'No.'

'You're lucky you didn't kill somebody.'

'I had the lights on. And I was perfectly capable of stop-ping.'

Once more, Gareth's shoulders trembled with that sudden subterranean laughter, and once more he settled as quickly into stillness. 'You fancy yourself at driving a bus?'

Roger grinned. 'I don't know how I'd get on once the engine was running.'

'Oh, it's easier,' said Gareth quickly. 'She runs as sweet as a pony. The way you did it was much harder.'

'Who's Dick Sharp?' Roger asked suddenly.

Gareth was silent. His eyes followed a double-decker bus that moved slowly out of the ranks and away across the square.

'I'm sorry I took your bus,' said Roger. 'But it wouldn't have mattered much, would it, by itself? I mean, it mattered be-cause of Dick Sharp, didn't it?'

Gareth looked soberly across at him. 'You're on holiday, aren't you?'

'I know what you're going to say. Keep out of our troubles and we'll keep out of yours. If you don't know Dick Sharp, don't get to know him and your holiday won't be spoilt. That's what you're thinking, isn't it?'

'I'm thinking you're a strange kind of a man, mister.'

'Strange or not, you're damn' certain you're not going to tell me who Dick Sharp is.'

Gareth got up abruptly and moved over to the driving seat. He switched on the interior lighting. Now the bus was once again the lighted oblong that Roger had steered down the hill.

'Ten to ten,' said Gareth. 'I go back up to Llancrwys at ten. They'll be getting on soon.'

Roger said nothing.

'Dic Sharp,' said Gareth, and all at once Roger visualized the name and understood that it had no 'k', 'owns two businesses round here. One's haulage and the other's building materials. A couple of years ago he thought he'd go into buses. All the main routes are worked by General, but the village services, up and down the mountains, were mostly small men, with two or three buses or with one, like me.'

A stout, breathless old woman approached the door of the bus, accompanied by a young woman who might have been her daughter or niece. They opened the door, then halted and began the final bout of their evening's conversation. Their high, plangent Welsh flooded into the bright stillness in which Roger and Gareth sat.

'Dic Sharp didn't get on well with the buses,' Gareth went on steadily. 'He's still got them, but he reckons they're too much trouble to run. He wants to sell out to General. And they won't buy from him until he's got all the local services. They're only interested if they can buy the complete set, everything this side of Pwllheli.'

Two thin men walked round the old woman and climbed on to the bus. Arguing softly, they went to the back seat.

'Dic Sharp's a rich man,' said Gareth. 'He started with nothing. I went to the village school with him at Llancrwys. But he's a clever head on his shoulders, isn't it? He's not telling anybody what he's worth, specially not the tax man, but it's plenty. The other owners sold up, one by one. Some were glad to sell, some didn't care much, and one or two didn't want to sell at all. But somehow, they found it wasn't worth hanging on. Not with Dic Sharp against them.'

Gareth put the key into the ignition and started the engine. The lights dimmed for a second, then shone brightly again; the bus began to throb gently. The two women stepped up the pace and volume of their conversation.

'I won't sell,' said the hunchback, looking straight ahead of him through the windscreen. 'I'm the only one left and I won't sell.'

Several more passengers entered the bus. The fat woman finally kissed her niece or daughter several times, addressing her as 'cariad', and slowly mounted the steps. Roger now understood Gareth's situation. He had the answer to his question;

it was time for him to get off the bus, to take himself out of the situation and out of Gareth's life.

'I have to collect the fares,' said Gareth. He took a leather bag from beside the driving-seat and slung it across his shoulder. Then he began moving deliberately down the bus, inquiring destinations and taking fares. Roger, watching him, had to fight down an absurd impulse to go to him and offer to collect the money while Gareth drove the bus. Absurd? Well, illogical at least. He felt, obscurely, a need to help Gareth, to succour him in his struggle against Dic Sharp. Without help, how could Gareth hold out? He remembered the voice of Mr Cledwyn Jones: 'If Gareth can't run the service he ought to sell out.' And Dic Sharp, no doubt, had his methods of making sure that Gareth would not be able to run the service.

Gareth came back down the bus, his bag clinking. He paused by Roger's seat, looking down at him with something like a friendly expression. He looked like a huge bird of prey, schooled by never-ceasing adversity, trying to smile with features not adapted for smiling.

'I won't ask you for a fare,' he said. 'It's a one-way run up to Llancrwys. You won't want to be stuck up on the mountain again.'

'Not twice in one night,' Roger agreed. Gareth nodded and went to the driving-seat. It was time to go, time to bid a final adieu to this strange little adventure. With reluctance, he rose. The bus, brightly lit and full of animated talk, seemed an oasis of life. Outside was the dark, windy square; beyond it, the mausoleum of the Palace Hotel and his lonely room.

Gareth looked round inquiringly, seeming to ask whether Roger had, after all, decided to travel. Roger smiled, shook his head and climbed down the steps. The bus shuddered into motion, rattled across the cobbles and moved slowly away down the street. Roger stood watching it go. After it had disappeared round a corner, he still stood looking after it, till a cold gust of wind brought his attention back to his own concerns. He was cold, he was not quite dry, his belly was sore, his mouth had a bad taste. He looked up: the statue of the local worthy, with its expression of perfect confidence, was gazing straight ahead, above him, as if teaching the world, by example, to ignore Roger's existence.

He had left his shoulder-bag in the saloon of that dismal pub. Well, let it stay there. He would buy a new one, with no unpleasant associations. Slowly, he moved off in the direction of the Palace Hotel. As he went, it occurred to him that at no time during their conversation had Gareth expressed any regret at having punched him in the stomach.

Fired by an energy whose source was obscure to him, Roger got up early the next morning and after a quick breakfast settled down in the hotel's writing-room with Dr Conroy's *Beginner's Steps in Welsh Grammar*. He worked fast and efficiently for three hours; then his brain suddenly switched itself off, refusing to take in any more without a rest. Never mind; he had surveyed the persons and tenses of the verbs Bod, Cael, Gwneud and Dod; he had noted the seven ways in which Welsh can form a plural; and he had absorbed the procedures for mutation (soft), mutation (nasal) and mutation (aspirate or spirant).

A brisk walk would oxygenate his bloodstream and prepare the brain for another bout of assimilation. He went to the lift and pressed the button for his floor, intending to leave Dr Conroy and pick up his raincoat, but as the lift moved upwards he suddenly realized that he had last seen his raincoat on Beverley. Good God! He had forgotten the girl completely. How was that possible? Only eighteen hours ago, she had been the focus of such intense feeling of one kind and another; yet he had gone through almost a whole morning without recalling her to consciousness. Unlocking his door, putting Dr Conroy down on the dressing-table, he searched vaguely for an explanation, but none came. Unless it was – the thought formed itself mistily, evading the full grasp of his mind – that the whole episode with Beverley had been unreal, had been founded on unreality, and that he had since been through a real experience: the real drives out the unreal, Gareth and his predicament had blotted out the shallow, tedious trap-laying into which his physical need had led him. That need was still real enough (he sighed), but the long-legged puppet with whom he had hoped to quench it had twitched away out of his life.

On the other hand, he would have liked to get his raincoat back.

For the moment, the weather was fine enough to go out

without it. As he emerged from the swing doors of the hotel, the salty air lifted Roger's spirits and seemed to take the weight out of his limbs. He walked, he breathed, he admired the sunlight on the brave old towers of the castle, he looked with approval at the small boats riding the water of the harbour and the gulls riding the wind above them. Where a few words of Welsh reached him from a conversation in some shop doorway or sheltered corner, he slowed to listen, and it seemed to him that the shape and texture of the language were becoming familiar to him. In another few hours, that mysterious switch would turn itself on in his brain, and he would suddenly find that the intelligibility barrier was broken. Onward! The joy of learning a language, of exercising his professional aptitude, gave him a bracing sense of power and usefulness, matching the exhilaration that came from outside, from the sun and the strong air. His walk had refreshed him, he was ready to work again; not quite at full pressure, though. His eye fell on a newsagent's window. Yes! Get a Welsh newspaper, and sit quietly looking at it, getting some idea of mutations, puzzling out the vocabulary where possible, over a pint of beer. An excellent idea, typical of experienced and efficient Roger, scholarly, intellectual Roger, the brain-manager.

The shop yielded an unexpected treasure: the local paper, it seemed, put out a Welsh-language edition. Roger bore it away with a real sense of excited anticipation. He pushed open the door of the next pub he came to, careless of its quality, his eyes already picking out words on the front page.

Absent-minded (outwardly), his mind athletic and fully engaged (inwardly), Roger bought a pint of beer and carried it over to the corner. For some time, he sat sipping and absorbing. Then, as the place filled up with lunch-time drinkers, he found it harder to concentrate. Bursts of laughter intruded on his hearing: waves of Welsh talk broke over him, offering themselves to his understanding and yet cheating it, like Beverley over again: he *almost* understood, there was so much that only just didn't fall into place. Finally, he raised his head and looked round. Yes, it was one group, standing near the bar, who were the centre of the animation. Two men in particular seemed to be making the most noise: one slight, quick, mobile of features, a knitted woollen cap on his restless head, was talking in an almost continuous stream; the other, square, gap-toothed, bald, was laughing a great deal, and getting in such words as he could find room for, in a voice husky and rather high-pitched. Roger watched, fascinated; this, after all, was as good as the newspaper. The man in the woollen cap was telling a story, acting each part in turn with lavish use of grimace and gesture. His stocky bald companion was participating with much nodding and corroborative laughter, conveying that he had been present at the scene described. Around the pair of them was a ring of attentive faces, some smiling continuously, some lapsing into seriousness and then breaking into grins and guffaws at each new turn in the absurdity. The landlord, his elbows on the bar, was a study in himself. His face registered every emotion called for by the story – indignation, tolerance, delight, convulsive mirth – with great vehemence, as if he were doing it for a wager. Each successive expression obliterated the one before, played itself out furiously, then gave place to another. Welsh? He was oval-faced, sallow-skinned, with a great thatch of black hair that started from just above his eyebrows and grew violently all over his head, grudging every inch of space it had to cede to his prominent ears, halted in its rush down his back only by the collar of his jacket. Then, in a gap in the narrator's recital, this landlord spoke a few words, and Roger noted that he had a different accent from the others. Their Welsh was guttural, his was liquid. They barked, he sang. Was he South Welsh? Ah, soon he would map out all this fascinating linguistic territory.

The woollen-capped man's story reached its exploding climax amid snorting, skirling laughter. He looked round, with the satisfaction of an artist, at the effect he had produced. Roger, putting down his empty glass, was infected by the presence of so much laughter, and a spasm came up unexpectedly from his belly. He was laughing, yes, laughing loudly, at a story he hadn't even understood. Then his brain registered something. A very fat young man, with curly brown hair, sitting next to him on the bench, was saying something to him.

'Da iawn' wir,' the fat man chuckled.

Roger turned and blinked. For the space of half a second he could not grasp why the words meant nothing to him: his ear was so attuned to Welsh that it seemed impossible he should fail to understand it. Then he smiled apologetically and said, 'I'm afraid I'm a foreigner. I don't speak Welsh.'

The other gestured, puzzled, towards the newspaper. 'But you can read it.'

'I was just trying to spell out a few words. I'm interested in learning Welsh.'

'Oh.' The fat young man gave Roger a glance in which there was a hint of a question, but it was soft, damped-down; 'Tell me why, explain yourself,' the glance said, 'but only if you want to.'

Roger did not particularly want to, but he was glad to get into talk. He could not size up this man, assign him to a background; he wore a shiny blue suit, obviously bought off the peg and not designed for anyone with his bulk of flesh, and this made him look comical; on the other hand, his eyes were large and fine, and his forehead, under that clustering mop of dark-brown curls, was high. Roger, in the mood for exploration, wanted to know about everyone he met in this odd, unexpected place. To initiate a conversation, he nodded towards the recitalist in the woollen cap, and said. 'That chap makes me wish I could understand Welsh. He was having everybody in fits.'

'Yes, Ivo's got a gift,' the fat youth agreed. 'A natural *jongleur*. And he and his mate, Gito – that's the thick-set fellow – they have plenty of chance to gather material for these stories. They go about in a lorry all over the district. They're in the scrap-metal business. Snappers-up of unconsidered trifles if ever there were any.'

A *jongleur*, eh? The man's accent was the standard guttural honk of the district, but he seemed capable of going outside his own orbit when it was a question of *le mot juste*. Or were they all like that?

'Does – what's his name? Ivo tell just as good a story in English?' he asked.

'His English is very good,' said the other, considering carefully, 'but it lacks a dimension. It's comedian's English. It doesn't smell of Cambrian soil.'

'Have a drink,' said Roger suddenly. He wanted to prolong his talk with this man who used language with such relish. 'I mean,' he said, retrieving the abruptness of his sudden invitation, 'I'm just going to get another – may I fill yours up while I'm there?'

Again the fat young man shot him that watchful inquisitive but soft look. 'Well, thanks. I think I've got time for one more. Just the ordinary bitter of the house.' When Roger brought him his refilled mug he smiled and said, 'The name's Madog.'

Roger nodded in salutation. 'Roger Furnivall,' he said. The name, as he uttered it, sounded ridiculous. It was so farcically alien to be called 'Roger' and 'Furnivall' in a place where everybody had names like Ivo and Gito and Madog.

'That's only my bardic name, of course,' said Madog. 'On my National Insurance card I'm Hywel Jones. But in Gwynedd it's still the privilege of a poet to be known by his bardic name.'

'What kind of poems do you write?' Roger asked, really wanting to know.

'Epics,' said Madog.

Epics? A fat young fellow in a reach-me-down business suit, sitting next to him in a pub and drinking pints of bitter, wrote epics?

'I'm half-way through one now,' said Madog. 'It'll be almost as long as *Paradise Lost*. But not in blank verse, of course, Welsh revels in rhyme. And in variety. Switch from one style to another – a sort of *collage*.'

'Has it got a title yet?'

'Gwilym Cherokee,' said Madog.

'Gwilym . . . ?'

'Cherokee. You know what happened to the Cherokees, don't you?'

'Well . . . not specifically . . .'

'Specifically,' said Madog, fixing his eyes sternly on Roger's, 'what happened to them was this. When the European settlers got to North America, they were faced with a way of life, among the Indians, that was altogether unintelligible to them. Most of them were merely ruthless towards the Indians, but some of them had do-gooding fits in which they wanted to educate the Indian, to turn him into a white man. And whenever they found that the Indians were resistant to this, and preferred their own ideas, they called them feckless savages and started to massacre them again. For instance – am I boring you?'

'Not at all. I've always found it very –'

'Take land ownership,' said Madog. 'The Indians didn't have the concept of individual plots of land. Their ownership was collective. But the white invaders didn't understand any other way of owning land than in piecemeal little farms, handed down from father to son. Their image of a thrifty man was a European peasant. The Indians couldn't grasp that idea and so they were thought incapable of thrift. Right?'

'Right.'

'Now,' said Madog. He took a great pull at his beer. 'We come to the Cherokees. They were adaptable and clever people. The white man preached progress to them and they listened. Of all the Indian peoples, they were the ones who went furthest down the white man's road. They drank in all his advice – till the land, sell your produce, adopt our values and we'll treat you as we treat one another. So they did it. They took to being farmers and blacksmiths and weavers and spinners. In the early nineteenth century, they invited a syllabic way of writing their language and even brought out a newspaper. The *Cherokee Phoenix*, it was called. But that was one phoenix that never rose from the ashes. It died on its burning nest.'

'What happened? I'm afraid I don't –'

'Andrew Jackson's Indian Removal Act,' said Madog. 'Eighteen-thirty.' He uttered the syllables with harsh distinctness, his voice loaded with distaste. 'They were pushed out from the good lands and sent to the wilderness. Good Indians and bad Indians. The adaptable and the unadaptable, the wise virgins and the foolish virgins. The Cherokees went with the rest, forced out at gun-point, leaving behind their farms and roads and shops and forges and their newspaper-press and their libraries. It all made no difference, you see, because the white man wanted their land.'

Roger looked across at the bar. Ivo, in that absurd woollen cap, was beginning a new recital, and the dark rubbery face of the landlord was grinning insatiably. He turned back to Madog.

'All right, that's the Cherokee part, and a good subject for an epic. But Gwilym?'

'You can call the Cherokee Gwilym,' said Madog in a fierce,

quiet voice. 'You can call him Dai, you can call him Ianto, you can call him Huw or Hywel or Gareth or Gito or anything you like.'

Roger thought for a moment. 'I see. You're manipulating a continuous parallel.'

'Call it that if you like,' said Madog.

'But,' Roger persisted, 'what was the precise historical equivalent? What did the English do to the Welsh that was the equivalent of driving the Cherokees off their homesteads?'

'Anglicization,' said Madog. 'Interior expropriation. Ripping up the South Wales valleys for coal-mines and turning the population into troglodytes who didn't even speak their own language. Taking untold wealth out of the earth of Wales and never ploughing a penny of it back.'

He looked ready to go on, but Roger shook his head despairingly. 'That's enough. I get the point.'

They sat for a moment in silence and then Roger said, 'Well, at any rate I'm a Saxon who'd like to make some amends by studying the Celtic languages.'

'Like buying a blanket on the reservation,' said Madog.

'That's unfair and you know it is.'

'Perhaps so,' said Madog. 'At least I shouldn't say it and drink your beer.'

'To hell with the beer. I hope I'm a civilized man, with a civilized man's interest in the arts. I ask a poet a question about his poetry and the next minute I'm a genocidal brute, driving the Cherokees off their land and despoiling South Wales, all on my own.'

'Not you. Your nation.'

'I'm not a nation. I'm me.'

'It's an old problem,' said Madog. He suddenly smiled. 'Let's talk about poetry again.'

'Yes, let's. I'm interested in Welsh prosody. Perhaps you'll give me some help with it, as I get on.'

'I'd be glad to, any time you have a question. You'll have to get your Welsh up to a certain standard first, of course. And in particular, to get some idea of mutations, because they affect the verse-forms.'

'Well, I'm getting the hang of those. Dr Conroy –'

Their talk jumped from crag to crag. Madog took up the

newspaper and, his finger wandering over the sheet of print, found examples of word-mutation. 'Now, try and get your ear accustomed to the quantities,' he said. 'I'll recite you a quatrain. Keep as much track as you can of the *cynghanedd*. It's basically a system of –'

Something large and square loomed over them. Gito, his bald pate gleaming anxiously in the electric light, wanted a word with Madog. He shot a quick, apologetic glance at Roger, seemed almost about to speak to him and excuse himself for breaking into the conversation, then thought better of it and began a rapid, nervous stream of Welsh. Madog listened and shook his head. Gito fired off two or three questions on a rising note; at least it seemed to Roger, from their interrogative inflection, that they must be questions. He decided to turn his attention to the paper and wait for Gito to finish and go away, but as he bent his head he suddenly heard 'Dic Sharp' amid the cluster of Welsh syllables.

Sitting quite still, listening with an intentness that surprised him considerably, he distinctly made out 'Dic' in Madog's reply. He laboured to catch any fragment of meaning, but the rapidity and complexity were too much for him, and he let his mind drift across the printed words in front of him and took an idle sip at his beer, affecting a relaxed idleness that he was far from feeling.

Gito seemed distressed. He began to say something, stopped in mid-sentence, gave an angry shrug of his wide shoulders, and went back to join Ivo at the bar. Madog sat looking after him for a moment, then turned back to Roger.

'Something important?' Roger asked.

'Oh, just a bit of local business. Always a lot of horse-dealing going on.'

'Literally? Real horses?'

'Well, no, I was speaking figuratively,' said Madog. His face, Roger thought, seemed rather blank, as if the subject displeased him. 'Now, take the *cynghanedd* in the following example. It's a little –'

'Just a minute,' Roger interrupted. 'I can't give my mind to higher things till I've satisfied a bit of vulgar curiosity that's nagging me.'

Madog sighed, but said, 'Well?'

Roger leaned forward. 'Do you know a man called Dic Sharp?'

There was a very slight pause before Madog answered, 'Of course I know him.'

'What sort of a chap is he?'

'How d'you mean?'

'Well –' Roger felt that he was getting nowhere. 'If I knew him, d'you think I'd like him?'

'I don't know you well enough to know who you'd like,' said Madog.

'Well, you know some things about me,' said Roger. 'You know I'm interested in classical Welsh metres, for instance. Now suppose Dic Sharp were here. Would you be able to talk about poetry to him, and recite *cynghanedd*?'

'I might,' said Madog. 'I might perfectly well. And that still wouldn't add up to a judgement on the kind of man he is. This is a living culture. People who appreciate verbal art aren't in a small leper-colony of their own, like in your country.'

'Oh, my country,' Roger sighed. 'You really are anti-English, aren't you?'

'I'm a Cherokee,' said Madog.

It was clear that he was angry with Roger for having questioned him about Dic Sharp, and that this anger had brought with it suspicion and xenophobia.

'Well, perhaps I ought to give up the subject,' said Roger. 'You've made it pretty clear that you don't want to discuss this Dic Sharp character and you're not at all pleased even to hear his name mentioned. But I feel in the mood for one more try.'

He looked across at Madog. Like most fat men, Madog was not good at looking angry for more than a few seconds at a time; his double chin insistently imparted an air of benevolence to his face. But he was doing his best, with much eyebrow-clenching and mouth-straightening.

'What if I told you I wasn't just prying into local affairs?'

'You said yourself it was vulgar curiosity,' said Madog.

'That was just self-deprecation.'

'We don't understand self-deprecation round here.'

'All right, here's something you will understand. I'm a friend of Gareth's.'

'Gareth who?'

'The hunchback.'

Madog turned slowly in his seat and looked at Roger. 'And you think that puts you smack in the middle of every local feud?'

'Ah, so you admit there is a feud?'

'I don't admit anything,' said Madog.

'What was Gito so worried about? Is Dic Sharp persecuting him?'

'What are you, a journalist or something?'

'I'm a philologist. I have a professional motive for learning Welsh and that's what I'm doing in this district. I haven't the slightest intention of involving myself in any vendettas or brushing up against the local Mafia.'

'Don't talk in that strain. We don't find it amusing.'

'I'm beginning not to care. And if you behave like people living under the threat of a Mafia you must expect to have the fact remarked on.'

'You *are* a journalist. That's the way journalists talk. Smart, one-up London journalists.'

'I am from London,' said Roger slowly and distinctly, 'but I am not a journalist and I am very un-smart. By profession I am a philologist. My work has hitherto been in the field of Old Norse, Old English and Old High German, with a historical interest in the development of modern Scandinavian languages. I am the author of a well-known paper called "The transformation of 'mutation variation' into 'mutation allophone' in Scandinavian languages, especially in relation to final *i* and *e* in Old High German". My motive for learning Welsh is to try to understand something about the philology of the Celtic languages.'

Madog was mollified. He looked ready to make peace. 'Right, I believe you, I accept that you have an honourable motive for being here and taking an interest in local life. I withdraw my charge that you must be a journalist, now what?'

'Now nothing very much. I ran into Gareth, under circumstances that might make an amusing story if we had time, but I'll leave it on one side for the moment. And I understand that Gareth is the last of these country bus operators to resist the merger that Dic Sharp wants to put through. So what I wonder is, can one do anything to help or encourage him?'

Madog sat staring in front of him for a moment. The newspaper lay on the table before them, forgotten now.

'When you see a whaling ship go out,' he said at last 'complete with every kind of radar equipment for tracking the whale and every kind of harpoon-gun for killing it, with a full complement of technicians and wireless officers and a sick bay and recreation room for the crew, with millions of money invested in the company behind it and no thought in anyone's head except to make a profitable trip and make more money, do you ever feel a twinge of pity for the whale?'

'As it happens I've never seen such a ship. But if I did, that would be my reaction.'

'Well,' said Madog, picking up his glass, 'that's your reaction to Gareth.'

'Then it's hopeless?'

'I didn't say that. Sometimes, by very patient negotiation, you can get some nations to sign an agreement that they'll give the whale a breathing-space, in certain areas of certain seas. You can never get them *all* to sign, of course – there'll be some who'll go in and enjoy the fat pickings left for them by the ones who've got some scruples and some notions of conservation and so forth. But there are just a few things you can do for the whale. For a time.'

Roger nodded. 'And have those things been done, for Gareth?'

'Probably not. Those of us who live here, who watch it all happening from day to day, get a bit numb about things. There may be things we could be doing to help Gareth that we're not doing.'

'And Dic Sharp – what sort of methods does he use?'

Madog jerked his head in the direction of Ivo and Gito, who were just raising fresh pints to their lips and conferring in quiet voices. 'Ask them. They ran a bus service till twelve months ago. Just the one bus between the two of them, but it kept them and their families. They gave a good service and always kept their bus in A-1 condition. But after a few months of Dic Sharp's treatment, they gave up. And they're not fellows who give up easily.'

Roger waited for Madog to say more, but he finished his drink in silence and got heavily to his feet. 'Well, I have to go. Must get a bite and go back to the office. My employer needs me to help him grind people's faces.'

'I hope I'll be seeing you.'

'If you're about the place,' said Madog, 'you'll be seeing me all right. Keep after those mutations now.'

He smiled cheerfully enough, and took himself off. But Roger could not quite dispel a brooding sense of worry. Had Madog broken their conversation off short because he was unwilling, or afraid, to enlarge on the topic of Dic Sharp and his activities? Was the subject dangerous? Our just distasteful? Madog obviously took pride in the language, the life, the traditions, of 'Gwynedd', as he called it. Was Dic Sharp the representative of everything in that life that Madog, and his kind, feared to acknowledge? Or was it rather that Dic Sharp was a dangerous man to meddle with, even to discuss where ears might hear?

He shrugged. What was it to him? But it must have been something, for, though he spread out the newspaper on the table and made a determined effort to continue his studies, his mind refused to concentrate. The great human structure of language, at once intensely concrete and entirely abstract, had, for the moment, lost its fascination. There, a few yards away, were two strong and determined men who had suffered as Gareth was suffering, and had given up. Well, what of it? Again he tried to push the subject away. Economic forces were like forces of nature: they worked impersonally, but they manifested themselves through individuals. Small businesses, local services controlled by local men, were doomed everywhere in the world. Gareth was doomed; all the Gareths of the world were hastening to extinction faster than the flightless rail or the white rhinoceros.

These thoughts made him restless, and he rose and walked out into the street and then, aimlessly, along to the square. Yes, there was Gareth's bus, standing among a long, uniform line of General buses. The hunchback was behind the wheel, waiting to set off for the hills, and a few last passengers were climbing up, carrying parcels and cases. Gareth's bus was bright yellow. Roger's eyes took in the colour sharply, under the gleaming sky. The last passenger clambered aboard; Gareth, with the leather bag slung across his shoulder, moved like a crab down the length of the vehicle; Roger, taking in the scene from the other side of the square, could imagine the talk rising in a living fountain, all the greetings, information, quips, condolences, thanks, invitations, hints, challenges, that would go rolling up the mountainside, as if the bus were a mobile inn without the drink. He saw Gareth go back to the driving-seat, saw him stare ahead through the glass, heard the cough and roar of the engine, and watched as the yellow shape moved out and away. How many more trips? How many more days or weeks before Gareth was driven to sell out, and only the drab, identical line of General buses, in their unvarying chocolate-and-cream livery, stood like a shelf of ledgers under those ancient battlements?

Well, that was Gareth's problem. Roger's was to get some lunch. His feet carried him automatically back the way he had come. The same pub? No, the sandwiches had looked rather curled-up and the hot pies, forlornly marinating in a heated glass case on the bar, obviously came from a factory. Roger was just walking past the door, to try some other place, when he remembered that he had left the newspaper on the table. Might as well pick it up: fivepence is fivepence. He went into the bar. Ivo and Gito, who had decided to brave the factory's hot pies, were sitting on the bench where he had been with Madog, eating and talking earnestly. His newspaper lay neglected on the table before them.

Roger went over and picked up the paper. This brought him within their field of vision, and they looked up at him. He smiled. 'Just picking up my paper.'

'If you find any good news in it, let me know,' said Ivo. He turned back to Gito, but Roger, suddenly impelled to linger and talk, was unwilling to be dismissed. He stood there, carefully folding and re-folding the paper, looking down at the two men. They looked strong, hard; inured to evil and fatigue, tanned and roughened by the weather. But Dic Sharp had beaten them down. What the hunchback faced and was determined to go on facing, these two had tried to face but in the end had turned and run. If he could talk to them, if under any conceivable circumstances he could get them to open up, he might understand the exact nature of Gareth's troubles. Certainly Madog wasn't going to talk, nor was Gareth himself.

Ivo, with his quick intuitive mind, must have understood that Roger was trying to think of something to say, because he nodded towards the paper with a grin and said, 'Looking for a job, eh?'

'Well, yes, in a way.'

'But you don't speak Welsh. Just learning it like.'

'Exactly.'

'I've seen it before,' said Ivo. 'People trying to brush together enough Welsh to get a job with the education. There's some very good jobs going, but the education won't have anybody that doesn't speak Welsh.'

'Not round here, at least,' said Gito, nodding.

'I see I can't keep any secrets from you,' said Roger. Pulling up a chair, he sat down and faced them across the table. 'You've guessed it, I *am* looking for an educational job.' (At Uppsala, among the blondes. But why go into every trivial detail?) 'And I am learning Welsh. But I've only just started and I've got quite a bit of time to put in before I'll be good enough.'

'Not a bit of it, man,' said Ivo with a wave of his hand. 'A couple of weeks and you'll know more than most of 'em do. That's not saying much. They only have to speak a few words of Welsh to the committee when they go up to get their job. If you can say *sut yr ydych chwi heddiw*, you're in.'

'The kids'll teach you the rest,' said Gito. 'Specially the rude words.'

'All the same,' said Roger, 'I know I'll come on faster if I can get into some position where I'll hear Welsh spoken round me and have a chance to speak it myself.'

'P'raps Mario'd take him on, doing bar work,' suggested Gito.

'Not a chance,' said Ivo. 'You have to be in the union. Anything to do with catering or bar work, it's union labour or nothing.'

'Who's Mario?' Roger asked.

'Landlord here,' said Ivo. 'He's Italian. Came to Wales as a P.O.W. in nineteen forty-three. Calls it his home, now. Never goes back. Speaks Welsh like a native. A native of Italy.'

'It's English he can't master,' said Gito.

'Doesn't want to, man. Never forgiven 'em for taking him prisoner.'

Roger glanced across at the proprietor, who, with sleeves rolled back over brawny arms, was polishing the same glass over and over again while he disputed vehemently with a customer. At least, Roger had to deduce from his eyebrow-play and lip-jut that he was disputing; he may have been sympathizing with the man in some misfortune.

'Well, he won't take on anybody but a union man. And he probably wouldn't employ an Englishman anyway,' said Gito.

'Yes, he would,' said Ivo. 'He'd like to order an Englishman about.'

'I was thinking –' Roger began.

'Yes?'

'I don't need any salary, you see. I'm on secondment from my job while I improve my Welsh. So it's not a question of earning a wage. Anything that would bring me among people, Welsh-speakers –'

'Go round selling things, on commission.'

'Take a stall in the market.'

'Make the tea on a building site. No, excuse me, that's union.'

'Sell programmes at the football matches.'

'Be serious,' Roger appealed to them, laughing.

'We're dead serious, man,' said Ivo. 'It's the hardest thing you could have asked us. What boss wants a man who says he'll come without wages? He'll think there's a catch in it and he'd best steer clear, isn't it?'

'Well, I don't insist on not having wages, of course. It's just that it doesn't matter either way. I tell you,' Roger's heart beat faster as he drew nearer to his target, 'one idea that did occur to me. You know Gareth from Llancrwys?'

Both men became still and watchful.

'I've noticed,' Roger ploughed on, 'that he runs that bus without any help.'

'That's putting it mild,' said Gito.

'Department of disexaggeration,' said Ivo.

'Do you think he could use some help? Just someone for a few weeks to . . .'

'To what?' Ivo asked.

'Well, do some of the donkey-work,' said Roger. He felt that his voice sounded false and weak. Yet, after all, he was not trying to cheat anyone. Why should he feel like an impostor? 'I mean, help to collect the fares, keep the accounts, take a hand in servicing the bus, anything that Gareth wanted . . .'

Ivo put down his glass and stared at Roger. His dark brown eyes held Roger's for a long time.

'All right, mister,' he said at last. 'That's where you've been circling round to, is it, all this time? Well, what's the game?'

'Game?'

Gito leaned forward. 'Who are you working for?'

Roger suddenly felt terribly tired. How could he, how could anybody, cut through this colossal tangle of suspicion?

'I'm working for myself,' he said, 'but it doesn't matter. My story seems to you so utterly unlikely that nothing I could say, nothing at all, would make you believe it. So let's just leave the matter there. I have to learn Welsh and I'm in the district for that purpose and I might as well have a job as do nothing, and I thought it would be good for my Welsh to get about on a bus and be among villagers who talk Welsh all the time. And I met Gareth and I know about him and Dic Sharp.'

Ivo gave Roger a long, appraising stare. 'You know about that, do you?' he said musingly. 'And just what do you know?'

'In detail, nothing. Just that Dic Sharp is harassing the life out of Gareth to make him give up and sell his bus to him so that he'll hold the complete pack of cards and can sit down to play for high stakes with General.'

'And that Gareth's the last,' said Gito as if to himself.

'Yes. So you can see why I thought it might be worth while to join forces with Gareth, if only for a few weeks, and give him what help I could. I mentioned it to you two because I thought –'

'All right, mister, you thought this and you thought that,' Ivo interrupted in something like a snarl. 'Where d'you come from?'

'London.'

'Well, you know what you'll do if you've got any sense?'

'What?' But Roger already knew the kind of thing Ivo was going to say.

'You'll go straight back to London, mister, and learn Welsh from the bloody television.'

He stood up, Gito joined him, and they left. Roger went slowly to the bar, ordered another drink from Mario, who served him in silence (fatigue? anti-Englishness? inability to speak English?), and sat thoughtfully drinking it until the place closed. The pies had all gone. But he did not feel like any lunch.

'Yes, there'll be eight of us,' an English voice was saying as Roger went past the reception desk. 'Eight for dinner, that is. I've no idea how many exactly there'll be joining us for drinks beforehand, and some of them might want to stay for dinner, but they can take care of themselves. I'm assuming responsibility for eight and that's all.'

The speaker was a man in his mid-thirties, horn-rimmed, pin-striped and buttoned-down. He stood confidently addressing himself to the dark beauty behind the desk, exuding efficiency. His neatly-shod feet trod the thick carpet as if they had never known a thin one. A slicker, an operator. So they had them here too.

Roger was approaching the lift, to go up to his room for no better reason than to get away from the man's voice and because he had just had tea in the lounge and the lounge depressed him even more than his room, when he was surprised to hear himself addressed by name. He turned. Yes, it was the girl at the desk. As the pin-striped man moved away, she repeated in her soft, Liverpool-tinged voice, 'Mr Furnivall.'

'Yes,' said Roger, approaching.

'I've got your coat here.'

'My . . .?'

'The young lady left it for you.'

She reached under the desk and produced Roger's mackintosh, neatly rolled. What was going on here? Had Beverley left it for him on a sudden impulse towards fair play? Or had she dropped it off at the desk in haughty and contemptuous mood, pausing only to brand him as a hot-handed lecher, a pitiful satyromaniac whose schemes had resulted only in a wetting? What, in short, had she told this girl about him?

'Oh, thanks, I'll take it.'

As the girl handed him the coat, their eyes met. Was it pure imagination, or did she hold his gaze a fraction of a second longer than was entirely necessary? Was there a hint, the tiniest grain of a suggestion, of amused ... amused what? complicity; satire? was there a flicker of the look that says, 'I know something about *you*'?

Well, let her know. He had no character to lose, no fair appearance to keep up. He was perfectly willing to give her a signed statement, if necessary, that he needed to make love to a woman and was ready to take off after any female shape that crossed his path. The dreadful truth, he suspected, was that such a statement would simply fail to interest her. No revelation about his state of mind, however lurid, would shock her, because it would not succeed in engaging her attention at all. A girl like that ... she must have men buzzing round her like amorous bluebottles. Clutching the mackintosh, Roger turned back towards the lift, then halted again. His room? Dr Conroy? No, now that he had his coat he would take a long walk. The light was fading and rain was coming down, but in his perplexity he needed fresh air and physical fatigue. Quickly buttoning his raincoat, he walked along the road that would take him clear of the town.

Rain fell steadily, hissing in the puddles. Roger found a lane that climbed, between stone walls, towards the dark-purple frieze of mountains. Remorselessly, driving himself to walk a little too fast for comfort, he beat back the hard road like a man on a treadmill. Before long his step was heavier, slower. He had left the last houses far behind, and across the roadside walls there stretched, now, not enclosed fields with black cattle, but the open hillside on which sheep nibbled restlessly, grey as the rocks they moved along. At last, the road levelled out; he had reached a plateau from which, in the distance, the mountains reared themselves stiffly. There was no point in going further. He turned, and for a moment forgot his troubles in the sudden shock of the sunset flaming over Anglesey. The rainy light glowed like fire on the sea; below him, the castle stood in its antique, collected strength. Even the works of man, if they accumulated enough of the dignity bestowed by time, could take their place in this work of rock, water and flame. Where nature was so dramatic and uncompromising, man too could hold his head up, if he were prepared to be as intransigent as she. Melancholy thoughts broke in; Roger shrugged and began his downward march. Where was that race of men who could build a masterpiece in rough-hewn stone? Dead, vanished, and their successors had the marrow sucked from their bones by the dishonest paltering world of modernity. Unreality, substitute, falsity, compromise everywhere.

He walked back to the hotel, satisfactorily wet, blown and exercised, but still gloomy. Darkness fell before he got back, and the light spilling from the hotel doorway helped to focus Roger's attention on a group of people who were getting out of a taxi at the kerbside just as he arrived. Glancing at them indifferently, he saw that one of them was the dapper man he had heard arranging to be host to eight people at dinner; of the other four, he registered only that two of them were women. Yes, women everywhere; even a complacent slob like that, with his horn rims and his city suit, doubtless had a woman to call his own, didn't have to carry his seed around like a convict.

Sick of the world, sick of himself, Roger sensibly went up to his room and had a bath. The hot water took the stiffness out of his limbs, relieved his fatigue, and gave him the beginnings of a more optimistic mood. If only he could get lined up with a woman, his other problems might be soluble enough. Dressing, he looked at himself critically. Well, older and more horrible-looking men did attract women; he had seen it happen. Back to the game, and may the dice roll for him this time.

He decided on a drink in the Lounge Bar (to see if there was anything to be picked up), then dinner (to set him up for the evening), then a systematic search of the town (assuming that the Lounge Bar yielded nothing). His spirits raised by a plan of action, he entered the Lounge Bar, mentally debating whether to drink whisky or gin.

His spirits dipped again as he heard a hubbub of voices. Of course, that smooth type was having his party. Were all these people with him? Roger's eye raked the assembly, who had just got rid of their hats and coats and were settling down to drink and talk. A dozen at least, if not fifteen. Mostly English; only one or two looked dark and long-skulled, and the predominant note in the babel was not North Welsh and guttural, nor South Welsh and lilting; it was English, and English of that fluting, narrow-vowelled kind that suggested the Home Counties.

Scowling, Roger moved towards the bar. Who the hell were they, anyway, invading a public place like this? He glanced right and left. They looked vaguely intellectual – or, if that was putting it too strongly, vaguely educated. One woman, a mere girl actually, still in her twenties, looked quite ... well, in a silly Bohemian way, almost quite ... attractive? Once again, the word was too strong. A really attractive woman standing beside her would have made her invisible. On the other hand ... a heavy fringe of dark hair from beneath which she peered with large eyes; sulky, discontented, obviously lonely and yet unwilling to seek involvement in the banal chatter of the party ... all right, all right, Furnivall. She's a woman, that's enough for you, isn't it? Well, she's with somebody else's party and you're not. Get a drink. A whisky. Roger turned his eyes to the bar. Then he saw Bryant.

Bryant was watching him; he had recognized Roger first. 'Why, hello,' he said, taking care not to show too much surprise. Bryant never liked to let anything ruffle him; his *persona* was of a man whom nothing could disturb. 'Fancy meeting you. I'd no idea you were in this neighbourhood.'

'I'd no idea *you* were,' said Roger. Bryant was a philologist, once briefly a colleague of Roger's in the lower reaches of some university department, before they had both moved on to other jobs. Soft-mannered, business-suited, he had always seemed more like a well-conducted tradesman than an intellectual. Rumour had it, indeed, that he had embarked on a career with an old-established house of wholesale jute importers in the City before being smitten by the more potent charms of philology. Making an obvious deduction, Roger remembered that there was a university college in the district, and a perfunctory catechism soon revealed that Bryant was associated with the place, as were most of the party of which he was a member. 'They've made me a Reader,' he purred gently, watching Roger's reaction from under deceptively drowsy lids. A Reader, eh? Mediocrity as you are, Bryant, you must be good at something. The great gift of impressing committees of other mediocrities, that must be your secret. Well, good luck to you, jute-buying Pharisee.

64

'Are you having a holiday up here?' Bryant probed gently.

'Sort of. I want to learn Welsh.'

Bryant's eyes lit up with a subdued wariness. Roger could feel the waves of his attention suddenly mounting in volume. 'Oh? Find it interesting, do you?'

'I like the whole Celtic group.'

'Mm. Not much doing in them, these days.'

'There is at Uppsala,' said Roger blandly. Then he could have bitten his tongue. Purely from a wish not to look like an unpractical fool in the eyes of this worldling, he had revealed his plan. For of course Bryant would twig it in an instant. He knew all about the job structure everywhere. 'Furnivall's got his sights on Uppsala,' the word would run round.

'You fancy it there?' Bryant was saying casually.

'Not necessarily,' Roger lamely tried to extricate himself. 'But if they run a big Celtic department others might follow suit.'

'There's always America,' Bryant added.

'Yes, thank God. Anyone who can teach anything usually ends up teaching it there. What was the figure I heard? – twenty-five thousand institutions of higher learning?' Suddenly, he thought of the outline of Beverley's mammaries.

At this point the dapper host bore down on Bryant and said, 'Recognized an acquaintance?' Smiling and watchful, the plump pig wished to have full knowledge of every development, however trivial.

'Yes, this is Roger Furnivall. We were colleagues once. A philologist. Roger, this is Gerald Twyford.'

The two murmured greetings, eyeing each other with dislike.

'You've taken a job up here?' said this Twyford.

'No. Just doing a bit of research,' said Roger, to blank off the topic.

'He's learning Welsh,' put in Bryant, with what seemed a tiny undercurrent of malice.

'Welsh? Good God. I suppose it's useful for philology in some way.'

'It's a language people speak,' said Roger.

'Not if they can help it,' Twyford chuckled.

Oh, Roger thought. One of those.

'Of course it's always open to people to choose poverty,' Twyford went on lightly. 'All one can do for them is to give them the choice to have prosperity if they want it.'

'Does speaking Welsh make people poor?' Roger asked.

'Of course it does. It aligns them with everything that's restrictive and old-fashioned and a nuisance.'

'Of course, the larger unit is the more efficient, in some ways,' Roger said carefully. He began to edge towards the bar.

'It's not even that. It's just that the larger unit, whether efficient or not, is the only one that's possible now. The small locality unit just doesn't exist as an alternative.'

'So people who speak Welsh, or Breton, or Romansch, or Latvian, or Marathi, are simply lining themselves up with an alternative that doesn't exist?'

'Oh, they have a *function*,' said Twyford. His spectacles flashed with contempt. 'They exist to make nice picturesque noises that people like you and Jim Bryant can study and make careers out of.'

'Excuse me, I need a drink,' said Roger. He turned away and pushed through to the bar. Whisky, and plenty of it, man.

'Yes, they're all taking it up now. Ken was telling me only last week.' The speaker, who was standing close beside Roger at the bar, was a balding man wearing rimless glasses. He was addressing someone on the other side of Roger, so that the waves of his voice boiled round Roger's head like surf on a lighthouse. 'Actually the man to watch is Doug Bum.' (Or some such name.) 'He's writing a book on contemporary satire. He asked me what I thought would be a good title for it and I suggested *Daddy's Gone Affronting*. That ought to do, don't you think?'

To stop himself from driving his fist into the balding man's face, Roger deliberately paid clinical attention to his accent. It was South-East London, devotedly overlaid with a drawling imitation of the upper-class lingo of fifty years previously. Roger signalled frantically to the barmaid. This evil farce must end. One stiff drink, now that he was actually at the bar, and then out. Better a stale cheese roll in a pub than a full meal within earshot of this shower.

He succeeded in getting a large whisky, and moved away from the bar to drink it in peace. Standing near the door, ready for exit, he took one appreciative gulp, paused to allow it to burn its way down before tossing back the rest, and found that he was standing close by the girl with the heavy fringe and large discontented eyes. Oh, you not-quite-beautiful doll. Let my put my arms about you, I can never live without you.

'Rather a crush,' he said. Let her snub him, let her slap his face. His dignity was not worth guarding in a world that contained people like Twyford and the balding South-East London man.

'They want to have a good time,' she said, looking round with a kind of distant amusement. 'They don't get so many good times. It's my husband's birthday and he always likes to observe it.'

'Which of them is your husband?'

'Gerald Twyford.'

This came as a genuine surprise to Roger. She was not the type he would have expected Twyford to have chosen. Her accent was faintly northern; wearing a damson-coloured woollen dress with a large gold chain round her waist, she seemed to be trying for an impression of slightly *outré* simplicity, whereas most of the other women present were dressed up to the nines in conventional fashion. A literary or artistic type? But if so, what on earth could she have seen in Twyford?

'So if you live up here,' Roger said, musing aloud, 'these are your circle of friends.'

'Not mine. My husband's.'

Somewhere deep inside Roger's mind, a tiny bell sounded. All personnel to action stations!

'Your glass is empty. Let me get you something.'

'Thanks.' She handed him the glass. 'I'm drinking sherry. Not that I like it, but I've started with it and I'd better not change, or I'll feel awful.'

'If you don't like sherry, why did you start on it?'

'I wasn't consulted.'

He hesitated. 'Dry or sweet?'

'Medium dry, I think they call it.'

Roger jockeyed his way back to the bar. His desire to get away had left him. There might, just possibly, be something doing here, and even if there were not, he felt a genuine pity for this girl, trapped in the Gerald Twyford menagerie. Where, by the way, had he come across that name? Economics? Articles in the weekly papers? Something about the money market?

He collected a medium dry sherry and another large whisky, and went back.

'I seem to know your husband's name.'

'A lot of people do. He's quite a success.'

'I don't want to be insulting, but what's he a success *at*?'

'Economics. He teaches it here, but most of the time he's in London being a consultant or something. And he goes on television and explains what's happening to the pound. He knows all about it.'

'And you? Do you make trips to London too?'

'Oh, me,' she said dismissively. 'I've got two children to look after. Besides, I don't know anything about economics.'

This seemed to be one of those statements that say a good deal more than their surface content; on the other hand, it closed the door on its immediate subject, for the time being at least. The only way forward was by some avenue such as *Why did you ever marry him in the first place* and, while Roger would have enjoyed putting this and similar questions at the right moment and in the right place, it was hardly possible on five minutes' acquaintance. So he asked her if she liked living in Wales. As she answered, the unhappiness in her face seemed to lift for a moment.

'I've hardly known anywhere else, except as a child. I was a student here – Gerald was a young lecturer, that's how we met. In my adult life I've never lived anywhere but in North Wales. It's like the part of England I come from, Lancashire, but better.'

'Why better?'

'Well, I like it more. It's still foreign to me – I haven't travelled much and I still find that exciting. Not that they aren't like North of England people, in a way – hard-shelled and economical with words but full of driving emotions just under the surface. I'm like that myself, I suppose. But the Welsh are – more so, you might say. More twisted!'

'Twisted?'

'Well, they've got more to twist. Their feelings are more

knotted up, with being a conquered race and then with nationalism and Methodism and being clannish. Oh, yes, they're almost like Jews the way they still have families and they take it seriously being someone's third cousin. They hate more and perhaps they love more.'

'I see.' Roger drank off his whisky. 'The love is perhaps but the hate isn't.'

'Well,' she said, looking straight in front of her, 'that's generally the way, isn't it? You can trust people to find something to hate more easily than something to love.'

Before Roger could answer, a loud bray of insincere laughter sounded from near his elbow. The balding man with the stifled South-East London accent and the rimless glasses was swaying about and spilling his glass of wine.

'That's priceless,' he was saying, between puffs of mirth. 'I must tell Karl the *very* next time I see him.'

Gerald Twyford, who had evidently made the joke at which the other was labouring to be convulsed, smiled nattily.

'I expect he'll be at that party of Robert's,' he said. 'I shall make a point of getting up for that. I've got something I want to discuss with John and Marion. Will you be there?'

'If I can get away,' said the other. Something about the extra drawl he gave to the second syllable in 'away' made it plain that he had not been invited.

Roger wanted to move out of earshot of their voices, but if he just walked away this would mean the end of his conversation with Mrs Twyford. How could he move her along with him? He had barely started to work on the problem when Twyford approached and, ignoring Roger, spoke shortly to his wife.

'It's time to go in to dinner. Are you ready?'

'I'll come when I've finished my drink.'

'The table's ready now. They won't hold it for ever.'

'They won't have to.'

'If you're not in in five minutes,' said Twyford, controlling his voice, 'don't bother to come.'

He turned away. The South-East London man, who had been watching the scene with undisguised interest over Twyford's shoulder, followed him in the direction of the dining-room.

'Oogh,' she gave a sudden, uncontrollable shudder. 'Isn't he *horrible*?'

To Roger, they both seemed horrible, but as she had said 'he' and not 'they', he felt impelled to ask, 'Who?'

'Donald Fisher. That awful false face of his makes me feel sick. And he looks so *unhealthy*. He looks as if a good dose of something would do him good.'

'It's his voice I can't stand,' said Roger. 'If you only heard him talking behind a screen you'd know he was a snob and a liar.'

He assumed, correctly, that Donald Fisher was the man from South-East London.

'Oh, yes, his voice,' she agreed, closing her eyes in disgust.

'Who on earth is he?'

'Oh, he's some ghastly literary type in the English Department here. He spends his life in the train, like Gerald. Always rushing up to town to further his career at cocktail parties. But at least Gerald really does know the people whose names he drops. I mean, to be fair, he isn't just pretending to be a success, he *is* a success. In that world,' she added, then stopped. It was plain that she had suddenly decided not to launch a full-scale attack on her husband's values in the presence of a stranger.

Bryant now came past, moving as purposefully as a giant eel on its way to the spawning-grounds. 'Coming in to dinner, Jenny?' he said as he passed Mrs Twyford. His voice conveyed its usual calm, impersonal cheerfulness. Roger was thinking, *Jenny*. The name told him so much about her. He knew, or thought that with a little imaginative effort he could visualize, exactly the kind of north-country parents who, twenty-five (twenty-seven? twenty-eight?) years ago, would have called a baby girl 'Jenny'. Or was that another of his daft illusions, of which he seemed to have so many just now?

'I must go,' Jenny said. Her husband was an important man with connections in London, her two children were at home being looked after by somebody, her place at the table was empty.

'Have a last drink,' Roger suggested, 'to prime you.'

She shook her head. 'It isn't drink I need. There'll be plenty of that with dinner.'

'You can wave it aside. It's now you need it, before you go in.'

70

She turned to him, her large eyes taking him in as if she had not really looked at him before. 'Are you married?'

'No.'

'Then how d'you understand so much?'

Roger was about to push this away with 'Do I?' when it occurred to him that he might as well be as candid as she was. 'I can see you're having a quarrel with your husband and that you'd like to punish him by not going in to dinner, but I can also see that you can't bring yourself to hit him that hard.'

'No, I can't,' she breathed, 'but I will have that other drink.'

Roger moved swiftly to the bar and got a large glass of sherry. (Pity she was drinking such miserable stuff.) People were thinning out, and he got served quickly, but not quickly enough; when he turned round with the glass in his hand, the jackal Donald Fisher was bending confidentially over Jenny, giving her a smile in which the sympathetic and the satirical were horribly blended. Obviously he had been sent out by the husband to bring her in.

'Here's your drink,' Roger said unconcernedly, handing it over.

'Jenny's just coming in to dinner,' said Donald Fisher.

'I'll have this first,' she said. 'Thanks,' and she took it. 'Tell Gerald I'll be in in a moment. I'll skip the soup. I don't want any.'

'We're not having soup. We're having grapefruit.'

'I hate grapefruit. I'd rather have this extra glass of sherry and round off my conversation with Mr –'

'Furnivall,' said Roger.

'With Mr. Furnivall. Could you go and soothe Gerald for me?'

Fisher lingered, mutinously. 'I should have thought you'd be better at that than I would. You're his wife. You know how to handle him.'

'Oh, God,' she said wearily. 'Do wives know how to handle their husbands?'

Donald Fisher managed one of his false laughs. 'I've avoided matrimony myself because I felt it would complicate my life. And here you are asking me to undertake delicate missions between you and Gerald.'

'No, I'm not. I'm simply asking you to be kind enough to

tell him I'll be in in a few minutes and don't want any grape-fruit.'

'Besides,' said Roger insultingly, 'I'm sure you're good at undertaking delicate missions.'

He meant to imply that Donald Fisher struck him as a perfect back-stairs type, a go-between, a natural pander. From the way Fisher looked at him, it was clear that his remark had landed on target.

'I'll deliver your message,' Fisher said coldly to Jenny. 'And leave you to bring your conversation with Mr Furnivall to its so delicately rounded conclusion.'

He walked away. Roger had a sudden vision of him sitting down at the table and attacking a half-grapefruit with a cherry stuck in the middle. He would eat quickly because he was behind the others, and because it would cause him pain to miss anything.

Jenny was staring gloomily into her glass. 'Why do I have to be surrounded by people like that?'

'Well,' said Roger, 'Gerald must like him.'

'I don't think he does. He just tolerates him. All that fine talk about delicate missions. It's good, coming from him. It's as much his fault as anyone's that everything's so awful.'

Roger was silent, but he looked his inquiry.

'In a way I suppose it's my fault, the whole thing. Gerald wanted to have a party. He always does, on his birthday – he has all these creeps and hangers-on to the house and they get drunk and stay till three in the morning and they're *awful*. Each year it's got worse and worse and finally this year I said I wouldn't have them and he could have the party at an hotel. He was furious, but I stuck to it and then he tried to hire a room here, the banqueting room or something, and they can't let him have it because it's being repapered or something and he ended up with his party so *diminished*, just a few drinks in the ordinary lounge bar and then eight people to an ordinary hotel dinner, and it's not good enough for him and in a way I quite understand and I feel awful.'

During this rapid recital, Jenny's Lancashire intonations became more pronounced, but her vowels remained no more and no less Lancashire than before. Roger noted this and he also noted that her voice was soft and had a dimension of pure velvet. She seemed to him more attractive now; unhappiness dramatized her face like joy.

'Well,' he said, in order to say something, 'if all your husband's friends are like Fisher, having one's house filled with them would seem to be a more than wifely penance.' What the hell was the matter with him? He seemed to have fallen into Fisher's own idiom. 'But haven't you any friends of your own you could leaven them with?' he asked.

'My friends,' she said slowly, 'wouldn't be seen dead with that lot. I've tried it and it leads to pure hell. Last year on Gerald's birthday, Donald Fisher nearly got himself murdered. He spent about two and a half *hours* being heavily patronizing to a marvellous Welsh poet called Madog. Madog's fifty times the man he is, but Donald Fisher's too stupid to see it and he thinks Madog's quaint because he writes in Welsh and doesn't read the *New Statesman*.'

'I know Madog,' said Roger. 'I'm glad he's a friend of yours.'

She said nothing, but seemed to be listening.

'It makes me think I'd like to be a friend of yours too.'

'Well, be one, be one,' she said. 'There's nothing to it.' She was very off-hand all at once, but was this a mask for excitement? Did she know, deep in her being, that a new man was offering himself?

Roger's mind whirled as he tried to think of a suitable next step. But it whirled in vain. A silence fell, and in the silence Jenny finished her sherry and set the glass down on a nearby table.

'I must go now. I can't fight Gerald any more on his birthday, not when I've ruined it already.'

'He'll be glad to see you.'

'He will at first,' she said, 'because it'll mean I've come to heel. Then he'll forget I'm there.'

She turned and walked towards the door. Roger watched her go. He was not insulted that she gave him no farewell, just walked away in the middle of their talk. It meant, he knew, that she was willing for the talk to be picked up again as casually.

He turned back to the bar, but a slight lurching and kicking inside him warned that he had had enough to drink for the present. What next, then? Food? His system rejected this idea too. The only hunger he felt was a hunger for action. Well, why not? He glanced at his watch. Gareth would have brought the bus down. It was almost nine o'clock; Gerald Twyford's party were dining fashionably late. He thought briefly of Jenny, taking her place among closed faces, with here and there a face too falsely open, too eagerly inquisitive, like the face of Donald Fisher. He hoped she would be all right. On the other hand, he must give his energies to his own problems before thinking any more of her. He needed involvement, needed a human reason for being in the district, not just poring over Welsh verbs and weaving fantasies about Uppsala. Gareth! Now was the time to brave him, to beat down his guard. A position, however humble, alongside Gareth would be the equivalent of enlisting as a soldier in the war against Dic Sharp, against the General Omnibus Company, against the giant squid with the clammy tentacles. To help Gareth would be to give tangible expression to his dislike of the Twyfords and the Fishers. And – the small, canny thought poked itself up – it would give him idiomatic Welsh in a month or two.

He had left his mackintosh hanging on a peg outside the men's cloakroom. Putting it on, he thought of the mysterious peach behind the reception desk, with that meaning look of hers from under the dark ledge of her hair. He looked over at her as he walked jauntily across the foyer, his step lightened by alcohol. Here I am, darling. Wearing the coat she left behind. I don't care what she told you, it's not as sexy as the truth. Come up and see me some time. But not now, I'm on business.

The night outside was fine and dark, though the world was still wet from the rain and the street-lamps made shiny, shifting patterns on the pavement. Where would Gareth be? In that dingy pub across the square, where he had gone straight from the bus the night before? Try there first anyway. Full of purpose. Roger swung along the street, enjoying the smell of the sea and the knotted talkers in the bright shop-doorways. There was life in this place, not shut up in the houses but spilling out into the street, even in weather like this. The strong stone towers did not yet look down on a settlement of the dead, a burial mound with a fuzz of television aerials, like an English small town. Welsh talk washed over him as he rounded a corner. Didn't these people know they had been officially classed as an anachronism? Who gave them permission to go on living above ground?

Gareth was in the pub, sitting in what was evidently his usual place, as Roger bustled over the threshold on a tide of alcoholic courage. Drunk again, he accused himself. Was he turning into a lush? Would he never again face any challenge, explore any new situation, without the aid of drink? Yes, yes, he hushed his conscience. If this goes all right, I'll ease off.

He sat down boldly beside Gareth, who turned his beak-nose towards him and peered out of the caves of his eye-sockets.

'Can I talk to you?'

'Talk away.'

'A drink first?'

Gareth shook his head. 'I shall be taking the ten o'clock up and I've had my ration. There's the breathalyser to think about.'

'Well, I've come to ask you something,' said Roger. 'It's this. Could you use an assistant?'

'An assistant?' Gareth echoed, as if he had never before heard the word.

'Unpaid,' said Roger quickly.

Gareth was silent for a long moment and then he said, 'Who wants to know?'

'I do. You see, here's the situation. I'm staying in the district for a few weeks, months possibly, while I learn Welsh. For the education. That's my job – languages. I need to know Welsh so I got some leave from my job and came up here. I've got a bit of money to last out on. I don't need a job from the wages point of view. But I do need something that'll bring me into contact with people who speak Welsh, d'you see?' He felt false, a hypocrite if not actually a liar, as he brought out this glib simplification of his real motives, but why should Gareth be interested in all the ramifications? Keep it crisp, or the man just won't listen. 'So I wondered if you could well, use me. In a temporary capacity,' he added, vaguely feeling that a bit of labour-exchange lingo would complete the act.

Gareth looked at him steadily, making it clear that the flimsy story did not impress him. Finally he said, 'And what do you want to assist me with?'

'Anything. Running your bus service.'

Gareth picked up his empty glass, examined it, and put it down. 'I've always carried on by myself.'

'Well,' said Roger carefully, 'there are always times when a man could use a bit of help.'

'For one thing,' said Gareth, 'I should have to know a bit more about you. I don't know who you are nor what you are.'

'By profession,' Roger began promptly, 'I'm a philologist. I study languages. I've written a monograph on the transformation of mutation variation into mutation allophone in the Scandinavian languages. I work at a university – they gave me a term's leave and if I want to extend it to two terms, they'll let me. There isn't much work for me to do. They may find they don't want me back at all, but if I get a good grip on Welsh I can get another job somewhere else. That's my *curriculum vitae*.'

Gareth had listened patiently. Now he said, 'Has your curricle veet eye brought you in touch with buses at all?'

'No.'

'Garage work ever?'

'No.'

'Have you got a commercial vehicle licence?'

'You know I haven't or I'd have said so.'

Gareth stirred his vast shoulders inside the leather jerkin. 'Doesn't sound as if you'd be much use helping anybody with a bus service, does it?'

Roger flushed with anger. 'I'm willing to learn and I'm willing to work for nothing. And you need help if it's only in the form of moral support.'

'No, I don't,' said Gareth stubbornly. 'I'm not ready to ask for help yet.'

'Yes, that's how you see it, isn't it? It's all a matter of pride. If you have to *ask for help* you've lost the game. You know where that attitude lands people? By the time they give up and ask for help it's too late, they're over the edge.'

'You know a lot about it, don't you?'

'I know what anyone with his eyes can see from the sidelines. I could tell the other night that your patience was very, very stretched. If Dic Sharp –' Roger stopped. He had meant to avoid that name.

'Oh yes, Dic Sharp,' said Gareth. 'I was wondering when you'd bring him in.'

'Why shouldn't I bring him in? Everybody knows he's at the root of all the difficulties you're having.'

'I never said that.'

'You said better than that. I heard you myself say you'd kill him.'

'I got my own reasons for that.'

'Look, are we talking like grown men or are we playing some silly game? If it suits me to help you out, and I'm willing to do any humble job and don't want pay, what difference can it make to you? Do I smell or something?'

'Perhaps you do, mister,' said Gareth. His face was perfectly without expression. 'Perhaps you smell a bit of Dic Sharp.'

All of a sudden Roger understood. 'Good God,' he said gently.

'That's a gentleman that leaves his smell in many places,' said Gareth. 'Like a fox in a farmyard.'

'So you think I'm a *saboteur*,' said Roger, still gently.

'I can't very well think that when I don't know what the word means.'

'It means an under-cover agent. Somebody who pretends to be working for you so that he can damage your business from the inside.'

'And do you think,' the hunchback suddenly demanded, his voice rising with temper, 'Dic Sharp hasn't got that dirty trick in his bag?'

'I don't know what tricks he has.'

'No, you don't, and there's a lot more you don't know. Dic Sharp has contacts clear over to Chester. Yes, even Liverpool men he can employ if he wants them, Irish, the lot. Round here, we know who we're dealing with. But Dic Sharp can bring strangers in any time.'

'And I'm a stranger,' said Roger slowly, 'so I might be a man brought in by Dic Sharp?'

'Work it out for yourself,' said Gareth. 'I'm taking the ten o'clock up.' He slid along the bench to the end of the table, and rose. But before moving off he stood for a moment, his fierce sardonic eyes blazing down at Roger.

'Gareth,' said Roger. This was the decisive moment, and he deliberately used the hunchback's name, which he had not done before. 'I'm not in the pay of Dic Sharp. And if you think I am, you've got a damned bad intelligence service and besides that, you're a damned bad guesser.'

'And so?' said Gareth. His worn leather jerkin shone under the electric light like a sweaty forehead.

'And so good-bye. People who are bad guessers can't fight clever men like Dic Sharp.'

The hunchback bent down, bringing his face close to Roger's. 'Now I know you must be working for Dic Sharp. He sent you along to threaten me. To try to get me worried so I'd lose faith in myself.'

'Go ahead,' said Roger. 'Believe any rubbish you like. I've given up.'

Gareth walked to the door, nodding to the landlord in salutation as he went past. He opened the door, then let it swing shut again and stood for a moment staring at it as if trying to see through its panels. Then he turned and walked back to Roger.

'If you're in the square at eight-thirty tomorrow morning,' he said, 'I could show you the time-table.'

'I'll be there,' said Roger.

'I'll look for you,' said Gareth. He nodded several times and went out.

Part Two

The strap of the leather bag was too thin. It cut into Roger's shoulder. Last night, undressing, he had found a red strip of soreness; today he had worn the bag across the other shoulder, but it had been inconvenient, forcing him to sort the change with his left hand. Now the day was over, it was the ten o'clock run up to Llancrwys, and he was tired. The remedy, he decided, would be to get one of those donkey-jackets with leather across the shoulders.

Thinking these thoughts, Roger watched Gareth's arms resting lightly on the big steering-wheel as he brought the bus gently over the last quarter-mile of its run. Most of the passengers had got off. The half-dozen who remained were going all the way to the windswept road that marked the upper limit of Llancrwys. They must be people who lived either in the last huddle of houses or in the scattered cottages on the mountainside. One of them, sitting primly by herself on the back seat, was the spectacular dark beauty from behind the reception desk at the Palace Hotel. Roger had been amazed to see her get on the bus in the town square, flabbergasted when she took a ticket to the end of the run. Was she visiting someone in this rainy huddle, this world's end of wet slate and staring sheep? But whom would a girl like that be visiting? Did she, could she possibly, *live* in Llancrwys? Taking her money, Roger stared at the girl with such undisguised interest that she coloured and turned to look out of the window. She was dressed in a green suède coat that had cost a lot of money. Of course she would have rich boy-friends, a girl who looked like that. Retreating to the front end of the bus, Roger stared at her some more, before going on to think about his sore shoulders and how he ought to get a donkey-jacket.

It would be a waste, of course, to buy a donkey-jacket if

Gareth did not intend to keep him on. Surely Gareth had nothing to lose, much to gain, by letting Roger ride on the bus and take the money? (They did not issue tickets. With very few exceptions, the passengers went to unvarying destinations, handed over the right fare and stood up when they wanted to get off.) Gareth, however, had not uttered. Roger had been on every journey the bus had made since the previous morning, except the eight-fifteen run down from Llancrwys to Caerfenai. He had had to miss that one because he was still staying at the Palace Hotel, a fact which also explained why he had walked the four miles back into town at half-past ten at night. It looked as if he would do the same tonight.

Gareth brought the bus to a gently shuddering halt, and the passengers, who had been chattering loudly among themselves, fell silent as they filed between the seats and down the steps, all except one woman in her fifties whom Roger recognized as Mrs Arkwright, the woman who had held forth in the pub about her Hubert and going back to Bolton. 'I asked them if they weren't ashamed,' Mrs Arkwright was saying over her shoulder. 'Ashamed to let an unprotected woman carry a load that 'ud kill a horse.' She was addressing a man who nodded with weary docility. Roger wondered what the woman could be talking about, then instantly forgot her as the dark beauty undulated past in her suède coat, her eyes fixed on the middle distance as an acknowledgement that she knew what was in Roger's disgusting mind.

She walked away into the gathering darkness. By herself? A girl like that, walking about on a lonely hillside without protection? Roger was just about to formulate the thought that there was, after all, something to be said for sexual assault as a pastime for a man in early middle age when Gareth's voice recalled him to actuality.

'Mrs Arkwright was on her favourite subject again.'

'You mean the one that was in the pub the other night?'

'The Englishwoman,' said Gareth tolerantly.

'And what's her favourite subject?'

'Dustbins,' said Gareth.

Roger waited, but it seemed that nothing more was forthcoming. They stood beside the bus, which gave out a series of faint hissing sighs from its cooling engine, like an animal sinking into sleep after a day's work. It was dark and rather cold, and Roger's bed was four miles away.

'Well,' he said, and stopped.

Gareth stood like a dolmen in the deep dusk. In most places it would have been dark by now, but on this western edge of the land there was still a faint light cast by the long gold and silver streaks that lay above the brooding purple sea. Roger could see Gareth's dark shape, though whether the hunchback's face bore any expression he could not tell.

'I'll take the fares,' said Gareth.

Roger unslung the leather bag and handed it over.

'Coming along tomorrow?' Gareth asked.

'If you want me.'

'You're learning. You'll be quite a help if you keep on, isn't it?'

'So you do want me.'

'I want you, yes,' said Gareth lightly, 'as long as you've got nothing better to do.'

'It helps me to learn Welsh,' said Roger. Without farewell, he began to move away down the dark slope.

'Going?'

'I've got a long way to walk.'

'I've been thinking about that. I reckon I could get you fixed up with somewhere to stay up here.'

Roger stopped. 'When will you know?'

'It's Mrs Pylon Jones. She lives at the first house on the right past the thirty-mile-an-hour sign. We could go and see her to-morrow morning.'

'Mrs Who?'

'Mrs Pylon Jones. Her husband had a big fight with the electricity board to stop them putting a pylon in his field. Fought them day and night for three years, lost his case, and went into hospital the day the lorry drove up with the first sections of the pylon. Never came home alive. That's when she took to letting rooms. A holiday flatlet it is, really. For the summer visitors.'

This, for Gareth, was a long speech. Roger felt that some unusual response was called for, but could not decide what form this should take. 'Mrs Pylon Jones, eh?' he said softly.

'She'll fix you up. Her place has been empty for three weeks.'

'Out of season terms, of course,' said Roger.

'It's a buyer's market,' said Gareth. He chuckled grimly. A gust of wind carried his words and his brief laugh away over the mountainside.

'Who's that girl in the suède coat?' Roger asked.

'Rhiannon Jones.'

'She works at the Palace, doesn't she?'

'Receptionist,' said Gareth shortly.

'Must be her night off,' Roger mused.

'She comes home when it suits her.'

Roger understood the drift of this remark. 'Well,' he said defensively, 'a girl like that's bound to have plenty to do in her spare time.'

'Um,' said Gareth.

There was a silence in which they could hear the cooling radiator make a slight tapping sound, as if trying to warn them.

'Well, good night,' said Roger.

'Good night,' said Gareth. He stood looking on as Roger started his long walk, then called after him, 'Perhaps you'll be able to get a lift.'

'Yes,' Roger said over his shoulder. 'And perhaps it'll rain half-crowns.'

Gareth chuckled again. Then he turned and moved away towards home. Roger walked briskly downhill. In front of him, the last fiery bars of gold lay on the horizon. The bleat of a ewe reached him from some hidden field. He realized that he did not know where Gareth lived.

To keep himself warm, he began to think about Rhiannon.

There was a high wind the next morning. Roger, standing in the square, remembered the time when it would have lifted the girls' skirts and afforded appetizing glimpses of knee and thigh. Now, however, inexorable fashion decreed that knees and thighs should be laid out for inspection like slabs of meat, and the wind was reduced to meaningless displays of aerobatics with scraps of waste paper. Roger stood beneath the statue of Sir Somebody Something with his benevolent bronze face, and looked about. A few General buses stood nearby, waiting to take off for important places with a load of typists and counter-clerks. The space reserved by custom for Gareth's yellow bus was empty, but already Gareth must be rolling along the main road into town.

Madog came stepping briskly along the windy pavement, on his way to work. His bulk was surprisingly agile. 'Hello,' he said, stopping. The estate agent's office could wait a few moments while one passed the time of day.

'Hello. How are the Mohicans coming along?'

'The Cherokees,' Madog corrected. 'I wrote almost a whole section last night.' He intoned ten or a dozen lines in a high, resonant voice. Roger listened as closely as he could, but the intricately-knotted Welsh would not come untied so easily. 'I didn't get any of that,' he said regretfully, as Madog ended.

'Don't worry, man. You'll be able to read it in translation soon.'

'Oh? I wonder what an English version will sound like.'

'Not English,' said Madog. 'French.'

The wind gave another great sigh; scraps of waste paper fluttered round the bronze limbs of Sir What'sit. Madog looked somehow crafty in his blue office suit, like a man wearing a disguise.

'French, eh?' said Roger. He did not know what question to follow up with. 'A new cultural force? The Paris-Caerfenai axis?'

'Not Paris,' said Madog. 'Quebec. Now d'you see?'

'Well ... not quite ...'

'I'll tell you all about it some time,' said Madog. 'Late for the office now.'

He walked on, but without haste. He did not look like a man who was late for the office. More probably he had decided not to give Roger any more information about his deal with Quebec, whatever it was, until he had thought the matter over some more.

Roger's gaze wandered across the square. Ivo and Gito were going into the café. Ivo saw him looking and gave a slight wave of the hand. Derisive, or friendly? Half-friendly at best. Well, his position was bound to look strange from where Ivo stood. Strange, and suspicious.

And yet it was all so utterly opaque. Did he, Roger, really look like someone who might be employed by Dic Sharp to infiltrate and sabotage Gareth's bus company? Would Dic Sharp employ such an obvious outsider, an Englishman, a *bourgeois*? Or did his appearance somehow not suggest that he was English and *bourgeois*? What, in that case, did his appearance suggest?

A yellow shape nosed into the square, an oblong of metal and glass, full of Llancrwys thoughts and feelings. Llancrwys was about to add its daily transfusion to the life-blood of Caerfenai. Gareth grinned briefly at Roger as he brought the bus round in a tight circle and came to a halt beside the statue of Sir Who'sit. The passengers began to get down. It pleased Roger to find that he recognized several of them already. There was, for instance, Mr Cledwyn Jones, plump and grave in his dark suit, as befitted a man who kept the minutes for the Society of Something-or-other and whom they would not be able to get on without. There was the thick-set young man with the huge fists, who had scowled in a corner of the pub on that wild, wet night after the debacle with Beverley (did she really exist? On the same planet?) There was, oh, God in heaven, Rhiannon in her suède coat. He had already noticed that she was not on duty at the hotel. Close behind her came another person he remembered from the pub that night: the dark, shy watchful youth who had sat under the lee of the bar and held his peace. When Rhiannon got down from the bus, looking straight in front of her like a queen, this lad moved with her as if determined to keep his feet on her shadow, and his dark eyes never left her back.

They had gone, and Gareth had switched off the engine and was coming out after them, his huge crooked bulk filling the doorway of the bus.

'All ready for work, eh? Well, there's nothing to do till we go back up at ten-thirty. We'll have a cup of tea first.'

They walked together across the Square. Inside the café, Ivo and Gito were sitting at a formica-topped table among the cardboard placards. On the wall, an out-of-date calendar dustily celebrated the female form. Cigarette smoke drifted upward, and the tea-urn gleamed under the naked light-bulb like tarnished silver.

'We're fortifying ourselves,' said Ivo, tapping the thick white clay of his teacup. 'There should be half a bottle of brandy in this tea, if my physicians hadn't warned me against high blood pressure. We're just off to do a deal with the tightest skinflint in Wales, man.'

'There's a lot of contenders for that title,' said Gareth, lowering himself on to a rickety chair.

'Ah, but this is Fivepercent Jones,' said Gito.

'That's a tough nut,' Gareth agreed.

Roger, listening, drank his dark, oversweetened tea.

'Know what he's buying now?' Ivo demanded. 'Lampposts.' He pulled back his woollen cap and scratched his head vigorously. 'Old gas lamps. He reckons they'll be all the go. In people's gardens. Like coach-lamps. So he's got dozens of 'em, in a special warehouse.' He leaned towards them over the table. 'Know what he did last week? His old grandmother died. Had her buried by the Co-op funeral-service. He went to the funeral in a black coat and striped trousers. And then what? Got straight in his car and went down to the Co-op office. They were just shutting for the day, putting their coats on. But before he'd let 'em out of his sight he collected the dividend stamps and took them home to stick in his book. Wanted the divi on Grandma's interment. Business is business, dead or alive.'

Was the story invented? Or just exaggerated? Roger could not tell from Gareth's grim chuckle or Gito's delighted, squash-faced grin. Still, it was a relief that Ivo and Gito were amiable and ready to talk. Without actually addressing a remark to him, Ivo had seemed to glance several times in Roger's direction during his story about Fivepercent Jones and the Co-op. He decided to test his welcome a little further. If Ivo had given up the insane suspicion that he was a paid agent of Dic Sharp's, let him show it now.

'Who is this chap Fivepercent?' he asked, casually, as if to join in the conversation were his undisputed right.

Ivo showed no trace of annoyance. Neither, on the other hand, did he show any sign of having heard. He continued his stream of talk, directed mainly at Gareth, but now, easily and without any change of expression, he switched languages and spoke in Welsh.

Roger had to admire the adroitness of the snub. Without truculence, without anything that came remotely near making a scene, Ivo had told him that he was not welcome. Gito also modulated into Welsh: so did Gareth, though he could hardly have understood the background to the situation. Gravely, calmly, they talked in their impenetrable language.

Roger knew that he ought to feel insulted, but he could not summon up any resentment. Their pride pleased him. It fitted in with the way he thought they ought to behave. All doomed ethnic groups should be proud; it would be too horrible if they were servile, apologizing for their lingering existence. As for the affront to his own pride, he could not feel it as real. So little of his character, after all, was involved in these relationships. If the visiting anthropologist is insulted by the Stone Age hunter, that insult makes an interesting entry for his notebook.

Presently, Ivo took out a large gun-metal watch, consulted it, and said what was evidently the equivalent of 'This'll never do.' He and Gito stood up, said their farewells, and even gave Roger a friendly enough nod as they moved away.

'Pob hwyl,' Roger said over his shoulder, 'Good luck,' keeping up face by pretending that he knew enough Welsh to have followed their talk and had been silent from choice.

'Good progress,' said Ivo, poker-faced. 'You'll be ready for a job in the education any day now.'

The pair pushed through the door and out into the Square. Had Gareth noticed how Ivo had put Roger in his place? Perhaps not. His face seemed merely businesslike and preoccupied.

'I've seen Mrs Pylon Jones already,' he said. 'She'll be in when we take the ten-thirty run up. I'll take you to her.'

Gareth had spoken of showing Roger the time-table, but this seemed to have been a general euphemism for starting work. Gareth's concern was not the sort that put out printed timetables. There was not, as far as Roger could make out, even a typewritten sheet. He had to follow as Gareth explained it verbally.

'We fit in with what the people want to do, isn't it?' (Philologist Roger was beginning to watch for that 'isn't it,' an exact equivalent of the French n'est-ce pas which these people used when they talked English, and to try to hunt it down to a Welsh original.) 'There's the morning trip down for those that go to work, and school kids. Up at ten-thirty – usually no-body much on then, except a few women who shopped early, but we've got to get up ready to come down at eleven. That's nearly all women going to the shops, and we get the same lot back up at twelve, in time to cook whatever they've got for dinner. Down again at twelve-thirty, then the time's our own till the four-fifteen up (school kids), then down again at five, up at five-forty-five – very full, then, everybody coming back from work. Seven o'clock down –' (Roger winced: this was the run he had rendered impossible the other night), 'then stay down till we take the ten o'clock up.'

All this, Gareth had volunteered in the café in the square, as they sat over their empty cups and waited for ten-thirty. Roger felt elated by the flow of prosaic detail as by inhaling oxygen. It meant acceptance. Yesterday, Gareth had given him no overall view of the time-table during the whole long day, merely telling him at the end of each run what time they would be making the next one. Now, they were colleagues.

They rattled up to Llancrwys with the bus almost empty, and Gareth was ready to take Roger to Mrs Pylon Jones. Leaving the bus to sigh out the heat from its engine in the fine morning air, they walked down the hill a little way. Mrs Pylon Jones's house had a brown front door which was for her, and a green side door which was for the holiday people. She had had her house converted, after the death of Mr Pylon Jones, so as to give the holiday people two rooms plus kitchen and bathroom, self-contained, with a view over the Irish Sea and a coin-operated gas meter. All was in order, it had cost Mrs Pylon Jones good money, out of the late Mr Pylon Jones's carefully amassed savings, and now the summer was over and it was standing empty. So much Gareth indicated to Roger as they approached the brown door. When Gareth knocked, Mrs Pylon Jones opened it immediately, as if she had been crouching just inside the door and looking at them through the letter-box. She was like a wild grouse of the moors: small, drab, quick and watchful.

They exchanged three-cornered greetings and then Mrs Pylon Jones came out of the house, produced a key, and led the way in again through the green door. The holiday people's flatlet looked clean and anonymous, with the sort of furniture that had never, in its life, belonged to anyone personally but had been bought at furniture sales in order to fit out rooms of just this kind. The impression of a non-place, of a habitat or biotope that could never be battered into the semblance of a home, was overpowering, but Roger knew at once that he was going to take it.

'I charge five guineas a week for it, in the season,' said Mrs Pylon Jones, standing just inside the door.

'This isn't the season, though,' said Gareth.

'I'd come down a bit, of course,' said Mrs Pylon Jones.

'I expect I could manage three pounds,' said Roger.

'Two 'ud be more like it,' said Gareth.

'I couldn't be doing with two,' said Mrs Pylon Jones softly and quickly. 'It wouldn't pay for the wear and tear, not two.'

'He wouldn't be in much,' said Gareth.

'Three would be all right,' said Roger.

'There's your heating on top,' Gareth warned.

'And lighting,' Mrs Pylon Jones murmured.

'I shan't be in much,' Roger smiled.

They clinched it.

That night, alone and melancholy in Mrs Pylon Jones's holiday people's bed, he lay and listened to the wind walking over the rough hillside. The wind mocked him as it stirred the thin grasses and ruffled the fleece of the resting sheep. *Over half of life is gone*, it sighed through the keyhole and down the chimney.

Sleeping, he saw Margot. She still seemed to him beautiful, with her red hair drawn back and her challenging green eyes. No human being has green eyes. He knew that and yet Margot's had always seemed to him the colour of unattainable emeralds.

Unattainable? But he had attained her, he had worked long and honestly at the task of wooing her, she had grown to love him, she had yielded to him all her womanliness, they had been naked together and laughed and played and sighed and laughed again. She had panted and shivered and been his. But then it had come, the insurmountable difficulty. And now in his dream, stirring heavily in Mrs Pylon Jones's bed, it came again.

'But there are hospitals that *exist* to look after people like Geoffrey.'

'Geoffrey isn't people like Geoffrey, he's Geoffrey and he's my own flesh and blood. He's not going into one of those places.'

'Well, it's him or me. I can't stand it.'

'You'd get used to it. I have.'

'As you say, he's your flesh and blood.'

'Well, so are you. He's my flesh and blood through being my brother and you are because we love each other.'

'Yes, I've heard that before.' Her eyes were emerald-hard. 'The twain shall become one flesh.'

'Don't you believe it?'

'And what if I do believe it?' She whirled to face him. 'With children? I bear children for you and they have to grow up in the same house as *that*?'

'Geoffrey isn't *that*, he's Geoffrey, and don't exaggerate, it's not as if he was disgusting or anything.'

'Well, he is to me. He's disgusting because he's so pathetic. Life's no use to him, why doesn't he die?'

After that, the dream became wild. Lust gripped them, and they slavered and bit at each other. Margot panted. 'Wait, let's get undressed,' but while they were snatching off their clothes a wall of plate glass grew up between them, thick, and cold. Naked, they rushed to it, pressing with all their might to try to get some feel of each other's bodies through its implacable surface. The glass flattened Margot's nipples. Roger had a tremendous erection but it was no good, the glass was there, and from somewhere behind him, Geoffrey was saying, 'I'm dying, Roger. I'm dying.'

About dawn he woke and flung aside the bedclothes. Standing in the middle of the room, still dazed with the unhappiness of his dream and the bitterness of the truths it had forced him to taste over again, he saw through the window the dark shoulder of the hill and the grey, dawn-streaked sky. Quickly putting on his clothes, he went out through the green door, buttoning his overcoat as the cold morning air came buffeting at him, but rejoicing as a strong swimmer rejoices in rough cold water. Then, bareheaded, his eyes still blinking away his wretched sleep, he began to walk: up the hill, through a metal gate, along a path that followed the windy curve of the hillside, with the miles of sea glistening far below on his right hand, and on his left the mountains lifting their hard green heads to the new light. He walked quickly, mindlessly; sheep got to their feet at his approach and bolted away, casting resentful looks; even the shepherds were not abroad so early; wide-winged crows circled above, observing him.

Roger walked until his limbs were thoroughly irrigated with warm blood, his lungs refreshed, his eyes washed by the bright air. Then, as suddenly as he had begun to walk, he stopped. There was no point in moving any further; he was at the centre of the universe, the focus of form and meaning. Above him, the new day climbed up from behind the mountains, pouring flood after flood of pristine light across the washed sky. Away to the west, the sea, much darker than the sky, drew into itself all solidity until it seemed heavier than the mountains, a flat solid plain on which the mind could build its pyramids. On the hillside, everything was pared-down, economical : the small trees, made cunning by the wind, hugged the slope of the ground with perfect strategic economy; not far off, a long, single-storeyed cottage pressed itself to the ground for the same reason, but challenged the wind with a quick, tumbling stream of smoke from its chimney. People were waking, they were having tea and porridge, they were looking through their windows and estimating the weather. Somewhere round on the other side of the hill, in the village, Gareth would be stirring and grunting in the last few minutes of his sleep, his tight back pushing blankets into a mound. And down towards the sea, in some unguessable spot, Dic Sharp was opening his eyes to smile at his money-bags.

The sun broke free of the mountains and prodded a long finger of light down towards Roger. Everything was new-minted, gilded, ringed with an entirely beautiful fire. On the wicked, on the weak, on the sensual, on the broken and disappointed, on every man and woman and bird and animal the sun would shine, and the wind would breathe, that day.

After so lyrical a beginning, today seemed encouraging, holding out possibilities of luck, a day fit for practical action and the facing of difficulties. Since the Beverley fiasco, Roger had been aware of a dragging lack of energy; he had been moving, a step at a time, in this strange unknown world, but always with a sense of having nothing in reserve. Now, he felt that he might assault his problems, sharply and on a broad front.

The first problem was money. He had brought a few traveller's cheques with him, but these were almost gone. Now that he had decided to stay in the district for a while, he must make some definite arrangement with the bank. And also find out (he shudderingly told himself) what his balance stood at. And also check out of the Palace Hotel, and pay his bill; for he had not even done that yet, though the bargain with Mrs Pylon Jones had been struck.

For this last vacillation, however, Roger had a motive. He wanted if possible to make sure that when he paid his bill and checked out of the hotel, Rhiannon would be on duty behind the desk. It would give him a golden opportunity to get into conversation with her. The trouble was, Rhiannon's spells of duty had no pattern that he could discern. Sometimes she was on the first run down in the morning, sometimes on the midday run up, sometimes on the last run down as if she were going on night-duty. Perhaps, when he had been on the bus for a few weeks, he would begin to see the outlines of a system in her peregrinations. But at the moment, it was guess-work. He had already gone along to the Palace Hotel, in one of his off-duty spells, and looked into the lobby to see if Rhiannon were there. She had not been, and he had gone out again, preferring to pay for his room for another day or more, if it meant that he would be able to strike up an acquaintance with her. She was so beautiful, so young, so marvellously turned out, so unapproachable by anyone who did not have a fast car and a wad of ready cash and a safe family business and a tanned face that crinkled easily into a grin and broad shoulders under an impeccably cut suit, that Roger knew quite well he was wasting his time. Even so, he bent his steps towards the Palace Hotel. It was eleven-twenty, and he was free till they went up again at twelve.

She was there. Fresh, dewy, dark-haired as an Egyptian but with a cool and rosy bloom on her perfect skin, she was sitting on a high stool behind the reception desk as if it were a cocktail bar and she a calmly watchful customer.

'Hello,' he said.

She smiled at him without speaking, and managed to put a slight tinge of the interrogative into her smile. (Why do you address me? And why so familiarly?)

'I'd like my bill, please. I'm checking out today.'

'Certainly.' She turned, and spoke to another girl who was working behind a glass partition. 'The bill for four-two-eight, please.'

She knows the number of my room without having to search her memory. Did she take special note of it? Was she ready at any time to . . .

'Here it is, sir,' she said, crisp and courteous, pushing a piece of paper across to him.

Sir?

'I'm on the bus run now, you know,' he said, signing his last traveller's cheque. 'Helping Gareth.'

'Yes, I've seen you.'

'I live up your . . . in Llancrwys. I've found a place.'

She turned to give the traveller's cheque to the cashier.

'Thank you, sir. Here's your change.'

'It sounds funny when you call me *sir*. As between fellow-residents of Llancrwys – we should be more democratic.'

'It's how I always speak to the guests.'

'Well, I'm not one. Any more.'

'All right,' she said dismissively.

He bowed out, defeated. At least she had dropped the *sir*, that barbed wire fence. Still, no doubt she had other forms of barbed wire left in reserve.

As he turned away, she slipped down from the stool, and he noticed that she was wearing a short and highly elegant black leather skirt. Her blouse was coral-red. The whole colour-effect was so beautiful that it affected him like a sandbag on the back of the head. Going towards the door, he felt himself walking unsteadily.

Get a grip on yourself, Furnivall.

The head porter was at his elbow, asking if he wanted his bags brought down from his room. Oh, God. Was there anything still up there? Could he face going back to Rhiannon and asking for the key? But no, the man had the key in his hand.

'I think I've taken most of my stuff – if you could just send someone up to look round . . .'

Dr Conroy was there, for one thing. And some underwear in the drawer.

'Ask him to check the drawers ... Look, perhaps, I'd better go up myself ...'

The head porter was bland and firm. Roger must not go. He summoned a menial, gave him the key. In a few moments, Roger's few scattered possessions were brought to him in a paper carrier-bag. His case was already at Mrs Pylon Jones's. What an exit: scrappy and undignified. Why had he been so unmethodical? Was Rhiannon looking across at him? Was she suppressing a giggle, or smiling faintly with contempt? Savagely, he took the carrier bag and, quickly rummaging in his pocket, handed the head porter a sum sufficient to install a heated swimming-pool in the garden of his bijou suburban residence.

'Oh, thank you, sir.'

'Not at all.'

He hurried out, sweating. Perhaps he would catch Rhiannon on the mountain one dark night. Not too dark, though – he wanted to see what he was doing.

He had just time for the bank, which was further down the street, before reporting to Gareth for the twelve o'clock run up. There, he explained his business and waited while they took down all the details. 'As soon as we clear it with your London branch, sir, you can have a temporary arrangement to cash cheques here. Up to what limit shall we say, per week?'

'Twenty pounds,' he said. There wouldn't be much money in his London account; exactly how little, they were going to find out for him. Probably about a hundred or a hundred and fifty pounds. And nothing coming in until January 1, when he would get a salary cheque from the university, with all sorts of deductions at source. What a dog's life. Why hadn't he saved money, why had he got to the age of forty without having a couple of thousand stashed away? He knew the answer before he had formulated the question: women. Forced, as he had been, to grab what sexual satisfactions he could on a casual basis, he had equally been forced into the role of big spender. Standing now in the cool, impersonal bank with the polished counters and engraved glass partitions, he felt faint at the thought of the money he had handed out, by the cartload, to restaurateurs and hotel proprietors, the quantities of rich food he had swallowed without feeling hungry, the delicate wines he had swilled without tasting them; and always the swift nemesis of the folded piece of paper on the plate. No wonder he was a poor man. It had cost him so much to satisfy his biological urges, and here he was, after disbursing the ransom of a score of kings, as unsatisfied as ever. The benefit was felt for such a short time, that was the unfair thing . . . Nodding to the trim cashier, he left the bank and walked quickly back to the square.

'I shall have my lunch-time pint in the Grapes,' said Gareth, after they had made their next run up and down. He was referring, Roger knew, to the pub that smelt of smoke and carbolic. The tone in which he gave the information was almost an invitation. Roger understood that if he were to ask, 'Mind if I come along?' Gareth would say that he did not mind. Inch by inch, they were moving towards some kind of *camaraderie*. But instead he said, 'Oh, I think I'll try the Italian's place myself.' It was better to keep some pride, not to thrust himself on Gareth.

'Right,' said Gareth. 'See you at half-past four,' and he carried his bulk away on pin-legs, across the square. Roger, his shoulder blessedly free of the cutting strap, walked down the slope to the pub kept by the Italian, promising himself a delicious hour of idleness and then, perhaps, a walk by the sea.

Mid-week, the Italian's pub was not very busy at lunchtime, though if Ivo and Gito were present there was always the illusion of a crowd. A few men in caps and raincoats were drinking pints in corners. Leaning against the bar, in quiet, deep conversation with the Italian, was Madog.

Roger was not sure of the etiquette of the situation, so he stood a little way down the bar and waited to be noticed. Madog's blue suit was crumpled and shiny; his hair needed cutting, and the fat round his midriff caused him to lean against the bar in an ungainly posture. Could he really be any good as a poet? Roger determined to hurry forward with his Welsh studies and read some of Madog's work as soon as possible. Certainly the commonplaceness of the man's appearance was no barrier to his being a genuine poet. That he looked quintessentially like a young man employed in a provincial estate agent's office was, if anything, a point in his favour, since poets who looked like poets were so often blatant impostors. The Italian, for his part, looked ready to go on stage in the chorus of a Verdi opera, to shout and huzza and pretend to drink out of a cardboard wine-goblet. His hair was like the pelt of a wolverine. It surged like dark surf around the bravely jutting rocks of his ears. He and Madog were looking at a cutting from a newspaper.

After a few minutes one of the raincoated men called out to the landlord in Welsh, addressing him by name, 'Mario!', and evidently pointing out that there was a customer waiting. The landlord glanced up impatiently and, seeing Roger, said something to him in his liquid Welsh.

'Sorry,' said Roger, smiling apologetically, 'I don't speak Welsh yet. Still taking the first steps.'

At the sound of his voice Madog looked up from the newspaper cutting and greeted him with a gesture.

'English,' said the landlord. 'What you like? I serve you now. We were reading something interesting. About Bree-tanny.'

'Oh. Oh? A pint of bitter, please.'

'Yairss, Bree-tanny,' the landord repeated. 'They are breaking the shop windows. The what you may call. Plate glass.'

'Oh?' said Roger cautiously. Who were? What was the man talking about?

'One an' nine,' said the landlord, pushing the beer gently over to Roger. His demeanour was not hostile, nor was it friendly; 'triumphant' would more or less describe it.

Roger handed him one-and-ninepence and said, 'Plate glass windows, eh?'

'Yairss,' the landlord beamed. He swept the money into the till. 'All adown the main street in Combourg. Is commandos.'

Roger shot a mute glance of appeal, over the rim of his glass, towards Madog.

'It's the Breton commandos,' Madog explained. 'Here, see for yourself.' He brought the newspaper cutting over to Roger. 'They've been blowing up shop-windows with plastic bombs. At night, so that no one got hurt. But if that has no effect –' he paused eloquently.

Roger picked up the piece of newspaper. 'I'm afraid I don't

know who the Breton commandos are,' he said, still feeling the need to apologize. 'Is it that they're –'

'Hah!' The landlord gave a great boom of satisfaction. 'Is just what they are saying in Paris. Who are these people? Where they coming from, these leetle people calling themselves commandos?' He shook with silent mirth, holding himself up against the bar. 'Then one day BAZOOM!' He whirled his arms in the narrow space in front of the bottles.

'They regard the French as occupiers,' Madog explained more gently. His smile had something tolerant, even sadly forbearing, which irritated Roger more than the landlord's theatricality. 'They want independence from Paris. Their requests through the usual channels have been ignored, so they're moving on to force. They're trained and they have weapons.'

'Weapons, yairss,' the landlord said, 'and money. Plenty of everything. Next time, is not only the shop-windows.' He smiled in delight.

'Well,' said Roger, drinking, 'that's their affair, I suppose.'

'Oh, Mario's all for joining in,' Madog grinned. 'He's going over to Brittany on his fortnight's holiday next September, and he's hoping to make contact with the commandos and join them in a bit of action.'

'Not really?'

'Yairss, really,' said the landlord, bending forward over the bar. 'Is coming here. Independence from Westa Minister too slow. Somebody got to help it along. So we get some practical experience. Go with the commandos. First the shop-windows at night. Then burn a few parked cars. Strike here, strike there, melt away. Show them we mean business. Then Westa Minister give way before violence comes. Set up Home Rule, Welsh parliament. English people shows passports at the frontier.'

Roger drank a long draught of his beer. He did not wish to be involved in some lunatic discussion, but on the other hand he felt that the landlord would become dangerous if he merely tried to fob him off. Besides, Madog was watching closely for his reaction. What did he read in Madog's face? Bland interest? A slightly malicious pleasure?

'What's your attitude to all this?' Roger asked Madog, bluntly.

'What would yours be,' Madog smiled, 'if you were a Cherokee?'

'You're impossible,' Roger shrugged, meaning it.

Madog was still bland. 'The English always have this difficulty. It's impossible for them to believe that they really do have enemies.'

'Not any longer, surely. In this century we've been made to believe it.'

'It hasn't changed. The English still grow up believing a version of their own history that's all light and no shade. They literally know nothing of the injustices they've perpetrated. They avoid guilt by keeping their minds a blank. Of all the thousands of English tourists who flock to Ireland every summer, how many have the faintest conception of what the English have made the Irish suffer? Question one in ten as they come off the ferry-boat. Try to find one who's even heard of the fact that the English government's policies led directly to the potato famine of the 'forties, when a million Irish died of hunger in a land of plenty – plenty they were forbidden to touch.'

'Oh, come on – it's a matter of –'

'English soldiers guarded the food stores so that the starving Irish populace shouldn't get it,' said Madog. His smile had gone now. 'The Irish agricultural worker had produced a surplus of everything, but he couldn't share in it. Potatoes were his food, and when the potatoes rotted, he starved amid plenty.'

'Yes, I know, and I'm not defending –'

'English people show passports,' the landlord said. 'Check up on them. Wales a rich country, steel, coal. Listen,' he said. 'Irish have their rebellion in nineteen-sixteen. Here, we wait too long. Too dam' long.'

'Well, perhaps you'll get your freedom by constitutional –'

'Nineteen forty-three,' the landlord said. 'Two Englishmen take me prisoner. Two of them together. They tell me they going to cut my balls off. All the way back to base they keep saying, When we get back to base, Eye-tye, we cut off your balls. Then they laugh.'

'But surely you didn't believe them.'

'Yairss, I believe them. Mussolini he told us –'

'Yes, but for Christ's sake, if you're going to bring Mussolini –'

'What the Welsh have always needed,' said Madog suddenly, 'is a Haile Selassie.'

Roger looked at him, speechless. The landlord, still brooding on his threatened *cojones*, went to the other end of the bar to serve a customer.

Almost angrily, certainly with an exasperated wish to get to the bottom of all this, Roger turned to Madog. 'Now, have a drink and tell me all about this political hornets' nest I seem to have walked into.'

'Oh, Mario's an activist,' said Madog, shrugging humorously. 'Perhaps I would be if anyone had ever taken me prisoner and threatened to castrate me. You see, after that he became a P.O.W. in this district and he put down roots here, married a local girl. He has a raft of kids and none of them speak much English, he sees to that. But people round here were kind to him during the war. I imagine they would have been the same in an English country district, but the way it registered on Mario was that the Welsh had been dragged by the English into a quarrel that wasn't their own and they had no feeling against a soldier from the other side.'

'Well, he can't have had much feeling for his own country if he –'

'He never knew it except under Mussolini. He's never been back. He thinks of himself as a Welshman now, of Italian extraction, and it irks him like hell to have to carry a British passport.'

'Oh, he's a British subject, is he?'

'What d'you think he is,' grinned Madog, 'a foreigner?'

They looked down the bar to where Mario was wiping glasses on a striped cloth that looked like one of his old shirts, and muttering to himself about that dreadful day in 1943.

'He left the land as soon as he was free to,' said Madog, 'and got a job as factotum in this pub. It was kept by an old lady who'd lived in Caerfenai since Victorian times. He was good to her and when she finally got too old to run the pub she recommended him to the brewery and he got the licence.'

'But doesn't he insult the English visitors in the summer? Put powdered glass in their –'

'Not him. That was a rare outburst we've just heard. Usually he's like everybody else, he keeps business and politics in very water-tight compartments. Beer-tight would be more accurate.'

They called Mario back and ordered a round and some sandwiches. He served them without apparent hostility, only remarking, 'My holidays, I go to Combourg.'

'You do that,' said Roger. He paid for his share of the beer and sandwiches and carried them over to a table.

'Actually,' said Madog, 'it's the cultural offensive that seems the best bet to me.'

'But isn't it terribly frustrating to write in a language that has so few readers?'

'Things aren't moving that way,' said Madog. He took a sip at his beer and looked rather secretive. 'That's not the way they're going, by any means.'

Roger waited for him to elaborate, but he added nothing except, 'You'll see something if you're around these parts for a while.'

They were silent, as if to let that part of the conversation sink down out of sight, and then Madog said, 'Now if I were going to Brittany I'd want to establish contact with some of the poets.'

'Oh yes?' said Roger, chewing.

'Some of the Breton poets are excellent,' said Madog. 'You'll have no difficulty with them once you have a grip on Welsh. I could show you –'

Their conversation became scholarly and technical, and once more Roger felt that he liked and admired Madog. A little earlier, he had not been quite so sure.

They talked until the pub closed and Madog went back to the office, so full of beer that he must surely slumber over the details of superior modern residences with all main services. Roger, standing on the pavement, looked up at the sky. It was full of tumbling clouds against a background of steady blue. The air was gloriously fresh. Ah, that walk he had promised himself! He moved quickly along the quayside, by the moored fishing boats, and over the salt-dusted planks of the harbour bridge. Now his back was to the town. The narrow, crumbling road, hardly used by traffic since it came to a dead end at the harbour bridge, followed the winding outline of the shore. In summer, visitors' cars found their way round from the main road and pulled on to the grass verge like metal beasts put out to graze, while their owners splashed and shouted in the sea, or dozed in shelters behind the newspaper, or licked ice-cream cornets. Now nothing remained of those three pleasure-seeking months except a tattered scrap of paper here and there in the brambles that lay across the low wall on the landward side, and on the beach a plastic bucket, forgotten by some town child now dreaming of Christmas, sticking fast where the tide could not float it away.

Roger walked, breathing deeply, delighting in the bareness and loneliness of the scene, the bearded rocks with shellfish clinging to them, the low hulk of Anglesey across the dully shining water, the stretches of mud patrolled by wading birds. In the holiday season, this stretch of shore was probably insufferable, but now, with the winter well set in, there was nobody about, and ... but as he rounded a curve, he saw that there was somebody about. A bright blue mini-car was drawn up on the meagre grass verge about fifty yards ahead of him. His eyes searched for the human figures that belonged to it, and after a few seconds he found them, down on the margin of the lapping sea: two small, absorbed children bending over the rocks, and beside them, their young mother. For an instant his eye rested on the group indifferently, taking pleasure in them simply as a focus of the human that gave composition to the picture he was enjoying. But, almost at once, the mother's figure straightened up and looked back towards the shore, and he saw a heavy thatch of dark hair, and in the same instant something familiar about the carriage of the body. Yes, it was. It was Jenny.

She had not seen him. One of the children, then the other, asked her something. He could hear the piping little voices so clearly in the quiet afternoon, though he could not tell what they were saying, and he heard her own voice, answering and reassuring – her voice that seemed to him, though it was lower in tone, as fresh and as young as their eager fledgling-cries. That was how they struck him, the three of them, as he paused to take in the scene for a moment without being recognized: a trio of children, equally lissom, equally delicate and unmarked and ready for life, jumping quickly from stone to stone or bending with sudden eagerness in whatever quest it was that absorbed them: the mother's figure larger than the offspring's, but merely, as it were, scaled up.

Standing motionless, he took her in, avidly. She was wearing levis, the inevitable leisure wear of her generation, and her upper half was encased in a chunky dark-red sweater within which her own outline was lost, but enticingly so. How slim she was, how eagerly her body moved. He knew, suddenly but finally, that he wanted her: not just as that abstraction, a woman, to be drawn into the vortex of his impersonal need for sexual contact, but as herself, as the unique, individual Jenny.

But she was married. All that about her being like a child, a third, larger child in that group of innocent children, was fantasy. She was a married woman. Unhappily, unsuitably married, as he was unhappily, unsuitably lonely. And both states were about equally hard to break out of.

He hesitated, wondering whether to walk past her, or turn and slink back into Caerfenai, shirking an encounter, or pluck up his spirit and go to her and talk. He needed her, and his need made him afraid. If she rebuffed him ... resented his interfering in a brief idyllic interlude in her trying life. ... But, as often happens, by standing still he had become conspicuous. One of the children glanced towards him, then the other, and now Jenny was looking at him. She looked away, then back at him again, as if wondering whether this was someone she recognized. In desperation, he waved some sort of half-hearted greeting and began to walk on towards her.

'It's Roger Furnivall, isn't it?' she called up, when he drew level, across the ten yards of rock and weed that separated the water's edge from the road.

'Yes,' he said, and immediately, as if her words had been an invitation, dropped down on to the beach and began to pick his way toward them. 'Hunting in the rock-pools?' he asked, drawing near. (Take a kindly interest. The favourite uncle. Get into conversation somehow.)

'There aren't any rock-pools here,' she said, straightening up and giving him that level look that made the candour of her eyes seem almost painful. 'It's the only thing I've got against this coast-line. It's just plain shingle.'

'We're looking for pretty stones,' the elder children informed him. Coming to a halt, Roger focussed the children and saw that the one who had just spoken to him was a girl, about five years old, and the younger, who was still looking at him in shy silence, was a boy who seemed a year or so younger.

'Pretty stones, eh? Have you found a lot?'

'Yes,' said the tot, self-possessed and proprietary. 'They're in this bag.' And she held up a stitched woollen bag in gay colours. 'All these are mine. Robin's got his in his pockets.'

'I'm only getting white ones,' said the boy, his voice shy and hardly audible. He put his hands quickly into his pockets, as if to guard his treasures from theft by this staring newcomer.

'Mary, Robin, this is Mr Furnivall,' Jenny introduced them gravely.

'Is he a friend of Daddy's?' Mary asked, her eyes summing up Roger's potentialities for entertainment.

'No, he's a friend of mine.'

That's something, at least.

'Is this a favourite spot of yours?' Roger asked. It sounded fatuous, one of those questions like *Do you come here often*, but she answered it in all seriousness.

'Very much so. I got into the habit of coming here when I was a student. Long, lonely walks while I wondered what Life would Hold.' She laughed, mocking herself, but without self-pity. 'And now I know what it Holds, I still come here. Nearly always with the children, now. They're going to grow up in a world of suburbs – I want them to have some early memories of a bit of the earth's surface that isn't suburban.'

'I'd guess,' he said, 'that you have some early impressions of that kind yourself. Something to set over against suburbia.'

'You're right, thank God. My father used to go fishing a lot. He'd take us to Dovedale, my brother and me, and let us run wild all day long, when we were hardly bigger than these two.'

'Here's one, Mummy,' said Mary, pouncing. 'A lovely red one.'

Her mother duly admired it before it disappeared into the bag. 'The colours are so delicate,' she said to Roger. 'Some of them are a lovely dark green – that's my favourite. It's green slate, I suppose, shaped by the sea.'

'I like the bright ones best,' said Mary. 'My dolls like them. They have a big house to live in and they need ornaments and jewellery. My Daddy says all ladies like ornaments and jewellery, and my dolls are ladies.'

Roger, now that he looked closely at the children, could see that Mary had the same shaped face as her father's: it was rounder than Jenny's, and when it was grown it would have less delicacy. Nevertheless, it was not like Twyford's face: nothing calculating looked out from the eyes; it was innocent, untainted. The boy, who now approached, was much more a replica of his mother.

'I've got some white ones in my pockets,' he said, looking up at Roger as if he had decided to trust him. 'White as milk, white as pillow-cases, white as clouds. That's what we said when we had the game.' (He did not explain what game.) 'Would you like to see them?'

'Very much.'

The chubby hand disappeared into the pocket, then the other into the other pocket. Five white stones were solemnly deposited in Roger's expectant hand. They were utterly smooth, and the light that shone through them was pure and milky. One or two of them had tiny veins of crimson.

'I don't put mine in the dolls' house. I don't play with dolls. I'm using mine to make a garden.'

'Oh, yes?'

'Yes. A moon garden.'

'A moon garden?'

'The kind they have on the moon. All white.'

Robin took the stones back into his small, clutching fingers. 'Have you looked at them enough now?'

'Yes, thank you.'

'I'll put them back in my pocket then.'

He put the stones back and returned to his quest. Both children, now, withdrew their attention from Roger and went back to the serious business of the afternoon. It was as if, now that they had processed him into their consciousness, they could ignore him and leave him to their mother to deal with.

Roger looked at Jenny with a new intensity. How much more he wanted her than he wanted, say, Rhiannon. Of course Rhiannon was the more beautiful girl of the two. But she was too damned beautiful: she excited him to the point of unbalance. Even if, by some fantastic chance, he managed to win her, he would never be able to live up to her. With Jenny, he could imagine a happiness that was credible, realistic: a domestic happiness that had room in it for these two children, condemned otherwise to grow up in the stifling money-atmosphere created by Gerald Twyford, and in a *milieu* where they would be constantly exposed to the sight and sound of loathsome body-ticks like Donald Fisher. He needed her: he could give her what she needed too: why not try? The wind blew over the wrinkled water, cold and salty, dispelling falsity.

'D'you ever get an evening free?' he abruptly asked her.

'Sometimes.' Her voice was flat, deliberate.

He crowded in. 'Will you spend one with me some time?'

She looked away across the water. 'Doing what?'

'Anything you like. Eating, drinking, talking.'

She frowned. 'Restaurants are out. There isn't one round here that's any good and anyway,' her voice stopped, but he understood what she meant to convey. She was married: restaurants are public places.

'I wasn't thinking of a restaurant,' he said quickly. 'I'll cook you a meal at my place.'

'Oh,' she said, turning to him with a flash of mocking amusement, 'you have a *place*?'

He laughed. The word was so loaded with the sad and funny associations of bachelorhood. 'Everybody lives somewhere.'

'But you live somewhere where you could have me to dinner and cook for me. How snug.'

'I won't be mocked,' he said. 'I'm an honest working man and I've taken one of those holiday flatlets that people pay huge prices for between June and September. I get it for a song.'

'That's good,' she said, the mockery vanished.

'I finish early on Wednesdays. It's at Llancrwys. First house on the right after the thirty-mile-an-hour sign. I've got my own door, at the side.'

'Goodness, what a flood of information. I haven't said I'll come yet.'

'You can, though. One Wednesday night when the children are in bed and your husband's away in London and can't complain that you're neglecting him, and there's nothing to do at home and nobody to talk to, you can get into your blue Mini and drive to Llancrwys.'

'I can, yes. But I don't see why I should.'

'Well, do it for no reason. Do it — just because you're invited.'

'Can you cook?' she changed her ground.

'Simple dishes. You'll be fed.'

'Shall I come and cook something for you? What kind of stove have you got?'

Roger's heart thumped. He was winning, she was going to accept. 'Never mind all that. You must have enough cooking to do, the rest of the time. Sit back and be pampered for once. The point is, will it be this Wednesday or the next?'

'Neither,' she said, flat and Northern. 'If it's anything, it'll be the one after that.'

'The third one from now?'

'Yes. Gerald's on a television panel in London that evening and nobody'll need me at home.'

An argument had broken out among the children. 'Mummy,' they cried, running to her, 'do fish eat sea-weed?'

'Some kinds of fish do,' she said.

'There you are,' said Robin to Mary.

'But,' her face puckered in disappointment at losing the argument, 'they haven't got teeth to chew it with!'

'They lick it with their tongues,' said Robin. 'They go, *lick, lick*.' He demonstrated.

'You're both wrong,' said Jenny. 'They do have teeth. You put your finger in a fish's mouth, you'll soon see if he has teeth."

This calmed them; neither had been wholly right, there was no undisputed victor. They moved away, Mary saying to Robin, 'Fancy thinking fish could lick!'

'They *can* lick. Moon fish can lick,' he said.

Roger felt he must cede the ground with a good grace. He had what he had come for; he must not get between the children and their afternoon with Jenny.

'Well, I'll be off,' he said. 'The third Wednesday from now. I'll look for you at about eight.'

'I don't know that I'll be able to stay long,' she said over her shoulder, as she moved over the slippery rocks towards where the children clambered.

'Doesn't matter,' he called, smiling. She gave him a quick answering smile, then turned away. Stepping from rock to rock, he reached the low sea-wall. There was the road, running back to the town between its strips of thin, salt-coated grass: the road that would lead him away from her, back into his emptiness. He turned to look once more; the three of them had their backs to him, bending down, staring into the frill of foam at the edge of the sea. 'There's one!' he heard Robin shout.

'Good luck in the hunt!' he called. But the wind, which had been increasing as they talked, was now too strong, and carried his voice away, back towards the harbour and the immovable towers of the castle. With a faint shrug, he set out to walk back the way he had come.

Gareth had a corrugated iron garage for the bus. It stood in a windy space between two garden walls near the top of the village, and it was slightly too small to contain everything he tried to get into it: the bus, cans of fuel, tools and a workbench, spare tyres, and so forth. Backing the yellow monster in and out was a delicate manoeuvre, calling for an awareness of three or four inches on either side, that Gareth would never have trusted anyone but himself to perform. He put it away after the last run at night and took it out in the morning; in between times, whatever the weather, the bus stood on the firm grass verge of the road near the centre of the village. This was where Roger had first seen it, as he walked down the mountain in that memorable downpour.

Now he had been working for Gareth nearly two weeks, and it was raining again. Waves of rain were lashing the village streets and the few passengers who wanted to go down on the eleven o'clock run to Caerfenai were already sitting in the bus amid a smell of wet mackintoshes. Gareth was winding his watch; they would be off in a moment. Roger was sitting in one of the vacant seats at the front, watching the rain and listening to the Welsh conversation behind him. He could make out a lot of isolated words, and quite often whole sentences, by this time.

The Corporation refuse-collecting lorry came into sight along the street, driving a few yards and stopping while the men collected half-a-dozen dustbins, emptied them into the mysteriously humming maw at the rear of the vehicle, and re-placed them, then driving on again and stopping again. Roger watched idly through the rain-blurred windscreen. There were three men collecting and one driving. The ones who were col-lecting wore oilskins and one of them had draped a heavy sack across his shoulders to absorb the rain. They worked silently and steadily, and all the time the hidden machinery chewed away at the refuse, crushing and storing it. Progress had come to Llancrwys.

Suddenly there was a long, squawking cry from somewhere along the street, and Mrs Arkwright appeared, hatless, her blue rinse already soaked and straggling. She was waving at the lorry and shouting, 'You'll have to come back! You'll have to come back!'

The three men hastily finished with the dustbins they were handling and climbed up on to the platform at the rear of the lorry. 'Drive on!' one of them shouted to the driver.

'We haven't finished the street yet!' he called, twisting his head out of the window.

'Never mind! Drive on!' they urged him. Mrs Arkwright had quickened her pace and was almost on them.

Inside the bus, the passengers craned to see the drama. The lorry accelerated away, the three dustmen hanging on to the back like meat-flies, and Mrs Arkwright, after one last gallop-ing spurt, came to a frustrated halt.

'I'll report this!' she yelled through the rain.

'It's not part of our job to get assaulted!' one of the men called back. The lorry turned the corner and was gone.

Mrs Arkwright wheeled and came towards the bus, a ready-made public meeting. 'I've shown 'em the plans!' she was shouting, even before she got her foot on the step. 'I've been down to the Council offices and shown 'em my plans and they've *admitted* I'm within the collection boundary, they've *admitted* it!'

There was a murmur of sympathy and one gaunt man said, 'It's all trickery these days, all trickery.'

'The dustmen say I've got to carry it down to the road junc-tion,' said Mrs Arkwright. 'A widow woman. I'd like to see them treat their own mothers like that.'

'Some of them would, some of them would,' said the gaunt man.

'Are you travelling, Mrs Arkwright?' Gareth asked. 'We're due away.' He spoke with all the pride of the driver of some great express train.

'Yes, I'm travelling,' she said grimly, shaking back a wisp of wet blue hair. 'Take me down to the square. I'll be in that office and I'll not leave till I've had my rubbish removed. If this goes on there'll be rats and typhoid, that's what there'll be, rats and typhoid. Here's my fare, young man,' she said to Roger.

Roger felt pleased at being called 'young man', but all the same he wished Mrs Arkwright had not got on the bus. She depressed him by the pathos of her life and the narrowness of her situation. She was alone in the fine new modern bungalow with the beautiful view of the bay, and the only event in her life was the weekly struggle to get her garbage collected.

Moving down the bus, holding on to the backs of seats to steady himself, Roger hoped that Mrs Arkwright would have an enjoyable *fracas* with the officials of the Corporation, without actually scoring a victory that would leave her with no life-fuelling grievance.

At last the Wednesday came, Jenny's Wednesday. Ever since making the date, Roger had alternately wished for and feared its approach. Of course he wanted Jenny to come and see him; of course he welcomed the chance to explore the possibilities, see how difficult was the terrain that would have to be crossed: to dispense with comfortably blurring metaphor, to estimate the chances of prying her loose from her husband for long enough to give him some necessary consolation. Yet, of course, it was just this inevitable work, this exploring and probing and prying loose, that he dreaded. It was all so much *trouble*, so damnably disturbing and effortful, and more so with every year that one lived.

He finished work at six o'clock, having come up on the early-evening run to Llancrwys. There was a ten o'clock run but it was never so heavy on Wednesdays; a lot of people had the afternoon off and they tended to go further afield and not just to the Caerfenai pubs in the evening. Gareth could take it himself; he had agreed to. Roger went in to his quarters, letting himself in through Mrs Pylon Jones's holiday people's green door and muttering to himself. 'Meat, vegetables, butter. Wine, corkscrew. Coal, firelighters. We have not reached conclusion, when I stiffen in a rented house. Potatoes. Get the window-catch fixed.' He felt tense, unconfident, miserable. Setting the scene for an encounter with a woman, cosily plotting a bit of quiet adultery in a Calvinist village, why was he having to go through this farce at his age? It was unjust, it was horrible. He sincerely pitied himself, and he even pitied Jenny a little.

Still, the fire lit well, the electric cooker shimmered with heat; he would give her a good meal at any rate, and some comfort, before he had to disturb her peace.

Mrs Pylon Jones was as quiet as a spider in her part of the house. Would she know everything that went on? Suppose Jenny, mad with unhappiness in her marriage, fell into his arms, into his bed? Would Mrs Pylon Jones be watching through a knot-hole? Would she summon the Llancrwys equivalent of the Vigilantes or Ku Klux Klan? And, after all (as a great weariness possessed him, standing in front of the electric stove) if she did, would it matter?

The hour came. She was expected, she was late, she was ten minutes late, fifteen minutes, he began to curse, then wheels crunched to a stop outside. He had meant to let her knock, and take his time about going to the door, but he wrenched it open. It was the bright blue mini-car, it was Jenny.

She came in, shedding a short, fashionable overcoat. Underneath she had on the same dress in which he had first seen her: simple, well-cut, damson-coloured wool, short (shortened?) a good dress (her best?); carefully selected for him, or automatically dug out as her only decent one? All this whirled in his mind as she spoke her opening, prepared sentences about why she was late.

'Let's eat,' he said. 'I'm hungry. I've been working.' Nervousness made him brusque.

'So'm I. I've been working too. Looking after the children and getting them to bed. What kind of work have you been doing?'

'Tell you later.'

'Is it a secret?'

'Not at all. I work on a bus.'

'On a bus? What d'you do, drive it? You don't seem like a –'

'No, I conduct it.'

'You conduct a bus? Are you doing it for a bet or something?'

'No, as a kind of holiday. To get a change.' He adjusted the hotplates as he spoke, clattered saucepans, moved as briskly as a chef.

'You seem very busy,' she said, coming up to his elbow. 'Can I do anything?'

'Yes, you can help yourself to a glass of sherry from that bottle over there, and you can draw the cork of the wine and put it on the table. Just menial things. I want to do all the essentials myself because my pride is involved in cooking you a good meal.'

'All right, I won't do anything that isn't menial, then I shan't bruise your pride.' He heard sherry being poured into a glass. 'Some for you?'

'No, thanks.' He had been at the gin, before she came.

What was her husband doing now, as she sat in Llancrwys and drank his sherry in Mrs Pylon Jones's summer visitors' flat? Appearing on a television programme, she had said. Would he be doing that now, at this moment? If he had a set would they be able to switch it on and sit in front of it and watch his horrible smooth face?

Wouldn't it be marvellous to take her clothes off and give it to her right in front of the television screen with her husband looking straight at them!

'What kind of work do you do normally?' she was asking.

'I'm a philologist.'

'Like boring old Bryant?'

'Like him.'

'What kind of thing does that mean you know about?'

'Northern European languages. English and Scandinavian are my favourite areas.'

'Yes, but what *kind* of thing d'you know about English and Scandinavian languages? Is it just the grammar and stuff?'

'Well, I wrote quite an important paper called. "The transformation of 'mutation variation' into 'mutation allophone' in Scandinavian languages, especially in relation to final *i* and *e* in Old High German".'

She stopped twisting at the cork and looked at him narrowly. 'You must be joking.'

'No, I'm not. That's the kind of title that philological papers have. And I've got one in the pipeline called "*ia* as a special diphthongal phoneme in Scandinavian languages of an intermediate period".'

'But who cares about that kind of thing?'

'Well, it's a matter of researching into the way these languages developed. You have to study old runes and the inscriptions on seventh-century sword-blades and so on, and then try to systematize what you can deduce from them about the evolution of the language. If you work it out clearly enough you can help the archaeologists to date things they've dug up."

'Only if they've got writing on them.'

'Yes, but a lot of things have.'

'Is it what you really like doing?'

'I like it the way some people like researching on chromosomes. The rice is done and the meat's almost done. Are you hungry?'

'What kind of meat is it?'

'Shish kebab.'

'Then I'm *very* hungry.'

He had grilled thick chunks of meat, speared them with pineapple and onion in between. It was his show-piece.

'You're a chef as well,' she said, sitting down.

'Only this one dish. Boiled eggs the rest of the time.'

They ate. He poured wine. She enjoyed her food, drank and talked; her face was towards the firelight. He had never seen her alone before. The first time, she had been weighed down by her husband and her husband's friends; the second time, she had been a mother, putting forth authority and love. Love! Her nature would be receptive to that, she would be fertile in it. But love was a grave matter, it altered people's lives, and at this moment what she was showing him was simple friendliness and pleasure. There was no weight on her; she was at leisure, escaping from her problems, enjoying a treat.

He poured more wine, brought cheese and fruit, and they ate, drank and talked on. But the thought of love had saddened him by reminding him of his needs, which were so pressing, and his loneliness. He had invited her because he hoped to draw her into his life, to get from her some of the things he needed, and while it was pleasant to be relaxed and casual, it would be hypocritical folly to try to prolong that relaxation and casualness beyond the point at which serious business ought to begin. Roger threw back a glass of wine, trying to key himself up, to gather resolution, but it was useless. He felt suddenly leaden and fatigued. He had allowed himself to be reminded of what serious issues were at stake, and it was too late to get back to gaiety; the few minutes of holiday were over and it was work, work, work once more.

Jenny, finishing a pear and wiping her fingers on a thick paper napkin, got the message that his mood had changed. 'What's the matter?'

He liked her simple frankness. Oh, well, get it over.

'Let's sit down, if you've finished,' he said.

'I am sitting down.'

'I mean on the sofa,' he said. It was drawn up invitingly close to the flickering firelight.

'If you like,' she said, her tone neutral, but when they were side by side on the sofa he could not bring himself either to speak or to make any movement towards her.

'That was a lovely dinner. Thank you,' she said.

'Thank you for coming to see me. It's much more trouble to drive all this way than to . . .'

'That's not what we're talking about, though,' she said quietly, 'is it?'

'What isn't?'

'Trouble.'

He was silent for a moment, then said, 'In a sense it is what we're talking about. That and nothing else.'

'I thought it was just for fun,' she said, looking at the fire.

'People of my age don't need fun,' he said. 'If they do, if they go round looking for fun and trying to set it up, that's a sign their lives have gone wrong somewhere.'

She said, 'And what about people of *my* age?'

'Quite different. They've got more time and that makes them calmer. There's time for them to build up a life, tear it down and build up another one that's more to their liking.'

'If they have to.'

He said, carefully, 'Perhaps it's better if they have to. It may be a mistake to get things too right at the beginning.'

'Why? You mean all that old stuff about a broken bone knitting up more strongly at the broken place?'

'Well, partly that, but other things too. People who just waltz into a happy life without making their mistakes and going through a period of unhappiness, don't realize what they've escaped from and so they're not grateful enough for their luck, don't appreciate it enough.'

Jenny drank from her glass. The firelight made the red wine glow with a rich, deep light that seemed to come from inside the glass.

'Roger, are you just philosophizing for the pleasure of hearing your own voice uttering wisdom? Or is there some personal reason why you're saying all this to *me*?'

In the short silence, he drank from his glass. But the wine had no effect on him. The threshold of his tension was too high to be reached by alcohol.

'Yes, there is a personal reason.'

'Well, let's hear it.'

'I want to make love to you.'

'Don't be silly,' she said in her northern accent.

He drank again. 'Why is it silly?'

'Because I'm a married woman with two children.'

'But you're married to the wrong man. Your marriage doesn't bring you any happiness.'

Instead of answering, she leaned forward and picked up her handbag from the floor. He thought she was rummaging for a cigarette, to parry his thrust and gain a little time while one was selected and lit. But in fact she surprised him by producing a pair of glasses with heavy dark rims. She put these on and looked at him attentively.

'Why do you do that?'

'I want to see your face,' she said. The thick, dark lenses, under that fringe of black hair, made her face seem like a child's, delicate-boned and vulnerable. Her eyes looked out through the lenses like those of a pet owl. 'I'm too vain to wear my glasses most of the time. But I need them if I'm to see anything closely. And really the light's not very good in here.'

'It never is in a rented place,' he said.

'Don't change the subject. I wanted to see your face clearly because it might give me some clue as to what's going on in your mind when you start talking about my husband and bringing my marriage into it.'

'Oh,' he said, 'you can put your glasses away as far as that goes. There's no mystery. I'll tell you exactly what's in my mind.' And yet, even as he spoke, he wondered how he would ever put it into words simple enough for him to understand, let alone her.

'Well, do it,' but she kept her glasses on.

'I'm lonely and not at all happy. I don't think I have much self-pity – I try to see my situation quite objectively. My life's come to a bleak, windy cross-roads and I don't know which way to go. I can plan for my comfort, but comfort alone won't make me happy. I've lost my bearings.'

'What happened to make you lose them?'

'My brother died. He was an invalid and I used to look after him.'

'Well, I'm sorry he died, because you must have been fond of him, but surely in a way it's rather a liberation for you?'

'Well, that's the hard part to explain.'

'Try,' she said, settling back.

'The reason I kept Geoffrey with me all the time wasn't that I was the only person who could look after him. Obviously there were lots of people who could do that, and many of them would be qualified people who'd do it better than I could. I often got irritable with him and sometimes I was quite the wrong person to be in charge of him.' He hesitated, then went on, 'When I said Geoffrey was an invalid, that was a bit of prudery, not using the right word. What he really was was a nervous wreck. A mental case – mental and nervous.'

'Was he born like that?'

'No, it was the war.' He paused again. 'I'd rather not talk about that part.'

'If you don't, how can I understand?'

He turned to her. 'D'you want to understand?'

'You want me to, don't you?'

He nodded. 'I think all you need to know, essentially, is that my parents didn't survive the war and Geoffrey and I were left alone and he was in this dreadful state. On his good days he could dress himself, except for the odd button here and there, and get his food up to his mouth somehow, but he couldn't concentrate or hold the thread of anything in his mind and I knew if he went to an institution they'd just tidy him away like some obscene piece of human débris. Not that I was ever tempted to let him go to one. I needed him as much as he needed me.'

'Why?'

He shrugged. 'My emotional pattern just settled down into that shape. In any case, I was only seventeen when the war ended, and it was years before I could earn money and have a place where Geoffrey could be with me. He was in hospitals of one kind and another for almost ten years. But I went to see him all the time and kept telling him he was going to come and live with me as soon as I was established, and he understood, or at least he understood on his good days.'

'What did he do on his bad days?'

'He cried.'

'Just that?'

'Just that and nothing more. He sat on his bed and cried all day long because of what had happened to him.'

Jenny stood up, smoothed her skirt down over her hips, and stood looking down at him. 'Now tell me what all this has got to do with my marriage to Gerald.'

At first, Roger could not answer. His mind was choked up by the memory of Geoffrey's red, crumpled face, and he could hear Geoffrey's voice sobbing *It's too hard, Roger. I can't do it, Roger. It's too hard for me.*

Then his mind cleared itself and filled with hard, white light and he said, 'It's easy. Unhappy people always seek one another out. I'm left without Geoffrey, which means that Othello's occupation's gone, and it also means that such love as I was able to show him wasn't enough to keep him alive beyond the age of forty-five. So I feel lost and I also feel guilty. Then, as it will hardly surprise you to hear, my sex-life is in a mess.'

'It doesn't surprise me to hear that about anybody. There are more ways of —'

'For a long time I ran around with a girl called Margot and I was very fond of her, I wanted to marry her. She was very pretty and she was on the run from a Puritanical upbringing. That meant she wanted to enjoy herself all the time, without stopping. She enjoyed herself with me and, to my knowledge, with three or four other men during those five years. To say nothing of casual encounters. She was a great one for stand-up sex in the bathroom at top people's Chelsea parties.'

'You say that as if you hated her.'

'I honestly don't. Only it made me the same way. I wanted to settle down but I loved Margot, and she wouldn't settle down with me, first because she hadn't finished having a good time with men, and then afterwards because I wouldn't have Geoffrey put away in an institution. Finally we split up on that. It took me about twelve months to believe it had happened. I needed Geoffrey so much myself that I couldn't believe anyone could reject him as thoroughly as Margot rejected him. She couldn't bear the sight of him.'

'I don't blame her, if having a good time was what she needed most of all.'

'No, I don't either. The sight of someone like Geoffrey does rather bring to one's mind all those sides of life that can't be assimilated to good times. If he'd been potent she might have tried to work it with him. They say some women are excited by idiots.'

'You're getting bitter.'

'*Getting!* I'm as bitter as hell, always have been.'

'All right,' she said, 'be bitter. But don't be proud of it. Don't think it makes you holy.'

'Jenny, that's unfair.'

'I'm not interested in being fair, why should I be? And anyway, people who are bitter against life always think it makes them superior. They think if you aren't bitter it just shows how shallow you are.'

Roger poured out more wine, for himself and for her. 'Possibly you're right. Anyway it doesn't matter. My bitterness doesn't go deep. It's just something that's settled on the surface of my life, like dandruff. It could be taken away without altering my character at all basically. Whereas that other business – needing to protect Geoffrey – that does go deep. It took root in adolescence.'

'You know what I think?' she said. 'I think all this'll melt away as soon as you find a woman you can love, I mean love properly.'

'I'm sure that's what the books say.'

'You're being bitter again. It isn't only the books. Everybody knows it.'

'All right,' he said, looking at her delicate-boned face, with its serious expression, in the firelight. 'It could happen, I'll grant that. But till then I'm stuck with what the books would doubtless call the Geoffrey-syndrome.'

'So you're looking for another Geoffrey.'

He nodded. 'But it needn't be anybody like Geoffrey. It can be anyone who's loaded with handicaps and in a mess. A hunchback, for instance, would do perfectly well, if he was in bad enough trouble.'

'A hunchback in trouble? What are you talking about now?'

'Oh, never mind.' He suddenly felt sick of going over his own situation. 'Let's talk about you. I want to have some picture of your life. Tell me about your children, for instance.'

She sat down again. 'Mary and Robin? Oh, they're just ordinary children. I have that deep unreasoning fondness for them that comes naturally out of a person's biology. I know I'd give my life to save theirs, any time, without feeling particularly brave or unselfish. It's just a law of life that you put yourself completely at the disposal of the new human beings you've produced. But there are times as well when I can just stand aside and see them like a neutral person, and they seem to me nice children but nothing special. Mary's got a practical little nature. She's good at doing things with her hands and she likes helping me. I think she's going to be a kind person. Perhaps one of those women who go through life quietly getting on with it and making the lives of everyone they come in contact with just that bit easier and happier. That's what I wish for her anyway. Robin, it's too early to say. He's got a nice voice and I think he's going to have absolute pitch when he gets old enough for his ear to develop.'

'So one will be the matron of a Cottage Hospital and the other an operatic tenor.'

'You asked me to tell you about them.'

'I'm sorry. I wasn't mocking.'

'It sounded like it. But perhaps you're the kind of twisted person who can't say anything without sounding as if you were mocking.'

She was angry. Turning away from him, she snatched off her glasses, as if she no longer wanted to see his face.

Roger spoke carefully. 'I'm not sure which of us is right. But if my remark sounded to you like mockery, then perhaps it was mockery, because your instinctive reactions are probably sounder and less warped than mine. So all I can do is to apologize. Perhaps it was an unconscious revelation. I asked you to tell me about your life, and to start by talking about your children, but it may be that I can't really bear it when you get going. Perhaps I'm jealous. It'd be quite natural. After all, here I am, lonely and unsatisfied, my whole life out of shape, and there's your husband Gerald Twyford, with the excellent luck of being married to you, having you in his house, around all the time to talk to or just to look at.'

'You're shooting a line now,' she said, looking at him indifferently. 'Don't forget a woman gets very skilful at detecting line-shooting. We have to listen to so much of it between sixteen and twenty-five.'

'Once again, what you say may be true, but if so it's unconscious. I thought I was being quite sincere. What my hidden motives might be, I don't know.'

'Are you sure of that? I thought you just said you wanted to make love to me.'

'That isn't a hidden motive. I've avowed it.'

She shrugged, but the cold expression had gone from her face. Roger decided to move in more closely to the attack.

'Is Gerald at home, looking after the children?'

'Good lord, no. Gerald's in London, as I told you before. You don't think I'd be sitting here with you if he –'

'Why not? It might do him good.'

'I don't know that I'm out to do him good.'

'Then what are you . . .'

'Oh,' she shrugged, 'just self-preservation. Gerald caught me so young, before I'd had a go at managing life by myself. And now, I don't know if I'd be any good at it.'

Roger settled his shoulders back against the sofa. He felt ready for plain speaking on dangerous topics.

'But if you're not making a happy marriage together, you'll have to face the prospect of breaking up sooner or later.'

'Why?'

'What d'you mean, why?'

'What *d'you* mean?'

'Well,' he expostulated, 'you can't sit down calmly under the prospect of half a century of misery.'

'I love the children,' she said as if thinking aloud. 'I'd even love Gerald if he ever came out of this phase he seems to be in, and started acting like a human being.'

'Was he ever really a human being?'

'Well, probably not. Of course I didn't realize that when I first married him. I didn't realize *anything*.' She gave a short, helpless laugh. 'I mean, if he seemed odd I just thought all men were like that. What I see now is that he was moving up towards being what he is now. Only in those days he didn't know any influential people so he couldn't be always rushing off to see them. He used to shut himself up in his study and write articles and letters to the papers instead. Desperate to get a bit of notice taken of him, I suppose, and get started on his career. I thought all men were like that. It's only now that he's become so open about it . . .' her voice trailed off.

'No, do go on. I think it might be good for you to talk and I do want to understand.' That was me, Roger thought, sounding like a cosy old seducer. Actually it was true. He did think it would do her good to talk and he did want to understand her situation.

'Well, I think Gerald's in just as much of a mess as I am, perhaps a worse one. He doesn't love me and he doesn't get much satisfaction out of the children, so it's hard to see what he's getting out of it all. Of course I run his home for him, but a housekeeper could do that.'

'Yes, but you sleep with him, don't you?'

'Yes.'

'Well, that's something a housekeeper wouldn't. Not the sort of housekeeper they have in respectable university circles, anyway. So that's his sex-life taken care of. He doesn't have to waste his time and energy running after women to get his needs satisfied.'

She put her glass down on the floor and sat up straight.

'I see.'

'What do you see?'

'Why you asked me here.'

'Oh, Christ.'

'That's what you're doing, isn't it? Wasting your time and energy running after women to get your needs satisfied. Well, I'm not women, I'm me.'

Incensed, Roger fought back. 'Didn't you know that situations could develop? You speak with such fine contempt about my needs but they aren't just needs any more, they're my feelings about you.'

'You're good at dressing things up in fine words. I suppose being a philologist helps.'

'That was unworthy of you.'

'Well, I feel pretty brassed off,' she said. 'You've hardly got me here before you're telling me your sex-life is in a mess, as if I were the district nurse or something.'

'All right, I ought to have kept the mask on and we ought to have talked about the weather and where we're going for our holidays. But I thought we'd somehow overleapt all that.'

'How could we overleap it when we've hardly –'

'Oh, don't let's be so *elementary*. Surely you've realized it's possible to get to know a person quite well on very slight acquaintance, if you focus them intently enough. I know you better than I did when we last met, because in the interval I've thought about you so much. I've called back into my memory every expression that passed over your face, every gesture you made; not only all the things you said but the tempo in which you said them, the pauses, the things that seemed to look out from behind the words.'

'It sounds,' she said, flat and North-country again, 'like a damned bad way of getting to know somebody.'

'But I can prove it isn't. I can tell you things about yourself that you'll have to admit are true.'

She put on her glasses and looked at him, searchingly and with caution. 'Well, suppose you can? Where's the fun in that?'

He laughed. 'Have some more wine. Don't worry, I'm not trying to make you drunk. I'd rather have you sober. I want to talk with you, really talk, really exchange something meaningful.'

'You're going so *fast*,' she said, holding out her glass.

'You have to, at my age.'

'Oh, stop talking about your age as if you were a million. I bet you've never been any different. I bet you've always tried to rush it with women, and frightened them off.'

'Is that what I'm doing with you? Frightening you off?'

There was a short pause before she said, 'I'm not quite sure how to answer that. I mean – you've gone so fast up to now that I don't really know, yet, whether there's anything to be frightened off *from*.'

'Well, here's what there is,' he said, putting his glass down and looking straight into her face. 'We're both people who haven't found happiness in life yet, and we might find it together.'

'Who says so?'

'I do. And don't tell me what you say because you're not in a position to know yet. I am, because I know myself and I know you.'

'Well, you don't aim to spoil your case by being too modest about it,' she sighed, 'that I do see.'

'It's too late for anything but straight truth-telling now.'

'Too late, too late,' she said with real exasperation, 'why d'you keep saying that, as if the world were just about to come to an end?'

'For anyone of forty, the world *has* come to an end. One world has gone over the hill and there's another one at your feet. It can be a good world if you seize your chances, and you might as well seize them if you can, because if you have a normal life-span you'll have to live in that world for thirty years. If you let your chances go, all you'll have is thirty years of sitting by a hearth full of cold ashes.'

Jenny put her glasses back on. 'I see what you're driving at. You're telling me in a roundabout way that I ought to leave my husband. And what would I do then? Come and live with you? Is that the idea?'

'A minute ago you were telling me I was the one who went fast.'

'Oh, I'm not going fast,' she said. 'It's just an interesting theoretical discussion as far as I'm concerned. But tell me, Sir Oracle, what *should* I do?'

'Give me a kiss,' said philologist Roger, Uppsala forgotten.

'Certainly not.' She swivelled her knees away. Since modern

clothes for women are designed to make the idea of chastity seem ridiculous, this only had the effect of drawing attention to her legs and kindling Roger's lust. 'I'm a respectable married woman.'

'You're a married woman and your children are asleep and you've got somebody looking after them and your husband is God knows where with God knows who, and you're sitting on a sofa in front of a bright fire with a man who's unprincipled enough to want to kiss you.'

She leaned over and kissed him. Fire crackled along his veins, and all of a sudden the wine he had drunk began re-decorating his blood-cells.

'Again,' he said as she pulled away.

'No. One thing leads to another.'

'Well,' he said earnestly, 'don't you want it to?'

'I don't think I do.'

'When will you know?' he demanded.

She collected herself neatly into a corner of the sofa, legs drawn up under her. A child's body, yet a woman's; with her cheekbones so high and her hair so dark and heavy, she might have been one of Madog's Cherokees, and her inward essence was just as wild and unguessable – ah, come to me, come to me.

She was speaking, her eyes fixed on the burning coals. 'I suppose if I did what you want me to do, I'd come with you now into the next room or wherever your bedroom is, and make love, and then get up and dress and go back to my house and drive the baby-sitter home and then go and lie down by myself in my marital bed. Well, it's too awful, it's too hor-rible.' she shook her head violently and went on shaking it, 'I won't do it! Think of the loneliness – think of all the thoughts that would go through my head after I got into my bed – Gerald's and mine.'

'Gerald might be in bed with some girl in London at this moment. What d'you think he's thinking of?'

'I don't believe it,' she said. 'I don't think he's interested in women. His career's his mistress and he wouldn't have time for a flesh-and-blood one.'

'Does that make it any better?'

'I didn't say it did. But I can't go to bed with you. If you want your needs satisfied at short notice, go to a whore.'

The sudden coarse bump down to earth disconcerted him. 'Don't talk like that,' he said gently.

'Why not? You're thinking like that.'

'Jenny, I am not. The coitus, for its own sake, is not so important to me.'

She laughed, in genuine child-like amusement. 'Why, you're a professor!'

'You've just advised me to go to a whore. I'm simply saying that even if I knew where whores are to be had, that isn't what's uppermost in my mind at this moment.' As he spoke he realized with mild surprise, that he was telling the truth. 'Of course, I'd like to take you to bed. But mainly as a way of bringing you close to me, building a permanent bridge between us.'

'Perhaps it wouldn't do that.'

'No, perhaps it wouldn't, but it's worth a try all the same.'

She stood up and shook her head. 'I can't. I'm sorry, I just can't. I've often thought about it. I mean, not being confident about my marriage, not feeling that I'm bringing any happiness to Gerald, I've lain awake many a time and faced this moment, just exactly *this* one, in anticipation. I mean, that some man would suggest becoming my lover. And I've always shied away from it.'

'Why? Love of Gerald? Fear of the consequences?'

'Nothing clear-cut.' She gave a slight shiver. 'Just a feeling. A dread.'

'Dread? What of?'

She said slowly, 'Of crossing a bridge, really. I mean, I know how silly this would sound to some people. They'd think of sex as just a physical spasm that doesn't change anything, like sneezing except that two people do it at once. But I can't get my mind to work that way. I'm frightened. It's like – well, messing about with something very powerful, that could destroy me. Well, don't you see?' She ended on a note of appeal.

'Yes, I see perfectly well.'

'My reason tells me it wouldn't matter at all. Gerald wouldn't have to know and it may be that if he did know he wouldn't necessarily care all that much. But there's something down below that layer, something deeper than reason, more primitive, that tells me if I give myself to another man I've finished my marriage. I can't go on pretending to Gerald after I've had that with another man. I can't see it as a shared fit of sneezing.'

'Oh, do stop talking about sneezing. Every woman feels as you do about sex unless she's done psychological violence to herself. It's the root of the old double standard in morality, which people laugh at nowadays but which actually had a lot of sound sense in it. If you went that far with another man, you *would* feel that you'd ended your marriage. But perhaps that's what you ought to feel.'

She shook her head, not in denial but helplessly. 'That's like telling somebody they need a surgical operation.'

'Well, people sometimes do.'

She had been gazing into the fire, but now she looked up at him. 'And what relationship does that put you in? My physician, recommending me to have an operation?'

'Jenny, you're very clever, but don't box me in with your definitions. I find you marvellously attractive and I ache for you and I think we could be lucky together and perhaps even make each other happy for the rest of our lives.'

'What's that, a proposal of marriage?'

'No, I don't propose to women I haven't slept with.'

She stood up. 'You won't be proposing to me, then.'

He paused for a moment and then said, 'All right, but no hard feelings.'

'No, Roger.' She smiled to show that it was true. 'And now I must go home.'

He, too, stood up. Suddenly the room seemed full of the sour breath of disappointment. The dishes on the table, the emptied wine-glasses, the fire that still glowed hopefully though there was no longer anything to glow for, all united to club him down into depression.

'Jenny, don't let it end like this.'

She shrugged. 'I like you, Roger. I dare say it's even true that we could have made each other happy. I'd have done better with you than with Gerald, anyway. But the fact remains that it's Gerald I've got.'

'Well, get rid of him.'

'I just can't. Don't let's have all that again. Anyway, whatever I may feel about my relationship with Gerald, I couldn't leave Mary and Robin.'

His shoulders drooped. 'I never knew marriage was so strong.'

'Oh, it is, Roger. It's primitive. Primitive things are the strongest always.'

'If you were married to me, would it be strong?'

'Terribly,' she said.

He laughed shortly. 'Well, that puts me in the Gerald class at least.'

Jenny found her coat now. 'Well, I'll be off. It was nice of you to feed me.'

'It wasn't nice. I did it for my own sordid motives.'

She turned her eyes full on him, and for a moment her hand rested on his arm. 'Roger, don't say that. I know your motives aren't sordid. You're an unhappy person who wants to be happy, and you're prepared to work hard at it and not just grab it at somebody else's expense. I don't think any of that's sordid.'

'All the same, you can't go along with it.'

She shook her head.

'Well, I'll see you out.'

There was a cold wind blowing across the mountainside. They did not linger. Her little car was waiting to trundle her back to the warmth and safety of Mary and Robin and the baby-sitter.

'Shall I see you again?'

'I expect so,' she said brightly, 'if you're staying in the district.'

'Can I telephone?'

'It's in the book,' she said, and started the engine. He shut the door for her, and behind the glass he saw her hand lift from the wheel for an instant in valediction. Then there was nothing but twin rear-lights disappearing down the mountain.

Roger went back into Mrs Pylon Jones's holiday people's flat and shut the green door behind him. Its slam seemed to close off the whole of life, love, experience, hope. He wanted nothing any longer, except to go to bed and sleep.

Without troubling to wash up or even stack the dishes that were on the table, he went into his bedroom and began to undress. The cold, neat, impersonal bed mocked at him. Never mind, there was always oblivion; he was tired from standing so many hours on the swaying and trembling bus, juddering along now towards the mountains, now towards the sea, as in some endless quadrille; sleep would come; that at any rate Gareth had done for him.

Once in bed, he turned over once and dived steeply towards unconsciousness. To forget, to sleep. Not to hunger, not to wander. Jenny, Margot, back through every infantile dream of satisfaction, the leech lips, the warmth . . . warm . . .

Someone was knocking insistently on a door near him.

Not for me, they can't mean me, I'm in bed, sleeping . . .

Knock, knock, knock knock knock knock.

There was one interconnecting door between Mrs Pylon Jones's part of the house and Mrs Pylon Jones's holiday people's part of the house. It was normally never used; Mrs Pylon Jones had firmly locked it, at an early stage, and kept the key in some fastness. On Roger's side, this door was covered with a long curtain, and he had got into the habit of ignoring its existence. Yet now Mrs Pylon Jones, or somebody, was on the other side of this door, knocking and knocking.

He leaned on one elbow. 'Yes? Is somebody –'

'Mr Furnivall!' It was the landlady; her voice was quiet and frightened.

'Yes, Mrs Jones? Can I do anything?'

A key grated and she came through, pushing aside the curtain. Light spilled in from behind her.

'Wait a minute, Mrs Pyl – Mrs Jones, I'll put the light on. Just go into my sitting-room, would you?'

Her thin, tense figure scurried along the passage into his sitting-room. She would see the mess, the litter of a cosy supper for two. What did she want? To see that he was not harbouring a woman? He had heard of the Puritanism of these slate villages with their frowning chapels. Roger grabbed at his shirt, pulled on trousers. Wanted trouble, did she? It was a pity he couldn't supply any. Mrs Pylon Jones, if you want to check up on my sex-life, I regret to report that I have no sex-life. If you keep careful watch on me for the whole winter, I'll try to manage a bit of self-abuse. Everything else is denied me by a cruel fate. Come away, come away death. I am slain by a fair cruel maid. Yet the landlady's voice had sounded frightened, more than disapproving. Frightened what of?

Dressed roughly, Roger joined Mrs Pylon Jones in his sitting-room. She had switched on all available lights and was standing in the middle of the floor. For some reason, his eyes rested on her hands; she was twisting them together nervously, and in the harsh light he saw for the first time how arthritic and swollen were the knuckles.

'Mr Furnivall,' she said, 'has your visitor gone?'

'Yes,' he said. 'About half an hour ago, I suppose. Why?'

'Because I can hear somebody outside,' she said.

Her fear, which now looked out plainly, made this simple statement important and terrible.

'Somebody outside?' Roger said roughly. 'Why shouldn't there be somebody outside?'

'Not just walking past down the road,' she said almost in a whisper. 'Hanging about.'

Her fear flickered like weak lightning in the neutral space between them. For a moment, Roger shared it: not fear of anything specific, but fear of the night, of the dark hillside and the crying wind.

'I'll go and see,' he said, and quickly, not giving himself time for hesitation, he walked to the green door and opened it, rattling the latch with a loud, decisive sound.

Outside, it was very dark, and rain had started to crawl across the mountainside. Roger's eyes could not penetrate the blank wall of darkness, but his ears caught a faint scraping of shoe-leather. It was not quite the sound of walking; more like the sound of someone drawing his foot gently down a wall.

'Anybody there?' Roger called. His voice lost itself, at once, in the blanketing rain. 'Anybody hanging about there?'

He waited for the reply that obviously would not come, then went back into the house. Mrs Pylon Jones, too nervous to stay in the room by herself, had followed him out into the passage and stood just behind him as he called into the night. Now, as he turned, she faced him.

'Well,' he began, 'there seems to be no –'

'Your feet!' She suddenly cried in a high, panicky voice.

He looked down. At first glance there seemed nothing unusual about his feet, which were in slippers, but suddenly he saw that he had left bright crimson footmarks. He lifted up one foot, then the other. The soles of his slippers were soaked in thick crimson.

Mrs Pylon Jones leaned against the wall. 'What is it?' she whispered, her eyes beady with terror.

'Well, it isn't blood, at any rate,' said Roger roughly. 'Blood isn't that colour. This stuff smells like ...' He took off one slipper and sniffed the sole. 'I thought so. Paint.'

'Paint?' she echoed, a note of outrage replacing the fear in her voice. 'But there's no wet paint on my ...'

'There wasn't,' said Roger. 'But I think there is now.'

He went back to the door and opened it again. This time, because he was not straining his eyes to see out into the darkness but looking at the door itself, he saw the abomination. A large tin of crimson paint had been chucked over the door and had run down into a sticky pool on the whitened step.

He stepped aside for Mrs Pylon Jones to see. 'That's what you heard,' he said. 'Somebody, or some collection of somebodies, came along and threw a tin of paint over the door.'

Then he remembered the scraping footsole on the ground, and an idea struck him. Moving quickly outside, he stood motionless, cupping his ear. From far down towards the coast road came the distant bellowing of a motorcycle. He heard it clearly: not even the pouring of the rain could blot it out.

'They were on a motor-bike, whoever they were,' he said, going back into the house. 'They must have got on the bike and let it coast down the hill until they were clear. I thought I heard someone's foot scrape along the floor – just the sound you'd make if you were starting to coast off on a motor-bike.'

Mrs Jones was twisting her hands together more rapidly than ever. Agitation peered out of her eyes and expressed itself in the lines of her body and the furrows of her face.

'I can't think who'd do a thing like this. I've always kept myself to myself and got along well with everybody, isn't it? I haven't got any enemies. There isn't a soul wishes me any harm, not that I've ever heard tell of. It must be you.'

'What d'you mean, it must be me? I haven't got any enemies either.'

'You don't know that. You're a newcomer. People are funny

sometimes. Nobody'd do anything against me. I've lived here thirty years, always at peace with everybody isn't it?'

'Now, listen, Mrs Jones. Let's have a cup of tea and –'

'Nobody'd throw paint like that to spoil my door and who's going to pay for it?'

Roger took her arm and half-led, half-propelled her shivering little body into his sitting-room. 'I'll just make up the fire,' he said, bending to the coal-scuttle, 'and then we'll have a cup of tea which I'll make in my nice little kitchen, and we'll get our calm back. It's a nasty shock. But of course it doesn't mean anything.' He settled two big lumps of coal on to the fire and poked it gently till flames licked up.

Mrs Pylon Jones sat where Jenny had sat, and looked into the fire as Jenny had done, and she too talked of her fears. 'I don't understand who'd do it when I've never had a cross word with anybody.'

Roger let her mumble it out to herself. He made no further attempt to get through to her until he had two cups of tea poured out and one of them, a good strong one too, in her thin, knuckly grasp.

'Now, Mrs Jones, drink that and listen to me. We've just been touched by one ripple from a storm that's raging all over the world. Delinquency, hooliganism, all the backlash of the frustrated energies of the young. I've no doubt at all that if we'd managed to get hold of those lads, because I'm sure lads is what they were, we'd have found they were typical hell-raisers, with boots and leather jackets, probably adolescent acne and low foreheads. Working at a blind-alley job and already branded as failures. It's easy to see the resentments that must build up inside them – and there's no outlet except taking it out on somebody. Well, they can't take it out on their own mates, and rival gangs are apt to fight back if provoked, so they look round for a defenceless outsider. Somebody different. Me, for instance.'

'Well, I still don't see why they have to throw paint over my –'

'Of course not. To you it's just senseless and monstrous. To me it's those things too, but at the same time I'm glad they decided to victimize me in a fairly mild way. Paint splashed over the door will cost me some money but it doesn't actually land me in hospital. I can just see them getting the brainwave and having a tremendous giggle over it. *Let's go down to the store-room and knock off a nice big tin of paint and chuck it all over his door one night – that'll have him guessing.*'

She was looking at him narrowly, over the rim of her tea-cup. 'You know who it was then?'

'No, of course I don't.'

'But you seem to know all about them.'

'I'm just guessing. Using my imagination to reconstruct the crime.'

'You were making all that up,' said Mrs Pylon Jones bitterly. 'I thought you knew all about it and who they were, with all that about what they were wearing, and their kind of job, and going to the store-room for the paint, I thought you'd know where they *worked*, at least.'

'Look, Mrs Jones, for all I know definitely to the contrary, that paint might have been chucked by a leprechaun.'

'We haven't got any of them round here. There's no col-oured nearer than Bangor.'

'What I mean is, I don't know who threw the paint any more than you do, but usually when this kind of silly destruc-tive trick is played, it's played by the kind of person I've been describing.'

Is it said a small voice inside him. *How very comforting.*

'This very evening,' said Roger, 'there have probably been thousands of incidents, from Stockholm to San Francisco, all of much the same kind as this. Ours was just one of them. As I said, a ripple from the storm.'

Oh, that's all right then, said the voice. *An institutionalized problem.*

'Look, I used to work at a university,' said Roger to the dis-believing Mrs Pylon Jones. 'I'm used to young people. Many's the incident of this kind I've seen.'

Ever had paint thrown at your door.

Shut up, said Roger to the voice.

'Have another cup of tea,' said Roger to Mrs Pylon Jones.

'I thought it was your visitor when I first heard somebody moving about, isn't it,' said Mrs Pylon Jones, following a trail of her own. She shot Roger a reproachful glance, as if by hav-ing a visitor he had hopelessly confused the issue.

'Have some more tea,' said Roger, rising.

'We ought to get the police,' said Mrs Pylon Jones.

'The police? But where's the nearest –'

'Caerfenai. There'll be somebody on duty if we telephone.'

Roger knew that the nearest telephone was half a mile away, in a box outside the Post Office. 'You're surely not suggesting –'

'A thing like this, it's got to be reported.'

'Look, I've got to be up early in the morning to go down on the eight-fifteen. I'll report it as soon as I get down there. They won't send anybody up here now, anyway.'

'They might,' said Mrs Pylon Jones, timidly obstinate. Roger began to see how it was that her husband had taken to his bed and died as soon as it was clear that he had lost his battle with the Electricity Board. If he was as softly persistent as she was, defeat, once he acknowledged it, would immediately give him cancer or a thrombosis according to his physical type.

'What did your husband die of, Mrs Jones?' he asked.

'I don't see that's got anything to do with it,' she snapped.

'I was just trying to change the subject.'

'If my husband was here,' said Mrs Pylon Jones, looking at Roger with hate, 'he'd have had the police here by now.'

'No, he wouldn't. He'd have put his overcoat on and struggled up the mountain and put some money in the box and rung the police station in Caerfenai, and they'd have taken the particulars and told him they'd be up in the morning. Well, that's what I'll do.'

'Thank you,' said Mrs Pylon Jones. 'It won't take you long to walk to the –'

'I mean I'll do it in the morning. And now let's go to bed and get some rest. Don't be anxious. Those silly boys won't come back, not tonight, not ever. I'll pay for the door to be cleaned and repainted. And if you're nervous, just listen out and if you hear anything, give me a knock and I'll be out there and grab hold of whoever it is. Only there won't be anybody.'

She murmured something, drank up her tea, rose and went off through the interconnecting door. It struck him, as he saw her off and bade her good night with fresh reassurances, that he had prevailed over her to just about the same extent that Jenny had prevailed over him. Neither was convinced; but each, recognizing an unalterable situation, had gone along with it.

He went back to bed. Outside, the wind walked about the mountainside. The tea made him wakeful, and lust invaded his veins. He burned for Jenny, for Margot, for Rhiannon. He tried to construct a fantasy involving all three of them, but in the end it was Rhiannon who dominated his thoughts. Perhaps, tomorrow, she would be on the bus. He would find where she lived, and one dark night he would throw a tin of paint over her door, as a symbol of the prolonged, spouting ejaculation he owed her.

Roger's Welsh was taking its first few real steps, and he could by now manage a certain amount of backchat with the passengers on the bus. They were gratifyingly good-humoured and cooperative, as if feeling that by making the effort to speak their language he was paying them a compliment. He did not, naturally, disabuse them of this idea by explaining that he had a weakness for blonde Swedish girls who might be studying Celtic philology at Uppsala. In any case, all that superstructure of his life seemed very remote just now. In one way, of course, his plans for Uppsala were more real than Gareth's bus because they were in a straight line with everything else in his life, including his professional career. But Gareth's bus insisted on *seeming* very real.

The passengers, who were nearly all regulars, had begun to take on recognizable faces and names. The shepherd with the too-large boots and the resonant voice, for instance, whom he had met on that first evening in the pub, often travelled with them. So did the two younger men who had been there at the same time, the dark shy one and the boxer-like one. The dark shy one was called Dilwyn and he was a childhood friend of Rhiannon's. They had played together over the mountainside fifteen years earlier, and now she had grown up into a beauty, expensively dressed, the target of men's glances, and left him hopelessly behind. Or had she? When she travelled on the bus, he always sat near and kept his eyes on her, and sometimes they would exchange a few words of conversation. She spoke to him unconcernedly, easily, as to a relative. Dilwyn's other passion was for model aeroplanes. He belonged to a club that held meetings in a large level field just outside Caerfenai, guiding their marvellous adult toys on long aerobatic flights high above the ground, while they themselves stood peering up with single-whiskered radio control sets in their hands. Dilwyn sometimes got on the bus carrying a model aeroplane almost as big as himself, and with his pockets bulging with tools and little cans of fuel. He lived in one of the terraces in Llancrwys and sometimes, on a fine afternoon, the high rasp of his plane's engine would be heard, scrawling its thin signature on the sunlit sky, as he practised and tried out modifications. But the season was coming to an end.

The other youth, the one who looked like a prize fighter, was called Iorwerth. Roger was afraid of him. His face wore a set scowl, and this scowl seemed to deepen whenever his gaze rested on Roger. When asked for his fare, he would hold it out in his great calloused fingers as if debating whether to flip the coins up into Roger's face. Since Roger had first seen Iorwerth in a pub, he knew he was not a teetotaller, but he hoped he was a moderate drinker who never took too much. He did not know what he would do if Iorwerth ever got on to the bus drunk and aggressive.

Iorwerth's manner was distinctly unwelcoming, but most of the passengers accepted Roger's presence among them very naturally and freely, and it often seemed to him hard to remember that he had ever been anywhere else. As he collected warm pennies from people's hands, listening to the high chatter of the women as they raised their voices above the grumbling of the bus, and watched the mountains, or the sea, come into focus within the oblong of the windscreen, it seemed to him that this life had almost enough reality to blot out any other.

Almost. But a few things were still not quite in alignment. His relationship with Gareth, for instance, seemed in an odd way to be standing perfectly still. As day followed day, and the number of hours he had spent in Gareth's company mounted to scores and then to hundreds, he felt that Gareth was getting to know him but he was not getting to know Gareth. There was something about that beaky face, with its bird-of-prey eyes staring out from their deep hollows, that repelled easy intimacy. With such a being, it was not easy to fall into a casual intimacy. Roger found that he could not, for instance, try out his Welsh on Gareth. If he essayed a Welsh phrase, Gareth would give that rather caustic smile of his, and answer in English.

Still, Gareth did sometimes initiate a conversation. The morning after the paint-throwing episode, bringing the ten-thirty up, they stood beside the cooling bus and looked over at the vast expanse of sea, with the narrow green fields running down to the coastline and the dark wedge of Anglesey, and Gareth said, 'How is it at Mrs Pylon Jones's? Quite comfortable, are you?'

Roger felt a brief impulse to tell Gareth about the red paint. But he decided to keep the matter to himself. The bus took a fork in the road just before reaching Mrs Pylon Jones's house, so that Gareth had not driven past and seen the paint-splash for himself. Doubtless gossip would reach him sooner or later, but he was not going to learn about it from Roger. Gareth's troubles were sufficient; he should not be burdened with Roger's petty misfortunes as well.

'Oh, fine,' he said. 'I feel quite at home in Llancrwys already.'

This in itself was a loaded remark; Roger realized as much, as soon as it was out. To be at home in Llancrwys was to be one of Gareth's neighbours, yet he had only the vaguest idea of what part of the village Gareth lived in, and certainly could not have pointed to the house. Gareth, at the end of their day's work, simply disappeared in the general direction of the upper part of the village, where the smallest terrace houses were. Roger assumed he lived by himself, but, again, he had no evidence one way or another. For all he knew to the contrary, Gareth might have had a wife and six children.

'Llancrwys is all right when you get used to it,' said Gareth. 'I have known people who found they couldn't live anywhere else. Never tried to, myself. But it seems to draw people. Take Mrs Arkwright.'

Roger nodded. Mrs Arkwright travelled on the bus nearly every day, usually indulging in a good hearty grumble, in which the words 'Corporation', 'refuse collection', 'scandal', and 'when Hubert was alive' recurred frequently.

'Her husband was a wholesale grocer in England,' said Gareth, as if England were one tiny self-contained area that did not have to be particularized. 'He used to come here for his holidays. Every year from his boyhood he stayed somewhere in one of these villages round here, and when he got married to her he started bringing her with him. All through the years they were here every summer, and when he got around the sixty mark he decided he'd got enough money and he sold his grocery business and built a nice little house for the two of them. Then he died.' He gave a short, grating laugh. 'She'll live another thirty years. She wasn't much younger than him, but she's a lot stronger. And it was him that was in love with the place, not her.'

'Why doesn't she pull up stakes and go back to her own world?'

'Can't do it,' said Gareth indifferently. His curiosity about Mrs Arkwright seemed abruptly to have run dry. As if searching for another and more interesting topic, he stared over the wall. 'That ewe's in trouble,' he said. 'Shouldn't be limping like that. I don't think Huw knows what he's doing.'

'Have you got experience with sheep?' Roger asked.

Gareth gave the same dry chuckle. 'Spent enough hours with them,' he said. Characteristically, he did not give any details of what it was he had spent hours doing.

Gareth now opened the bonnet of the bus and peered into the engine. 'This magneto won't last much longer,' he said. 'I heard where they were breaking one or two buses over Portmadoc way. I think I'll go over on Sunday. Might get one that's got a bit of life in it.'

'Mm-hm,' said Roger listlessly. He saw no reason why he should make polite conversation to a man who kept his confidences as buttoned-up as Gareth did. So, leaning against the bus, he thought briefly of Jenny. She was a nice girl. If he had met her when she was single, he might have done a lot worse than marry her. Marriage, a home. A woman permanently in attendance. He could hardly imagine it. Would it be worth making a serious effort to get Jenny away from her horrible husband and marry her? Well, but what about the children? Did he like children enough to take over two of someone else's? Perhaps so. They would keep Jenny happy, anyway. It was all another puzzle. Life seemed to hold so few things that were unambiguous and free of complications. To rest his mind, he turned, as Gareth fiddled with the magneto, to images of pleasure.

'Where does Rhiannon live?' he said to Gareth's bent back.

'Oh, along,' said Gareth. He poked at the magneto with a screwdriver. 'Doesn't seem to want to come off.'

A few days later, he found out for himself where she lived. He tailed her home one evening, skulking near the wall, while ahead of him the rich green of her expensive suède coat seemed to glow in the deep dusk, its effulgence conveying to his mind both invitation and warning. They had left the centre of the village, passed the clump of Council houses, and gone some five hundred yards out along the open hillside when suddenly, to his surprise, she opened a gate and went into a cottage he had noticed before on his solitary early-morning walks. This cottage was old. Like most of the outlying houses it ante-dated, perhaps by centuries, the Victorian terrace houses that were the oldest buildings in the actual village of Llancrwys. Single-storeyed, thick-walled, it hugged the mountainside, crouching behind a barricade of whitewashed wall and thorn hedge, ready for the worst fury of any gale blowing in from the Irish sea. Like all these long houses, it had originally been a smallholding, and the little barns and cattle-byres were built on to the house in a straight line, human beings and animals living under the same roof as frankly as in the old Swiss chalets, except that the arrangement was horizontal and not vertical.

The place was a smallholding no longer. Farming on that tiny scale was almost completely extinct, even up here. The family still kept hens; Roger had seen the creatures stumping about, pausing amid their restless clucking to stare through the gate, as if mesmerized, at any chance passer-by. But the cattle-shed had been turned into a garage, with neat modern doors in rustproof metal; the old windows had been replaced by large-paned modern ones in steel frames; the whole ensemble shone with fresh whitewash and paint, lace curtains were elaborately arranged in the windows, and two large television aerials surmounted all.

Change had come, yes. But the cottage was still a cottage, it still stood behind its hedge-and-wall barricade on the bare hillside; hens still pecked and clucked about; quite possibly the place had no bathroom – certainly the neat whitewashed *ty bach* stood primly on the other side of the narrow yard. Roger walked back to the village in bewilderment. He could not fit Rhiannon into this picture. Down in the hotel, among the soft carpets and the discreet lighting, she seemed so entirely a creature of *la dolce vita*. Had she really grown up in this long house, inside those thick, sturdy walls, so close to the bare earth? As a child, had she sat in the yard among the hens, skipped over these slopes, waded in the flashing streams? And did she still own some dowdy, chapel-going couple as her progenitors?

What puzzled him was not that Rhiannon, with her luxurious beauty so perfectly band-boxed and turned out, should *come* from a place like this, but that she should still go back there, still acknowledge it as her home. Why on earth should she? Cheapness? He chuckled scornfully at the thought. A girl like that would have no need to economize. If she wanted to set up in a flat in the town, or for that matter in any town, any city in the world, it wouldn't take her long to find someone to pay the rent.

But perhaps she would have scruples about accepting the money, about forming immoral relationships. No, surely. There was something so – what would be the best word? so *experienced* about her. She must have been around. But perhaps he was wrong. Perhaps her clothes and make-up just made her *look* like that. A pure village maiden? Content to settle down, in another year or two, and marry someone like Dilwyn, with his quietly intense adoration and his model aeroplanes? No, he couldn't believe that either.

Roger, in short, could not size up Rhiannon. But then, neither could he size up Gareth, or Ivo and Gito, or Madog. That, however, did not mean that he was not going to try. Some mysteries were worth investigating, some were not. The people round here were, on the whole, attractive mysteries.

And if that was true of the rest of them, it went double for Rhiannon.

He waited his chance, and it came one evening when she came undulating out of the mist and boarded the bus to go down on the seven o'clock run. She climbed up the steps;

looking straight in front of her. God, how beautiful she was. Had she a lover? Was some lucky swine getting *that*, all of it, as often as he wanted it? He could hardly believe that any human being was so lucky. But if so, it was somebody who didn't deserve it, that much was absolutely certain.

'A shilling, please,' he said unnecessarily, approaching her. She was already holding out the correct sum in a neatly gloved hand.

Since they did not, on Gareth's bus, rise to the luxury of tickets, there was no chance to touch Rhiannon's hand again as he gave her one. But he smiled encouragingly, catching her eye, and she threw him a look that was half-way, or perhaps a third of the way, towards an answering smile; at any rate, he told himself, quite a comradely look, as from one resident of Llancrwys to another.

That settled it. He would plunge now. Quickly he collected the rest of the fares, then stood at the front of the bus beside Gareth, peering through the windscreen as if intent on the road ahead. Actually he was screwing up his courage. He could see Rhiannon reflected in the dark glass. She was not wearing her suède coat this time. She had on a belted mackintosh and knee-length boots. The effect was plain and sensible on the surface, yet at some deeper level alluring and somehow extravagant, as if the mackintosh and boots were not designed to be worn outdoors, in real rainy weather, but only indoors, within the scent of expensive cigars and with champagne corks going off in the background.

When the bus rolled into the square and halted, Roger mumbled something to Gareth and set off in pursuit of Rhiannon. She seemed unaware that she was being followed, or perhaps merely indifferent; at any rate, she went up the steps of the Palace Hotel without hurrying or looking back. Roger paused in the shadowy car-park. He had for some days been carrying a tie in his pocket, ready for just this situation, and he now took it out and carefully tied it round his neck. His badge of respectability. It would have seemed wrong to wear a tie on the bus, but without it he would have been refused admittance to the Palace Hotel. Such are the magical properties of an eighteen-inch strip of cloth. Then he took a deep breath and went up the steps.

The Head Porter recognized him and presumably knew, since everybody knew everything, that he now collected the fares on Gareth's bus, yet managed to greet him in a way that suggested that he did not know this. So did the barman. In this hotel, decent social pretences were kept up. Besides, they may have been allowing for the possibility of Roger's being an eccentric millionaire. Why not? It was no more intrinsically unlikely a thing than an eccentric philologist. He downed a couple of quick whiskies, straightened his shoulders, and went out of the bar and into the lobby, Rhiannon's domain.

She was at the desk, looking absently out across the expanse of carpet, that uncharted sea which in the fullness of time floated toward her everything she needed. Roger, the whisky warming his veins, went boldly up.

'Hello,' he said to her.

She looked at him impassively. 'Hello. What can I do for you?'

'It's not on hotel business,' he said. 'It's personal business.'

She continued to look at him without change of expression, seeming neither surprised nor challenged.

'Could you tell me,' Roger pursued, 'where people in this area go when they want a good evening out? A good meal, a good wine, perhaps a band.' Ought he to add, 'a floor-show'? Or would that be laying it on too thick?

She took the question as if it were a routine inquiry. 'Well, it depends how far you want to go.'

'Anywhere that a car'll take me to in an evening.' Or did she think he went everywhere on a bicycle? Or only to places that were on the route of Gareth's bus?

'Well, the nearest that's quite good is over on Anglesey. There's a place that does a good dinner and wine list, and it has a little dance floor.'

'Have you been there?'

'Yes,' she said non-committally.

'You think it's the best within, say, twenty-five miles of here?'

'Yes.'

'Would you come there with me one evening?'

He had said it.

Rhiannon looked at him as if deciding what to say. Her big

dark eyes played over Roger's face as if seeing it properly for the first time. As, indeed, they were, since this was the first time he had offered himself for inspection within the range of things that mattered.

She opened her lips to say something or other, but before any words could come out, her attention was abruptly jerked away from Roger by the surging approach of a fleshy, fair-haired young man who came rapidly up to the desk, leaned half across it, and said, 'Evening, beautiful.'

Rhiannon looked at him with scarcely masked loathing. To Roger, standing where both their young faces appeared to him in profile, it seemed that there was some very special quality of insolence about him, some furious inner resistance in her. For his own part, Roger took an immediate dislike to the youth. It was not so much that he resented having his conversation interrupted, at such a crucial moment. After all, the young man could hardly have known how important a point they had reached. It was rather that everything about the newcomer exuded a kind of greasy insolence. His yellowish hair was brushed back in a quiff, and arranged over his ears like a duck's plumage. His voice was light and rather creamy in texture, and fitted in well with his generally pampered and over-padded appearance. His walk was the worst of all. He seemed to swim along with his shoulders barging the air, as if secretly yearning to come across some person defenceless enough to be pushed to one side. It was easy to imagine him shoving a blind person into a ditch for a joke.

Staring straight into Rhiannon's eyes, the young man now leaned a little closer to her, ignoring Roger altogether, and said, 'All right for the twenty-first?'

'No, it isn't all right.'

'That's bad. I expected you'd have it straightened out by now.'

Rhiannon got down from her stool and stood squarely on her legs, facing him. 'You had no call to expect anything. I told you when you first asked. All the rooms are booked up for that evening.'

'My father spoke to Mr Evans and he said he'd try and put one of the other parties off.'

'He may have tried,' said Rhiannon with finality, 'but if so he didn't succeed. All the other arrangements are still down in the book and the book is in my charge and if you want your party on that night you'll have to have it somewhere else.'

'That's bad,' said the young man again. 'Perhaps we'd better talk to Mr Evans again.'

'There's nothing Mr Evans can do,' she said, turning away.

'There's plenty he can do,' said the young man, 'if he wants favours done for him. And everybody wants that, don't they?'

She did not reply. He hesitated as if about to add something more, but she bent down and began to rummage on the shelf under the desk for some imaginary lost article; the gesture was so dismissive that his insolence was not proof against it, and he surged away.

Rhiannon slowly straightened up and stood looking hard at nothing. Anger had caused her normally damask skin to flush a dull red. As Roger watched, this red slowly drained away, disappearing first from her neck and then from her forehead. It stayed longest in two bright patches on her cheeks. She appeared to have forgotten Roger's existence, but he felt that the situation was too delicate for him to risk breaking in on her thoughts, and merely stood there in silence. Finally she turned to him and said, 'An hotel can't make space out of empty air.'

'No,' said Roger.

'He thinks he can have everything he wants,' she said with sudden viciousness, 'that's his trouble.'

'And what is it he wants? In this instance, I mean,' said Roger carefully.

'It's his twenty-first birthday and they want to have a slap-up affair and spend a lot of money and let everybody in Caerfenai know how much they're spending. That's why they want to have it here, right in the middle of town, instead of in some place just as good a few miles off. He didn't get round to trying to reserve the room till it was too late and we were booked up, but he thinks that's a detail.' Then annoyed with herself for having said so much, she turned her annoyance on Roger. 'Was there something else you wanted to ask me?'

'You haven't told me yet,' said Roger gently, 'whether you'll have an evening out with me at this place on Anglesey.'

'Oh, yes, yes,' she said dismissively, as if among a host of minor annoyances she could not be bothered to fend off one more. 'I'll come.' She turned back to her ledgers, flipping the pages over, pretending to be busy.

'Next Thursday?'

She looked at him with sudden attentiveness. 'How d'you know that's my evening off next week?'

'I've been noticing the times you travel on the bus.'

She half smiled, then suddenly laughed outright. Her teeth shone in the shaft light from the desk, and also he suddenly saw what a beautiful throat she had. But then, everything about her was beautiful.

'You must be the noticing type,' she said.

'Well, I've got nothing else to do when I'm on the bus.'

They fixed a date and she told him the telephone number of the Anglesey restaurant.

Now that he had at last got the Rhiannon-target in something like range, Roger decided to spare no effort. He would spend money, cut a dash, ladle out charm, as never before. However small his chances of success, the reward for that nearly-impossible success was so fantastic that, as in the case of the football pools, it did not make sense *not* to try.

He decided to hire a car. The negotiations for this took longer than he had expected, and he missed the four-fifteen run up. This meant that Gareth, without warning, had to cope single-handed with a bus full of noisy school-children. When Roger reported for the five-forty-five up, he apologized.

'I had a bit of business to do.'

'I managed,' said Gareth.

The bus was loaded and ready to start, so Roger said no more until they reached Llancrwys and the passengers filed off. Then, in the empty bus, he began again.

'I'm sorry I missed that run. I was hiring a car.'

'Oh?' said Gareth. 'Wedding or funeral?'

'I'm having an evening out. A break in my Spartan life. I'm afraid I shan't be on the ten o'clock up tomorrow night.'

'All right,' said Gareth. He took out a duster and began wiping down the instrument panel.

Roger tried to find some way of working round to telling Gareth that it was Rhiannon he was taking out in the hired

142

car. He wanted, for some reason, to see what Gareth's reaction would be. But he could not think how to put it.

'I felt I'd earned a bit of gaiety,' he said feebly.

Gareth finished wiping the instrument panel and put the duster away in his pocket. Roger watched him, helplessly. Was Gareth ever gay? Had he a personal life at all, with needs and wishes? Was he loved, did he love? Or did he simply disappear into the mist at the end of each day's work?

Perhaps he was metamorphosed into an eagle, clinging to some high crag, staring unblinking into the night.

'So I've hired this car,' said Roger, 'and I'm taking ... a girl out.'

'Good luck to you,' said Gareth. He switched off the lights of the bus and went down the steps.

Roger, standing in the darkened bus, felt a sudden flare of resentment, almost of hatred. Why should Gareth slam this iron door, in his face all the time? He felt like running down the steps after Gareth, seizing him by those vast shoulders, and shaking him with all his strength. But of course he did nothing.

'See you at seven o'clock,' Gareth's voice came to him through the darkness.

'See you,' said Roger despondently.

If he had talked and forced Gareth to listen, if he had found words for his loneliness and his pain and his needs, Gareth would just have looked at him with that bird-of-prey face. Above a simple, practical level, there was something in Gareth that repelled all communication.

Then the thought came: *Of course. That makes him more like Geoffrey.*

Thoughtfully, buttoning his raincoat, Roger walked down the hill to Mrs Pylon Jones's.

The next evening, his mood had changed again. His clothes were not new, but they were well brushed; his face had also seen its best days, but it was well shaved; and the hired Ford in which he drove up to the Palace Hotel, where Rhiannon had arranged to meet him, was glittering and new enough for both of them.

He parked neatly in the forecourt of the hotel, the car

purring smoothly to a halt. Diamond Jim. Last of the big spenders. His bank account had taken another beating that morning and the loot was safe in his wallet. Rhiannon would find she was batting in her own league. No Llancrwys penny-pinching, no smell of bus-oil, tonight. He would make up the ground he had lost on Beverley.

He went quickly up the steps of the hotel. Rhiannon was not behind the desk, which was what he had expected. She had arranged to meet him in the Lounge Bar. He went in. She was not there. Never mind, she had to be late. Probably she had come off duty and was upstairs putting on a different dress and dabbing at her face. Roger ordered a drink and waited. When the drink was finished, he ordered another drink and waited. When the drink was finished, he ordered another one and waited some more. At last, four drinks and an hour after entering the hotel, he went out into the foyer and asked the girl at the desk where Rhiannon was.

'She's not here tonight.'

'Yes, but surely she . . . When did she come off duty?'

'Are you Mr Furnivall?' the girl asked, suddenly giving him a close, scrutinizing look.

Roger knew what was coming. All at once he saw the whole thing. His knees sagged a little 'Yes,' he said.

'Rhiannon left a message,' said the girl. 'She said she's sorry but she can't manage tonight.'

For a wild instant, Roger wanted to open his mouth and say to the girl, 'Then I'll take *you*.' She was a girl, wasn't she? Even though she was undeniably plain, she belonged in the same class as Rhiannon, though Rhiannon was at the top of it and she was somewhere near the bottom.

Actually all he said was, 'Oh.'

The girl gave him a placid look and went back to writing something on a message pad. Roger turned away.

The car was waiting. The table was booked at the Anglesey restaurant. Perhaps the best thing to do with his disappointment was to look straight at it and stare it down. He got into the car and, driving carefully, found his way along a maze of country roads to the place in the middle of Anglesey where the restaurant was. The table was still not taken. He apologized briefly for being one instead of two, and then settled down and deliberately chewed his way through the most expensive and elaborate meal the place could provide. He forced himself to concentrate on eating and drinking, not merely swallowing the stuff but doing what the untranslatable French word calls *déjustation*. The avocado pear and shrimps, the sole, the *bœuf flamande*, the cheese and celery, all had their appropriate wines. Finally, a good brandy with his coffee, and a small but excellent cigar.

As he consumed all this, Roger glanced now and then at the empty chair opposite him. Someone should have been sitting in it, but not Rhiannon. He realized, now, that he had been on a wrong scent there. He felt no bitterness. It had been absurd: a fragment of fantasy, thrown up by an imagination that had been heated by privation and loneliness, and by a life jarred loose from reality. Pacing the bare hillside, or sitting alone in Mrs Pylon Jones's holiday people's flat, any kind of sexual life seemed as remote and fantastic as any other. But down here on the level ground, with fellow-diners who looked like building contractors and wholesale fishmongers, two and two made four. Rhiannon! He might as well have wished for Cleopatra reincarnated from the dead.

Ballasted by the heavy load of food and drink in his stomach, he waddled out to the car and drove gently back to Llancrwys. Gareth would have taken the ten o'clock up just a few minutes before. As he drew up outside Mrs Pylon Jones's and switched off the engine, Roger suddenly heard Gareth's voice saying in that flat, dismissive way, 'Good luck to you.'

And good luck to you, Gareth. Move over, I'm coming to join you on that windy ledge. I'm going to be an eagle like you, and live in a pile of sticks on the mountain, and forget that I was ever a man.

Forget, forget, forget, forget.

As he walked up the hill to report for work the next morning at eight, Roger laid a bet with himself that Gareth would not ask him how he had enjoyed his evening out. He put a hypothetical ten thousand pounds on Gareth's not saying anything about it one way or another. And of course he won. This made him feel somehow reassured. The hunchback's taciturnity, his wonderful consistency in refusing to countenance any area of life that existed away from the bus and its concerns, was soothing and good.

They rattled down at eight-fifteen, up at ten-thirty, and then Roger excused himself and said he would see Gareth in town. He had to take the hired car back. Gareth nodded. Even now, he expressed no curiosity about Roger's leisure activities.

It had rained in the night, and the air was sweet and cool, as if washed by the soft downpour. The sun shone coldly on to the flat sea. Winter was almost on them. There had been no frost as yet, but Roger could feel it in the air.

The expensive hired car was as fresh and glittering as the rest of the world this morning. It seemed pathetic, unused, like a bride turned back at the altar. Without allowing himself to think, Roger got in and started the engine. He took off the brake and the car rolled gently forward and down. At first he could use third gear, but as the road got steeper he went down to second. How well he knew this road : he would never forget it. Every curve, every camber. He knew it through the soles of his feet, going up and down on the bus.

The freshness of the morning tempted Roger to wind his window down. He let go of the wheel with his right hand and began to turn the handle, at the same time taking a right-hand bend between high stone walls. Then it happened. The front end of the car suddenly dipped and canted over, the steering-wheel twisted violently and almost pulled itself out of the grasp of Roger's left hand. The car wallowed like a launch in heavy waves, and tried to throw Roger over to his left, into the passenger's seat. Snatching his hand away from the window-handle, he brought it very quickly on to the steering wheel, but even within that half-second the car had pulled further off course. He had a quick, blurred vision of a wheel bouncing down the hill ahead of him, and then the front of the car was violently shouldering into the stone wall at the roadside. A wing crumpled. Metal scraped on the road. Roger was jolted hard from side to side. A projecting corner of stone pushed neatly through the near-side window, covering the passenger's seat with cubes of safety glass. Then they stopped.

Trembling, Roger got out. The only thought in his mind was that he wished he had a flask of brandy on him. Walking round to the front of the car, he saw at once that the damage was not very extensive. But it would cost a fair amount of money to put right. The near-side front was a mess. The head-lamp on that side was beyond repair, and the crumpled wing would have to be straightened out and several deep scratches and dents taken out of the door. The smashed glass would be easy to replace, but it looked shocking now, with a great jagged hole and all those shining cubes, like costume jewellery, lying everywhere. He looked down the road. The escaped wheel was still running and lurching. As he watched, it mounted the narrow pavement in front of a row of houses. The accident had happened just at the beginning of the next village below Llancrwys. He did not like to think what might have happened if the wheel had come off while they were running down the village street.

As he watched, the wheel ran along the pavement in front of the low wall that shielded the tiny front gardens of the houses. Then it seemed to hit some obstruction; perhaps a stone or a child's toy left on the footway. It jumped into the air, changed course, and, travelling at perhaps forty miles an hour, made straight for the door of the General Stores and Post Office.

Roger wanted to yell and wave his arms, but it all happened too quickly for him to do anything. The door of the shop was reached by two steps. Up these steps the wheel bounced. The door itself was made of wood up to half-way point, and above that of glass. Owing to the slight check caused by the steps, the wheel hit the wooden part of the door. That was blessing number one. Blessing number two was that there was no one standing right in the doorway, just coming out or just going in. Roger had a swift, sick vision of a child, or a quavering old age pensioner, being bowled over and killed. But at once he saw that this was not going to happen. The wheel struck the door full on the wood and bounced back; the glass in the top part shivered and the pieces fell all over the steps. The wheel settled and lay still in the gutter, its shining metal innocently reflecting the sky.

Roger ran down the hill, his legs slightly shaky under him. As he went down the village street, doors opened, and women, some wearing scarves round their heads, looked out at him. He did not pause to examine their expressions, which he felt sure would be disapproving. Inside the General Stores and Post Office he could hear, as he approached, a hubbub of female voices crying out in Welsh. He thought the place must be full of women doing their morning shopping, but when he ran up the steps and breathlessly entered the shop he found that there were only two. Both had high, clear voices, and both were taking short, scurrying steps up and down the shop, like frightened hens. The postmaster, an elderly gnome-like man with a gleaming bald dome across which several long wisps of hair were carefully plastered, was standing behind the Post Office part of the shop, staring with quiet dismay through the wire grille. He was too old to do the general shop trade and his daughter usually helped him with it, but this morning she was away for an hour or so in Caerfenai.

When the two women saw Roger they switched to English, explaining to him at considerable length that it was dangerous to roll motor-wheels downhill where they might run into people. The fatter and paler of the two added that she had suffered a shock to her heart and there ought to be a law.

Roger replied with the counter-explanation that the wheel had come off his car while he was driving it down the hill, and that this had happened without his intention or foreknowledge. At the third repetition he managed to establish this as the generally accepted account of the occurrence.

Much tongue-clicking followed. The less plump woman picked up a bag of onions from the counter and said she must be going home, but continued to stand in the same spot. Two more women, an old man and a child entered the premises.

The postmaster now unclicked a section of the counter and emerged into the shop. Advancing to the door, he examined it and declared that not only was the glass broken but the wooden panelling was split.

'Somebody'll have to pay for it, isn't it?'

'I'll pay for it.'

'A new door will be needed, new from top to bottom.'

'I'll pay for it.'

'I was in the back, getting a postal order. Mrs Jones wanted a postal order for two and sixpence and I keep them in the back. I didn't witness the incident. It was the wheel off your car, wasn't it?'

'The wheel, yes. I'll pay for the door.'

'A new one will be needed. The wood has gone as well.'

'Get any kind of door you like. I'll pay. I'll write down my name and address.'

'If Mrs Jones hadn't happened to want a postal order, I'd have witnessed the incident and then I could have given my –'

'It doesn't matter. I expect these two ladies don't mind my asking for their names in case witnesses are needed. The insurance company is bound to –'

'Yes,' said the postmaster. 'That door is useless now. Except possibly for firewood.' He bent to examine the door, his dome gleaming palely in the autumnal light from the street. 'I daresay the lock could be put to some use. The lock isn't damaged as far as I can see. I could get the lock taken out and –'

'It doesn't matter. Just get a new door and I'll pay.'

Order was finally restored. The two women expressed their willingness to repeat their detailed account of the incident, already given several times over (the audience had now been augmented by a woman carrying a baby and a young man in a bloodstained apron, perhaps a butcher's assistant). Roger asked them their names. One was called Mrs Arwel Jones and the other Mrs Iolo Jones. They both lived in the village street.

Roger walked back to where the car stood forlornly canted over, its naked axle resting on the tarmac like an exposed bone after a fracture. He took the wheel with him. The crumpled wing would not prevent the wheel from revolving, if it could be put back. He hunted for the jack and finally located it in a well under the back seat. With it was a bundle of tools. Slowly, his hands trembling, he put the jack in what he thought was the right place, and turned the screw until the car was almost upright. Then he tried to fit the wheel back on. Fortunately, the thread was not stripped from the bolts. And yet, however much he fiddled and wrestled, the wheel would not go on. Something was wrong. The car was not jacked up high enough. He lay on his back and studied the mechanism. He was doing badly. But then, would any philologist do better? Would Bryant be any use at this?

A long, slow whining announced that a vehicle was climbing the hill. It shuddered and halted, throbbing. Roger looked up. What new threat was this? But no, not a threat. Ivo and

Gito, their faces expressing sympathetic concern, were climbing down from the cab of their scrap-iron-carrying lorry.

'Trouble, isn't it?' said Ivo, the woollen ball on his cap bobbing as he bent down to look. 'A puncture, eh?'

'No. The wheel came off.'

'The wheel came –' Ivo and Gito exchanged glances. 'Is it your own car?'

'Hired,' said Roger. He sat upright, feeling suddenly very tired.

'A hired car ought to be in better condition than that,' said Ivo.

'The jack's wrong,' put in Gito, looking over his shoulder.

'So it is. That jack's on the wrong position, man. Here.' Ivo's clever, black-nailed hands darted in among the stubborn mysteries, wound the jack down a little way, moved it a few inches, wound it up. The axle rose much higher this time. 'Here, let's have that wheel.' A few deft, twirling movements, and Ivo had done in a moment what Roger would probably not have managed in an hour. 'Thanks,' he said, meaning it.

Meanwhile, Gito had been casting an eye over the car. 'A lot of damage here,' he said in his husky toot. 'The hire company'll want to know.'

'I can let them have the details,' said Roger shortly.

'These modern cars are all the same. They should stick to old-fashioned fish glue,' said Ivo.

'Just flew off without warning, did it?' Gito persisted.

'If I'd had warning I'd have stopped,' said Roger. He felt he needed a drink before facing the explanation to the hire company.

'Where did you leave it last night?' Ivo suddenly asked him.

'Outside where I'm staying. Mrs Pylon Jones's.'

'Mm,' said Ivo. He looked across at Gito.

'Could be,' said Gito.

'Could be what?' Roger asked crossly. He felt cold and very irritable.

Ivo took off his woollen cap. His hair, which Roger did not remember having seen before, was sandy and close-cropped. He stroked it with a meditative hand.

'Any idea who threw that paint?' he asked Roger.

'No. Just some hooligan who –'

'If they can throw paint over a door,' said Ivo slowly, 'they can just as easily loosen a few nuts on a wheel.'

Roger stiffened. 'But that's fantastic. Are you suggesting that somebody's trying to kill me?'

'Of course not,' said Ivo. 'It didn't kill you, did it? But it's going to mean a lot of trouble for you. You'll have to take the car back and explain why it –'

'Yes, yes, I realize that. The point is, do you think somebody's trying to ...' Roger stopped. He could not think how to say exactly what somebody might be trying to do.

'Make Llancrwys a place you want to get out of?' Ivo supplied. His voice was level, but his eyes were troubled.

'Oh, surely that's ridiculous,' said Roger. He got into the car and started the engine. It turned over quite smoothly. Obviously there was no damage in that quarter.

Seeing that Ivo was looking at him steadily through the glass, Roger wound the window down and said, 'You think somebody doesn't like me?' He tried to speak carelessly, but his voice came out with a heavy, anxious sound.

'That could be,' said Ivo. He put his woollen cap on again and climbed up into the cab of the lorry. Gito was already behind the wheel. In a cloud of smoke, the burdened vehicle staggered off up the hill.

Roger started the car moving. It occurred to him, as he picked up speed, that he had not checked the other wheels. The sooner he got rid of this car the better. But first he would have a drink.

The rest of that day was a nightmare. The interview with the car hire company was exactly the ordeal Roger had foreseen; the manager, an angry little terrier of a man, made him answer the same questions over and over again, and then imprisoned him in the office and made him fill in endless forms. While he was sitting there, laboriously writing out the answers to smudgily-printed queries, Roger's limbs began to shake with delayed nervous reaction. He felt faint, and several times had to stop writing; when he resumed, his hand was trembling so much that what he wrote was barely legible. He longed to go to Mario's for a stiff drink to brace him up, but the little terrier-manager was in an outer office, mounting guard, and kept opening the door to see that Roger had not made his escape by sliding down the drain-pipe. Finally, limp and bedewed with sweat, he made his way to Mario's in time for a drink and a late, hurried lunch before they closed.

The trembling stopped, but for the rest of the day he felt heavy and tired. The leather bag felt incredibly heavy on his shoulder, and his legs ached as he walked up and down the shaking floor of the bus. He longed for the day's work to be over, with a longing so intense that it blotted out everything else. He hardly gave a thought to last night's humiliation, or to the possibility that someone was trying to crowd him out of Llancrwys. All that mattered was to get to his bed and sleep.

Just before they left for the seven o'clock run down, Rhiannon got on. Roger made no attempt to ask her why she had stood him up. As he saw things now, through the cloud of his fatigue, she was just another passenger. He went round and collected the fares, and when he got to Rhiannon he simply stood and held out his hand like a robot. As she put the shilling into his palm she looked up at him, quickly and inquiringly. He gave her a half-smile through his weariness, to show her that at any rate he was not sulking, and went back to his place beside Gareth.

When they reached Caerfenai, rain was hissing gently down out of an intense darkness. The passengers got off. Roger sat slumped in his seat at the front, staring through the windscreen. He did not turn to look for Rhiannon, but he could not help seeing her reflection behind him. She had waited till everyone else had gone, and was standing close to him. Gareth, perhaps from an instinct to leave them in privacy, followed the other passengers out of the bus. Roger saw him walk off, across the square and towards his usual pub, without looking back.

Rhiannon came straight to the point. 'I'm sorry I didn't turn up last night.'

Roger stood up slowly and faced her. 'It doesn't matter.'

She gave a quick shrug. 'I didn't know what else to do,' she said. 'I thought it over, you see, after you asked me in the hotel. And I decided it was better if I didn't come.'

'Better for you or for me?'

'For both. I mean, there was nothing in it for you and I didn't want you to start building up.'

Roger opened his mouth, but shut it again. Why protest? He knew exactly what she meant, and her frankness was a virtue.

'It's horrible having to disappoint people,' she said. 'Try to understand.'

'Oh, I understand all right,' he said. 'The only thing that isn't quite clear to me is how you knew. I mean, I might have had no plans more ambitious than just taking you out for the evening.'

'But you did, didn't you?' she said softly.

'I did what?'

'Have plans more ambitious.'

'Not plans, Rhiannon,' he said. 'Just dreams.'

She nodded. 'That's why it's better. Nip them off before they grow into plans.'

She gave him a little smile, in which there seemed to be some genuine friendliness, and suddenly she had left the bus and gone into the darkness.

Roger thought of the shiny hired Ford canted over on its side, the wheel leaping down the hillside, the postmaster's bald head with its long fronds of plastered hair, and suddenly he began to laugh. He laughed until his midriff ached almost as much as it had done after Gareth had punched him, on that first evening. The thought made him laugh again and he realized that his fatigue, his nervous shock and his churned-up emotions were bringing him to the edge of hysteria. The thought abruptly stopped him laughing. Moving slowly and with dignity, holding himself very erect, he went down the steps of the bus and across to Mario's.

The next morning, Llancrwys woke to a downpour. The heavy drops seemed to be pouring through layer after layer of cloud, with the bottom layer resting on the dark slate roofs of the houses.

Roger did not mind this. He rather enjoyed wet days on the bus; it was wonderfully snug, with the lights switched on and everybody chattering and commiserating with each other on having to stand and wait in the rain. Bad weather seemed to make the bus even more of a haven, giving it back some of the magic it had had for him on that first soaking night of autumn. Humming, he washed, shaved, dressed, and ate. He had slept away his fatigue; after the unpleasant excitements of yesterday, he was looking forward to a day of blessed normality.

Gareth's garage was at the top of the village. Roger laboured up the slope, taking great breaths of mist. He was wearing his new cap. Deciding that this was not a climate in which one could go hatless, he had treated himself to a large tweed cap, carefully chosen as being not too similar to the cloth caps worn by the sheep-farmers (that would have been simple imitation) and not too sporting-gentry (that would have been affectation). He liked his new cap. He had admired it several times in the glass, in the privacy of Mrs Pylon Jones's holiday people's flat. But he had, through some lingering vestige of timidity, some faint sense that these people were always weighing and judging him, not yet plucked up the spirit to appear in it. Now, the rain, heavy enough to license any headgear, had blotted out all such hesitations. Roger could have walked up the street with a tablecloth wrapped round his head without fearing to seem eccentric.

The rain was drumming on the corrugated metal of Gareth's garage as Roger approached. Gareth had propped the doors open and was inside, already at the controls of the bus, persuading the engine to start. It was giving a series of loud, complaining coughs. Always, on beginning the day's work, it was like this; as bad-tempered as a camel. Roger waited outside, away from the fumes, while Gareth coaxed the engine into a steady drumming and backed the large yellow oblong slowly out into the downpour. Then he shut the garage doors and joined Gareth in the bus. Gareth nodded in greeting and eased the bus round in a series of back and forth half-circles till it was pointing the right way. Then they waited, with the engine running cheerfully now and the windscreen-wiper making a big fan-shaped clear patch on the windscreen. Usually the first few passengers, those whose houses were close to the garage, joined them here. But no one came. Roger took off his cap and mackintosh, shook them out, and put them over the back of a seat. Then he took down his leather bag from the parcels rack. That made him ready for work. But there was, at the moment, no work to do.

'Time to go down,' said Gareth. He put the bus into gear and they moved down to the cross-roads. This was their second picking-up point, and usually there were ten or a dozen people waiting. But today, the rain-swept roads were empty of standing figures. For an instant, Roger wondered whether he and Gareth had made a grotesque mistake and turned out on a Sunday. But no, it was Friday and everybody should be going down to Caerfenai to work. Was it a Bank Holiday or something?

He could not see Gareth's expression. The immovable bulk of the hunchback's torso was propped in its seat as usual, the shoulders of the leather jerkin stained with rain; those immense hands rested on the wheel with no impatience, no gesture. They moved on. The next stop was empty. At the next below that, an old woman got on.

'I missed the bus,' she explained to Roger, wetly holding out her fare.

'What d'you mean?' he asked, bending to make sure of hearing her correctly. 'This *is* the bus.'

'I missed the other one,' she said impatiently, as if he were tiresomely pretending not to know what was happening. 'The one they all got on. I was coming along the lane but I couldn't hurry. The doctor's told me not to hurry. I thought I was just in nice time.'

'You were in nice time,' said Roger. 'You got there just as we did.'

He wanted to go on questioning the old woman, whose few meagre coins made the only sound in the leather bag that felt shrunken and uneasy at his side. But Gareth had suddenly begun to drive faster. Down the mountain, hugging the centre of the twisting, rain-sluiced road, he began to throw the bus round the curves at what seemed an impossible speed. The old woman's face puckered in alarm; Roger was forced to sink into a seat and hold on tight.

'What's he doing?' she moaned across the aisle. 'We shall have an accident.'

'Never,' Roger called cheerfully. But he was not so sure. Wet stone walls swayed towards them; sheep, grazing on the roadside banks, leapt up and scurried away. He felt a sudden wave of nausea. He was not quite recovered yet, from the shock of losing that wheel. His body felt shrinking, tender; he was frightened of being hurt.

The road began to flatten out under them, and, mercifully, they were running through level fields, approaching the junction with the main road. Gareth raced the engine, changed down, and began to pump hard on the brake pedal. Up-down, up-down. He was staring intently ahead as if something had caught his attention. Roger craned to see. Through the curtain of rain he saw another bus ahead of them. It was only about a hundred yards in front, just leaving the T-junction as they approached it. It was a bus about the size of Gareth's, but painted a dark red, almost purple, the colour of liver on a butcher's slab.

Gareth slowed down, looked rapidly both ways, and swung the bus over the white line without stopping. He was chasing the liver-coloured bus, that was obvious. Accelerating fiercely, he closed up until the two buses were running in line-ahead formation. The driver in front showed no awareness of being chased. There were no more stops to make, as they were now on a route dominated by a frequent service of General buses, so they both drove steadily on and drummed into Caerfenai as if the liver-coloured bus were towing the yellow one.

They rolled into the square, turned, and stopped. Then, for the first time, Gareth's composure broke.

'The bloody sod,' he said. 'He's got my place.'

The liver-coloured bus had in fact drawn up neatly beside the statue of Sir Somebody, in the place reserved by custom for Gareth's bus. Roger shared Gareth's outrage at this. It seemed like a cool declaration that Gareth had not only been supplanted but had become a non-person.

'We'll see about that,' said Roger. He opened the door and stood aside for the old woman to get off. She did so, tremulously. 'The doctor told me not to hurry,' was her parting shot. She felt, evidently, that by driving at an unaccustomed speed Gareth had caused her to defy her doctor, with possibly fatal results.

Through the window Roger could see that the passengers had nearly all disembarked from the liver-coloured bus. He could also recognize them as the Llancrwys regulars. As he watched, Mr Cledwyn Jones hurried away across the square, buttoning his raincoat, and close behind him went Dilwyn, the

Rhiannon-watcher. Gareth was already out of his seat and plunging down the steps of the bus. Roger followed quickly.

The rain was lighter here, hardly more than a sea-mist. The liver-coloured bus stood in Gareth's place, the last few passengers getting out. It had no markings, nothing to identify its company or town of origin. But its destination plate carried the one word CAERPENAI, and prominently displayed in the front window was a cardboard notice with bright chalked letters: EMERGENCY SERVICE.

'Emer –' said Gareth, then stopped. Roger glanced at his face. It was composed of straight lines and dark holes.

One of the regulars, a fat jolly woman whose name Roger did not know beyond the inevitable fact that it was Jones, clambered off the bus and turned to Gareth in surprise.

'You here, Gareth?'

'Why shouldn't I be here?' said Gareth. His voice was a deep snarl.

'The man said – well, perhaps I didn't understand him right,' she said, embarrassed. 'He said it was an emergency service and that was why it was free.'

'Free?' Roger asked. His heart, he noticed, was beating very fast.

'Nothing to pay,' she explained. Then, flushing, she moved away rapidly. But her words had held them on the pavement for a few seconds, and that was long enough for the last passengers, a woman and two children, to come down the steps of the liver-coloured bus. The driver now leaned across and slammed the door shut.

'Just a minute, you!' Gareth shouted in a voice that echoed across the square. But the driver, ignoring him, moved the gear-lever and the empty bus started forward.

Gareth made a savage grab for the door-handle as it went by him, but the handle was recessed and the smoothly enamelled side of the bus was wet. His hand skidded impotently past the handle and the bus moved on, out of reach. As it went Roger looked up at the driver's face. It was pasty, with a short button-nose and expressionless dark eyes. It looked like the kind of face a child might make out of dough in its mother's kitchen, using currants for eyes and pressing the pale dough into shape with clumsy, earnest little fingers.

The bus was gone, the rain was beginning to fall more heavily, and they had only the old woman's fare to show for the run down. Near them, a big brown General bus coughed out a derisive cloud of oil-smoke and moved away, full of office-workers going to Bangor or Llandudno. Gareth said, 'Let's get a cup of tea.'

The car hire company had asked Roger if he could produce witnesses of the accident that had happened while he was driving their car. It was not a question of going into a court of law, since nobody was bringing a prosecution, but merely of satisfying the demands of the insurance company, who would probably wriggle out of paying if it could be proved that Roger had driven recklessly. It was unfortunate that no one had actually seen the occurrence; still, if the two women who were in the village shop would sign statements to the effect that they had seen the wheel smash into the door some sixty or seventy yards further down from where the car had come to rest, that would be satisfactory evidence that the wheel had flown off of its own accord. The fact that the wheel could be re-attached and the car driven back to the garage proved that the axle was not damaged, so the wheel must have come off through the slackness of the nuts that held it. This much was all they needed to put through a smooth deal with the insurance company. Roger supplied the names of the two witnesses. Mrs Arwel Jones and Mrs Iolo Jones, and the hire company undertook to write to them, enclosing a typewritten statement of what had happened, and requesting from each that if the account tallied with her memory of the incident, she would append her signature, in which case there would be no need for her to be troubled further.

A week or two went by. Each day was heavy with its own preoccupations, and for days on end Roger forgot completely, except in odd moments, about the wheel-throwing episode. The liver-coloured bus harried them continually. It was not present on every run, but they never knew when it would be there. It materialized out of nowhere, sometimes on the run up and sometimes on the run down, and ran ahead of them by two or three minutes, always with that prominently displayed board: EMERGENCY SERVICE. Sometimes it carried a conductor, a ferrety sharp-faced youth in a shiny peaked cap. At other times the dough-faced driver was alone. But fares were never charged. When the conductor travelled, he merely sat among the passengers and answered their questions. If they asked him who was responsible for operating the emergency service, he invariably replied, 'The transport board'. Sometimes people went further and asked him what transport board he meant, and then he would smile craftily under his peaked cap and say, 'The service you've got is being withdrawn, see? The transport board are just making sure the people aren't left with no bus to travel on. This is an emergency service.'

All this, Roger gathered from village conversation and the slightly shamefaced confessions of people who, though sympathetic to Gareth, travelled free on the Emergency Service when opportunity arose. Sometimes he would discuss the situation with Gareth, but always one-sidedly; Gareth stared savagely into the distance, like a starving hawk, and kept his counsel. And their takings drifted lower and lower, and the bills for fuel and spares had still to be paid.

Then, one day, Roger received a letter from the car hire company. Neither Mrs Arwel Jones nor Mrs Iolo Jones had replied to the request for a signature. They had simply left the letters unanswered. The car hire company requested Roger to call on the ladies and find out the reason for this. In view of his possible liability, they added threateningly, it was to be expected that he would do this at his very early convenience.

Roger called on both women that same day. He got Gareth to hold the bus for a moment, on the ten-thirty run up, while he knocked at Mrs Arwel Jones's door. Getting no answer, he ran along to Mrs Iolo Jones's house, while Gareth still held the bus with its engine quietly drumming. Mrs Iolo Jones had an electric bell as well as a knocker. He pushed the bell and knocked at the same time, to indicate that he was in a hurry. But no one answered. He tried again on the four o'clock up and the five o'clock down; no answer, both times, in either place. After that he gave up asking Gareth to stop the bus. Instead, he waited till they had taken the five-forty-five run up, then walked down the hill from Llancrwys to the village where the two ladies lived. Being free from about ten past six, when they arrived at the top, till seven, when they went down again, he usually went back to Mrs Pylon Jones's and got himself some kind of evening meal. But this time he gave his free hour to walking down to visit Mrs Arwel Jones and Mrs Iolo Jones. He had a copy of the typewritten statement in his pocket, and was hoping to collect both their signatures and have done with the matter. But once again, he was unlucky. At Mrs Arwel Jones's, he could hear what sounded like the noise of a large family, with the clattering of crockery and the noise of a television or radio. But no one came to the door for a long time, until finally a small boy with bright, baleful eyes opened it a few inches and said, 'There's no one at home.' Roger was about to ask what he could possibly mean by such a statement, when the boy abruptly shut the door again. Roger knocked again, but no one came. He wondered whether he would be within his legal rights to open the door and go in without further ceremony, demanding to see Mrs Arwel Jones. He tried the handle, tentatively. The door was locked. He hesitated. Perhaps the boy had meant that his parents were not yet home, and that only the children were in. He looked a shifty, dishonest, rather malicious boy. But perhaps this was the form of words he had been told to repeat if any neighbours, salesmen or welfare visitors should happen to call while his mother and father were out. It did not sound very likely, but Roger could not be entirely certain that it was not the case. Sighing, he decided to give it one more try at another time, and for the present to go to Mrs Iolo Jones. He went along the street to Mrs Iolo Jones's house, knocked, waited a few minutes, rang, then knocked and rang alternately until he was certain that whoever lived there was either out or determined not to come to the door. Then, hungry and tired, he walked back up the hill, in time to join the seven o'clock down with an empty stomach and a sense of frustration.

That evening, he felt too tired to chase the Jones ladies any further, but on the evening after that he decided on a bold course of action. Coming up on the ten o'clock run, he got off the bus at the village where the ladies lived. All the fares had been collected by that time anyway, and he put the leather bag on the floor beside Gareth and said, 'See you tomorrow.' Gareth nodded. Roger went down the steps and stood on the pavement watching the bus drive away through the darkness.

Then he went to Mrs Arwel Jones's house. Certainly there were enough people at home to answer the door. Light streamed from an upstairs window; the downstairs window was dark, but by the sound he could tell that people were watching television in there. He knocked on the door. There was a long pause, during which he had the distinct sensation of being watched. Then the door opened, this time by a plump, unkempt adolescent girl. Her face was dirty, but she had made a commendable effort to hide the dirt by plastering make-up over it.

'Our mam's gone to bed,' she said promptly, on meeting Roger's gaze.

'How did you know it was your mam I wanted to see?' he demanded.

She paused for a moment, one hand firmly gripping the door-handle, then repeated, 'Our mam's gone to bed,' and shut the door in his face.

Roger kept his temper. If for some reason the woman was determined not to let him in, she held all the cards. He would lie in wait for her, keeping his eyes open every time they passed through that village, and if necessary leaping off the bus to grab hold of her on the pavement. Meanwhile, there was Mrs Iolo Jones. He moved along the pavement. Yes, her window was lit up. Mrs Iolo Jones was the slimmer and less pale of the two women. She had seemed a slightly more intelligent person, and moreover appeared not to be carrying through life the handicap of a large and educationally sub-normal clutch of offspring. More hopefully, he knocked with polite moderation.

This time the door was opened at once, and Roger found himself confronting a little dried-up man in a dark suit, looking like a chapel deacon.

'What can I do for you?' this man said, or rather barked. His voice was high and resonant, his delivery abrupt.

'I wondered if I might speak to Mrs Iolo Jones for a moment,' said Roger. 'It concerns –'

'If you have business with my wife,' said the chapel deacon, 'it will be convenient if you discuss it with me.' He retreated a few steps and they faced one another in a small, brightly lit parlour with a coal fire burning fiercely in the grate.

'She witnessed an accident,' said Roger. 'I was driving –'

'Beg pardon. She did *not* witness it.'

'Well, strictly speaking I know she was in the shop, but you see, the wheel –'

'She did not witness any wheel,' said the chapel deacon. 'I have her authority for saying that she does not wish to make any statement.'

'Well, could I just speak to her a moment? You see, I'm –'

'There will be no necessity, I can assure you.'

'But when she was in the shop that morning, she told me –'

'When Mrs Jones was in the shop,' said the chapel deacon rather loudly and very distinctly, 'she was there without me. Since then, she has been able to discuss the incident with me. Her husband,' he added sternly.

'And you've told her she didn't see anything?'

'She prefers not to be brought into it,' said the chapel deacon. 'And now, if you'll excuse me, I have –'

'Now look here,' said Roger. His breathing had become short. 'I'm not asking your wife to do anything.'

'Very fortunately.'

'She was standing in the shop and a wheel came bouncing up and broke the door to pieces. No, don't interrupt me, please. The door was smashed. She can't help having seen it. She was standing within a few feet of the door when the – the impact happened. All I want her to do is to say so.'

'Impossible,' said Mr Iolo Jones.

'But why on earth is it impossible?'

Mr Iolo Jones turned his rather prominent brown eyes on Roger's. 'Some things are,' he said simply.

Roger was nonplussed. 'You mean –' he began, stopped, hunted for words, hunted for the thoughts he wanted to put into words, gave up and said, 'You mean she won't make a statement?'

'Yes, I mean that,' said Mr Iolo Jones.

'But this is . . . Why on earth? Has she been intimidated or something?' But even as he uttered the words, Roger felt their absurdity. 'Damn it, this isn't Chicago. There aren't gangsters about. The idea's ridiculous.'

'The idea is, as you say, ridiculous,' said Mr Iolo Jones. He pronounced it 're-dick-kiwless'. 'Now, if you'll excuse me.'

Roger went out of the parlour door and into the passage. Mr

Iolo Jones followed him a few paces behind. When they got to the street door, Roger opened it, but instead of going out he turned suddenly and confronted Mr Iolo Jones in the dimly-lit passage.

'What is it you're frightened of?' he asked abruptly.

'My wife –'

'Your wife nothing. When she was in the shop it hadn't occurred to her to be frightened of anything. It's you who've told her to keep her mouth shut, and it's you who're making damned sure I don't come face to face with her for fear of what she might let out. Well, why not be honest? Is there somebody trying to make my position impossible? And have they passed the word along that it won't be healthy to co-operate with me? Can that really be so? And what kind of ill-health would result from it? Violence? Surely not. In a country district, people remember faces. You can't cosh somebody and disappear down an alley, not up here. What is it then?'

'I have nothing,' said Mr Iolo Jones, 'to discuss with you.'

As he spoke he darted forward as quickly as a snake and gave Roger a sudden push with his little dried-up arms. Roger stumbled over the doorstep and at the same instant he heard the door slam behind him.

Without turning round, he set his face towards Llancrwys and began the long walk up the hill.

Sometimes, amid all this, Roger thought of Jenny. It gave him pain to remember her, and he avoided it as much as possible, but her presence in his life seemed inescapable. It was like sitting in an L-shaped room and knowing that she was there, in the part of the room that was hidden from him, sitting quietly and never moving to where he could see her. Very often, as he sat with Gareth in the bus, waiting in the square at Caerfenai till it was time to move off, he had the sudden very clear feeling that at any moment she would come walking across the square, with that matter-of-fact expression, perhaps wearing her glasses, and get on the bus. Of course this was pure fantasy, but he could not shake it off. One day, crossing the square, he thought he saw Jenny go into a shop down by the castle; he hurried after her, surprising himself by the speed and urgency of his movements, his legs seeming to move into rapid action of their own accord. But when he got to the shop and went in, he found that it was not Jenny he had seen, only a girl wearing a raincoat similar to the one he had seen Jenny wearing. Her face, as she responded in lethargic half-surprise to his staring at her from the shop doorway, was quite different. Roger's body felt heavy and inert as he walked away. The intensity of the sudden disappointment was a revelation to him. He needed Jenny, perhaps even loved her, certainly could have loved her if circumstances had allowed their two lives to be braided together. He had been trying to cheat his emotions by concentrating on Rhiannon, that masturbation-fantasy. But it was Jenny he needed.

For the whole day after that, her face was constantly in his mind's eye, the large dark eyes peering at him from under that thick rug of hair. Towards evening, he could stand it no longer. After coming down on the seven o'clock run, he told Gareth he would not be with him at ten o'clock. Gareth, with his usual determined incuriosity about Roger's personal affairs, merely nodded. Roger walked rapidly away. Drink, that was the answer; or, at any rate, the only answer left to him. If there had been a brothel in Caerfenai, he would have gone to it. But if such an amenity existed, it had escaped his attention. Alcohol, and plenty of it, was the only thing that remained. He would float Jenny's image away on a tide of fermented liquor.

Mario's was empty and dull. No one Roger knew was there, and Mario himself seemed to be in one of his sulky moods, answering only when spoken to and polishing the glasses bad-temperedly. Roger drank up quickly and moved to the next pub, and the next, and the next. It started to rain with quiet intensity, and he had only a thin coat. That ruled out pubs that took more than five minutes to walk to. He toured the places in the centre of the town, throwing down drink after drink without success. His legs became a trifle unsteady, but his mind remained sober and gloomy, and that gnawing feeling of deprivation remained. So did Jenny's image; it became, if anything, brighter and more three-dimensional. Oh, curse it. He must be in love with the girl. Nonsense, nonsense, that was all over years ago – being 'in love' belonged to adolescence, like chocolate creams and Chopin. It was worse than being in love: it was recognition of something genuine, something real and life-giving that might have been his, but wasn't. Oh, blast the girl and blast her smoothly contoured windbag of a husband whom she was too timid and hidebound to leave!

He came out of the last remaining pub, a sour little box of smoke, and stood in the rain. Where now? Home? Oh, God, no. He would commit suicide up there on the windy hillside, with nothing to look at but the non-furniture of his non-home, Mrs Pylon Jones's holiday people's flat. This was rock-bottom. He realized, for the first time, that it was possible for people to die of sheer unhappiness and discouragement.

Well, better to die of drink than that. There was one place left: the Palace Hotel. Roger fumbled in his pocket and took out the tame tie. Knotting it, he walked towards the hotel through the mocking rain. It was risky; he might meet Donald Fisher or some other poisonous centipede; even Twyford might be there, God forbid the thought. Well, perhaps that wouldn't be so bad. He could pick a fight with Twyford, do him grievous bodily harm, spend three months in prison; it would be an interesting experience. Better than this aching desert of non-life anyway.

Tottering slightly, he went up the steps of the Palace Hotel. Fortunately he had plenty of money on him; he had drawn out another wad of notes that day, leaving his bank account thinly-clad and shivering. Stumbling into the foyer, he looked over towards the desk. Rhiannon was not there. Her place was occupied by a much less attractive girl. That was one mercy. Another was that Donald Fisher was not in the Lounge Bar. Nor was Twyford, nor anyone he recognized. A few shadowy people sat in corners. There would be no need to talk – just drink, drink, drink, and if he got too blotto to go home he would just lurch over to the desk and ask the unattractive girl to book him into a room.

There should be a brothel in Caerfenai. It was absurd that such a simple and good idea had not occurred to the Town Council.

There seemed to be no waiter service, so Roger went over to the bar and got himself a double whisky. The barman's short jacket, the lighting, even the arrangement of bottles behind the bar, made him think of the first time he had met Jenny. She had stood over there, on that carpet, bravely and disconsolately drinking sherry and suffering her husband's toxic friends. The whole scene came back to him: Jenny's pale moody face, the confident gleam of Twyford's glasses, Donald Fisher ceaselessly ducking that sweaty dome of his in a gesture of mechanical deference. He heard the creamy, exploring voice of Bryant. God! What a crew!

As Roger, drink in hand, went over to a seat, four people entered the Lounge Bar and took up positions at a table not far from him. The soft armchair, and the drink he had already taken in, made him feel relaxed, and his attention wandered gently in the direction of these four people. There were three men and a woman. Two of the men were young and nondescript, and evidently disposed to defer to the third man, who was in his mid-forties. He was long and thin, and everything about him seemed to be long and thin, including his face, which was surmounted by a crest of curly brown hair so that he looked, when seen in full face, rather like a rooster; except that his nose was not beaky, merely downward-pointing and long. His eyes, set close together, were dark and watchful. What attracted Roger's half-attention, however, was not so much the man's appearance as his attitude towards the woman. She was obviously his wife; they had the look of people who are utterly accustomed to each other; but it was equally obvious that he was in love with her and thought himself lucky to have her. He settled her comfortably in the most draught-free position, took pains to find out exactly what she would like best to drink, and in general showed that he enjoyed looking after her. Not that she struck Roger as needing much looking after; a big, well-fleshed woman about the same age as her husband, handsome in a simple, euphoric way, with blonde hair that probably needed only a little chemical help to gleam brightly, as it did, under the electric light.

'You let Cedric run you home now, love,' the rooster-man was saying. 'You can watch the telly and make yourself a cup of something and I'll be along inside an hour.' His voice was light, but with the heavy North Wales consonants. 'Cedric'll have you home in five minutes.'

'It'll be a pleasure,' said this Cedric. He stood up and waited politely.

'I might as well,' she said, 'if you're sure you won't be long.'

'Not long at all,' her husband assured her.

The woman picked up her handbag and went out with Cedric. As she walked to the door, Roger watched her with the faint, baffling sense that he had seen her face before somewhere.

The other young man, after a few words from the long thin man, nodded his head vigorously, got up and took himself off. Left alone, the long thin man ordered another drink. Roger noticed that he did not go to the bar for this, but merely held up his finger to a waiter who had appeared from nowhere in the last few minutes. When Roger had first come into the Lounge Bar there had been no waiter on duty. Even now, the waiter did not seem to be very thoroughly on duty, since he ignored all Roger's attempts to call him or catch his eye, so that in the end Roger was forced to walk over to the bar and buy himself another drink. Apparently this hotel had waiter service for some guests and not others. Or did they simply despise him, Roger Furnivall? Knowing that he worked with Gareth, did they regard him as a social misfit who, even with the price of a drink in his pocket, had no right in the town's best hotel?

Irritated, the whisky in his stomach beginning to glow dull red, Roger glared like a bull at the rooster-man. How could this gangling bastard get V.I.P. treatment while he, a scholar and a gentleman, was a carpet for the staff to walk on? Standing apart from himself, watching his own reactions as he so often did in the early stages of drunkenness, Roger knew this mood to be coarse, obvious, unworthy of his ingrained subtlety, but something (the whisky? his sexual disappointment?) made him welcome and indulge the mood all the more because of its crude over-simplification. He stirred in his seat and clinked the ice in his glass; he felt an impulse to lean over to the long thin man and speak to him, ask him if he had any explanation of the fact that the waiter seemed to wait only on him.

The long thin man had not seemed to be watching Roger, but they were the only two customers in the bar, and without giving any sign of it he must have become aware of the mood of irritation building up in that quarter. Suddenly, now, he turned to look full into Roger's face across the ten feet or so of carpet that separated them, and spoke.

'It's a problem sometimes, isn't it?'

'A problem?' Roger was genuinely startled.

'Getting a bit of service,' said the long man. 'Nobody's running round for a bit of custom the way they used to be. All gone slack, it has.' He beckoned to the white-coated waiter. 'Gentleman here wants a bit of service, Phil.'

'I'm all right,' said Roger hastily. 'I've just got myself a drink.'

'Well, I'm just going to have another and I think we're on the same stuff,' said the long man. He nodded towards Roger's glass. 'That is whisky, isn't it? Thought so. You'll join me, won't you? Two doubles, Phil.'

Roger felt as if a lasso had been deftly thrown to encircle his legs just above the ankle. He did not want to join this stranger in talk. Yet, once again, it was his own fault. He had allowed his attention to be caught by the small, uninteresting mystery of the man's authority with the waiter and his own complete lack of the same.

'Thanks,' he said resignedly.

The long man uncoiled himself from his seat and moved over to Roger's table. 'Pardon my intruding, isn't it? The place gets very dismal out of season. The visitors have gone and the locals just sit in front of the television. No life at all.' He dropped his eyes for a moment, then suddenly raised them to Roger's. 'Not much in it for a man like you.'

Roger opened his mouth to speak, but at that moment the waiter arrived back with the two double whiskies.

'Chalk it up, Phil,' said the long man.

'Yes, sir,' said the waiter.

'And get yourself and Siân one.'

'We're on duty, sir.'

'Well, chalk it up and have it when you're not on duty.'

'Yes, thank you, sir.'

Phil went away and they were left with the two glasses and the tray.

'Water or soda?' the long man asked.

'Neither, thanks.'

They were silent again. When Roger's drink was mixed he took a sip of it and said, 'You say there's nothing much here for a man like me.'

'That's how it looks to me,' said the long man.

'And what kind of man am I?'

'You know that best,' the long man smiled.

All at once Roger knew who he was talking to.

Foolishly enough, the first thing that flashed into his mind was to wonder whether or not to drink the glass of whisky he held in his hand. To put it down untasted, then stand up and with a chill nod take his departure – wouldn't that convey, better than words, that he meant to go on fighting on Gareth's side? That he refused to be compromised or scared?

No, he quickly decided, it wouldn't. The whole situation seemed to have taken a shape that forbade any such simple, unhand-me-sir gestures.

Instead he said, flatly. 'There's a lot in it for me. I find life in these parts quite interesting.'

The long man looked at him again with that quick, flickering glance that went straight to the eyes and away again. 'How's the Welsh coming along?' he asked.

'O, gweddol.'

There was a short silence in which Roger could hear himself breathing.

Then Dic Sharp drank from his glass, set it down carefully and said, 'All the same.'

'All the same, what?'

'You're doing it the hard way, like.'

'I find it quite an easy way. At least,' Roger added levelly, 'it would be, if we were left alone.'

'Look,' said Dic Sharp. He leaned suddenly towards Roger. 'You could learn Welsh without any of this – trouble and bother. If it's a job in the district you want, a job for three months, six months, I could find you one. Much more interesting work and better pay.'

'That's what you tell them all, isn't it?' (Inwardly Roger said, *So he doesn't know I work for Gareth for nothing. That's interesting.*)

'Yes, I tell them all that,' said Dic Sharp easily. 'And they all listen.'

'Perhaps they all have, up to now. But now you've struck one who isn't going to listen.'

'But *why*?' Dic Sharp demanded. His eyes, as he flicked them on to Roger's and back again, showed a sudden flash of intensity. 'What's the point of it? Tell me that.'

Roger leaned back, and took a long swallow of whisky before answering. 'I'm not up here for long. Not much of my life is invested in this, I'll admit it straight away.'

'So you're just amusing yourself. Just killing time. And messing things up for them that have to live here.'

'You interrupted me. That isn't what I was going to say. My attitude's just the opposite. Even if this is only an interlude in my life, I want to do something useful with it, besides just picking up a bit of Welsh for my own ends.'

Dic Sharp was watching him carefully. 'Well, there's plenty of useful work a man like you could do up here. An educated man. But why Gareth Jones?'

'Why not? It's keeping something alive.'

'If you'll excuse me saying so,' said Dic Sharp, 'we'd get on a lot better up here without people like you coming in and interfering.'

'You sound like an Alabama policeman,' said Roger, throwing punches now.

'I don't know what you mean by that and I don't care. You come in here and start talking about keeping things alive. You don't slow down long enough to see that the trouble with North Wales is that too many things are kept alive when they're dead on their feet.'

'Like what?' Roger snapped.

'Small farms. Small businesses. Small ideas. A bloody fool like that Eyetie, Mario, with his plastic bombs.'

'Has Mario got plastic bombs?'

'He will have soon, if he isn't stopped, man. That mad look in his eye gets worse every time you see him. One of these days he's going to put a plastic bomb into a suitcase and blow half somebody's face off.'

'I hadn't expected to find you so articulate,' said Roger, moving in to fight at close quarters.

'Why should you expect to find me one thing more than another?'

'I don't know. Call it intellectual arrogance, if you like. I thought you were just a crooked local business man in a hurry to get his hands on any money that was going about, and ready to use what means came to hand. The sort of backstairs small crook who employs even smaller crooks to loosen the wheel-nuts on people's cars. What I didn't expect was that you'd have theories.'

'I understand,' said Dic Sharp. 'I'm born and bred here and know every corner of it, but I haven't got the brains or the book-learning to have reasons for what I do. You come in and take one look and straight away you can explain everything. Even me.'

'Hold on, hold on,' said Roger. He was beginning to get interested. 'It may be that I'm making an unjustified claim to understanding. But you're making an unjustified claim to power, and that's worse.'

'What power am I claiming? Just up-to-date ideas and being a good business man, that's all.'

'Don't be hypocritical. Up to now we've been honest with each other, let's keep it like that. You know perfectly well you're claiming power. You're the little Caesar around here, and everyone has to give way. If that hired car had somer-saulted going down the mountain and I'd been killed, you wouldn't have lost ten minutes' sleep.'

'You keep talking about cars,' said Dic Sharp, drinking.

'Oh, come off it. You were behind it and you were behind the paint-throwing. And all for the same reason. You don't be-lieve Gareth Jones has a right to live.'

'No,' said Dic Sharp. He settled his shoulders against the back of his chair. 'I don't believe he has.'

'Well, I do. It's as simple as that.'

'Oh, no, it isn't, my friend. There are laws.'

Roger laughed shortly. 'I never expected to hear you speak of laws.'

'Careful, that's libel.'

'Be your age.'

They glared at one another, openly hostile at last.

'When I say there are laws,' said Dic Sharp, his crest of brown curls nodding like a rooster's comb, 'I mean real laws, not the kind that get on the statute-book.'

'Don't tell me. Economic laws, the only kind that people like you ever –'

'Have you ever seen a hedgehog,' Dic Sharp asked, 'that's got in the way of a car?'

'Oh, I know that's the kind of argument that you're bound to trump up. You think it justifies your –'

'The hedgehog,' Dic Sharp ploughed on, his voice cutting through Roger's protests, 'broke a law when he got in front of the car. Not the sort of law you recognize, but the sort I recognize. He curled up, didn't he, when he saw the car coming? If the car'd been a horse, the hoofs would have kicked him clear. But it wasn't a horse. Cars had been invented, isn't it?'

'All right, don't bother to spell it out. You're the car and Gareth's the hedgehog, and he ought to wake up to the fact that you've been invented.'

'Well, let's put it his way. He doesn't have to wake up to it. But nothing can stop him getting hurt if he doesn't.'

'Yes,' said Roger. 'And that lets you out, doesn't it? You can break Gareth or any other small operator, you can use any ruthless method you like, up to and including violence, and there's nothing to blame yourself for because it isn't you that's doing it, it's Laws.'

'I ought to get pretty nettled at some of the things you're saying, mister. But somehow it doesn't touch me. If you understood more of what you're talking about, you might move in close and get me on the raw. But it doesn't connect. One thing I know, you've never been in business.'

'Oh, that explains everything, doesn't it?'

'Not everything. But most things. You call me a crook, a thug. That's how you think of me. Well, I'll tell you what I really am. I'm a man who's gone into business from very simple beginnings. No capital. I started as an ordinary workman. Then I broke away on my own and did a job here and a job there and got a few chaps to work for me. Do you know what it means to go into business without capital? It's like trying to run a zoo without cages. Nothing'll stand still, nothing'll wait. You have to have the money for everything in a hurry, isn't it? You're in competition with chaps whose fathers did well, yes and their grandfathers too, and they've got stocks and bonds and money in the bank and they can bide their time. You can't. You fill one hole by digging another and then you have to fill the second hole quick, else you'll fall into it. I make money fast. I have to. They think I'm rich, the people round here, the ones I grew up with. Well, I'm not. I could go smash tomorrow. I make plenty of money but it all goes out again. I push it out as soon as it comes in. Because I've got to keep expanding. Now take this business with the buses. I spent money I couldn't afford on buying those operators out. They got a fair price. One or two of them were a bit slow in deciding to sell, so I helped them along a bit. If I'd had capital, I could have afforded to be a gentleman and use gentle methods. But I hadn't. The money was eating its head off and I needed it. So I got them all in the bag. All except Gareth Jones. My old schoolfellow. Listen, we used to take sandwiches to school at Llancrwys because it was too far to go back up the mountain to eat and they didn't do school dinners then. I used to give him some of my sandwiches everyday because his own were always so poor.'

'And you think he ought to give you his bus for a packet of sandwiches?'

'You know damn well what I think. There's no reason for Gareth Jones to have any grudge against me.'

'No reason at all, eh? You're just trying to take his livelihood away.'

'Oh, I'm not just trying, Englishman,' said Dic Sharp tolerantly. 'I'm *doing* it. I need that money in three months from today and I'm prepared to spend a little extra money to make sure it comes in within that time.'

'By fair means or foul.'

'There aren't any fair means,' said Dic Sharp. 'It isn't fair when a car runs over a hedgehog.'

He looked at Roger with an expression of kindly interest, as if waiting to hear how this thought struck him. But Roger was looking over his shoulder at a person who was approaching them. This was the fair-haired young man he had seen badgering Rhiannon at the reception desk. As the youth walked towards them with that peculiar lunging movement of the shoulders, Roger saw that he was the much-indulged son of Dic Sharp and his stately blonde wife. Obviously the pup got his fair hair from his mother, his aggressiveness from his father, and his selfish demanding attitude from years of cosseting by both parents.

Ignoring Roger entirely, he now straddled carelessly before his father and asked, 'Ready for off, Dad?'

'Just about,' said Dic Sharp, pushing back his chair and rising.

'The man just rang up,' said Sharp *fils*.

'He did, eh? Everything all right?'

'Spot-on.'

The two of them moved away. Roger looked at their backs with hate. At moments, during their exchange, he had been almost ready to like Dic Sharp, or at least to understand his point of view and make some allowances while still opposing him. But seeing him with his horrible son put a stop to all that. The effect of Dic Sharp, and all the men of his generation who were similarly minded, would be first to make the world into a chromium-plated desert, and then hand over that desert to their unspeakable offspring. What Dic Sharp was after, basically, was a world in which youths like his son need never go to the trouble of joining the human race.

Roger got up and went to the hotel entrance. Outside, the rain was swishing gently down. It was getting late. The evening was over. Should he get a taxi up to Llancrwys?

No. He would walk. His bones needed fatigue, or that long watchful rooster's face would come between him and his sleep tonight. And he needed plenty of rest. Things were not going to get any easier.

The walk was long, and by the time he reached the steepest part of the climb, just before entering Llancrwys, Roger felt that he had earned his night's sleep. Neither Dic Sharp nor Jenny, however much their images haunted his bedside, would have the power to keep him from diving into unconsciousness. The night was cold and blustery, but at least the rain had stopped. His decision to walk the four miles home had been a wise one, laying to rest all his anxieties. Laying to rest. What was that in the distance? His anxieties. Why were those lights shining? His anxieties ... Laying to rest ... What was afoot, what new threat, what disturbance of the repose he so desperately needed?

Mrs Pylon Jones's house was blazing with light as if for a wild party. Every window streamed with yellow. Roger covered the last fifty yards, steep as they were, at something like a run. The brown front door was shut, and he knew that the green side door would be shut too, but he knew also that this must be just to keep the cold air out. The house was awake, alarmed, waiting for him.

Then, as he drew near, he saw it. A huge star-shaped hole in the front window of Mrs Pylon Jones's holiday people's flat. In his front window.

Roger walked up to the green side door, opened it, and went in. The light was on in the passage as well as in every room in his flat. And he had company. Mrs Pylon Jones was standing in the middle of his sitting-room, nervously twisting her hands together and looking at the smashed pane and away again. Beside her stood her neighbour, Mr Cledwyn Jones. Mr Jones's quiff stood up accusingly and his bespectacled eyes, fixed on Roger's, showed all the relish of an upright citizen called in to redress a crying wrong and determined to extract every drop of enjoyment from it.

'So you're back at last,' he said.

Roger had been about to address the pair of them in Welsh, but it was evident that Mr Cledwyn Jones thought English the more suitable language for cold hostility.

'I fetched Mr Cledwyn Jones when they did it,' said Mrs Pylon Jones. 'I was so frightened. I couldn't stay here by myself. Gave me a shock, it did. A shock.' She seemed to be trying to shed a few convincing tears from eyes that remained obstinately dry. But there was no mistaking her distress.

'When they did what?' Roger asked. 'Can't we all sit down?' he added.

'Did what?' said Mr Cledwyn Jones with measured scorn. 'Why, did *that* –' he gestured convulsively towards the smashed pane – 'some of your fine friends. While you were out enjoying yourself.'

Roger sat down wearily. 'Look, don't let's start on *that* note,' he begged. 'Somebody broke the window, but not one of my fine friends. It happened when I was out, but not enjoying myself. You needn't work so hard to push the blame on to me.'

'You'll have to go, Mr Furnivall,' put in Mrs Pylon Jones quickly. She had stationed herself slightly to the rear of the dumpy figure of Mr Cledwyn Jones, so as to look at Roger as if round a tree-trunk. 'I should have asked you to go when they threw that paint. I ought to have known, then, what I was in for.'

'Well, spell it out. What were you in for?'

'Your fine friends,' said Mr Cledwyn Jones, unwilling to give up the phrase, 'have paid us another visit tonight.'

'What you mean is,' said Roger, 'some lout's broken a window and you suspect it's somebody who doesn't like me.' Oh, if only he could go to bed. If only he were not so tired: tired by Rhiannon's refusal, tired by Dic Sharp's menacing presence, tired of these mountains, tired of Welsh, tired of effort.

'The vandals,' said Mr Cledwyn Jones, giving the word a splendid fullness of pronunciation, 'the vann dalls who have taken to infesting this village, may not be friends of yours. But they are, if I may so put it, friends of yours in a deeper sense.'

'No, sir, you may not so put it.'

'They are here because you are here. They commit these –' again he gestured largely – 'outrages, because of some feud they have with you. Nobody in living memory has witnessed such scenes in Llancrwys.'

'You'll have to go tomorrow,' chirped Mrs Pylon Jones, peering round him.

'Oh, don't be silly,' Roger snapped. 'How can I go tomorrow? I shan't have time to look for another place and clear my stuff out until the week-end at least.'

'That's fair,' said Mr Cledwyn Jones magisterially, turning to Mrs Pylon Jones and nodding so that his quiff trembled in a stately manner.

'Well, Sunday, then,' said Mrs Pylon Jones, twisting her hands very quickly. 'I can't keep him a day after Sunday. I'm too nervous. It's the shock, isn't it, the shock.'

'We gave a statement to the policeman,' said Mr Cledwyn Jones. 'He wants a statement from you too. He hasn't long gone. He left word to call in at the Police Station in Caerfenai tomorrow morning and no later.'

'With pleasure. Not that I can tell him anything.'

'You're sure of that?' said Mr Cledwyn Jones, shooting at Roger a look full of deep watchfulness.

'Of course. How should I know what hooligan might take it into his head to –'

'This was the instrument used,' said Mr Cledwyn Jones suddenly. He brought his hand out from behind his back and held up a billiard ball.

'Well, what about it? What's so special about a billiard ball? Has it got somebody's name and national insurance number engraved on it?'

'It came through this window less than an hour ago,' said Mr Cledwyn Jones.

'Well, don't keeping holding it under my nose,' said Roger. 'It makes you look silly. You look as if you ought to have a balloon coming out of your mouth with the words *Perhaps this will refresh your memory* written on it.'

'There's no call to be insulting.'

'Doesn't it occur to you that you're insulting me?'

'Well, no, it doesn't,' said Mrs Pylon Jones. 'Nobody asked you to come here.'

'But ...' Roger was speechless for a moment. 'Do I have to wait to be asked? Isn't North Wales full of people who come here from outside?'

'It's out of season,' said Mrs Pylon Jones quickly and soothingly. She seemed to be trying to de-fuse the situation by giving a logical and non-offensive reason why Roger ought not to have come to Llancrwys.

'If you go,' said Mr Cledwyn Jones, 'these outbreaks of vandalism will stop and we shall be able to go back to our normal life.'

Roger opened his mouth to ask him what kind of normal life Gareth Jones would be able to go back to, if his last bit of moral and physical support were scared away. But, looking at the two of them standing there with their closed, accusing faces, he said nothing. Why waste his breath? As far as Mrs Pylon Jones was concerned, she wanted to see the back of him and that was that. Mr Cledwyn Jones, for his part, would regard the persecution of Gareth by Dic Sharp as a very minor matter, and certainly nothing that concerned a busy, intruding *Saeson*, Saxon, Englishman, clumsy fool.

Seeing the matter, suddenly, as they must see it, Roger decided to carry it off with what dignity and good humour he could muster.

'Mrs Jones,' he said, 'I'm more than sorry that my presence in your house should have caused you this disturbance. I'll take myself off at the first possible moment. It's now Thursday night – shall we say that I'll vacate the flat on Sunday?'

She nodded, birdlike, her swollen claws clasped.

'I've already paid the rent until then. And of course I'll pay for the replacement of that pane. And,' Roger turned to Mr Cledwyn Jones with a courtly smile, 'I'm sorry, Mr Jones, that you should have been fetched out late at night, and I hope at least that you'll keep the billiard ball for your trouble.'

It was a small, petty, unworthy triumph, but a triumph. He saw them out of the green door and went straight to bed. Let Dic Sharp's mobsters come back again, let them break every window in the damned place, as long as they let him sleep, sleep, sleep.

Sunday came. Roger, as he ate his breakfast, half expected Mrs Pylon Jones to come shrilling in and demand his immediate decampment, but she chose instead to stay in her own part of the house and send waves of silence at him through the curtained door. Wordlessly defying her, he sat in front of the electric fire for an hour or so, but the intensity of her wish to be rid of him was such that he felt almost physically lifted to his feet, in the end, and carried towards the door. Buttoning his mackintosh, he went out, with no aim in view, simply to be away from the waves.

Outside, the world was bathed in white mist. It lay in long ridges in the lee of the walls, formed a still pool in every hollow, and on the bare slopes it swirled slowly as the sheep walked about. It made the air damp and cold. Roger felt exposed, helpless.

He walked towards the crossroads at the centre of the village. Nearby stood the high naked shape of the chapel, its edges softened by the pale mist. There was no one about. In another half-hour or so, the meagre congregation would converge on the chapel, stand outside for a few minutes gossiping and shivering, and then go in to keep their date with their notion of the force that had shaped them from the clay. For once, Roger was tempted to join them: just to be with people, to participate in something that would lift him and them, for a time, above their jagged litter of personal concerns. Then he thought of how they would stare at him over their hymn-books. And, after all, he had no right, at this late stage, to claim so boldly to be one of them. The minister ran a small car and was never on the bus.

Roger walked past the chapel without slowing down. Then he saw Rhiannon coming towards him through the mist. She was wearing her green suède coat. Where could she be going?

He stopped, watching her come towards him. She saw him and kept unconcernedly coming on. As she drew nearer he saw that she had a soft woollen scarf, of a warm flame-colour, round her neck. Her cheeks were freshened by the cool air. All at once he realized that she was, after all, a country girl.

'Where are you going?' he asked her.

'Nowhere. My father wanted me to go to chapel with him. I said I had a headache and wanted to take a walk and I'd meet him there at service time.'

'And will you?'

'I don't suppose so,' she said indifferently.

Someone, perhaps the verger or warden or something, opened a door at the side of the chapel, studied them for a moment, then closed the door quietly.

'And you?' she asked. 'I should have thought you'd lie in on a Sunday morning, after taking that early bus down every-day.'

'I'm being thrown out of my digs,' he said tonelessly.

'What? Out of Mrs Pylon Jones's?'

'Yes.' He told her about the billiard-ball episode. As he spoke, they found themselves walking together down the road. It was not planned, it was entirely without volition, but they were walking along together. It was too cold to stand still – that was it, yes, it was only that.

Rhiannon's lovely eyes opened wide as Roger rounded off his story. 'What d'you think's behind it?'

He shrugged. 'Someone wants me out.'

'Is it Dic Sharp?'

The question came out so naturally, so simply. Yet he could

not match this naturalness, could not stop himself from shooting her a hooded glance. 'You've heard that, too?'

'Everyone's heard it,' she said carelessly.

He envied her detachment. It must come from a real sense of not being involved. She really did have one foot in the larger world outside, if only through the rascally businessmen with whom she jetted off to Majorca. A whore. Was it true? He would never know. She would tell him nothing, and what right had he to know?

'What will you do now?' she was asking.

'I haven't any idea. Nobody in Llancrwys will take me in. If they did, they'd only get the same harassment – perhaps worse. And I'd be out again. It's better not to wish it on them.'

They had reached the point where a small road, no more than a lane between high banks, came snaking down the mountainside and joined the road they were walking on. Rhiannon turned into it and began to climb.

'Where are we going?'

'I want to show you something,' she said. Her face was solemn, as if with suppressed excitement or sudden resolve.

Show me, Rhiannon. You are so beautiful, so gentle in your perfect confidence: your triumph within your own world is so complete. I will accept anything, question nothing, if it comes from you.

They climbed until the road turned, levelled out, and began to lead away round the shoulder of the mountain. There was a last short terrace of houses, looking blank and square through the mist, and then the village died out into scattered cottages. Where was she taking him? For a walk across the lonely mountain? Ah, Rhiannon. To be alone with you in some cup of luminous mist. Naked on the soaking heather.

The road clung like a worm to the steepening slope. It edged cautiously round to the point where the ground fell away and they could look out over a valley full of small, gnarled oak trees. The trees were almost bare, but some branches were still clothed in brown leaves. From among the brown-and-grey tangle, huge outcroppings of rock reared themselves up, here and there, above tree level. The mist lay softly over all. The beauty of the scene made Roger want to cry out: but the quiet mystery of it silenced him. This was a place of the druids.

He had still no idea why Rhiannon had brought him here, but now he noticed that she had halted and was looking at him expectantly. He saw nothing that called for a response from him, except the magic of the valley at their feet, and she had surely not brought him to look at that. Beside them was a small deserted chapel he had noticed before on his lonely walks. It was surrounded by a brick wall with iron railings and a wrought-iron gate. The wall, railings and gate were in quite good condition; on the chapel itself, he had never bestowed a second glance.

'Well?' he said.

For answer, she clicked up the latch of the wrought-iron gate. He followed her up two steps and into the tiny yard that served no purpose except to indicate that the chapel was a sacred building and ought not to rise straight out of the bare earth. It had flag-stones, badly cracked but firmly set. Rhiannon was walking purposefully ahead of him, round to the back of the building. He let her go ahead while he paused and looked in through the cob-webbed window. Inside was one large, bare space where benches and pulpit had been, and, at the end, a door that presumably led into some cramped vestry. But the worship-area had been cleared, refurbished, domesticated. A large double divan was pushed up against the wall; the pot-bellied iron stove with a long pipe may have been there in the days when the chapel was a chapel, but it had more the air of Montmartre; canvases were stacked against the far wall, furthest from the reach of damp.

'A studio, by God!' he muttered in mounting excitement.

Rhiannon came back round the corner of the building, shaking her head. 'I can't find it.'

'What?'

'The key. I thought they might have left it somewhere.'

'Who might?'

'The people, silly.' She was raising herself on tiptoe to look in through the window. 'Not much point if we can't get in.'

He loved the 'we'. 'But whose is it? What are those paintings?'

'The Fräulein's.' Rhiannon laughed shortly. 'She's in Morocco now.'

He waited, then said, 'Is that all you're going to tell me?'

'For the time being, yes.' She was being deliberately annoying. 'If we can't get in, there's no point in going into it anyway.'

'Get in?' Roger demanded. 'Is that the only problem?'

'That's the first problem.'

Resolution welled up inside Roger's chest like rage. He walked quickly round the building, to see if there was a glass door at the back. No: the back door was of solid timber. It would have to be one of the main windows. He went round to the side that was not seen from the road, and pulled himself up on to the windowledge. This one would do. Its upper section opened widely enough for a slim man to squeeze his body through: he could see the catch that fastened it, separated from him by a simple leaded pane. Quickly, grimly eager to act before he had time to think of reasons for not acting, he jumped down, searched for a suitable stone, found one, clambered on to the window-ledge again.

Two or three supplementary blows with the sharp end of the stone, and the pane was a clean empty space into which he dived his arm. The fastening came undone, the window swung outwards. He heard Rhiannon's footsteps coming round the end of the building, and urgently, not wishing her to see him in an undignified struggle with his legs waving in the air, he crammed his head and shoulders through the open space, kicked wildly two or three times, and fell forward with his hands on the inner sill of the window and his knees resting painfully on the metal frame. A second's pause to steady himself, another wriggle, and he was down on the boards of the floor among the dust and broken glass. Quickly, he stood up, knocked his hands together – no cuts, no serious bruises even – and then he was striding confidently towards the main door of the chapel. It opened easily: a modern Yale lock, he noticed, had been fixed and evidently kept lubricated. Then he was poking his head out into the crisp mist, calling softly, 'Rhiannon! Walk into my parlour.'

She came back round the end of the building. 'That was quick work. I was hoping to see you squirm in.'

'I did it quickly so you wouldn't see me. At my age one must keep some dignity.'

As he spoke, he stood back to let her in. She came past, her suède coat brushing carelessly against his arm, and on the word 'dignity' flashing him a quick look, mocking but comradely.

'Well,' he said, following her until they stood together in the middle of the bare floor, 'this is a surprise.'

'Didn't you know this place was here?'

'I'd seen it from the outside. Just another empty chapel. I'd no idea it was fitted up like this. Who's Fräulein? Has she got a name?'

'It was empty for years,' said Rhiannon. She seemed lost in her own thoughts, peering about the bare rectangle of the room as if it were a haunted grove. 'They used it for a chapel until – oh, about the time I was born.'

Nineteen forty-eight or thereabouts, Roger mentally supplied.

'Then the old chap who was most keen on keeping it going, I think it was his father who had started it, he died. The others – there were just half a dozen of them – decided to close the place up and go to the chapel in the village. They locked it up and for years it just stood here. The boys broke the windows and some slates came off the roof, but it's all quite sound. I used to play round it with Dilwyn. Sometimes he'd say, Let's go in. But I wouldn't. I was frightened of breaking into a chapel. Thought the Lord would strike me dead or something.' Again she gave that short, dismissing laugh. 'Then Mr Robertson started to come up here with the Fräulein.'

Roger knew better than to interrupt.

'At first they used to come to the hotel. She'd been the *au pair* in his family, and he'd taken up with her. He had a lot of money. He owned ships. The Blue Streak line, or something – some fancy name. His offices were in Liverpool. Anyway, this girl, her name was Inge. She had Mr Robertson and his cheque-book just where she wanted them. She must have stopped being the *au pair* by that time, but she was on the scene all right. She didn't like Liverpool and he wouldn't set her up in London because it was too far away. Wanted to keep an eye on her, I suppose. So she used to make him bring her up here for weekends a lot. And sometimes when he went back to Liverpool on the Monday, she'd stay at Caerfenai or somewhere near. Used to wander about with an easel, painting. Said she was an artist and she knew how to look at mountains. I shouldn't have thought it was so difficult. In the end he had a brainwave. Bought her this place and did it up as her studio. The only thing was, she wouldn't spend the winter up here. Nor in Liverpool. The last I heard, she'd fixed it that she spent the winters in Morocco. He has an office there too.'

Roger pictured Inge. He saw lank blonde hair and a self-willed, rather thin mouth. Mr Robertson would be bald and cigar-smoking. He moved over to the wall and turned some of the canvases round to the light. They were abstracts: meagre, bright, two-dimensional.

'She didn't paint the mountains, then.'

'No, she just looked at them.'

Roger turned the pictures back to the wall. 'Well, it's lucky for me that she conned this place out of Mr Robertson. But tell me, does he ever send anybody up to inspect it?'

'The key's at the Post Office. But they never come up.'

Roger bent down and opened the door of the stove. There were some clinkers in it, and the pan was full of ashes. Fräulein Inge had not bothered to clear it out after the last day's heating. 'It seems to work all right.'

'It ought to,' said Rhiannon. 'Fräulein didn't like things that didn't work.'

Roger glimpsed a history behind this remark, but it was one he would never know, and he felt no inclination to pry into it. Let Mr Robertson and Inge enjoy the sun of Morocco and meanwhile let him find a haven in their empty-chapel love-nest full of *ersatz* abstracts. Rhiannon had led him here, she was his good angel.

'What d'you think would happen if I moved in?'

She shrugged. 'What could happen?'

'Well ... technically I'd be committing a crime. And there are people about who'd find it very convenient if I were taken off to prison or something.'

'You mean Dic Sharp,' she said. 'Well, he'd have to get in touch with Mr Robertson. It'd be no good trying to get Fräulein back from Morocco in the middle of winter. She wouldn't come. And Mr Robertson wouldn't take it very well if anyone started poking into his business. The place is probably in his name, but that doesn't mean he wants everybody to know about it. He's got a wife and family, he wants to be careful.'

There speaks the hotel receptionist, Roger thought. Nothing is hidden from those eyes. SO YOUNG AND SO UNTENDER.

He moved across to the vestry door, opened it and peered in. The vestry had been fitted out as a tiny kitchen, with a sink, cupboards and a neat, four-ring cooker.

'Good God! I'm dreaming.'

'They got the electricity connected up again,' said Rhiannon behind him. 'It'll be turned off at the main switch. But I expect you can find it soon enough.'

Possessed by a sudden manic energy, Roger burrowed like a terrier, opening the cupboard under the sink, dropping on hands and knees to explore the shadowy corners. In a moment he had found what he was after: two neat fuse-boxes and a main switch. A single downward click, and the dials began to move round with the inevitability of fate. That settled it. They were criminals.

He turned to Rhiannon. 'You realize what we're doing? We're accomplices in a crime. Already I've smashed a window, and now we're occupying someone else's premises and stealing electric current.'

She looked at him placidly but without expression: stone-walling. Had he gone too far? His intention had been, of course, simply to involve her, to draw her more deeply into the situation for whatever the results might be worth to him. And her untroubled but watchful young face told him that she understood exactly.

'You need somewhere to go,' she said calmly, 'and it's not your fault you've got to leave Mrs Pylon Jones's. If those people, whoever they are, are going to see to it that no land-lady will have you, you'll have to be somewhere on your own.'

'Thank you for justifying it so logically. Now all I have to do is move out here and wait for them to come out one dark night and cut my throat. Nobody'd hear my screams down in the village.'

She shook her head. 'They won't do that. Harassing land-ladies is as far as they'd go. Dic Sharp, if it is him that's behind it, can find young mischief-makers who'll break windows and throw paint, but it's another thing to risk going to prison for twenty years.'

'That's comforting.'

They walked back into the main room. A three-bulb electric light burned in the ceiling. Evidently Fräulein Inge had left it switched on at the wall when she turned the main switch off in the kitchen. As Roger stood in the doorway, his eyes took in the room properly for the first time. It was large, for a domestic dwelling-room, but tiny for a religious meeting-place. The result was that the two atmospheres blended. At the height of its life as a chapel, it must have conveyed a hint of the domestic. Even when some beetle-browed preacher mounted the pulpit – that pulpit which had now been taken down, and, no doubt, chopped up for firewood, but which presumably had been situated at the end furthest from the door, just beside where he was standing now – even then, the pulpit must have dominated the room hardly any more than the patriarchal armchair in some roomy farmhouse. Most of the quarrymen and their families must have crowded in to the big chapel in the village: lost in reverie, Roger saw their dark Sunday clothes, mutton-chop whiskers, sober-faced bonneted women, and heard the thunder of their hymns rolling over the mountainside as far as the Sabbath-silent quarry: but up here, a few families had met together, the same people week after week for a lifetime. It must have seemed to them like a sacred annexe, a prayerful extension of their own homes. And why did they hive off in this way? Just the difficulty of getting down to the village in bad weather? He doubted it. For a few upland farmers, perhaps. But surely there was some fiercer reason, some spurt of that white-hot flame of Protestant certainty that linked these people with Huss and Wycliffe. They must have built this place, raised it painfully from the bare rock and thin soil, in order to *worship God in their own way*: that proud, stubborn European demand that had sent men to burn at the stake or drown in the dark Atlantic.

And here he was, the modern inheritor of European culture, standing beside a dark-eyed, soft-voiced girl of these mountains, a girl only one generation removed from the very people who had reared these walls with their calloused hands. And her motive in bringing him to the chapel had been simply random kindness, because he had nowhere to hide himself from the weather; and his motive for getting to know her in the first place was because he wanted to strip off her clothes and savage her like an animal. To this we have come. The great book of European history closes with a snap. He and Rhiannon, so different in so many ways, were alike in this: they were barbarians, staring round them at walls whose purpose they could not imagine.

Then he grinned at his own pomposity. Tell that to the eighteenth century, when Rhiannon would have been got with child by the first hard-riding squire who had met her on a lonely road. Victorian religious fanaticism had been no more than a local movement of the graph. If he and Rhiannon had been Ancient Britons, wandering these very slopes in skins and woad, he would have had exactly the same designs on her and she would have understood his motives just as well.

And yet, something remained: it was a chapel that had been part of the home-life of its members, and now that it had passed into the possession of those who could not even imagine the supernatural – for Roger knew well enough that Fräulein Inge and Mr Robertson would have only such thoughts of God as an animal might have – it had become a dwelling-space into whose walls many thousands of prayers had soaked. Its rafters, which now looked down on the childish art-play of Fräulein Inge, had once looked down on rows of bowed heads or resounded to fervent calls for repentance. And something remained: but what?

'I'll leave you, then.' Rhiannon's voice jolted Roger back to the present moment and his own assortment of dire needs. Suddenly, he knew that he could not bear loneliness: not now, not till he had had just a little more contact with a fellow human being, a little more time to prepare himself. This place would be unimaginably lonely, perched on its craggy slope with only the whispering druid-wood far below.

'Oh, please don't go,' he blurted out. 'I mean – it's terribly helpful and kind of you to show me this place, and I think it's the answer to my problems, given that all I need is a fairly short-term answer – but it'll all be spoilt if you just walk out now. I mean, well . . .'

'What do you mean?'

'Well, nothing, except that . . . I need someone to be around, someone to talk to and discuss things. God, I shan't make any demands on you – I'm a long way past that.' He was entirely

187

sincere. 'If I'm going to settle here, get the place warmed and dried out and dusted and get myself a meal, it's got to be today. I shan't have any time tomorrow or any day during the week. And the fact is, I'm too discouraged and tired out and, oh, I don't know, shaken up by all these things that have happened, to be able to face it on my own. If you aren't here to talk to. I'll just lie down and give up.'

It was a frank appeal to her pity. He felt better after making it. Now the last disguise had been thrown aside: he no longer pretended to dignity or self-sufficiency, he was a vagabond who existed on charity.

'I've got to go to chapel,' she said.

'You know you don't have to. You can always say your headache didn't go away and you walked on the mountain instead.'

'They'll expect me home at one. Mother's cooking a big dinner.'

'That's hours yet.'

Rhiannon thrust her hands deep into the pockets of her elegant coat, hunched her shoulders, abruptly turned to look straight into Roger's face, and she was laughing.

'You win. I'll help you to settle in. That'll be my good turn for the day.'

'Your serious crime for the day, you mean.'

'Oh, that doesn't frighten me. If we're arrested I'll just tell them you invited me here and I took it for granted you'd rented the place. And I'll expect you to back me up.'

'I'll do that,' he said. A rush of pure gratitude swept him on to add, 'I'll back you in anything you do. You're the best friend I've got.'

Once assured of her company, Roger felt all his energies liberated. He worked quietly and furiously. The stove needed to be cleared out. Was there a dustbin? Yes, and marvellous discovery – a fuel bunker with some anthracite left in it: enough for two or three days' continuous burning in the small stove. He could find no newspaper or sticks to start a fire, but he had that kind of thing at Mrs Pylon Jones's. It was time, he announced, to get over there and pull out.

'How will you manage?' Rhiannon asked. She was idly looking through Fräulein Inge's paintings, putting each one back after a brief glance and a short, incredulous exclamation.

'I'll just have to carry everything in my two hands,' he said. 'It'll take half-a-dozen journeys in all, but I shan't need to bring it all over today. At least half the stuff I can just pack up and leave till I'm going past in the week. All I need now is the bit of food I've got in for the week-end. And some warm clothes. And my washing and shaving stuff.' He ticked off the items on his fingers. 'And a hot-water bottle to air some of these very damp blankets – only I haven't got one.'

'I'll bring one this afternoon – I shall have to go home to eat.'

'Good,' he said, feeling secure and sustained in her benevolence. 'Shoes. A book to read tonight. Milk, if the man's left any. That's about it. I'll get over now. Will you wait here?'

'I might as well,' she said. 'I could do a bit of dusting.'

Dusting? Rhiannon? What was coming to the surface in her?

Without pausing to quiz her, Roger walked briskly out, closing the big door behind him. Outside, the weather had changed. The mist had cleared, except for a few streaks here and there and a cool lake of transparent haze in the valley beneath him. The sun was shining from a sky that was rapidly becoming clearer and bluer. One of those freak days of incredible perfection. Was this the turning-point of his life? Homeless, harried from human society, camping in a deserted chapel, breaking the law, was he about to enter on blessedness, peace, unbroken good fortune, a happiness never before dreamt of? He walked quickly along the lane towards Llancrwys. At one point he halted and looked for a long moment towards the mountains as they stretched away inland. Snow lay here, but only on the peaks. Shining white above, dimmer green and brown below, they gave an unearthly impression of weightlessness: bright masses of rock and snow floating in the washed air, an emblem of heaven.

The meagre drawl of a tiny petrol engine assailed Roger's sharpened hearing. He looked up at the slope above him. Yes, it was Dilwyn. His thin, eager face was turned to the sky, the whiskered radio-box in his hand, and above him his toy, his joy, his expensive obsessional love-object, his Rhiannon-substitute, his one-in-seventy-five scale model Piper Comanche, climbed the lovely noon in tight, clawing circles.

Roger felt pleased. He liked the solemn, creative madness of

Dilwyn. The aeroplane, busy and purposeful against a background of utter calm, seemed to him deliciously absurd. He waved cheerfully. Dilwyn showed no sign of having seen him. Was he squinting upwards at his droning charge, oblivious of everything beside? Or – the thought suddenly struck home – was there hostility, a blank rejection, behind the non-greeting? Did Dilwyn know that Rhiannon was with Roger? That she was waiting for Roger in that same chapel which he, Dilwyn, had never persuaded her, in those round-faced childish days, to enter?

Well, there was nothing he could do about it. A girl like Rhiannon must affect the lives of many men in a few short years, before her beauty faded. It was each for himself. Roger walked on, through the crisp sunlight, towards Mrs Pylon Jones's. As he did so, the thin scratching note of the engine ceased, and, glancing round, he saw the bijou contrivance begin to slant downwards towards the little magic box that brought his toy back to him in a series of long swoops.

Back at Mrs Pylon Jones's, Roger packed his bags in a silence that seemed as thick as porridge. Had Mrs Pylon Jones gone out for the day, in order to avoid seeing him? Or was she lying in bed with her hat and coat on? In any case, their relationship was as much beyond repair as the broken pane which now let in the bracing air. That reminded him: he must take some newspaper to stuff the similarly broken pane in the chapel. Or perhaps old rags would be better. A duster. Spying one beneath the sink, he carefully packed it. Even more carefully, he packed an almost full bottle of gin, securing it against breakage between two shirts.

At last he was ready: immediate requirements in a case he could carry, plus a duffle bag over one shoulder. The rest neatly packed in a larger suitcase, which he could pick up some time when the bus went past the door. It was over. Mrs Pylon Jones could wait in peace for next summer's holidaymakers.

Quietly closing the green front door (but keeping the key, for the moment, safely in his pocket), Roger went round to the brown front door and knocked. There was no answer, and he knocked again, waited a moment, and was picking up his suitcase to go away when he heard mouse-like footsteps scurrying towards the door on the other side.

So she had been in, after all : listening through the wall to his preparations for leaving. How glad she must be!

She opened the door a few inches. Already, in her fantasies, Roger himself had become an assassin.

'Well, Mrs Jones, I'm off. You won't be disturbed any more.'

'I hope not,' she said, but her eyes seemed to be looking on all sides at once. It suddenly occurred to Roger that she was like some French farmer's wife in 1942, who had allowed a crashed R.A.F. pilot to sleep in the barn and was anxious for him to clear out before somebody went and fetched the Gestapo.

'It's not as bad as that, surely?' he could not help saying.

'The window'll be ten shillings,' she said. 'You could leave it now.'

Roger was about to hand over the sum when he remembered his other suitcase. He must keep some sort of foot in the door. Otherwise, she was in a mood to bar and bolt the place against him like a fortress.

'I've got to move my stuff by hand,' he said, 'and I can't carry it all on this journey. So if you'll allow me, I'll leave one case behind and pick it up early next week. I could give you the ten shillings then.'

'It would be convenient,' said Mrs Pylon Jones, 'to have it now and settled with.'

'Perhaps,' said Roger stonily. 'But it happens to be Sunday and the banks are closed. What bit of cash I have on me, I shall be needing. After all, it's not my fault that I'm being turned out on to the mountainside on a Sunday morning.'

He picked up his case and turned his back on her. 'On Monday,' he flung over his shoulder, 'I'll come for the case. Before midday. I hope that's not too long to let it stay there.'

For answer, he heard the sound of the brown door being closed: without haste, and certainly without a bang, but with complete finality.

Walking back, Roger puzzled over the question of why Mrs Pylon Jones should so entirely reject him. Guilt by association? He remembered the accusation in Mr Cledwyn Jones's voice: *your fine friends.* Yes, that must be it. In their eyes, he was sullying the village. The day the gangs came to Llancrwys. It never happened until the Englishman took a room. He brought big-city ways. And what about that woman with the bright blue Mini and the black hair, the one he cooked a meal for and wanted to take to bed, right next door to where a decent woman was sleeping? Lucky for her she said no, the brazen hussy. He could hear the tongues deliciously wagging.

Thinking these thoughts, he was walking past the chapel: not his own chapel, commandeered love-nest of Mr Robertson and the Fräulein, but the big, central, still-in-business chapel. The trickle of worshippers was arriving; the usual blend of the very young (coerced into attendance by the old) and the old (coerced into attendance by the wingbeat of the angel of death). Yet their worship, he knew, would be genuine enough. They eyed him aslant as he walked past with his luggage, and he half expected to be questioned, especially as many of the faces he saw were familiar to him from his bus journeys. But no one addressed him. On weekdays, in the bus, they spoke readily, even volubly, to him; but today, they were a tightly knotted group, going about the business of Sunday, and he was a passer-by, a foreigner with a suitcase, a visitor out of the season of visitors.

Well, here was the chapel: his new, bizarre sheltering-place. The sun glistened on the old paintwork and bounced off the smooth slates of the roof with an effect of Mediterranean heat. Nothing in life was predictable any more: he had finally broken out of the cocoon of dailiness. Letting himself into the chapel, he found it dust-free but deserted: Rhiannon had written on a sheet torn from a diary and left prominently in view: SHALL COME BACK THIS AFT., MUST EAT AT HOME. Good luck to her! He would have the place in a fit state to welcome her. Dumping his belongings in a corner, he set to work in a cold frenzy. Operation one, to get the stove going. He had brought firelighters, and some small pieces of coal in a newspaper. When they had fairly caught, he added anthracite from the bunker outside. In a miraculously short time, the stove glowed with heat, and so did its long black pipe. Warmth! Life! Roger felt he had earned a drink; there was plenty of gin but nothing to put in it; never mind, he had sugar among the meagre stock of provisions he had brought over from his cupboard at Mrs Pylon Jones's. a couple of spoonfuls of sugar, a dash of cold water, top up with gin – it was possible to get it down, and alcohol was all he needed now.

Alcohol, and Rhiannon. He had barely finished setting out his belongings – provisions in the cupboard, cups and tea-pot beside the sink, kettle on the electric cooker, clothes hanging behind the vestry door – when there was a knock and she reappeared.

'Welcome back. You didn't take long over lunch.'

'I've been away an hour.' Then she looked round with an expression of approval. 'You've got the place comfortable already.'

'It's the stove. Thank goodness it works efficiently.'

'Yes. By the way,' she took a key out of her bag and handed it to him. 'I found this, hanging on a nail inside the cupboard.'

'What is it? A spare key?'

'Must be. It fits the front door, anyway.'

'How thoughtful of the Fräulein : this, and fuel too. And her paintings to look at, always supposing we want to.'

Rhiannon sat down, still taking stock of him and his situation. 'I've brought a hot-water bottle. You can air these blankets in time to sleep in them. But you've got no sheets.'

He was touched. The hot-water bottle seemed to him an immense symbol of goodwill. 'Oh, I can get a pair of nylon ones tomorrow. It won't hurt me to do without tonight.'

'Now,' she said, 'I'm a meal ahead of you.'

'But several drinks behind,' he said, showing the gin-bottle.

'You oughtn't to have too much of that without eating. You'll get drunk and I can't be alone in a deserted building with a drunken man.'

He hacked off a thick slice of brown bread, buttered it, balanced three great strips of cheese across it, and wolfed the combination before her eyes.

'That's better,' she smiled.

'Now,' he said. 'I'm entitled to another drink.'

He sloshed gin into the glass, water, sugar. 'Will you join me?'

She giggled softly. 'Gin after lunch.'

'It's a lot better than nothing to drink at all. And I bet you had a teetotal lunch.'

'Wrong, smartie,' she said. 'There was a glass of elderberry wine all round. In honour of Sunday.'

'Well,' he said, handing her a glass of gin-and-sugar, 'this is in honour of Sunday afternoon. Cheers.'

'Cheers,' she said idly and sipped without protest at the horrible mixture. She was sitting on the end of Fräulein's studio couch, warming one hand at the open door of the stove. Comfort! Who would have believed it? He sank down beside her.

'Rhiannon,' he said. His voice sounded different to him: dark with emotion. 'I want to understand you.'

'Why?'

'Not *for* anything. Just because I do.' He ran his fingers wildly through his hair. 'It's so long since I understood anybody. And since I came up here, I haven't met anyone I can even begin to understand. The only person who's troubled to offer an explanation of his motives was Dic Sharp. And that was only a very superficial one, to justify himself for behaving wickedly.'

'So you'd like to understand *me*, just to make a start somewhere?'

'Not for that. Because you're you. I shall never forget you, even if I never set eyes on you after today. I shall think about you for all the rest of my life. Don't you think I want to understand what I'm thinking about?'

'Sometimes it's better not to.'

'But not with you. There must be something –' he gestured helplessly. He felt drunk: the bread and cheese had not entirely done its work. Or was it the presence of this untamed beauty? 'I can't talk,' he said. 'I want to listen. Tell me about your life. How you look at things. What kind of stuff happens to you. It can't all be in that snug little long house on the mountainside, with Mum and Dad and the dog under the telly aerial.'

'Oh, heavens, no,' she said indifferently. 'Not much of it at all is there.'

'Well, where's the rest? What fills your life? What do you think about? Tell me, Rhiannon. I've no claim on you, no right to ask anything of you, but talk to me.'

'I'll have another gin,' she said unexpectedly. He had not even noticed that she was drinking the one she had.

He mixed her a good one. 'Now talk. It's warm and snug in here, the stove's going well, you have a sympathetic audience of one: doesn't that give you the urge to talk about your life?'

'I don't follow my urges,' she said. 'I'd be in enough trouble if I did.'

What had come over the girl? Roger had never expected her to admit to an inner conflict of any kind.

There were no comfortable chairs. They would have to be on Fräulein's couch. But it was tiring to sit there without any support for one's back. Impulsively, Roger swung his feet up and stretched out. There was plenty of room beside him. 'Come here,' he said.

'No, thanks.'

'Look, everyone who talks about themselves always lies down. A psychoanalyst –'

'Don't give me that. You're not a –'

'No, I'm not, but you'll never enjoy a good unwind unless you rest your spine. Honestly. The spine's the key to everything.'

'In that case I'd better keep mine straight.'

'Straight, yes,' said Roger soothingly, 'but horizontal.' Before he had time to wonder at his own effrontery, he put his arm round her shoulders and gently pulled her down beside him. For an instant her body stiffened in protest: then, as the springs of the couch received it, relaxed. Acquiescent, she lay beside Roger. Her bones were as delicate as a cat's: his pulses roared.

'This doesn't commit me to anything,' she murmured.

'Of course not. Only to talking.'

'Not even that,' she demurred, 'if I don't feel like it.'

They lay still for a moment. Roger's arm was lightly, unselfconsciously across Rhiannon's midriff. The windows of the chapel were steamed up and the stove glowed with a wonderful cherry-coloured heat. Outside, the mountains waited for news of the universe.

Gently, she lay beside him. It was as if she had decided to trust him, to breathe as freely in his presence as she did in solitude. And all this without for a moment doubting that his designs on her were carnal, rooted in the need to touch and cling and bite and dig. She had accepted him; not as a lover on whom she would have made reciprocal demands; simply as another human being before whom there was no need to wear a mask. Knowing this, he kept himself still and silent, listening as she began to talk in a soft, half-whispered voice that barely broke the silence of the tranquil room.

'My mother's always talking to me about getting married.

She thinks life begins then, for a woman, and not before. A lot of girls I know think the same. They think the part of your life before you get married just isn't real: it's only marking time. My mother's glad I've got this hotel job because she thinks it'll bring me into contact with successful men who can offer me a secure home. She ought to hear some of the things they offer me.'

'You don't tell her, then?'

'I couldn't. She doesn't understand and nothing would make her. She lives in a different world. As for my father –' her shoulder twitched slightly in the semblance of a shrug. 'I can't talk to either of them about anything that matters. My mother can tell me how to make an apple pie, so I just let her go on about that kind of stuff. But anything else, I'm on my own.'

'It must be lonely.'

'I've learnt to trust myself. I work things out and decide what to do. But they're always at you, the men, trying to persuade you to play their game.'

Roger was silent. He wanted to know if any of them got what they wanted, but knew better than to question her. Let it come out of its own accord.

'Sometimes I wonder if my mother's right, and real life'll start when I have a home to run and a husband to look after. And kids. I can't imagine that yet. Other times it seems to me just the opposite – that the real bit of my life is now. It depends who I marry. As I am now, I've got something the men want, and what they want they'll pay for. The money I've seen spent – it shocked me at first. But I got used to it quickly.'

She seemed inclined to fall silent, so Roger prompted gently: 'Have you always had your present job?'

'I worked in the bank, at first. I was trained for bank work – went on a course after I left school. But that only lasted a few months. The hotel job came up and it seemed much more fun.'

She was silent again, so he asked, 'And is it?'

'Fun, yes,' she said. He could not see her face, but he imagined her mouth making a wry shape. 'It's fun. I'll say one thing – compared with the bank, it's certainly where the action is. We get all the business men. Young and old. I don't know which are the worst, but one thing I do know, none of them leave you alone.'

'Is that what you want – to be left alone?'

'No, not that either. And I don't even mind that they're all out for the one thing. Why shouldn't they be? They're built that way. But it gets wearing. None of them'll take No for an answer. In the end you decide to pick one and let him call the tune, just to keep the others off.'

Outside, the light had moved round. It was now slanting in from the west. An evening was coming in that was unlike any evening in the history of the world. Roger lay still, listening to Rhiannon's voice, feeling her delicate hip-bone pressing lightly against his groin.

'That was why I took up with Mr Fielding. I don't mean I just picked him out of a hat. I liked him. His approach wasn't crude and he had a very nice side to him. He could be very nice, I mean, really. He told me honestly, he appreciated the happiness I brought into his life and he liked to show his appreciation. And because money was what he had most of, he liked to spend money on me, show it that way. He was nice to me, and as time went on he got so he hated to think of losing me. In the end he reached the point where he offered to divorce his wife and marry me. I said no. We argued about it all one week-end.'

'Wouldn't you have been happy with him?'

'I might have been. But to get married would have made it real. As things were, it wasn't real – it was just a kind of game. Marriage would have altered that. I'd have been Mrs Fielding and he'd have been running off with another hotel receptionist. Or perhaps he wouldn't – that's not the point really.'

'What is the point, then?'

'Well . . . that I'd have had to take him into the centre of my life if he'd been my husband. Build my world round him, my real world that I lived in. And I just couldn't see it.'

'But it was all right,' said Roger carefully, 'as long as you were just . . . going about together.'

'Yes. It wasn't all that important. He didn't have my virginity or anything. That had happened before – while I was still at the bank.'

In the vaults one slack afternoon, Roger thought to himself. *Or after hours, on a pile of credit slips.*

'Mr Fielding told me frankly he put two thousand a year on

one side for himself. Just for pleasure, for good times. He'd worked hard, he said, for thirty years, he'd got a grown-up family, and now he had enough money to meet everybody's needs including his own. And he said he didn't know how long his health would last. He had stomach ulcers – couldn't eat anything much. He used to look very puffy sometimes: I don't think his heart was very strong. I used to worry about what would happen if he died while he was in bed with me.'

'No doubt that's the way he'd choose to die.'

'I dare say, but what about me?'

'There's no law against your sleeping with him. Nobody would actually *do* anything.'

'Tell that to my father. He's a deacon. He had me to chapel twice every Sunday and Sunday school in the afternoon as well, when I was a kid.'

'Does he still matter to you?'

'It lasts,' she said. Her eyes wandered about the ceiling above her, as if seeking to trace a pattern. 'You don't get away from it that easily.'

Yet here she is lying in a chapel, he said to himself. *Full of gin and with a man's arm across her belly*. Then the thought came to him: *Perhaps that's why*.

'Mr Fielding took me everywhere,' she went on. Her voice was slow, almost hypnotized. 'He was always going to New York and Chicago. I'd fly with him on the jet, and be with him all the time he was seeing his business contacts. He used to introduce me as his secretary, and once or twice I did help him a bit, keeping his notes straight. Usually we'd catch a day or so in Florida before we had to come back. I'd be sun-bathing in February, in a bikini! And my parents would think I was with a girl-friend in Liverpool.'

Suddenly, agony tore into Roger's fibres like shrapnel. He had a quick, blood-misted vision of Rhiannon and Mr Fielding basking on a beach and then going back to their suite at the hotel, sun-warmed and with nothing in their minds but pleasure. He rolled over on to his back and covered his face with his hands.

'What's the matter?' she asked.

'I can't bear to think about it,' he said.

'Don't feel like that,' she said softly. And then, to his amazement, she leaned over, took his hands away from his eyes, and kissed him on the mouth.

For one wild moment the earth seemed to be tilting over, the laws of gravity suspended, probability banished to another solar system. Without volition, Roger's hands moved down Rhiannon's body to her hips. She was lying full on top of him, and her warmth came to him through their clothes.

'Why am I doing this?' she murmured, kissing him again.

Speechless, he made no answer.

She smiled down at him and said. 'This still doesn't commit me to anything.'

No. But this place used to be a chapel and that's the only thing you still haven't done, isn't it, to get back at your father? Open your legs in the very place where they used to have the prayer-meetings?

His grip on her hip-bones became more purposeful. Here goes to burn out the memory of Mr Fielding and of all the Mr Fieldings past, present and to come. It wasn't Miami, but it had a dimension Miami would never have. He would give it to her right where the harmonium had stood. In the shadow of the pulpit.

An angry, scratching drone suddenly drew itself across the still afternoon. It approached the chapel, wavered, flattened out, circled, surrounded them. Was some immense, surreal insect, the Kafka-dream of an oversized hornet, buzzing ferociously to attack them? Or was it part of Roger's delirium? Was he awake? Had he died?

The thin, ratcheting buzz came in at one window, then the other, then the other again. Whatever it was, the thing was circling just above the roof. Then, suddenly, Rhiannon was laughing. Great spasms of laughter shook her, so that her slender midriff vibrated between Roger's hands. The next instant, she had rolled on to one side, away from him.

'It's Dilwyn,' she gasped, beginning to laugh again. 'Dilwyn's aeroplane.'

And so it was. Roger, recalled to quotidian reality, knew that he was in Llancrwys, that it was Sunday afternoon, that he had to go down with the eight-fifteen tomorrow morning, that the broken pane had still not been stopped up, that the stove needed refuelling, that his colossal erection was fading to rag-limpness, and that girls like Rhiannon were not for him but for the Mr Fieldings of this world.

And perhaps, the aeroplane engine hinted, for the Dilwyns. The childhood sweetheart, after all, was the one who really held the cards.

Lying on his back, listening to the dry rasping as it spiralled round and round above him, Roger decided that it was the most prosaic sound in the world. To the eye, Dilwyn's aeroplane was lyrical, with its gull-swooping, its climbing and levelling; to the ear, it was an affirmation of the utterly mundane. And that, no doubt, was precisely what Dilwyn intended it to be. He had been watching and waiting; he knew Rhiannon was in there with Roger; he judged that they had been left alone long enough, and that it was time for an interruption. The idea of sending his toy to break their spell – it was brilliant, Roger had to admit. He had under-rated Dilwyn.

Rhiannon was sitting up, fiddling with her hair. He would never get her back now. The chance was irretrievably lost.

'Would you like a cup of tea?' he said. I've got all the materials for making one.'

'That would be nice,' she replied, suddenly as deaconly as her father.

Outside, Dilwyn's aeroplane scrawled a derisive line of sound across the mother-of-pearl sky, and flew back to its master.

A little later, Rhiannon left the chapel.

Part Three

The next day, as if to drive home to Roger the nature of the world he really inhabited, the liver-coloured bus harried them all day, carry its 'EMERGENCY SERVICE' placard insolently ahead of them on every run both up and down. The ferret-conductor was with the pastry-driver on every trip; perhaps this was the beginning of a more ruthlessly mounted offensive.

'If I could get my hands on 'em – just once,' Gareth breathed with fierce longing. It was the only remark he made all day that acknowledged the existence of the spoilers. Roger did not know whether to hope that Gareth would be granted his wish or to hope more fervently that he would not. In any case, there seemed to be no chance of it. The pair were exceedingly cunning. The liver-coloured bus never drew up beside the yellow one, either in the square at Caerfenai or at the top of Llancrwys village. It lurked at unpredictable points along the route, emerging from side streets a minute or two before Gareth's bus was due, and scooping up the waiting passengers. That Monday, the only people Gareth and Roger carried were those who assembled at the terminal points ahead of time; anyone who joined the run at any point *en route* was gathered up by the liver-coloured pirate and travelled for nothing. This fact began, as the day wore on, to strike guilt into Roger's soul. It cost a shilling to ride from Caerfenai to Llancrwys, if one went all the way, and it troubled Roger to take the shilling from the gnarled hand of some old pensioner who might easily, by walking a few hundred yards and starting out a few minutes earlier, have saved the desperately-needed coin for some small comfort.

On the other hand, his common sense told him, if Gareth went under and the route came under some soulless monopoly, nobody would ride for as little as a shilling again. By making a fight for it, they were doing the only thing that could protect the interests of these eternal victims, the old and the poor.

By the time they came to make the seven o'clock run down, Gareth's face was an immovable block of granite and Roger was buzzing like a hornet. They did not, this time, see the liver-coloured bus, but from the fact that they went down with only three passengers it was safe to deduce that it was there in the darkness ahead of them, sliding like a shark up to stop after stop and luring the innocently opportunistic fools into that horrible livid maw.

Gareth brought the bus to rest beside Sir Somebody's statue, switched off the engine and sat with his arms resting on the wheel. Something about the slump of his shoulders told Roger that hope had begun to desert him, seeping away from his mind like air from a tyre with a minute puncture.

'Well, what's the answer, Gareth?' he said quietly, standing just behind the driving-seat and watching Gareth's face reflected in the windscreen.

'I know where Dic Sharp lives,' said Gareth in a harsh, effortful voice. 'I could go round there now, ring the bell, and when he came to the door I could get him by the throat and –' he kneaded his titanic fingers convulsively in the air – 'watch his face turn black.'

To break the tension, Roger forced a laugh, and brought his hand down on Gareth's shoulder. 'Go and have a drink instead. We'll find some other way.'

With no further words – for how could either speak without revealing the despair that was in his mind? – they switched off the lights and left the bus standing in the square. Gareth went to his usual carbolic-smelling pub, but Roger made no move to accompany him; if they sat together from now till ten o'clock, they would only depress one another. It was better to seek neutral company. He went on to Mario's.

The bar was only just beginning to fill up. It was bright and cheerful, with good lighting and rows of variegated bottles. Mario's Continental soul declared itself in this at least: he was incapable of opening a place that purported to offer solace and refreshment and then making it nothing more than a morose little box of smoke. He had no Nonconformist background. Roger did not much care for Mario, but he liked Mario's pub, and for the moment he was glad enough to see Mario himself.

The landlord's hair seemed to have become even thicker and

more vehemently massed all over his skull, as if preparing at last to invade the rest of his body and turn him into a Yeti. He gave Roger a genial scowl.

'What is your wish?' he asked.

'My wish,' said Roger, 'is that men everywhere should be free, equal and benevolent.'

Mario's smile flashed. He drew a foaming pint of beer and pushed it across to Roger. 'Is on the house.'

'Thank you, but why'?

Mario shrugged delightedly. 'Already we make a *nazional-isto* out of you. You are living here only three months and already you are seeing the point about home rule.'

'I said nothing about home rule,' Roger said irritably. He looked down at his hands; they were trembling slightly. A whole day's anger had frayed his nerves. 'Home rule is an artificial problem. I speak of real problems – cruelty, greed, tyranny, the power of the rich to drive the poor to the wall.' He spoke loudly, not caring who heard him. 'Money can buy too much in this town, as in every other town. You won't alter that by being ruled from Cardiff.'

'Alter it, yes,' said Mario calmly. 'Every problem is more easy to manage when we have it on the human scale. Now, look at yourself. I don't know what has making you so angry –'

'I think you do,' Roger interrupted in the same carelessly resonant tones. 'If you don't, you must be the last one here to be in on the gossip. I can't believe you don't know what I'm angry about.'

'Something with the buses, no?' Mario conceded.

'Not just something. Everything. You must know that Gareth Jones, with whom I work, is having the economic life crushed out of him by someone who wants to expand at his expense. I won't say whom, because that's something else you know already.'

'So right,' said Mario. His face slumped into tragedy, then rebounded into bright, smiling confidence. 'Is all going to disappear. All those monopoly problems. Is resulting from *accentromento*.'

'Don't be silly. Dic Sharp –'

'Right, you name names,' cried Mario. 'I tell you, exact. Why is – our friend – wanting to take over Gareth's bus? Because he is in a hurry to sell. To General. And where is General central organization? In Caerfenai? No.' He shook his head till it seemed he would injure his neck muscles. 'In Cardiff like you say is no good? No.' Again the spasm of head-shaking. 'Is in England.'

Roger finished the beer and handed his glass back. 'Now you have a drink with me. I'm still not interested in nationalism and home rule, but you *have* got a point. Dic Sharp –' he took good care that the whole room could hear the name – 'wouldn't be resorting to gangster methods to get hold of Gareth's harmless little one-man bus company if it weren't that a big company like General has a built-in urge to expand, to take over more and more territory and mop up all the individual operators. They've got a line of talk that justifies it, full of pious economic platitudes about streamlining and efficiency, and some of that talk comes out of Dic Sharp's mouth if you put a coin in the right slot and press the knob. But they're all fools. General are fools on a large scale, and Dic Sharp's a fool on a smaller scale, with a dash of the crook thrown in, which they can afford not to know about. But fools is what they both are. Because the day is just about over when transport could be run for private profit anyway. Big Brother's standing behind them ready to gulp them down. And he'll gulp General as easily as General will gulp Dic Sharp or Dic Sharp'll gulp Gareth.'

Two men came over to the bar to be served with fresh pints of beer, and Mario gave his attention to them while Roger drew breath after this long speech. The pint-buying men, he noticed, were careful to ignore him. They created the same wall of silence round him that people create round a drunk who suddenly begins bawling patriotic songs in a train.

Perhaps that was what they thought he was: some poor devil with a grievance, who had had too much beer in an effort to give himself some backbone and now aired his loud complaints in the bar. Or was it caution? Had that rooster, that long thin puppet who doted on his wife and son, really the power to frighten people?

Mario was back again, leaning his powerful forearms on the counter while he enunciated carefully in his operatic English. Roger felt he ought to talk Welsh to Mario, but at the moment he felt too angry, too unsteady. He would hit all the thin patches in his vocabulary just when he wanted to talk quickly, power-fully, dismissively. No, no, they must meet him on his own ground, he had given way long enough.

'I am thinking like you,' said Mario. 'Transport is too big now. It can't be for private rich men any more. Any more than for private poor men. In five years, ten years, is all Government. But –' he slapped the bar and struck an attitude identical with that of the statue of Cavour in Milan – 'is all the more important to have home rule. Nationalize from Cardiff – Gareth Jones has a chance. Nationalize from London – Gareth Jones is *disfatto*.' He made the gesture of crushing an insect beneath his shoe.

'I don't see the difference,' said Roger. 'Why does it matter to Gareth whether he's bought out by a Government office in Cardiff or a Government office in London?'

'Because,' said a new voice at Roger's elbow, 'if he's bought out from Cardiff he'll be reinstated as manager and he'll still drive his own bus over his own route. If he's bought out from London, some Englishman will be promoted over him and he'll be sweeping the garage floor.'

Even before he had time to swivel round, Roger recognized the voice. It was Madog. And with Madog, Roger now saw, was a newcomer. This person was a young man of about Madog's age. He had pale, crew-cut hair and horn-rimmed glasses, and he wore a short coat made of some soft material and decorated with a bold pattern of large checks. His appearance, while pre-dominantly urban, carried a hint of the tundra.

'Oh, hello,' said Roger. In his present mood, the sight of Madog was not particularly soothing to him. 'Still wearing your Cherokee war-paint?'

'I'm exploiting a traditional alliance,' said Madog suavely. 'Je présente –' he indicated the horn-rimmed blond youth – André Something-or-other.' Roger did not trouble to register the unmemorable French name, but he greeted the young man politely enough.

'Are you making a long stay in Wales?'

'Comprends pas,' said the young man, looking sternly at Roger through his lenses.

'Oh – er, Vous faites une longue visite au pays de Galles?'

'Ça depend.'

'Et vous ne parlez pas l'anglais?'

'Jamais,' said the young man tersely.

'Il ne parle que le français et le gallois,' Madog put in. He seemed to be hugging himself with obscure satisfaction. His blue suit was as shiny as ever, and yet something about him suggested a new-found success and prosperity. What was it? His bearing was confident, his skin clearer than usual, as if high spirits had suddenly made him healthy.

'Vraiment?' said Roger without interest. 'Vous êtes de Bretagne, peut-être?'

'Canadien,' replied the young man. Having uttered this one word, he compressed his mouth into a slit and looked at Roger as if ready to stare him down.

'Oh, well, have a drink,' said Roger. He felt utterly weary. 'Beth ydych chi 'n yfed?'

The horn-rimmed man looked uncertainly from Roger to Madog and back again.

'Doesn't look as if he speaks Welsh very well,' Roger could not resist saying.

'He's learning,' said Madog defensively.

'Well, ask him in whatever language he cares to understand what he'd like to drink, would you?'

'Qu-est-ce que vous allez boire, André?' Madog asked.

This difficulty surmounted, drinks named and poured, they nodded to each other in rather distant salutation, and drank.

'Well, what's he doing in Wales?' Roger asked, more to keep the conversation going than because he felt the slightest interest in their visitor. 'Is he here to learn Welsh, like me?'

Yes, that's what I came here for, wasn't it. But all that seems a long time ago. I know Welsh well enough now, and yet it no longer seems important.

'Partly,' said Madog. 'His government have sent him.'

'His government? What is he, a foot-and-mouth inspector?'

'He's the Caerfenai-Quebec axis I told you about,' said Madog plumply. 'He's doing the official French translation of *Gwilym Cherokee.*'

'But –' Roger struggled to understand. 'You said his government was paying for him to be here.'

'That's right. He's on a grant from the Canada Council.'

'But he's –' Roger stopped and started again. 'Let me get this straight. He's come over to see you and translate your epic into French. For publication where? In Quebec?'

'In the first instance, yes,' said Madog. 'But it'll be a parallel-text edition, so they'll distribute it in Wales as well. And of course Paris always takes a good number of copies of anything published in Quebec. It's one of the ways they keep up their links across the Atlantic. By the time we've finished it'll amount to world distribution.'

Roger began to understand. 'So he's here on a nice trip, to collaborate with you, which means in effect that you'll do his work for him, since he obviously doesn't understand three words of Welsh. And no doubt, since there's a lot of gravy running over the side of this jug, you'll be off to Quebec any time you fancy a trip there.'

'No doubt,' said Madog. 'When I can be spared here.'

'Well,' said Roger. He drank deeply from his beer. His feelings were genuinely confused. On the one hand, he had no wish to stop anyone from spending money on spreading Madog's reputation as a poet, which was doubtless well deserved. On the other hand, it seemed as cock-eyed as everything in the modern world. If the word 'culture' had any meaning, which mattered most in any genuine cultural sense – that Gareth should continue to operate his bus, or that this phony, who pretended that he did not speak English and that he did speak Welsh, both demonstrably untrue, should wring from the bureaucrats of his country a sum sufficient to keep Gareth in business for a year?

'You look disapproving,' said Madog with gentle mockery.

'Oh, it's not that exactly. No, it's really not that. Only – well –'

'Well, what? Does it hurt to see a poet get a bit of backing from public funds?'

'Not at all, believe me. But there's backing and backing. I mean, this business of publishing your poem in Quebec. Isn't it a bit of a non-event? How many Quebequois have any genuine interest in Welsh poetry?'

'I'd expect them to have a great deal,' said Madog. 'After all, we're not expecting them to learn Welsh, only to read a translation into their own language by one of their own poets.' So the horn-rimmed blond was a poet, was he? Grub Street certainly looked different these days. 'Added to which, it's the minority cultures that are coming up into focus today. The central ones are running down; England, America, metropolitan France, are cultural deserts – the flowers are blooming in the marginal lands that have never been thought worth cultivating.'

'In other words,' said Roger heavily, 'the thing to be nowadays, if you want fat grants and subsidized publication, is a playwright from Marrakesh or a novelist from Barbados or a poet from the Seychelles.'

'Specifically,' said Madog, grinning, 'a writer of epics from Caerfenai.'

André, who had been openly listening, broke into a grin that answered Madog's. Roger decided to insult the man mildly by keeping up the convention that he must be addressed in French.

'Et vous, monsieur,' he said, 'vous vous intéressez á la litterature galloise depuis longtemps?'

André shrugged. 'C'est de la santé,' he said dismissively.

'La santé?' Roger pursued.

'La fertilisation mutuelle des cultures,' said André. He spoke pityingly, as if spelling it out to his deaf old grandmother. 'Et la lutte contre la centralisation.'

After that, Roger gave up. Perhaps they were right. In any case, he could not argue the opposite case, since it was clear that their only response would be to cast him in the role of Dic Sharp and the General Omnibus Company.

'Well, good luck,' he said, preparing to turn away.

'Watch this space,' said Madog with quiet exuberance. 'I've just arranged to hire the Town Hall for a big read-in by Welsh, Breton and Cornish poets. Next spring. I hope you'll be still here.'

'Oh, God knows,' said Roger. He signalled Mario for another drink and slunk off with it to a quiet corner, leaving Madog and André to their excited talk. Everyone was living, everyone was moving towards some cherished objective. Fräulein Inge was in Morocco (where Mr Robertson had an office). Madog would soon be off to Quebec (at the invitation of the Canada Council). Gerald Twyford was probably at that moment talking his head off on television; even Donald Fisher was doubtless creeping round the bum of some influential editor.

In all this merry dance, he could think of only three who were out of it. Gareth, being squeezed to the wall : Jenny, stuck immovably in her loveless marriage : and himself, one of nature's losers, drawn by some fatal flaw to every situation that ended in disappointment.

He drank his beer, which seemed to be rapidly losing its taste, in large, dissatisfied gulps. The whole thing was a mess, a bloody mess. He ought to get out now, while he could point to some definite entry on the profit side of the ledger. He knew Welsh, thanks to the daily chatter on Gareth's bus, well enough to feel his way into the technicalities of Celtic philology; what he ought to do now was to pull out, get back to London (had he really still got a flat there? Was it mutely waiting for him under its thickening layer of dust? The prospect of seeing it again filled him with an ever deeper sense of futility and distaste), and get into the British Museum for a good hard spell of work. Feather his own nest for a change. Get a good job, a comfortable home, money, a pension. And blondes, too, if there were any to be had. At this moment, he felt too tired and leaden to work up much enthusiasm about blondes. Perhaps – the thought came down on him like a consignment of slate lowered into the hold of a ship – perhaps his *débâcle* with Rhiannon had been his final, ignominious farewell to sexual love.

He sat in his corner, immersed in these thoughts, and feeling more and more ineffectual and bitter, until the clock above Mario's head warned him that Gareth would soon be waiting for him in the square. The ten o'clock run up! That, at least, was an intelligible reality.

Slowly, Roger stood up, moved out of his corner, and went out to the men's lavatory at the back. There was no lighting in the pub yard; the back door had glass panes, and through these enough light spilled out to guide one's feet into the lavatory, where a single weak bulb grudgingly enabled the customers not to void urine on their shoes. Roger, his mission fulfilled, came out of the lavatory and stood for a moment with his back to the pub door, looking at the new moon above the ancient battlements of the town wall. The moon was so delicate, so thinly-sliced, and the battlements so old and heavy and dark, that the contrast between them would have been impossibly abrupt, were it not for the lacy floating clouds that caught and held the nascent silver light, and the hushed murmur of the hidden sea.

Caught in an aesthetic trance, Roger stood looking up. Behind him he heard someone open the door and come out; another customer anxious to return the beer he had rented from the brewery. Roger paid no attention to the rattle of the door or the light foot-fall in the yard. Then he felt a violent impact in the small of the back, and without time to make the slightest movement to protect himself he went over as helplessly as a ninepin. Down went his undefended face, hard: not on the stones of the yard but on the corner of a crate of empty bottles. The crate was of wood, but the corners were reinforced with steel wire, and the wire sank deeply into Roger's upper lip. Pain blinded him. He rolled in the yard, clutching at his face. His knee hurt, but his mouth hurt more. Behind him he heard the same light footsteps retraced, and the door unobtrusively closed.

After a long time, Roger got to his knees and then to his feet. He stood in the yard, looking up at the delicate new moon, just as he had done a few minutes earlier: but everything was changed.

The pub door was opened again and two men came out. They were arguing cheerfully in Welsh. One thought Caerfenai Town should get a new goalkeeper, and the other thought the trouble lay in the poor quality of their forward play. Roger took out his handkerchief and pressed it to his lip. He took it away and looked at it: dark blood was already soaking in. He put it back to the wound and kept it there.

Across the square, Gareth was already in the driving-seat, and one or two passengers had settled in the bus for a good gossip before the journey. Roger climbed stiffly up the steps and took his usual place on the other side of the engine cowling from Gareth.

The handkerchief attracted Gareth's attention and he asked, 'Toothache?'

'No,' said Roger, muffled. 'Some drunk barged into me from behind and I fell on to a crate of empties.'

'Did you see who it was?'

'No, by the time I'd got on my feet and turned round, whoever it was had gone.'

'I see,' said Gareth. He turned to stare through the windscreen ahead of him.

The passengers were entering the bus faster now. It was impossible to discuss what had happened. By the time Gareth rolled the bus forward on the stroke of ten, every seat was filled. Perhaps the liver-coloured bus was lurking somewhere ahead of them, snapping up passengers from the isolated stops, but at ten o'clock most people started from the square. As he moved down the aisle, hiding the congealing lip behind the handkerchief, Roger's one free hand worked overtime putting the fares in his bag. The lurching of the bus made it difficult for him to keep his feet, unable as he was to hold on to anything. But the weight of the coins in his bag made him feel that they had won, nevertheless, a small victory.

But the next morning they made the run down with no passengers at all. The liver-coloured bus had turned up and smartly cleaned out the lot. Roger had covered his cut lip with sticking-plaster; it was badly swollen and he had difficulty in talking. Not that there was anything to say. Things had gone back to their bad normality. The liver-coloured bus was winning and they were losing. That was all.

Drawing up by the statue, they were in time to see their enemy discreetly leaving the square on the other side.

'Well, this can't go on,' said Gareth, switching off the engine.

'No,' Roger agreed.

Gareth sat absolutely still for a moment. Then he turned to look up at Roger and asked, 'Did you notice anybody in the pub last night who might have been the one that attacked you?'

'No,' said Roger. 'I was talking to Madog and a friend of his, and then later I was sunk in my own thoughts and took no notice of anybody. But I'm interested that that's how you see it. You don't think it was an accident.'

'It could have been an accident,' said Gareth slowly. 'But one thing I don't like. If it was a drunk who staggered into you, he wasn't too drunk to take himself off before you could get a look at his face.'

'Well, perhaps he was frightened at what he'd done.'

'Perhaps he was,' said Gareth. 'And perhaps he was more frightened of the people who'd sent him. What they'd do to him if he let himself get identified.'

'You think it's as bad as that?'

'The way things are turning out for us,' said Gareth, 'I'm in a mood to look on the black side.'

In silence, they left the bus and went across to get their morning cup of tea.

The rest of the day was a nightmare. Roger felt tired, discouraged, unwanted. His lip throbbed and his knee-cap ached. He was suffering for an idea, but what idea? Who cared? Who wanted his participation, wanted his presence at all? Even Gareth would hardly notice if, one morning, he simply failed to show up for the eight-fifteen run. He might be stricken, in his lonely lair, with pneumonia or a heart attack, and who would come near him? He would die like an animal on the bare hillside.

But that night, something did, after all, happen. After the ten o'clock run up, they put the bus away and then stood, for a moment, facing each other in the moonlight. The air was still and clear. It was beginning to freeze hard and the moon had grown a size larger since the night before. As soon as Gareth came out of the garage and stood facing him, Roger had the feeling that something momentous was about to take place between them. Was Gareth on the point of giving up? Was he going to say that this would be their last day's work, the end of the long fight against Dic Sharp?

Gareth stood silent for a moment and then said, 'That's it, then.'

'Yes,' said Roger. He felt the plaster shift on his swollen lip as he spoke.

'I suppose you're going home now.'

'Home –?' For an instant, Roger thought Gareth meant that he would be going back to London, to civilization, away from this empty hillside and this cold, hard struggle.

'To the chapel,' said Gareth.

'Oh. Yes. I suppose so.'

'Well,' said Gareth, 'if you're not doing anything, come and have a bite to eat with my mother and me.'

'Come and have – where?'

'Up at home,' said Gareth. He turned and set off up the road, but not without waiting for Roger to fall in beside him.

As they walked, Roger's disappointment and weariness fell

away, and this made him realise how much he had been oppressed by the apparently closed door between Gareth and himself. Now, at last, Gareth had opened the door, or at least set it ajar. Never until now had Roger so much as known where Gareth lived. Now, he was going to enter his habitat, to meet his mother, to be received as a guest and – surely ? – a friend, rather than merely tolerated as an inexplicable parasite who had his incidental usefulness.

They walked on in silence as these thoughts moved in Roger's head. At every moment Roger expected Gareth to turn in at a gateway or open a door, but they went on without pausing, and now the road became steeper and began to mount the last slope that led out of the village altogether. Where did Gareth live ? They had passed the furthest of the terraces. Of course, Llancrwys was a remarkably scattered village; Roger had noticed, in his solitary walks, that whenever he seemed to have left human habitation behind and to be emerging on to the bare mountain, there was always a cottage nestling in the angle between two stone walls, and another one beyond that. Some of these cottages were derelict, others were used to shelter cattle or store equipment for the small farms that still ringed the village; but some of the furthest-flung were still, he had found, occupied.

Even knowing this, Roger was increasingly surprised as they plodded upward. The village, with its scattered lights, was now quite definitely below them, and the dark, silent bulk of the mountain was plainly spread out in the unwavering moonlight. Away to his left, and higher up still, was the place where, in another lifetime, he had made his ludicrous attempt to satisfy his needs on the body of that slab of processed cheese from California – what had she been called ? No matter, it had all gone, far down the stream of his life. Directly ahead was the mountain's bald top, and beyond it, coming into view with each step upwards, the cluster of dark peaks that would never give up their secrets; swarmed over every summer, re-asserting their triumphant loneliness every winter. Over to the right, the direction in which Gareth seemed to be moving, Roger could see nothing but the long, levelled-off slate tips, thrown up a hundred years ago by the quarry which had called Llancrwys into being.

To break the silence he said, 'Is the quarry deserted now?'

'No,' said Gareth. 'They still send out a few loads a week.'

'How many men work there?'

'About forty,' said Gareth. 'I remember when it was three hundred at least.'

Roger was silent again. So forty men went up to that quarry every morning, and he, who thought he had come to know the district from the ground up, who considered himself to have earned his knowledge by discipline and sacrifice, had never suspected the fact. As he and Gareth took the bus down, these men silently left their houses and walked up, through the mist or rain or wind, past the cropping sheep and the derelict cottages. Probably they climbed along the grass-covered track that had once been a slate railway, and was still splendidly firm on its rock-solid embankment, not at all eroded by time though the rails had been taken up thirty years before and silence had swallowed the chuffing engines and the rolling trucks.

But where was Gareth's house? He could see a few lights, but nothing at all in the direction in which they were moving. Indeed, all Roger could see up there was the firm, level outline of the slate-tips: four enormous heaps of broken rock and slate, steadily taken out of the hillside, load by load, since the eighteen-forties, and carried out to build up into these great man-made cliffs. There they stood, dark against the moonlit sky and solidly opposite to the moonlit sea, shaped and levelled as carefully as marble chips laid on a grave.

Each tip was a long, dark finger running out from the hilltop, increasing in height in proportion as the ground fell away around it, and its top was as level as a billiard-table. At the foot of each gigantic pile, the humble fields began, every one enclosed in its four stone walls, sheltering a few sheep or a cow or two, and with the inevitable cottage over in one corner. Yes, he had seen this before. But where was Gareth taking him? Were they on the point of beginning to climb up the shadowy side of one of these monstrous man-made cliffs?

The road petered out, and was replaced by a path of beaten earth and stones. Gareth kept steadily moving along. But towards what? Did he live in some cleft in the rocks? Glancing sideways at Gareth's powerful, misshapen body, a man's head on a goat's back, Roger felt a flicker of numinous dread, as if he might find himself in the company of some grinning monster of the mountainside. He shook his head to clear it of foolish fancies. Then Gareth spoke.

'My father worked this small-holding. He had nine acres.'

It was too dark for Roger to see the fields in detail, but he knew what they would be like: poor soil spread meagrely over the rock, thistles, marsh-grass, the wind always sighing through the gaps in the stone walls. Poverty, hunger and incessant labour, with nothing to set against them except the grandeur of the mountains, the noble sweep of the bay, and the delicate gaiety of the wild flowers that somehow pushed up from the thin soil every summer. The harebells alone would almost compensate a man for each new back-breaking year, if he had the contemplative eye and could see beauty.

'Nine acres,' he said, and he knew that all those miscellaneous thoughts had gone into the two short words and that Gareth would read them there.

'It was a life,' said Gareth. 'He didn't have a job in the town and work the holding in his spare time, like so many of them. He gave all his time to the nine acres and he worked them properly. I helped him as soon as I was big enough to lift a bundle of hay.'

They were still walking steadily on.

'Then when he died, I could have carried it on. But I'd always been more interested in the motors. So we sold the sheep and the two cows, and the equipment, what there was of it, and I went into the bus business.'

'Oh.'

'That was about fifteen years ago,' said Gareth. His face was towards Roger as he spoke, but his voice was inward, musing, like that of a man talking to himself. He ceased now, his talk ending like an abandoned railway line among brambles and rust. The unspoken thought hung in the dark air between them: *Fifteen years, and then closed down by Dic Sharp that used to go to Llancrwys school? Is that to be the way?*

Suddenly Gareth halted and opened a metal gate. 'This way,' he said. Roger followed, swivelling his head about for any trace of human habitation. But the small field they had entered was as dark as the rest of the mountainside, as dark as the gigantic motionless tip that reared silently up from its further side. Again Roger had to fight down the fear of something nameless. He felt an impulse to demand where Gareth was taking him. But he held on to his taciturn dignity. If he once lost it, he felt, Gareth would despise him for ever, with no second chance.

They walked across the field, and as they did so the moon came out from a bank of cloud and shone straight on the dark, straight sides of the quarry-tip in front of them. In its sudden light, Roger saw what they were walking towards: a small cottage of one storey, lying flat at the bottom of the tip like a neat oblong doorstep at the foot of a mountain. The moon gleamed in its dark windows; no smoke came from either of the two chimneys. Evidently there was no one at home.

'Your mother must be out,' he said to Gareth.

'She's in all right,' said Gareth shortly.

In? Lying in bed? Or in the *tŷ bach*, reading a newspaper by candlelight?

The cottage's front door opened on to a small patch of paving-stones, with the remains of what might once have been a flower-bed. Nothing else stood between it and the bare hillside. Gareth marched straight up to this front door and opened it, at the same time calling out, 'Here I am, Mam. Got company.'

Roger followed a pace or two behind. The door opened straight on to a room, and this room was as dark as the rest of the house, darker than the moonlit field outside. So why did Gareth call out to his mother in the tone of one certain of being heard?

Because his mother was sitting there in the darkness. Because his mother had no need of light. Or rather she had need of it but she could not have it.

Gareth's mother was sitting in a rocking-chair opposite the door. This room was evidently the main living-room of the house. Behind her chair, a door led into what must be the kitchen. All this Roger saw as Gareth clicked on the light. He stood still in the doorway, unable to move, unable to think of any phrase of greeting. He was too confused, for a moment, even to decide whether to speak in English or Welsh. His mind seemed incapable of forming any thought except one: *how like Gareth not to have told me that his mother was blind.*

But why shouldn't he? What harm would it have done to prepare me for this?

Because Gareth is Gareth. And Gareth never prepares anybody for anything.

Gareth was speaking to his mother in Welsh. His voice, when he addressed her, lost its grating tone and became more velvety, deeper, more comfortably cadenced. The old woman spoke in English, evidently to Roger.

'Please to meet you. I tell Gareth he bring you up one night for supper.'

Roger struggled to collect himself. She was looking straight in his direction, as if realizing that he must be standing in the doorway. But there was no sight in her two stony eyeballs.

'A oes arnoch eisieu siarad Cymraeg, Mrs. Jones,' he said to her, 'rwyf yn ei deall tipyn bach.' But the old woman would not speak Welsh to him. She rocked back and forth a few times and said again, 'Please to meet you.'

'I've told her all about you,' said Gareth over his shoulder.

'I telling Gareth to bring you up to supper,' she said firmly.

Roger advanced into the room and shut out the night behind him. The room was warm and neat. Of course, a blind person would have to be tidy. A coal fire was laid in the grate, ready to be lit, but the room was warmed by an electric convector stove. Gareth went through into the kitchen; Roger heard him take the lid off a cooking-pot that stood on the hotplate and say, 'Looks about done.'

His mother answered in Welsh, and while they talked through the open door Roger found himself a chair, sat down, and studied the old woman. The first thing that struck him, now that he had got over the initial surprise of her blindness, was that she was very big. Lean and wasted as she was in old age, she had long limbs and a big frame; standing up, she would be a good six feet tall. Roger wondered if Gareth's father had been a giant also. Somehow, he felt that this was not likely; such offspring, powerful but cursed with crookedness, could more easily be imagined as issuing from the union of a female giant and a male dwarf. Gareth's father, he decided, had been a lop-sided gnome of the wet rocks, moving on short strong legs about his nine acres, peering keenly over his ragged stone walls.

Mother and son were talking. He found that he could understand their quick, familiar Welsh very well.

Did Siân come today?

No. She sent her brother.

Which brother? Arthur?

No, Maldwyn.

A grunt of impatience. – He's the daft one. Do they expect a shilling for him?

He did all right. He never let me stumble once and he kept me on the short grass. My shoes hardly got wet at all. And he put the bacon in all right.

Gareth turned to Roger. 'Mam does a lot of the housekeeping. It's surprising how much she can do. Three times a week she goes down to the shop in Llancrwys, walks all the way down and back. She has a little lad to guide her. He does it when he comes home from school. He takes her down to the shop and helps her to get all the things in her basket, then comes back up here and she sits in her chair and tells him what to do and he puts something on to cook. Like this, for instance." He tapped the enamel pot. 'A nice joint of bacon, boiled just right.'

Mam, who had been listening to this and turning her face attentively in Roger's direction, suddenly struck in with, 'I can't do potatoes. We having bread except when Gareth doing it.'

Roger wished she would speak Welsh, but evidently the pair of them had it firmly in their heads that English was for the visitor and Welsh for themselves. The old woman's English was what one would expect after a lifetime of neglect. Presumably she had been taught in English when she went to school, back in the eighteen-nineties, but since then she had seldom used it. Doubtless she understood it well enough, but in speaking it she seemed to distrust its complexities. Verbs, for instance, seemed to her best if firmly restricted to the present participle. He wondered if his Welsh would sound any better to her. But then, he was clearly not going to get a chance to try it.

'No, we can't do vegetables when we have to rely on Arthur or Maldwyn,' said Gareth. 'They put the pot on and then go. They don't switch the heat on. Mam does that. She gets the time from the wireless and she knows which is the right switch to turn. One turn to the right – low heat. Two turns – medium. Three turns – full.'

'I not using full,' she interposed, keenly following the account through every step.

'She sits with the door open,' Gareth continued, 'and if anything boiled over and started to smell burnt, she'd switch off the hotplate straight away.'

'I see,' said Roger. 'But what if something really went wrong? If a fault in the electric cooker caused a real fire to break out?'

Gareth smiled calmly. 'Look beside her chair,' he said. There, standing within reach of Mam's long arm, was a small, spray-action fire extinguisher. 'If the cooker caught fire,' said Gareth, 'and, mark you, the cooker is the only thing that ever might catch fire in a million years – well, Mam smells it at once, and hears it too, and she just picks up her little fire extinguisher and foams it out.'

'I never having to do it,' said the old woman gravely, 'but I always ready.'

'Oh, Mam's as safe as houses,' said Gareth proudly. 'You'd be surprised at the things she can do.'

Abruptly, as if deciding that enough time had been given to admiration and sentiment, he bent, struck a match, and lit the fire.

'Now, when that draws up,' he said, standing back, 'we'll be snug.'

Roger felt the truth of this. As Gareth, waving aside his offers of help, moved back and forth between sitting-room and kitchen setting out dishes, making tea, cutting slices off a large, fresh loaf, and generally preparing a hearty supper for three, Roger leaned back in his chair and savoured the contrast between this warm, brightly-lit room and the cold hillside beyond the door. He felt conscious, too, of the steep black cliff of slate that towered up behind the house. He felt he would like to ask Mam some questions about it. Had it always been there, as high as that, in all the years she had lived in the house? Or had it grown by unobtrusive wagon-loads, month by month, to that monstrous bulk? As a young bride, brought here by Gareth's father in some unimaginable springtime of their lives, had she started back in amazement and fear at the sight of the house where she was to spend her days, seeing it already overhung by this artificial mountain?

He dismissed the picture as idle fancy. She was doubtless a local girl, familiar with the tip from babyhood, and if it had grown a little during her lifetime she would have scarcely remarked the fact. The tip only seemed strange to him because he was a newcomer.

What, then, could he talk to her about? He searched his mind for a topic, but nothing suggested itself, and he was content to remain silent. Fatigue pulled his shoulders back into the chair; besides, his cut lip had begun smarting again. He explored it with his tongue. Yes, the swelling was going down. But it was still painful.

'Supper's ready,' said Gareth. 'Pull up to the table.' He was quickly and expertly carving slices from the smoking joint of bacon; already he had cut the loaf into thick, buttered slices and arranged a stack of them beside each plate. Before beginning to eat, he settled his mother into her place and saw that everything was within easy reach. His final gesture – the signal, as it were, for the meal to begin – was to pour out three large cups of tea, thick and dark as a witches' brew.

Eating the hot boiled bacon and fresh buttery bread, drinking great gulps of the reviving tea, Roger felt purely happy. He was accepted by Gareth at last; the portcullis was up. And, in his warmed and relaxed state, he forgave Gareth entirely for the delay in accepting him. To bring someone home to meet Mam – this was not, could not be, a light undertaking. If your mother was an ordinary housewidow living in an ordinary semi-detached, with a television set in the living-room and a framed photograph of her deceased husband (an inspector of plumbing with letters after his name) on the cold tile mantelpiece, it was nothing to take someone home and introduce him. But to come to this dark, secret lair on the mountainside, this hidden badger-set at the foot of the great silent tip, and usher a newcomer into the presence of the old blind giantess, was something altogether different. As he ate, Roger once more took stock of Gareth's Mam. She ate as blind people do, bending forward over her food and making slow, precise movements. Now and again a scrap of bacon or bread fell back on her plate, but nothing ever reached her clothes. She was not the sort of woman to let herself go and become a messy feeder. She had on a black dress, with a thick brown cardigan over it for warmth. Her hair, iron-grey, was drawn back into a bun; on one finger was a broad old-fashioned gold ring which would have to be buried with her, since the joint of the finger had swollen and cut off its escape. Her face had something Red Indian about it (Cherokee: suddenly Roger thought of Madog in his blue suit), the cheekbones high, the skin permanently tinged with brown after a lifetime of upland weather. Its expression had the calm that blindness often brings, the repose that settles on a character when abrupt movement and hasty action are for ever out of the question.

The fire was burning up; Roger could feel its heat on his cheek. Gareth heaped more slices of bacon on all their plates; evidently this was the main meal of the day, when they expected to do themselves well. Deep, drowsy contentment began to seep through Roger's being. How good it was here. He looked round, through a mist of gratified approval. The cottage might have been fifty years old, or a hundred, or three hundred; the design of long houses, once perfected for these wind-beaten slopes, had not altered. The small window looked out on the thistly field and the stone wall, and beyond that to the endlessly falling ground which sloped down and down to level out only on the shore, within sound of the ceaseless wash of waves and rattle of sea-rounded stones. Everything was as it had always been ... and yet not altogether so, for the old woman's way of life was made possible by the modern engineering that brought electric cables up the mountainside, so that she could cook for her son without an open flame, and tell the time by the wireless, and have a spray of fire-extinguishing foam by her rocking-chair. It was a complicated patchwork, but what gave it unity was that everything in it had logic in relation to everything else. And Gareth's struggle for independence, his determination to go on running his own bus service, had its logic in relation to what Roger was seeing now. The bus was to Gareth what the nine acres had been to his father. It was his life.

At last, as he cleaned his plate and leaned back, Roger understood what he had been doing for the past three months. He touched his swollen lip with pride. It had earned him this illumination. He had no doubt that it was the sight of his injury, the honourable wound he had suffered in their common cause – for surely, assault proven or unproven, it could be taken as such – that had prompted Gareth's invitation.

Their meal ended, Gareth, once more waving aside offers of help from Roger, took the dishes into the kitchen and washed them. Then, with Mam back in her rocking-chair, the three sat in the bright glow of the fire. A time for confidences? An opening of hearts? Apparently not. Gareth spoke briefly of magnetos and distributor heads. The gathering threat of Dic Sharp, the liver-coloured bus cruising like a shark to destroy their nets, were ignored. Roger understood this. Diplomatic relations must prevail on this, his first visit. The honour was already great; he was at Gareth's fireside.

After a while, Gareth went out to the lavatory at the back of the house. Left alone with Mam, Roger's instinct was to keep some framework of polite conversation going, staying safely among neutral topics and perhaps making another attempt to get her to speak Welsh to him. But her own mood, he suddenly saw, was quite different. Once the door had safely shut behind Gareth, she leaned forward in his general direction, her body stiffened and a look of urgency came over that broad face. He knew that she was about to say something of great importance to her.

'Gareth,' she said. He understood that this was testing, to make sure that it was Gareth and not Roger who had gone to the tŷ bach.

'He's gone out.'

Mam stiffened still further and leaned forward another inch or two.

'Mr Furnivall.' Her pronunciation made the name sound like that of a shaggy chieftain in some wild glen – Furn Ni-*Vall*.

'Yes, Mrs Jones?'

Guided by his voice, she suddenly put out a strong old hand and gripped his knee.

'Tell me.'

'Tell you what?'

As if for an answer, she squeezed his knee until he almost cried out. She was fighting for utterance.

'Speak *Welsh*, for God's sake,' he said.

Slowly, her head shaking to and fro with the effort, she got it out.

'They tell me in the shop. They telling me is bad with the buses. Another bus coming to take the trade. They saying it is with Dic Sharp. They saying they not knowing what will happen with Gareth. Some people saying he have to give up. To sell the bus and stop the service, soon. Tell me, Mr Furnivall. Tell me if it is bad. Gareth —' she shook her head vehemently — 'Gareth say nothing to me. Never once he telling me what happens with the bus.'

'He doesn't want to worry you.'

'I do worrying. All the time, and when I go down to the shop they always telling me bad things.'

Roger thought quickly. Gareth would be back in a moment, and if he found Roger in the middle of explaining their difficulties to Mam he would at once, and for ever, regard him as an enemy.

'Mrs Jones,' he said in a low voice. 'Don't worry. Dic Sharp would like to buy the bus. He wants us to give up. He has some tricks he thinks will make us give up, and for the time being he has managed to cut our money down a bit, but we shall win. We shall win,' he repeated fiercely. 'Fe newn ni ennill.'

The latch clicked; Gareth was back. Mam sank into her former posture. Looking across at her, Roger would hardly have known that the short, tense exchange between them had not occurred in some brief day-dream of his own. But the muscle above his knee still ached from the imploring pressure of her fingers.

Diplomatic conversation was resumed, but not for long. Everyone had to be up early in the morning. Within a few minutes, Roger had uttered his thanks and goodbyes.

'We hoping you come to see us again,' said Mam, now fully back in her role as gracious matriarch.

'Any time you like,' said Roger. It rested with Gareth, now, to invite him or not. Surely he had behaved correctly?

Gareth walked with him as far as the gate of the field. He seemed in a generous, expansive mood.

'Can you see all right? Take care of that lip. Better bathe it when you get home.'

'It's getting better.'

'See you in the morning.'

'Yes. Goodnight. Thank you.'

Roger turned and began to walk back down the path of beaten earth and stones. Neither of them had mentioned their troubles. Well, play it from day to day. In a week, in a month, if Gareth was forced to give up, he could pack a suitcase, close up the deserted chapel, go back to London and put in his application for Uppsala straight away. He thought of how he would phrase it. 'I have recently widened my range in the Celtic field by acquiring both written and spoken Welsh, and am ready to undertake research and teaching in these subjects.' The words sounded in his head, but they seemed to come from an immense distance, from somewhere as far away as the horned and watchful moon.

Reaching the point where the paved road began, he halted for a moment, turned, and looked back at the cottage. Its windows were still lit up: but as he watched, the light went out. And the great black tip stood silently over the house, as it had stood for a hundred years.

Roger's stove was his best friend. It provided him not only with heat but with companionship. When he came in at the end of the evening, or to rest for a while between runs, he approached the little pot-bellied, chuckling god like a grateful worshipper. There was always the small, wholesome ritual: to insert a smooth metal talon in the godling's navel and shake it up and down to stir up its entrails; then to carry out its neat little bedpan; then to feed the dying stomachic glow with neat oval pellets of compressed anthracite dust. These objects were known as 'stove nuts', but to Roger, as he weighed them meditatively in his dusty palms, they were not nuts but eggs. Each one was an embryo of delicious, comforting heat. And the little triumphant stove was the incubator in which the eggs were hatched into phoenix-life.

At first glance, because of its Continental appearance, he had taken the stove for an importation of the Fräulein's. But, as he got to know the Fräulein better by living among her diminishing emanations, he knew that the stove must date from the last phase of the chapel's religious life. Fräulein Inge would be a modern girl who thought of heat as something you summoned by the impersonal flick of a switch. She would have demanded electric central heating. Why had Mr Robertson not complied? What had caused the Fräulein to cover her impatient arty fingers with anthracite dust?

It must have been something to do with the wiring, Roger decided. Examining the electrical system, he saw that the not very high-powered cooking apparatus was the only thing with a power fuse. The rest of the fuses were all for lighting. No doubt Mr Robertson had gone into the matter and reported back to Fräulein Inge that the circuits would not stand any more power appliances. She must have sulked at that, and drawn her mouth into a thin straight line, and threatened to go off to Morocco there and then. Roger could imagine the pair of them, sulking and exhibiting their discontent to one another, till in the end they slumped down on to the divan and purged their irritability in sexual sweat and hostile, poisonous discharge.

The stove, however, had survived these scenes, and lived on to make the damp, neglected place into a home. Sitting in front of it, sometimes with the cheerful little doors wide open, sometimes with them thriftily closed, Roger understood why every civilization has called the hearth sacred, the seat of the household deities; and understood also why modern man, heating himself with thick, stale air from furnaces he never sees, has become anxious and uncreative.

That was all very well, but the supply of stove eggs was running low. He must go to a coal merchant and arrange for a load to be delivered. Roger knew this, and yet shrank from taking action. To place an order with a coal merchant, to give the chapel as his address, to receive a bill and pay it, all seemed impossibly overt, official acts for one in his position. He was living in the chapel for no better reason than that it was nobody's immediate concern to turn him out: he was squatting, entirely illegally, making use of the place exactly as a fox uses the untenanted home of a badger. He had no feeling of permanence; each day there might be his last; when the spring came, he would have to get out anyway, leaving as few traces as possible for Fräulein Inge to exclaim over. And before that, Dic Sharp waited with his polished rooster's beak, ready to peck, peck, peck. It could not be long before the news reached him that Roger was occupying the chapel, and then his only problem would be how to get Roger into serious enough trouble without himself arousing the antagonism of Mr Robertson, who was doubtless some bigger and more dangerous Dic Sharp in his own right.

As these reasons spooled endlessly on the tape-recorder of his mind, Roger allowed the stock of heat-eggs to dwindle until the frosty morning came when he combed through the bunker and, with difficulty, collected one last bucket of them. Soberly, he used these to make up the stove. That would keep it burning for four hours – five, possibly, seeing that it was a windless day. After that, cold would descend and the place would cease to be a home and become the cave of some shivering Neanderthal hominid. Since no coal merchant would deliver within four hours, it was already too late to avoid at least one freezing night and possibly two or three. Softly cursing his feebleness of will, he put on his overcoat and tweed cap, and went off to join Gareth on the eight-fifteen.

Twice that morning they were harassed by the liver-coloured bus, but Roger hardly noticed. His world had shrunk to a small iron digestion slowly fuming away its last meal. At lunch-time, he went into Mario's in a state of dejection. Mario had just served a pint to quiet, stocky Gito, who for some reason was there alone without his *alter ego*. When he saw Roger's face, the landlord spread his hands in a defensive gesture.

'Is something a matter. Your life is bad for you. Cattivo umore.'

'Yes,' said Roger, climbing up on the high stool. 'Damned caitiff humour. Give me a pint of your cheapest and sourest beer.'

'I give you,' said Mario promptly. 'But I charge you for the best. Then it taste good.' He drew Roger a pint of his usual beer. 'Drink up, tell us your troubles.'

'They said you've moved,' said Gito. He moved his rectangular bulk a little nearer to Roger so that they could talk quietly. His face, under the pale dome of his baldness, seemed gentle, welcoming.

'I suppose everybody knows,' said Roger indifferently. 'I had to leave Mrs Pylon Jones's because somebody who shall be nameless, called Dic Sharp, bribed a lot of hooligans to make my position intolerable.'

Mario cast a quick, watchful glance round the bar. It was not yet very full, but several heads had lifted at the mention of Dic Sharp's name. 'You like to get me in trouble, uh,' he said reproachfully to Roger.

'Dic Sharp doesn't own this pub,' said Roger defiantly.

'He can make a difference to what happens here, though,' Gito put in. His soft, husky voice was curiously commanding of attention, more so than anyone could have guessed who saw him only in his normal role of audience to quick-talking Ivo. 'You found that the other night, didn't you?' he went on, his eyes fixed on Roger with gentle persistence.

Roger fingered his lip; the swelling almost gone down now. Wordlessly, he nodded.

'Well, then,' said Gito.

'Well, what?' Roger snapped. 'We all just give in to him, do we? Let him do anything to us and never even mention his name in a public place?'

'Not where we might get our friends into trouble,' said Gito.

With a despairing shrug, Roger picked up his beer and took a huge draught. He felt utterly hopeless. He thought of his stove, steadily fuming down.

'At this rate,' he said, 'we might as well give up.'

'I didn't say that,' said Gito. Mario had now gone to serve a customer in the other bar, and they were left alone, their heads close together. 'Seems to me you can do a lot by hanging on.'

'A lot of what?' said Roger sourly.

'A lot of good. And a lot of damage to Dic Sharp. Ivo was talking to a chap the other night, who's in the transport business. He was saying that if Dic Sharp doesn't get hold of Gareth's bus soon – in five, six weeks, say – he'll be at the end of his money and he'll have to sell all the buses back.'

Roger considered. 'How many has he got?'

'Oh, fifteen, twenty, something like that. Some of them, he bought out the business and left the owner to manage it and do the driving and everything. No difference on the surface, isn't it? Only it's Dic Sharp's bus and he can sell it any time and the chap's'll be working for somebody else, or sacked maybe.'

'Did he offer those terms to you and Ivo?'

'He did, man. But we wouldn't take them. We put up a long

fight and when we got out we got out. I talked it all over with Ivo and he said No, give him the trouble of finding a driver and someone to service the old girl.' Gito looked into his glass, his face suddenly sombre. 'He'll never find anybody that can make her run as sweet as I could. Well, anyway.' He drank from his glass. 'We got out with enough money to put down on a lorry, and we get a living out of the scrap business.'

'But you'd go back to the buses if you could.'

'Yes, man, if he'd sell.'

Roger was beginning to understand. It was not only Gareth he was fighting for. If they really managed to hold out until Dic Sharp was forced to sell, a whole network of small businesses might go back to their original owners, and the tide of creeping anonymity would be held back, perhaps for years. He squared his shoulders. He had some value, after all, in the life of these people. And – it occurred to him – a right to ask help of them.

'Gito,' he opened up, 'is your lorry handy?'

'Down by the quay,' said Gito, preparing to sink his teeth into a cheese roll.

'Could you give me a bit of a hand with something I want to carry?''

Without hesitation Gito said, 'Yes,' chewing and nodding.

'I need some fuel, you see. We could call in at the coal merchant's and get a few bags.'

'No trouble at all. Only I got to be over the other side of the mountain at three o'clock. Got to pick Ivo up. He's over there doing a bit of business.'

Roger smiled. 'You'll be there,' he said. 'A meat pie please, Mario, and another pint for both of us.'

Half an hour later, Gito led Roger down to where the lorry waited by the quayside. The harbour was quiet without the yachts and catamarans of the summer people: two or three masts were sticking up from water-level, and one small fishing vessel was getting ready to go out with the afternoon tide, but for the most part the harbour was as dead as the car park. Under a flat steel sky, Caerfenai was deep in its well-deserved winter sleep.

Ivo's and Gito's lorry was a Canadian Dodge. It had seen its best days some twelve years earlier, but Gito's short patient fingers were always moving about in its entrails, tapping and healing, and when he got into the driving seat and started the motor it sounded hale enough. Certainly, battered as it was, the big olive-green shape gave an appearance of power and solidity. It began to move through the quiet streets like a big freighter nosing out from harbour into the roadsteads.

'The best coal merchant is Williams, up the hill there,' said Gito. 'We'll get quick service and good quality stuff. What kind is it you want?'

'Stove nuts. Those egg-shaped things.'

'Of course,' said Gito softly. 'I was forgetting. I know that stove. I used to sit as near to it as I could and go to sleep when the sermon came on.'

Roger was surprised and pleased. 'You know the chapel? You used to go there?'

'My family went there till my Dad got a different job and we moved six miles away. I was ten then. I don't remember much about the chapel, only the stove. I got to know that very well. We were old friends, you might say. Many a cold Sunday morning I blessed the stove more than I cursed the sermon.' He laughed quietly into the noise of the engine.

At the coal merchant's yard, Gito consulted briefly with the incendiary Williams, then hoisted five hundredweight bags of the best stove nuts on to the lorry. He waved aside Roger's help, and, when Roger approached the merchant and asked how much he owed, Gito said rapidly, 'On our account, Ben. We'll get you that back axle tomorrow.'

'I need chicken wire,' said Ben Williams. 'Fifteen or twenty yards. Twenty to be on the safe side.'

'We'll find you twenty,' said Gito. 'Come on now,' he said to Roger.

'But I want to pay for the —'

'On credit,' said Williams. He gestured towards Gito.

'Don't argue now,' said Gito. He pointed to the lorry. 'Get in and we'll take it up.'

They were climbing in low gear, the engine whining and thrusting, before Roger spoke again. 'I don't see why you should stake me to free fuel.'

'That chapel must take a bit of heating.'

'All the same, I don't see —'

'I don't see either,' said Gito. 'I don't see why anyone should attack you from behind so you cut your lip open. Or loosen the wheel-nuts of your car. There's a lot as I don't see.'

'There's an easy explanation there,' said Roger grimly. 'Dic Sharp.'

'Well, there's an explanation here too. Gito and Ivo.'

Roger smiled, shrugged, and said no more.

At the chapel they unloaded the fuel, and then Gito followed Roger into the chapel and watched while he lovingly replenished the stove, shaking out the ash and carefully feeding in the dark ovals. When Roger straightened up from this task, Gito asked, 'What are you going to do now?'

'Walk down the hill,' Roger answered, 'and get a General bus into Caerfenai, to be with Gareth for the four-fifteen up.'

Gito appeared to be thinking. 'That gives you a bit of time, then.'

'An hour and a half. Why?'

'I just thought,' said Gito. 'If you were free to come with me I could show you something interesting.'

After this, there seemed nothing for it but to go back into the high, draughty cab of the Dodge. This time Gito drove straight up the steep road that led out of Llancrwys, and they crawled slowly round the shoulder of the mountain till they were running easily down into the next valley. The road levelled out for a mile or two, then they were climbing again. Roger was in entirely unknown country by now. He waited in patience.

Finally they approached a straggling village, with a long street lined with houses in uneven clusters, and a stone bridge over a dashing little river full of white water and sharp rocks. Gito eased the big lorry over the bridge and pulled up beside the road. Nearby, a construction gang was working, bright yellow earth-moving vehicles were parked in a sea of mud, and a bonfire was making the winter air shimmer with summer heat.

Gito switched off the engine, and in the silence Roger said, 'Well? What are you going to show me?'

Gito nodded to show the direction of his eyes. Roger looked and saw a big Victorian house on the other side of the field. The lead and slates had already been stripped from its roof, and the windows taken out of their oblong anchorages. The place looked as raw and pitiful as a ship being towed to the breaker's.

'It's coming down, that house,' said Gito. 'Road widening.

Most of the inside has gone already. Me and Ivo have had some good stuff out of it. Metal grates, pipes, fenders, all sorts of stuff. Now.' He glanced down at Roger's feet. 'Are you frightened of getting your shoes muddy?'

'No.'

'All right, come with me.'

They walked across the grubbed-up field and round to the back of the house. Outside the back door, a conservatory had stood, but this had already been dismantled, and on the bare, level flag-stones stood what Gito was now, proudly, pointing at.

'The parlour floor,' he said.

At first Roger thought he was looking at a heap of bricks. Then he realized they were wood-blocks. Polished, hard parquet blocks.

'That lot's going,' said Gito casually. 'Nobody's got instructions to ask any money for them. They're just treated like junk, that'll have to be carted away. And it's good wood. Oak. You don't get it now.'

Oak! All at once Roger thought of the fine dust these blocks would burn down to, the lovely steady heat they would give. He stared greedily at the heap of wood-blocks, polished by the tread of generations, dully shining in the white afternoon. He needed them, he wanted them, he must have them.

'Could we really . . .?' his voice trailed away.

'The lorry's waiting,' said Gito.

Quickly, they stooped and gathered an armful each. Pity they had no sacks. But it could not be helped. With sacks, they would have loaded the entire heap on to the Dodge in, say, three journeys each. Using only their arms, it would be more like ten or a dozen. Never mind, the blocks were there and to be had. Roger felt rich as he loaded himself with the solid, beautiful rectangles. And as he saw Gito heap up the blocks in his powerful, steady embrace, he felt doubly rich: rich in friendship.

They slipped and staggered across the naked clay, returning empty, going back full. The workmen and their foreman all seemed to know Gito well, and to accept without question his right to help himself to anything from the site. It was quite possible that he and Ivo had paid a lump sum down for the privilege of such beachcombing. What was important was that the stove would glow, the chapel would be warm and cheerful, for the rest of the winter, and it was free, a gift, a kindness. Roger's heart overflowed. That mean, silent onslaught in the darkness of the pub yard – it had depressed him terribly at the time, but looking back now he could see that it had earned him a huge, disproportionate reward. He was accepted. His wounds had proved him. Those who hated Dic Sharp loved Roger Furnivall. And to be loved, it was worth being hated.

They were almost finished. One more load each, or two at the most, and they would be ready to drive back over the mountain. Roger, his arms barely meeting round an extravagant load of parquet blocks, approached the lorry from the rear, its tailgate down, its generous flat space strewn with his winter comfort. He was just bracing his muscles to heave the load after its fellows, when a metallic shape, coming towards him along the village street, claimed his attention. A car. A mini-car. A bright blue mini-car, driven by someone who was looking at him with heavy-rimmed glasses through the windscreen. A bright blue mini-car driven by Jenny.

Jenny's car. Jenny's two children. Jenny's eyes, looking at him under Jenny's heavy dark fringe of hair. Jenny's mind, registering him. She recognized him, he knew that. She saw his face surmounting the pile of wood-blocks. The little blue car slowed, almost faltered. She wanted to stop, to speak to him, to start their dialogue again. Perhaps she wanted to tell him what she had been thinking since they met. Lying in the dark beside Gerald, or lying in a half-warmed bed with a cold area where Gerald should be, or abstractedly moving about the house, soaping her children in the bath, standing in the chemist's or the greengrocer's waiting her turn, she had been familiar with his image, had seen his face and heard his voice, knew his need of her and what he had to offer.

Their eyes met. Roger clutched his wood-blocks and prepared himself for whatever was coming. But nothing was coming. Her face, behind its glasses, swam past him; her hand moved to the gear-lever. Mary and Robin looked at him incuriously from the back seat. Then they were gone.

'Just enough left for one load,' said Gito, coming up behind him.

'Yes,' said Roger. He shot his armful of blocks into the back of the Dodge.

He turned to look down the long street, but the car had turned a corner and his life was empty again. Stiffly, he walked over to the broken house to fetch the last of the wood-blocks. The winter was upon him, now; it was in his bones.

One morning that week, Mrs Pylon Jones was on the eleven o'clock down. As Roger approached for her fare, she gave him a gnome-like, sideways look.

'This came for you,' she said, and handed him a letter.

'Oh,' he said. 'Thank you. Tenpence, please.'

'I've had it two days,' she said. 'I didn't know where to send it so I had to wait till I met you.'

'You can forward anything else to my bank in Caerfenai,' he said and named it. 'Not that there should be anything.'

She looked even more gnome-like. 'You could give me your new address in Llancrwys.'

The rattling of the bus almost drowned her words, but the expression on her face conveyed her true meaning: *I know you're squatting where you don't belong. The law will find you out.*

'The bank would be best, thank you,' he said stiffly and moved back to his privileged seat across from Gareth's. But the brief episode made him feel hunted. He was a wild animal, without right, and everything organized was his natural enemy.

The letter, which looked unpleasantly official, lay in his pocket and radiated menace. As soon as they reached Caerfenai, Roger tore the envelope open. Yes, his worst fears were confirmed. It was the motor hire firm. Since no witnesses had come forward to establish that the accident to the car had not been Roger's fault, the insurance company had rejected the claim and Roger owed them seventy-two pounds.

He read the terse letter over several times with hate. Why seventy-two? Since the bill was obviously a fancied-up one anyway, why could they not leave it at the round sum of seventy, without insulting his intelligence with the feeble pretence of having worked out the cost minutely? He decided that when he got round to paying it, he would make out the cheque for seventy-one pounds nineteen shillings and elevenpence, and enclose a letter saying that his estimate of the work and materials involved came out a penny below theirs and they were at liberty to sue him for the penny.

But childish revenges, though they were permissible to a man in search of salve for his wounded feelings, would not get him out of this mess. Seventy-two pounds would make a cruel hole in the modest reserve of money that he had been counting on. The university would be paying him his salary instalment about now, but their attitude to sabbatical leave was ungenerous, and the bargain he had been able to strike with them was pitiful enough. The sum that was coming in would have been enough to keep him in fair comfort till Easter, but with seventy-two pounds scooped out of it this was no longer true. Bitterness dragged his mouth aslant. So Dic Sharp had scored a decisive victory; he had won, if not the war, certainly an important battle.

'Bad news?' said Gareth, who had twisted round in the driving-seat and watched Roger's face as these thoughts went through his mind.

'Yes, money,' said Roger. 'Or more precisely, absence of same. I owe seventy-two pounds on that car that got damaged going down the hill.'

He had, in fact, never mentioned this occurrence to Gareth. But in their new relationship, so much easier and franker and fuller, it would have been artificial to keep up any pretence that Gareth did not hear the gossip and know what was happening.

Gareth stared hard at Roger. His face was full of a listening intentness that made it seem, for a moment, as blind as his mother's. 'But that accident wasn't your fault.'

'The insurance company think it was. There are two women who could testify that the wheel flew off on its own, but they won't come forward.'

Gareth was silent.

'So it looks as if I'll have to pay the seventy-two quid. That'll teach me to go driving round in hired cars.'

Gareth drummed his fingers on the wheel. His eyes moved restlessly, then came back to Roger's. 'Finding life expensive, are you?'

'It's costing me about six pounds a week to live,' said Roger. 'I'm expecting that to level off now that I've got free accommodation, but on the other hand there's always the possibility that I might be prosecuted for moving in there in the owner's absence and then I'd be fined very heavily. That's if I was lucky and didn't go to prison.'

'I doubt if you'd get a prison sentence. There's no damage to the place and it'd be your first conviction.'

'Thank you for assuming that. It happens to be true, but still. There'd be a hell of a stink and the university'd probably ask for my resignation. All in all, it's a possibility I keep blanked off as far as I can – just never think about it. Meanwhile, I've got enough money to live on at the rate of five or six pounds a week till, well, sometime in February or March.'

Gareth's fingers became still. He lifted them gently from the wheel and folded his hands in his lap.

'That's all right then,' he said. 'Because we aren't likely to be still in business by then.'

'Are things that bad?'

'I could keep going for another three months,' said Gareth. 'even in spite of –' he nodded in the general direction of the liver-coloured bus and the hostile world beyond the windscreen. 'But there's the little matter of licensing. The insurance is paid up for a few months yet, but the licence is due on January the first. On January the second it'll be against the law to take the bus on to the road. And that'll be it. The money just isn't in the kitty.'

'How much is it?'

'Eighteen pounds ten,' said Gareth. 'That's for a thirty-two seater like this. If it was a forty-one seater like most of them, it'd be four pounds more.' He spoke fondly, leniently, as if the bus had done everything in its power to help them by not swelling into a forty-one seater.

'And you haven't got eighteen pounds ten?'

'Oh, I've got it,' said Gareth. 'But it's earmarked, see? If I spend that money on the licence, I shan't be able to get fuel and spares, so we'll go out of business anyway and the licence money'll just be wasted. You see,' he warmed to his theme, 'the front brake linings are near the end of their time anyway. In the next couple of weeks they'll wear down to the point where a Ministry spot-check'd fail the bus and it'd have to be taken off the road. So I'll have to replace them and I shan't be able to do it under eight quid. Then there's the worm-drive. I've had my –'

'Gareth,' Roger interrupted, 'we're staying in business till February at any rate and I'm paying the licence fee.'

'No. This has cost you enough already.'

'I say yes and I won't have any arguments. It's my money and if I want to stay here and work on the bus for another few weeks, that's my privilege.'

For a moment it seemed that Gareth was going to be stubborn. His shoulders moved under the scuffed leather jerkin as if he were shaping up for a fight. But before a contest could start, Roger got in with a decisive blow. 'Look at it this way. You owe it to the bus. She's run well and always done what we've asked of her. Wouldn't it be a bloody shame to take her off the road just for lack of a licence, when the money's ready and waiting?'

Gareth considered for a moment and then nodded. Without speaking, he got up from the driving-seat, went to the door of the bus, and slid it open. Then he turned to face Roger again.

'I'll take it,' he said, 'strictly as a loan. If we come through, I'll be able to pay it back out of the profits, in about May or June. And if we don't come through,' he paused, 'I'll get a job somewhere and pay it back out of my wages. You can send me your address if you're not here then.'

'Agreed.'

'Well,' said Gareth. He seemed about to thank Roger, but after a short hesitation all that came out was, 'See you at twelve.'

'See you.'

The little pot-bellied stove never went out. However dead and black it seemed, Roger only had to riddle it and then open the doors, and a beautiful combination of soft light and hard heat came glowing out. He did this at three o'clock next morning. He had been lying, broad awake, on Fräulein Inge's studio couch, staring up through the intense darkness to where he knew the ceiling was, only he could not see it. He could see nothing. Utter darkness reigned within him and without. He felt conscious of his body as a physical entity occupying a fixed position in space: the springs of the couch moved gently each time he stirred, adapting themselves to the contours of his hips and shoulders: beneath the bed was the plank floor, beneath the floor were the foundations of the chapel, beneath the foundations were the hard, ancient rocks, going down, down, through the granitic layer and the basaltic layer to the mantle of compressed iron-magnesium silicates, then down through the sulphide and oxide shell to the ceaselessly revolving core of the planet. He felt that core, as hard and hot and compressed as his own loveless heart. No, not loveless: unloved, that was a crueller and truer word. He loved, but he was not loved. So the love in his heart was untapped, unreleased. It would be more accurate to say that his heart was prepared for love, ready to give out love at the first sign that Jenny would be willing to let herself receive it ... *Jenny!* Unwittingly he had named her, lying alone in this darkness, feeling the roundness of the earth with his bones, knowing that only she could assuage the loneliness of lying on one's back on a revolving planet, enclosed in the troposphere, conscious of nothing but darkness.

Suddenly the thought of Jenny flooded his being so strongly that it was no longer bearable to lie still. He got up abruptly, tossing the blankets aside, and went first to the stove, to get it going, then to the window. The faint glow from the opened stove was just sufficient to guide him to the window without stumbling over anything, but the darkness remained intense: he could only just see where the window was framed, and the sky outside was totally black. Once more Roger had the feeling that his eyes were useless, that it was his bones, his nerves, his blood-vessels, that told him where he was and what lay about him. He could *feel* the mountains rearing up their enormous black heads all about him. It was his veins, muscles and joints that told him how the ground fell sharply away, over in the direction he was facing, until it ran down far enough to meet the tops of the strong, stunted oaks, that gnarled forest where the Druids had walked and chanted, and where their emanations would stay, intact and undiminished, through all the generations until the last tree was down.

Fancies. Feelings. Imaginings. Roger crossed the floor and snapped on the light, suddenly needing to banish the darkness, the loneliness, the motionless oaks and the moving Druids, not because these images were false but because they were true.

Sleep was impossible. He must talk, he must break this silence. And talk, to be meaningful, must be to the woman he stood ready to love. Quickly, savagely, he snatched up ballpoint and pad, dragged the one chair to a good position under the light and before the stove. Write, write, tell her. She'll put on her glasses and read it. Her glasses with their big black frames that make her face look even younger, its bones as fragile as a kitten's.

JENNY, Roger wrote,

I want to talk to you. Don't be afraid, just open your ears and listen. You'll read this with your eyes, but your ears will hear my voice. The vibrations of my body will flow into yours through the fingers that hold these sheets of paper, because I have held them in my hands that long to touch yours. But don't be afraid. The vibrations won't hurt you. If you think they might, keep the letter near you for a few days before you read it. Keep it in your dressing-gown pocket, or under your pillow if that smooth porker of a husband is away. Keep it somewhere that's near to you when you're relaxed and close to sleep. That way, the vibrations of your physical being will soak into the paper and make it harmless – take the sexual radioactivity out of it. That's a clumsy and ugly expression, sexual radioactivity. What I mean is love. I love you, Jenny, but you don't have to do anything about it. That's the only way to have a successful relationship – not to ask anything of the other person. Then, sometimes, they flow towards you.

That's enough about that. I want to talk to you about other things. About Geoffrey. I was so closed-up, so afraid to talk, about him when I had a chance to tell you face to face. When we sat on the sofa at Mrs Pylon Jones's, remember? When you said it must be a liberation for me that Geoffrey had died, and I said it was rather hard to explain and then funked it and talked about other things?

I don't live at Mrs Pylon Jones's now. I had to get out because hooligans were paid to throw paint and smash windows. That's something else again. It's to do with Gareth and his yellow bus. Not that it's really separate from Geoffrey. If there hadn't been Geoffrey in my life there wouldn't be Gareth now. I know that. But I mustn't start explaining from the wrong end. Perhaps it doesn't matter about explaining at all. But I want to tell you things, starting with the most important. It matters to you because I love you, and you might as well know what kind of person it is that loves you. And for me, it makes a sort of bridge to you, and gets over my loneliness. I live in an old chapel now, the one you come to if you climb out of Llancrwys on the little road that runs north, along the ridge looking down at the sea. I live here with somebody else's furniture and paintings. But the stove nuts are my own, and I have a store of lovely oak blocks, and I'll find some way of paying for the electricity. There's a haunted forest down the hill from here. Perhaps Geoffrey's there, with the Druids. But I don't think he'll do me any harm. I don't think anybody wishes me any harm, even Dic Sharp. I mean not personally, I'm just a bit of grit in a machine to him. He wants me to go away. But I don't think he hates me. I'm not close enough to anyone to have that kind of intense effect on them: I'm utterly alone. The big studio couch here makes me think about sex, but I expect that's over for me. I honestly don't think I'll ever have a woman again. I'm quite fit for it, but the ones I know don't seem to want me.

That makes me think of Margot. She was the great love of my life, till I met you. But perhaps it wasn't love at all. It certainly wasn't much like the feeling I have for you. Let me be straight about this, because I'm trying to sort out very complicated things and I shall go wrong if I don't keep it very clear and very honest. Margot was wonderful. I told you a bit about her, how she was getting away from a puritanical background. Getting away from it in all sorts of ways. Her father was a very tense man. He used to get into terrible nervous rages and dance up and down and scream at Margot and her sister. Perhaps he unconsciously wanted to rape them or something. The tension used to be colossal, and since the mother was a mousy little woman who scurried about and tried to hide behind the furniture, there wasn't any calm to be had. The sister was always having nervous breakdowns, but Margot was too strong for that. She got out and set up a life for herself that was as far removed from her family's as anything could be. One of the things she did was to cultivate this utterly cow-like calm. When I got to know her really well I could always tell when she was tense or worried about anything, because her movements slowed right down and she even blinked slowly, as if she were drugged or under hypnosis. It was her way of reacting against her father's high dramatic rages. I remember the first time we ever went to bed, when it all started. We'd spent one or two evenings together and then she invited me round to her place. Naturally I had my hopes, but I didn't know her at all well and

I couldn't see my way ahead. We had something to eat and then she sat down on a *chaise longue* that made her look like some adventuress from a novel of the early nineteen-twenties, and she kept looking steadily at me. Her speech-rate slowed down till it seemed as if she had some sort of impediment. Then she put a cigarette in her mouth and very, very slowly, she took out a match and struck it. But she moved her hand up to the cigarette so slowly that the match was half burnt out before it got there. Then she said something to me, some short sentence like 'Do you want a cigarette too?', something like that, just a few words, but it took her so long that the match-flame actually reached her fingers before she finished it. She moved the match on to the cigarette at exactly the same moment as it touched her fingers, and then of course she waved it out. It took her *three matches* to get that one cigarette alight. I was watching her in a trance. It hypnotised me. Afterwards, getting to know her, I realised that she was very stirred up inside. She was looking at me and deciding whether to get in at the deep end. The bed was waiting, I was waiting and it only wanted her to give the starting signal. Well, she gave it. And she kept on giving it. Sexually, she was terrific. Nothing will ever come up to that again. At least I don't see how it could.

No, I haven't forgotten whom I'm addressing. I know you're still with me, Jenny, reading this and turning over the pages and perhaps getting angry about all this brooding over another woman. But no. That misjudges you, doesn't it? I don't think you are a jealous person, and in any case, even if you were interested enough in me to feel jealousy, you wouldn't extend it backwards to something that's over. You understand. You know that the reason I'm going over it, and in your presence, is to make one last effort to sort it all out. Why did Margot mean so much to me? And why did it break up? I think they go together – the intensity of what we had, and the break-up. Because, as I told you, the official reason, so to speak, why we broke up was Geoffrey. I wanted to marry Margot and she wouldn't because she knew I would never send Geoffrey away to a hospital. And yet, is that all? Didn't I single out Margot, allow myself to be sucked right into the heart of her mystery, because – just because – I could never domesticate her, never make her go along with my life-style. Geoffrey was, if you like, the big, conspicuous concrete manifestation of that, but the more I think of it the more I realise that I didn't *want* her to be attainable. That was why her eyes attracted me so much. Yes, she had those strange green eyes, at least they seemed green to me. Ice-green. I looked into her eyes many hundreds of times, stared into them deeply, tried to get lost in them and never come out but I could never quite read what I saw there. *That was what drove me insane*. I'd look straight into her eyes while I was making love to her. Usually she'd start off with her eyes closed, but after I'd been giving it to her for a bit, taking it slowly to start with, she'd open these green eyes and look straight up at me with those undecipherable depths inside them. It used to make me feel I'd give anything, anything at all, to get right inside her, into her innermost fibres, right in where she lived, to find the central core that was Margot and nothing else but Margot, find it and shoot hot sperm into it. No wonder she was satisfied with me. I used to get such a devil's own erection that nothing she could do would break it down.

When we broke up over the issue of Geoffrey, I felt real grief. I don't think I was fooling myself. After all, a great chunk of my life was being dragged away without anaesthetic. Deep down, I may have willed it, yet we sometimes will our own agony and crucifixion. I needed Margot, even if I needed Geoffrey more. Even if the reason I chose her in the first place was because, at the centre of my being, I didn't want to share Geoffrey with a woman. He was my brother, and my penance, and my victim, and my support, all in one.

Now I'm talking wildly. What does that cluster of terms mean? I don't know, Jenny, not exactly. But I'll try to get near it. And thank you, dear love, for listening and helping me to get all this out. Christ knows I may not even post it. Your lovely eyes may never even see it, your eyes as lovely as Margot's but different altogether, hungry and attainable. I can read what I see in your eyes: need and pain and laughter all whirled together. Yes, and pride: pride that won't yield till it finds good cause.

Wait a moment, love, while I put some more stove nuts on. I don't want the place to get cold. By the time that late dawn crawls over the sky, I want to get everything said.

The stove's fuelled and I'm back in my chair. Let me put it all down about Geoffrey. He would want me to. If he's down there in the oak forest, he can come up here if he likes, and stand behind me and read this over my shoulder. If he wants to be in this too, I welcome him.

What was it that made Geoffrey so utterly necessary to me? Was it something to do with what I owed him? That seems a funny way to put it: I looked after him for years, organised my life round him, interrupted my work for him, sacrificed any hope of domestic happiness with a woman for him: surely it was *he* who owed me? From the outside, yes, that might be true. But nobody who was outside could understand what happened during those nineteen hours.

What nineteen hours? My darling girl, my Jenny whom I love for ever even if we never see each other again, I speak of nineteen hours between an early Friday morning and a late Saturday night in the year of Our Lord Nineteen Forty-Four. Were you born, then, Jenny? I think you were a little girl, having welfare orange juice and playing with a doll in the quiet front room of a well-run bourgeois house in the north. I hope you were happy that Friday morning, that you ate your breakfast and played nicely and that your Daddy was at home and came into the house for lunch and took you on his knee. I'll tell you what I was doing. I was lying bent double under a few tons of beams and bricks and rubble. I could breathe, but I couldn't straighten up, and for about ten hours I had cramp so badly that I thought I wouldn't be able to stand it, that the cramp would kill me even if the air didn't give out. Well, the air didn't give out. The cramp wore into numbness after about the tenth hour, and I kept on bending double and breathing, but I never expected to see daylight again. I was sixteen years old, and I kept thinking, 'Sixteen years isn't a bad life. Lots of people don't live that long. Whole species of animals don't live that long.' I expect my mental state was odd and dislocated. I was a bit concussed as well as cramped. But, for whatever reason, I didn't feel too sorry for myself. It was Geoffrey I felt sorry for. He was in the same room with me – we shared a big bedroom – and I knew he was trapped somewhere nearby, because I could hear him. He made every kind of noise. He was much more badly hurt than I was. Sometimes he sobbed, sometimes he cried quietly, sometimes he made no sound at all, and then at other times he lifted his voice up and howled, yes, howled like a wolf. His mind was going, but before it went he said goodbye to life.

It was a flying-bomb that did it, Jenny. I don't suppose you remember, but after the Germans stopped their air-raids, in about 1941, we had two or three years of respite, and then in the later stages of the war they started sending over these pilotless flying bombs, a sort of baby version of the big stuff we shall get next time, whenever it's to be. They weren't as bad as the earlier blitz, in a way, because they came in an isolated, desultory way, one here and one there, and nobody bothered to sound the air-raid sirens; there was no point in putting the whole town on alert for one bomb, and in any case there was no time. The thing would just appear in the sky, drone along for a bit, then cut out and fall in a horrible silence that was broken by the appalling bang. People got used to them. My father saw one land smack on a fish-queue. One minute they were all standing there with their string bags and brown-paper carriers, the next they were all in little pieces, and he came on home and had his tea. You didn't waste food in those days.

Well, that Friday morning it was our turn. My mother and father were asleep in the parental bed. Geoffrey and I were asleep in our room next to theirs, it was four o'clock in the morning and Geoffrey was on leave. He was twenty-one. He'd been on some sort of officers' training course and he was just about to pass out and get his commission. We'd all been up late the night before, mildly celebrating. Mother and Dad didn't have any military ambition and neither of them cared at all whether Geoffrey went through the war as an officer or a private as long as he went through it and came out at the other end, but since he had been selected as officer material, they were glad he had been successful and wouldn't be returned to the ranks as a misfit. They had all the normal emotions of pride in their sons. In the end, of course, it was they who didn't survive. When the rescue people finally got the house off us, at about one a.m. on the Saturday, they were both dead. I was all right except that I needed a fairly long spell of attention in a hospital, and Geoffrey was – well, Geoffrey was Geoffrey. The new Geoffrey, the one who had howled his fare-well to the life of a young, alert, well-washed, high-I.Q. young officer-to-be, and entered on his own particular *vita nuova*.

It was an accident you see. There was no reason why the beams and bricks should have fallen in that particular way, to leave me relatively all right but Geoffrey so agonisingly trapped and imprisoned that he never got well again. There was no reason in our characters, in anything we had done to deserve good luck or bad. War-time was like that even more than ordinary time is. One man survives, the man standing next to him doesn't. And if it had been a quick, clean death I wouldn't have thought more than that about it. I'd have buried Geoffrey decently, as (with the help of some grizzling relatives from Polperro) I buried my parents, and that would have been all. He'd have been a name on a war memorial: a brother I used to have. But those nineteen hours changed everything. All through them, except for a few short spells towards the end when I was unconscious, I listened to Geoffrey's noises and I knew what he was going through. And even while it was going on, I couldn't rid myself of the thought: *he is bearing it for me.* Oh, I know there's no logic to it. The whole thing was nothing but an accident. If I had been sleeping where Geoffrey was, I'd have got what he got. Come to that, I did sometimes sleep in his bed while he was away. It was by the window, and I liked it better. He had the choice because he was the elder, and he'd chosen that position. And it was that that did it for him. I listened to him, hour after hour, and I wondered if we'd meet in some future state of existence. 'The next world,' I called it. Well, the next world started, for both of us, when they dug us out on that dark Saturday night. A world in which the chief thing I wanted to do was bear some of Geoffrey's pain because he had borne so much that might have been mine.

It took me years, of course, to get myself educated and qualified and get a job. But as soon as I was getting a salary, I set up some kind of home and approached the hospital people to let me take Geoffrey under my roof. They probably wouldn't have let me, being so young and raw, if their own position hadn't been desperate: they were turning out anyone who had as much as a slum home to go to, as long as they could call it 'home'.

So I had Geoffrey, and he became my life. All my troubles came from that, but so did all my strength: in fact, I didn't know what other kind of strength there was, or where you could find it. Paying what I owed to Geoffrey was the only thing I understood. If I hadn't paid him, I'd have had to go back into that wreckage and be bent double again. My love for him was the sign that I was grateful for survival.

Strange, the ruts people get themselves into. I don't need to tell you that, Jenny, because you're in a rut yourself and you're perfectly clear-sighted about it. My rut had very deep sides. I clung to my suffering over Geoffrey because if I hadn't protected him and paid for it in the hard cash of deprivation, I'd have felt I had no right to live. Just as you feel that if you left your husband, and took your children away from their comfortable anchorage where they can be watched over and approved of by *both* parents, you'd have no right to live. And you'll understand me – I'm not using fancy phrases in a void. It does happen to people to become convinced that they have no right to live, and that's when they commit suicide. It's the sickness unto death. They feel that instead of sharing in the bounty of life, they're just standing about like uninvited guests, that nobody's going to speak to them or offer them a glass of anything, and they're condemned to stand there in a draughty spot near the door and be ignored. So they just move quietly to the door and leave.

If those last few sentences seem to hint that I've been considering killing myself, I must correct the impression. I never got that far down the slide. For one thing, Geoffrey was taken from me by the gentlest of all the sundering powers: death is always easier to take than separation or betrayal. I looked after him for all the days and nights that were allowed to him. Towards the end, when he couldn't get out of bed, I got a professional nurse in, but I still spent a lot of time with him. I drew strength from him right to the end: strength, and justification, and forgiveness. Not specifically from *him*, because he was never aware that there was anything to forgive me for. But I knew there was. I had to be forgiven for my good luck, for the way the beams and bricks had fallen.

I can't tell you what Geoffrey died of. They threw so many medical terms at me that I felt pretty sure they meant he just died because he had had twenty years of being Geoffrey, of being the Geoffrey who was lifted out after those nineteen hours in hell. He had cerebral ischaemia: that was what the doctors generally called it, during those twenty years. But various complications set in, all with long names, and the long names just meant that he was tired. He couldn't go on fighting for life any longer.

So it wasn't too hard for me, Jenny, and I kept calm. I quietly closed up the flat and put dust-sheets over the furniture and came up here with a programme to fulfil and beyond it a nice little scheme for feathering my own nest and taking care of my wants. Apart from looking after Geoffrey, I've always been a very selfish person. (And even the business of protecting *him*, as I've said, was done for my own sake, to keep away the nightmares.) All my other dealings with the world have been round the edges of Geoffrey, so to speak, and spiritually I've never felt it necessary to give more than the dregs of my energies. Except to Margot – I did feel I genuinely loved her, and certainly a great part of me wanted her – but I've explained about that. When I came up to Caerfenai, my conscious programme was to allow my selfishness full rein, to look after number one and damned well do it with conviction.

And now, as I sit here in the dark pre-morning, squatting like a tramp in a deserted chapel that isn't even a chapel any more but somebody's love-nest, just about the only thing I can see clearly is that that neat little programme has collapsed. I thought I was too old to change, I thought getting used to Geoffrey's being dead was the last major adjustment I'd ever have to make, and I was glad of that. Change is pain, that's how I formulated it to myself: April is the cruellest month. But now, before I finish this letter and tear it up or put it in the stove or perhaps, my darling, even post it to you for you to put your big black glasses on and read when nobody's about, what I want to confess to you, joyfully and humbly, is that I *am* changed: I wasn't too old, too dry, too stiff: the mountains have changed me and the sea has changed me, and the steepness of the road up and down to Llancrwys, and Gareth and his Mam, and Madog and Gwilym Cherokee and Mario with his hair, and Rhiannon whom I lusted for, and you whom I both lust for and love, and Ivo and Gito, all these have made me different. I'm no cleverer than I was when I got off that train last October, but I'm much wiser, and a bit braver, and a lot freer.

So, for all these things, take my blessing. Take it to yourself and let it radiate out from you to the life around you, because there are no nicely defined limits that show where it ends and you begin. And now, since writing all this has made me sleepy and gives me cramped fingers, I'm going to get into bed and sleep till it's time to go to my work – my funny, sad, brave, hopeless, going-through-the-motions non-work that is still the most important thing I could be doing except loving you.

Without reading through, he scrawled a big 'Roger' at the end of it, tossed the heap of crumpled sheets on to a chair, and, rolling into the Fräulein's bed, fell asleep. When the alarm clock woke him, he got up wearily, and moved slowly about, poking the stove, making tea and dressing, for nearly half an hour before he remembered the letter; then, gathering up the sheets and folding them roughly, he stuffed them, in any order, into an envelope. He did this more to quieten the letter, to keep it from bringing itself to his attention, than because he had decided to send it. But later that day, in a slack period between runs, he went into the Post Office and looked up Jenny's address in the telephone book, under 'Twyford, G.R.', and scribbled it on the envelope and quickly posted the letter. As it slipped irretrievably into the box he felt a quick urge to grab it back; then the thought came, 'I might have burnt it: but she will burn it, anyway, when she has read it: and why not let her know what kind of man it is who loves her?'

That evening, Roger felt gay. He spent more time and money than usual in the pub, where Mario taught him an Italian song and Madog, who had dumped his Canadian ally somewhere, discoursed long and swiftly of Meilyr and Gwalchmai ap Meilyr. Roger got slightly drunk, and, on the ten o'clock run up to Llancrwys, gave several passengers the wrong change.

Now the days were short and dark, and the shop windows were rectangles of yellow light that pushed itself out into the streets like something solid, so triumphantly did it assert its thick waxy brightness against the meagre, damp air and the cloud that lay inertly just above roof-level. The crowds on the narrow pavements grew thicker every day, for Christmas was coming. More people travelled, taking with them more parcels, till every available bus was jammed to the doors, and though the liver-coloured pirate did his best, running indefatigably two minutes ahead of Gareth, the long patient queues were glad enough to climb on to any bus that drove up to them, whether they rode free or paid, and there were many times during those three or four weeks when the yellow bus was as crowded as its predator, and the leather bag on Roger's shoulder felt blessedly heavy. But Gareth's face remained set and grim, none of its straight lines relaxed into a gentler curve, and Roger knew that, even with this slight gain in their takings, they were not holding enough ground. Christmas was not for them; the fat season saw them growing leaner every day. Good-will rang from the steeples, but to them the dark rainy roads seemed dangerous, full of unknown threats. One afternoon, trundling down the main street of Caerfenai, they thought for one heart-stopping moment that they had run over a child. The pavements were crowded with laden shoppers, and a little boy of about five, who had been pushed away from his parents by the shoving tide of adult bodies and saw them moving away ahead of him, grew frightened, darted into the gutter to get round the slow bulk of two fat women and a pram, and suddenly slipped and fell, going down on the greasy road right under (or so it seemed) their nearside front wheel. Gareth pulled the bus to a sharp halt, following drivers braked in a long line, and in an instant Roger was outside, the bag bumping on his hip, expecting to see a white, blood-splotched little corpse. What he saw was a child scrambling up unhurt and running away like a rabbit, what he heard was a chorus of clucking and high female Welsh voices. But the surge of relief that visited his heart, as he climbed back on to the bus and told Gareth that all was well, lasted only a moment, and the underlying fear and foreboding stayed cold and packed-down as old snow round the roots of a tree.

Neither of them mentioned the incident afterwards, but Roger had the impression – though it was quite impossible to say how far this might have been simply his own fancy – that a new and more dispirited phase of their life set in on that afternoon. Gareth seemed more silent, if that were possible, than he had been since the autumn: utterly preoccupied, sunk within himself, as if the inward sulphur of his troubles had choked his mind and reduced him to an automaton. There had been times, in the previous few weeks, when Roger had feared a violent upshot of their situation: it had been all too easy to imagine Gareth, white-hot with silent rage, cornering the dish-faced driver of the liver-coloured bus, or his ferrety confederate, and choking the life out of him with those great steely fingers. Now, this phase was past. Gareth seemed hardly aware of the hideous mirage that hovered perpetually in front of them. The driver still took good care to scuttle away to his unknown lurking-place, but Roger had the impression that now, even if he had sauntered over to Gareth one day in the square and stood insolently in front of him, Gareth would simply have regarded him uncomprehendingly with those unseeing eyes, like a hawk permanently wearing its leather hood.

Then, one day, Gareth did speak. It was a low, dark morning in the square, when the stones of the castle seemed to have drunk whatever light was in the sky and converted it into weight with which they pressed down on the earth as if trying to force their way down into it and be done with their long task of holding up. Rain was about, but it was not raining at that moment. Gareth and Roger were standing in front of the bus, and for some reason Roger's eye noted that the radiator cap was exactly on a level with Gareth's hair-streaked dome.

'Christmas,' Gareth said as if to himself, looking at two

women who laboured slowly towards them with armfuls of trumpery parcels. Then he turned and looked directly at Roger. 'What will you be doing?'

'Sitting in my chapel with a bottle of something and drinking myself to sleep,' Roger answered promptly.

'Oh,' Gareth considered this gravely. 'I thought you might be going off for a day or two. You know, to family.'

'No.'

'Well, it's no good being on your own at Christmas,' said Gareth. 'Come and spend it with me and Mam.'

Roger's chest felt tight. Without ever admitting it to his conscious mind, he had, he now realized, been dreading Christmas Day, dreading it to the point of panic.

'I'd love to,' he said.

'Just pot luck, mind,' said Gareth. 'But we'll get our hands on something.'

From that moment, the Christmas at Gareth's became the focus of Roger's life. As he rode up and down on the bus, or swept out the chapel and prepared his crude meals of tinned food, or sat resting in front of his gleeful little stove, his thoughts turned constantly to it. What would they eat? Drink? Do? Talk about? Would Gareth's mother wear her thick brown cardigan, or would she dig out some faded 'best' clothes for the occasion? Would they sit stiffly and watch the clock, or would the magic of the snug interior, the warmth and light, the day freed of effort, work on them and bring out confidences?

He weighed carefully, many times, the question of what gifts or contributions he should take along. Would Gareth take it amiss if he were to come staggering across the field to the front door of the cottage with his arms barely meeting round a great bundle of luxuries? He longed, fiercely, to draw out the rest of his pitiful stock of money and squander it on the sort of celebration that Gareth and Gareth's Mam would never, otherwise, know in their lives: hothouse fruit, really good wine and plenty of it, a turkey, dates, walnuts, some old port and a French brandy, cigars . . . What was the use of that miserable little sum lying against his name in the bank? It would keep him alive, at cheese-paring level, long enough to watch Gareth's final pecking to death by rooster Dic Sharp, and where was the fun in that? Wouldn't it be better to blow it all on one glorious day of reckless feasting, and then, in the cold dark of the morning after, close up the chapel and creep away, leaving Gareth to founder and go to the bottom with no other eyes on him but the pitying, blind orbs of the woman who had suckled him?

He longed to make the big, wild gesture; at times even planned to make it. Sitting by his own stove, he would decide to go into the bank as soon as it opened in the morning. But when the morning came, he never quite mustered the resolution to do so. It was not that he was afraid of misinterpretation, the gesture's falling flat. He knew Gareth, by now, well enough to be confident that any spontaneous act of goodwill would be acceptable in the hunchback's driven life. No, it was something beyond that. Gareth was so clear-sighted, so intelligent with the direct, grasping intelligence of one who has never had to waste brain-power on inessentials. And Gareth would know at once, if Roger drew out his money and splashed it out in a communal libation, that he was giving up. That money was Roger's fighting fund, and to spend it would be the announcement that he had no stomach to go on fighting. This, Roger could not bear. He did not intend to witness Gareth's final humiliation, but neither did he want to leave him encircled by his enemies as long as there was a cartridge or two in his belt.

In the end, he settled for a bottle of good white wine and a bottle of whisky. They could go into his deep overcoat pockets, one on each side. He could hang up his overcoat on getting there, judge the mood of the occasion, and say nothing about the bottles till the moment offered itself. Then he could bring out the wine, to drink with their food, and say nothing about the whisky till afterwards. Little by little, as they relaxed and the day wore on, he could make his contribution.

Lying in the dark, listening to the wind moving across the mountainside and sighing down below in the druid-forest, he realized that the tact he was bringing to bear, the patient strategy in avoiding offence, was not integral to his nature. It had been put there by the long years with Geoffrey.

A week before Christmas, Roger had a nightmare so terrifying that he could not shake free of it after waking up. He dreamt that he was walking on the mountain of slate that overhung Gareth's cottage. At first the footing was firm and the climb exhilarating: he bounded up the twisting path between the walls of piled slate as if his shoes had rocket-propulsion built into them. But when he reached the top, and looked out over the sea, it was covered with high white waves that came racing in towards the shore, horrible in their eagerness to drink the land and smother all its life. Rooted to the spot, he stared at the hurrying waves that flung themselves further and further up the shore and began to climb the mountain towards where he stood, and it was too late before he realized that they were not the real danger, only a fiendish decoy, and that the slate-heap was beginning to shift and settle under him. He struggled to keep his feet, and succeeded, but the neatly stacked pieces of slate and rock began to slide, to totter, to fall in crashing heaps and cascade down on to the cottage. Roger, strangling in his dream, tried to shout with all the power of his lungs, to warn Gareth and Mam to hurry out from under their doomed roof, even if it meant running down the mountain towards the white-headed waves that licked hungrily up, but no sound came from his tight throat, and silent, aghast, he watched the first wave of burial, and then the second, and then the third, thud and slither on to the roof far below. Every movement he made, whether forward or back, only dislodged more slates, and now the cottage had disappeared from sight, and he knew that Gareth and his mother were buried for ever, deeper than he and Geoffrey had been by that wicked bomb, deeper even than his parents, whose squashed bodies had been hastily hidden in the earth, beyond the reach of grain-storing memory or groping love.

Then he woke, and poked up the stove into a blaze, and put on his clothes and went out. It was six o'clock in the morning, and dawn was not to be looked for, at that season, till eight. But there was enough light to walk by, if one were frightened and distressed enough to need to walk: and his feet took him over to the top of the village, and up the narrow lane that turned into a stony path, and on between the black walls of slate, till he stood in the grey emptiness that was neither night nor day, and looked over at the sea, which lay flat and quiet in what might have been the last rays of starlight or the first premonitory lifting of dawn. Nothing moved. The slates lay as they had lain, one upon the other, for a hundred years: the sea was a broad plain with room for all the wanderers who would ever live; the slate-tip was a mountain packed with secrets. And there, below him, as he stood motionless and gazed down, the outline of the cottage roof slowly formed itself. Gareth and Mam were safe in there, sleeping, immune. His fears were calmed. But he could not bring himself, yet, to move away. He stood immovable, as the dawn moved on its slow hinge and opened a crack of heaven-coloured light somewhere behind the mountains at his back, and gradually the grass became green and the whitewashed walls of Gareth's cottage picked themselves out in bravery, and finally a square of yellow light appeared in the kitchen window. Gareth was up, he had put the kettle on, he would be making tea for himself and Mam, putting on his trousers and boots for another day. Dic Sharp had still not quite won, and Roger's dream had been nothing to do with Gareth and Mam after all: just a cry from the past, the falling-away of a scab from his own ancient, incurable wound.

Christmas Day dawned amid white, freezing mist. As Roger walked along the lane towards Gareth's, the bottles dragged at his pockets. The sun was a low red disc and the mist went all the way up to the sky. Even the tops of the mountains were not wholly clear.

He opened the gate, went across the field, and knocked on the cottage door. It was eleven o'clock; he had timed his arrival with some care, so as to be early enough to help with the preparations but not so early as to intrude on a scene of comfortable late rising. Evidently it was right: Gareth, in his shirt sleeves but shaved and combed, opened the door at once.

'Merry Christmas,' he said gravely.

'That's come true already,' said Roger.

He entered. The old woman was sitting in her accustomed place. She wore the usual brown cardigan, but over it, across her broad fleshless shoulders, she had arranged a fine fringed shawl, decorated with intricate needlework. Perhaps the needle that made those thousands of patient stitches had been her own, half a century earlier; perhaps her eyes, in their days of keenness, had put in all those hours of close and loving observation.

'Nadolig Llawen,' she said.

Roger felt exhilarated. His sense of occasion was roused by

her Welsh greeting and her embroidered shawl. Yes, this was to be a special day.

From now on, the three of them spoke in Welsh.

Sit down, Gareth commanded, drawing up a chair for Roger. The fire was hot and clear; it must have been lit at least two hours earlier.

But I want to help, Roger protested.

You can do that by keeping Mam company. Nobody's allowed in the kitchen. I'm cooking the feast and what I've got is a secret till I bring it in.

Roger, willingly allowing Gareth to be captain of his own ship, hung up his overcoat ready to sit down. But first (why not?) he took out the bottle of wine, an excellent hock that he had chosen very deliberately from the stock of the best wine merchant in the district.

Here's something to wash it down with. It needs to be cold so I'll stand it outside.

Gareth took the bottle for a moment in his great hand.

Wine, eh? he said.

I thought I'd like to bring something, said Roger simply.

I'm a beer man myself. But it does no harm to break out of your habits now and then. I've got a bottle or two of beer in, and to tell you the truth I've opened a couple already, in the kitchen, while I've been doing the vegetables. If I mix my drinks too much, you'll have to put me to bed.

Laughter forced its way up from the echo-chamber of his chest.

All cooks drink, said Roger. The heat of the kitchen lets them sweat it out.

He opened the door and put the bottle outside in the misty morning. A solitary crow alighted, eyed the bottle, and flew disappointedly away.

Closing the door, Roger went and sat beside Mam. Gareth had already disappeared into the kitchen and shut the door firmly.

Mr Furnivall, said the old woman.

I'm here.

There's something I want you to do.

For an instant, Roger felt an anticipatory twinge just above the knee, where her powerful old fingers had gripped him the time before, when she so urgently needed to ask him for news of Gareth's troubles. But there was no urgency this time: on the contrary, her serenity was palpable, authoritative.

There's a little drawer in the table.

He looked round and located it. Yes, he said.

Please open it and tell me what you find.

He slid the drawer open and took out two thick, round, crinkly shapes. Crepe bandages? No, paper streamers, egad.

Gareth didn't get anything to decorate the place with, said the old woman, smiling into the fire. I suppose he thinks it doesn't matter because I can't see them and he doesn't mind about such things. But the last time I went down to the shop with Maldwyn, the day before Christmas Eve it was, they said they had two of these big paper streamers left over and nobody would be buying them now and would I take them as a present. I said yes straight away. I thought it was very kind of them, because after all they could have put them back into stock for next year.

Roger turned the unwieldy packets over in his hands.

Shall I put them up? he asked.

Yes, she said eagerly. Do it while Gareth's in the kitchen. There's a little hammer and some tacks on the sideboard behind me.

Roger took the hammer and tacks, broke open the first packet, and, seizing a chair to stand on, began working fast and efficiently. In a moment he had the first streamer running right round the four walls. Then he took out the second one and looped it across from the centre to the corners.

How does it look? Mam asked.

Pretty good, to me, he answered, putting the chair back against the wall. I dare say a woman would do it better.

What colour are they?

One's red and silver, the other's yellow and green.

She sighed with pleasure and folded her hands.

I heard you, Gareth shouted from the kitchen. I heard you hammering. What's the game?

Just cracking nuts, Roger called. Go back to your work.

Gareth's chuckle flowed round them as they sat conspiratorially by the fire.

For a few minutes, neither of them spoke, and it crossed Roger's mind to wonder whether Mam would renew her questioning about the state of Gareth's affairs. But, as he glanced across at her calm face, he realized that this was a mistake. Nothing would make her pollute this day with the anxieties of the world.

To draw her on to a topic that she would enjoy, he asked her a question about her late husband and their life together in this house. Her answers were freely informative.

Gareth had already told Roger, as they walked towards the cottage on that first visit, that his father had been dead fifteen years. Now Mam added the all-important fact that it was only since his death that her sight had failed her. Their life together had been happy, he could tell that : small frugalities, the saving of candle-ends, a meal of butcher's meat only on Sundays and festivals; but tragedy and disappointment they had been spared – unless, Roger thought, you counted the grief it must have been to them that their only child had proved misshapen. Or was that deeply felt as a grief ? Wouldn't he have been, to his mother at any rate, simply her child, simply Gareth ? And the father, however it may have hurt him to see the lopsided whelp in its cradle, would have been reassured as the years went by and Gareth grew into a prodigy of strength, a knotted and twisted oak that nothing could push down.

Have you a photograph of your husband ? he asked Mam.

Up in my room, she answered.

It pleased him to think that she kept her Geraint's picture near her bed, where she could reach out and touch it on waking. For that, surely, was the motive. And he forbore to question further. Whether Geraint had been a man big enough to match her size, or the strong gnome he had originally imagined to be the only father for Gareth, would remain mysterious. It was right that some things should be left in the shadows.

A warning whoop from Gareth told Roger to get the table laid. Under Mam's direction he found the thick white cloth, the cutlery, the carving-fork and knife. There were no wine-glasses, but on the dresser he found what seemed to be a medicine glass, which he put beside Mam's place, and ordinary half-pint tumblers for himself and Gareth.

Appetites ready ? Gareth called from the kitchen. We'll be eating in two minutes.

Roger hurried to the front door. The wine was chilled to

exactly the right temperature by the nipping air. A hasty question to Mam, and he was directed to a corkscrew. Working fast, he had just got the cork out and poured the first glass when Gareth flung open the door from the kitchen.

Clear the way! he shouted. Clear the way for the head cook of the royal household!

He marched in, holding a large meat-dish proudly high. On it lay a brown richly smoking shape. A delicious smell of delicate roast meat and herbs came with him on his progress to the table.

A hare! cried the old woman. I can smell it, Gareth! I know I'm right!

Gareth set down the dish with tender pride.

Not just an ordinary hare, he said. A hare of the mountain. I snared it myself. I've been very busy these last few days. I snared three, as a matter of fact, but the first two weren't good enough for a feast like this. The first was just a leveret, and the second was an old female, very bony. But this one, ah!

Roger gazed with reverence at the dish.

I'll just get the vegetables, said Gareth, while you help Mam to the table and get her settled with everything she needs.

He disappeared, and came back with a huge pan of roast potatoes, a dish of Brussels sprouts, and three plates heated to such a temperature that even his work-inured hands could not hold them without a cloth.

Roger, having installed Mam in her chair on the side nearest the fire, was just about to take his own seat when he noticed that the old woman was sitting very still and upright, with one hand raised for silence.

Gareth?

Yes, Mam?

Are you ready for me to say grace?

Gareth laid down the carving-knife and stood, immobile, beside his chair.

Say it, Mam.

O Lord, the old woman said, here we are just about to eat another good Christmas dinner through Thy mercy and love. I've seen seventy-two Christmases and I've never failed to have something good to eat on them, since I grew my first set of teeth, and it's all Thy mercy and love, Lord.

Roger salivated as the smell of the roast hare came to his

nostrils, but the stillness was profound, and hungry as he was he did not want it to be broken yet.

This is a special Christmas, Lord, as Thou knowest, said Mam. Our lives have got much more difficult this year and they may get more difficult still, but Thou hast sent into our lives a new friend, who has come from we don't know where, and decided to give us his help we don't know why, but it gives us joy, O Lord, that he is here with us to share our feast this day.

Amen, said Gareth.

And to remember with us the birth in Bethlehem, she finished.

They stood for a moment without breaking the spell, and then Mam said briskly. Now, Gareth, carve! And Gareth carved.

I never knew before, said Roger with his mouth full, that you could roast a hare.

I've come round to it, said Gareth. I've stewed 'em and I've cooked 'em with belly of pork. But I think they taste finest of all when they're roasted.

He drank off his wine.

Goes well, that.

Have some more, said Roger, pouring.

I killed this hare cleanly, said Gareth. Snapped his neck like a matchstick. So he didn't lose a drop of blood.

How much did he weigh? Mam asked.

Before I cut his head and neck off, and skinned him, said Gareth in a calculating voice, his head slightly on one side, I should say about, well, six pounds.

They ate on in silence for a few minutes.

It's lucky that Gareth was able to turn his hand to cooking so well, said Mam, evidently to Roger. He never cooked a meal till I started losing my sight.

Ah, well, it wasn't sudden, said Gareth. You had plenty of chance to coach me while it was coming on.

Drinking the last of the wine, Roger looked quickly from one of them to the other. How strong they were, how matter-of-fact and without self-pity. Mam's blindness was a fact they had both accepted, and whatever agony it had caused them was now assimilated and conquered. That she was blind was simply one of the given conditions of life, such as that the mountains were steep, the rocks hard, and the wind from the sea always in their faces.

When they had cleaned out every dish and pushed away their empty plates, Gareth stood up.

I hope you've kept some room, he said. There's a Christmas pudding.

Good God, said Roger. What genius!

Oh, it's from the shop, said Gareth quickly. I know when I'm beaten. But I thought Christmas wouldn't be right without it. It's just a little one.

This was the time, Roger decided, to go to his coat pocket and produce the whisky. They arrived back at the table at the same moment.

Something to pour over it, he said, unscrewing the bottle.

You're the genius, said Gareth simply.

Roger poured some of the whisky on to the tiny pudding, and Gareth took out a box of matches and lit it. They watched gravely as the small blue halo flickered for a moment.

It should be brandy really, Roger apologized.

I'm sure this is just as good, man.

The pudding despatched, they stacked the dishes and sat down by the fire to enjoy the sensation of being full-fed, warm, peaceful, and permeated by alcohol.

Are you in a draught, Mam?

Not the least bit.

Outside, the short day was already sinking downward. Sheep would be penned together for fleecy warmth, and, soon, the mist would condense into freezing drops on the heather. The year was turning, turning on a bleak axle of darkness and cold.

Roger and Gareth were slowly sipping whisky from their tumblers.

Have a drop more,

It keeps the cold out, Gareth acquiesced.

Don't be silly, Gareth, said his mother. By this fire there's no cold to keep out.

It's lubrication, said Gareth calmly, pouring a couple of inches into his glass. Same as the bus. Keeps condensation out of the cylinders.

He drank, appreciatively.

They sat in silence for a few minutes. Roger noticed that the light coming in through the window, on the seaward side, had changed from a cheese-cloth white to a rich, warm pink. He was about to remark on it when a sudden qualm about Mam's blindness caused him to keep silent. Was it right to mention a fine sunset when sitting with someone from whose eyes the colour of sunsets had faded for ever?

The light grew richer: from pink it deepened to a wonderful crimson, that glowed in a square on the whitewashed wall behind Gareth's somnolent head. Roger, lifting his glass, saw that his hand was bathed in this same crimson. Then he noticed that Gareth's eyes were wide open, and that he was staring across the room and through the window.

Mr Idris, Mam, Gareth said suddenly.

Where? Is he coming to call? she asked.

No, said Gareth. He's going past the gate, with his dog.

Walking off his Christmas dinner, she said.

And getting a bit of peace from his wife's cousins, Gareth added.

Now, Gareth. Don't make a mock of Mr Idris. He's a good friend to you. And he may be a better one yet.

Roger turned and stared out into the unbelievable sunset. Across the flaring skyline a small human silhouette walked steadily, hunched a little against the cold, and with a dog-silhouette at its heels.

Who's Mr Idris? Roger asked.

Explosives man at the quarry, said Gareth briefly. He poured a little more whisky into his glass and set the bottle down within Roger's reach.

He's a good friend to Gareth, said Mam. Her voice was quiet, but there was a kind of insistence in it.

Roger felt he was in the presence of some situation whose outlines he could not feel. There was a moment of silence, and he wondered if he ought to move on to some other topic. Then Gareth spoke.

What Mam's talking about is this. I know how to handle explosives. Once I had almost a year at it, working up there – he nodded towards the quarry and I got pretty skilled at the blasting. I could take out just the area of stone they wanted, not a chip more or less. I got a natural feel for it, you see. And Mr Idris, he was just starting then, he worked with me. Well, he's retiring next year. And he's been down here two or three times to know if I want the job when he goes.

I see, said Roger.

Of course Gareth wouldn't take the job if he could keep on with the bus, said Mam. Her blind face was caught in the crimson light, and her work-squared hands lay still in her lap. But the way things are, it's good to know there's something else.

Roger did not know what to say, but he felt some answer was necessary. He looked into the fire and said, There's always something else.

Not for me, there isn't, said Gareth. I'm hard to please.

Suddenly, he gave one of his rare smiles.

If I can't keep on the bus, he went on, it'll be a question of getting a job. And all the jobs are down in the town. I want to stay up here.

Is it as important as that? Roger asked.

Gareth nodded vigorously. I live here, he said.

But said the old woman urgently, what about when I die, Gareth? You can't stay up here all alone. You'll need a little house in the town.

I shall stay up here, said Gareth. It's the only place where I feel right.

The square of sunset-colour travelled slowly across the wall behind him: now it was beginning to touch his shoulder and the edge of his face. To Roger, watching him, it seemed that the wild creature Gareth most resembled was not, after all, a hawk or an eagle, but a badger. Yes, a powerful grey badger, despite the red of his thin hair: living there in his set at the foot of the slate cliff, undislodgeable, shy, proud.

And implacably hunted.

I shall go back to the blasting, Gareth said. That's the way to stay on the mountain. I shall go up to the quarry to work and come down here to rest. Caerfenai'll see me no more.

You'll have to go down to shop, said Mam.

What for? Gareth demanded. I can get everything I need in Llancrwys, and that's as far down the mountain as I'll go, unless I decide to see if I can get a rabbit or two along the hedges near the sea. Or gulls' eggs – I know places where you can always pick up a few if you're not too stiff to climb rocks. For everything else, I'll stay up here.

Gulls' eggs, Roger thought, and a rabbit from the hedgerows. Gareth's instincts, his mental world, seemed indeed exactly those of a badger. It was easy to imagine him, if the bus were taken from him, turning back to the mountainside, finding not only a living but a deep, inarticulate satisfaction in digging in ever more deeply, blasting out great cubes of rock, hollowing caves in which he could live his secret life. Roger had a sudden terrifying vision of Gareth in twenty years' time, alone, with collapsed cheeks and a few white threads blowing round his dome of a head, moving purposefully among the wet stones with a pocket full of dynamite, his mind on gulls' eggs.

We mustn't think of that, he said quickly. Our luck will turn. Dic Sharp's making his last throw. If we hold on for only a few weeks, he'll give up.

They both looked at him in silent surprise, and he could see how much he had startled them by mentioning the forbidden name, and at their Christmas fireside too. But he was unrepentant. If Dic Sharp was in their thoughts, and he must have been for Gareth to dwell so intently on a future among the explosives, then let Dic Sharp be in their mouths too.

Gareth! Mam! Roger cried. Drink a toast with me: to our victory!

In his excitement, he stood up.

Mam hasn't got a drink, said Gareth. Here.

He took down a glass and poured an inch of whisky for her. The bottle was getting very low now.

I don't touch strong drink, she protested.

No, said Gareth. But you will this time, Mam. Roger's right. He wants us to drink a toast to the best thing we have in the world: our fighting spirit.

Christmas, she sighed, and you talk of fighting.

We talk of surviving, Mrs Jones, said Roger.

They raised their glasses. Mam coughed a few times as the whisky went down, but she seemed gladdened by it, or by something: a gentle, reminiscent smile came over her face.

Ah, Gareth, she said softly. You're Geraint's own son.

I hope so, Mam.

He'd have said just the same as you. He'd have said that our fighting spirit is the best thing we have.

Gareth smiled with her, so that it seemed to Roger, watching, that their two faces were very much alike.

Remember when Prince kicked me? Gareth asked.

Yes. I was frightened for you.

I never told you what happened afterwards, said Gareth. All these years I never told you, but I'll tell you now.

Afterwards?

When I got out again, said Gareth. He turned to Roger. We had a horse called Prince, that used to do the work about the place before we had a tractor. He was a good old helper – he knew every stone and blade of grass on the place better than my dad did. But once, when I was a little nipper, six or seven years old, a strange thing happened – he kicked me. I must have been fooling about near his hind legs. The kick was a pretty bad one – it didn't break any bones but it dislocated my arm. I was badly bruised as well, and they put me to bed and I was there for a couple of days at least. When I got up and started running about the place again, I kept very clear of Prince, and my dad must have noticed this, because one morning he called me over to where he and Prince were standing, just outside the stable door. Gareth, he says. Yes, dad. Would you like a shilling, he says. A shilling was a lot of money to me, and he got it out of his pocket and held it up so I could see how it glittered in the sun. It's yours, he says, all you have to do is pick it up – and with that he tosses it down right among Prince's hooves. I looked down and saw it shining there, and Prince's feet looked very big and very hard, and I was still aching from the kick he'd given me, but I wanted the shilling and there was something I wanted more than the shilling, you understand me?

Roger nodded.

So I went down among the horse's feet and picked up the shilling, said Gareth. He had turned his head and was speaking now to Mam. The ground was a bit muddy and the first time I went for it it slithered away. But I grabbed again, and Prince kept still as a mouse, and I came up with it and shouted, I did it, dad! I did it!

He laughed delightedly.

And I never knew, said Mam. Did he tell you not to say anything to me?

Not he. But I noticed he said nothing about it when we came in for our dinner, and little as I was I understood somehow that if he said nothing it was best for me to say nothing, too.

There was a silence. Roger thought of the small, misshapen

body, bruised and frightened, going down in the mud for the shilling that was to be his bright badge of manhood, shining in the shadows of his mind for ever. The sharp, still-frightened but exultant cry rang in his ears: *I did it, dad! I did it!*

You did it all right, he said to Gareth.

Prince was as good as gold, said Gareth. I was sick with grieving when he died, though I was nearly a man by that time.

The crimson light had paled, and the sky outside the windows was now almost drained of its magic.

Let's have some light, said Gareth, springing up, and a cup of good hot tea.

The afternoon trance was broken: the bustle of cheerful normality was back. The electric light splashed literalness over everything, banished metaphor, showed Gareth as less of a badger or a hawk than a hunchbacked man, Roger as a shabby smiler with an intellectual face, Mam as a placid ebbing life in an armchair.

They drank tea, and Gareth produced another surprise from the mysterious kitchen into which no one but he was allowed: a dark, rich, marzipan-topped Christmas cake.

Gareth, this is home-made, said Mam, eating judicially.

Mrs Arkwright, said Gareth, nodding. She makes cakes for something to do. Half the village gets one.

Roger had a sudden vision of Mrs Arkwright, alone in her spick-and-span bungalow, mixing dark sugary ingredients in a big china bowl and thinking of people who needed cakes. Under some circumstances, this vision would have seemed to him intensely melancholy, the time-killing of a lonely woman whose only other occupation was quarrelling with the dustmen, but now he saw it in a different light. It made him think of the courage and resourcefulness of human beings, their endless inventiveness, their readiness to fight back against the bitter siege of the years.

Mrs Arkwright! he cried. Lancashire's gift to Llancrwys!

God bless her for a kind heart, Mam said.

I hope she gave the dustmen a cake, said Gareth.

Roger felt light-headed. He was probably drunk; but, if so, what had inebriated him was less the whisky than the strangeness of the day and the delicate flesh of the roasted hare and the sombre splendour of the sunset, and the utterly individual faces of Gareth and Mam, and the thought of Mrs Arkwright and the dustmen and all the rich, inextricable human pattern that could never be unpicked.

The last time I ate this kind of cake was at a wedding, he said. The statement was not true, but he listened to it with interest and wondered what other statements he was about to make. And besides, what was true? The brain's truth or the heart's truth?

I went to a wedding just before I came up here, he went on. It was a tremendously happy occasion. My brother Geoffrey got married to this wonderful girl, Margot. I think they're going to be ideally happy.

They listened, and he talked on.

Margot's the most beautiful girl. She has red-gold hair and these amazing green eyes. All sorts of men have been trying to marry her but she stood out for the best. That's Geoffrey – if I do say so myself, being his brother and everything. Of course, he's always overshadowed me. He's some years older, and besides that he's far more intelligent and attractive. But he's always been gentle with me. I never felt jealous of him – all the things he did just seemed to be out of my sphere, so that it never entered my head to compete with him.

Geoffrey and I lived together, he went on. Of course, I knew I'd lose him sooner or later. The best thing, really. I mean, it's a shame for Geoffrey not to be married and have offspring. He'll be a marvellous father.

And you, said Mam into the kindly silence. You'll be looking round for a wife now.

And not before it's time, said Roger heartily. I had my eye on one or two up here. But they seem to be all booked.

Rhiannon's booked, that's certain, said Gareth drily. That fellow with the aeroplanes'll never leave go of her.

Dilwyn? D'you think he'll get her in the end?

When she's ready, said Gareth, nodding, she'll come to Dilwyn.

Well, I must get married, said Roger. Or I'll feel very out of it, with Geoffrey and Margot setting up house. They've found a wonderful place, in the country. Right off on its own, among the fields. Sixteenth-century, with a paddock and an orchard. They've both lived in London so much that they'll be glad to have quiet and elbow-room in the country. And there's plenty of room for a family.

Restless, he crossed the room and stood looking out at the long, still line of silver light that rested on the edge of the dark Irish Sea.

Yes, he said, so quietly that the others scarcely heard him. I've got to get used to doing without Geoffrey now. But he'll be all right with Margot. And it's nice to see two people as happy as that.

Smiling, he turned and faced Gareth and Mam. That's enough about me, he said.

They drank up the whisky, ate some cold ham, and sat by the fire in a comfortable stupor. Gareth produced an old pack of cards and he and Roger played, unskilfully but with much companionable joking, two or three games of rummy. Finally, at midnight, Roger noticed that Mam was asleep in her chair and judged that it was time to go. Gareth saw him down to the gate.

'No work tomorrow,' he said. 'Have a good lie in.'

'I will,' said Roger. 'Goodnight, and thanks again.'

As he turned away, a slight feeling of strangeness, of displacement, tugged at his consciousness. He had walked a hundred yards through the crisp, clear night before he realized what it was. Both he and Gareth, as the day of celebration ended and their thoughts turned to work, had spoken in English.

On the twenty-seventh of December they ran a normal service. The liver-coloured bus also ran a normal service, but to their glee they managed to steal its thunder on the all-important first run down at eight-fifteen. Heavy traffic had clotted badly on the outskirts of Caerfenai, and the liver-coloured bus, jammed with passengers that should have been theirs, was wedged between a knot of private cars and a heavy lorry that crawled doggedly on the crown of the road. Gareth, thundering up from behind with his bus nearly empty, managed to take advantage of a momentary slackening in the opposite stream of traffic, and with a loud, scornful roar, swung ahead of the liver-coloured bus and drew into the square decisively ahead. The dough-faced driver of the pirate bus found a spot at the other end of the square, dumped his passengers with unseemly haste, and drove hastily away, while Gareth and Roger laughed, crowed, and gestured derisively at him without leaving the shelter of their bus.

This triumph kept them going all day, though it became obvious as time went on that the liver-coloured outfit had orders to harass them as closely as possible. It foreshadowed them on every run, and the takings for that day were as low as they had ever been. But they both avoided any mention of the fact. An utterly stubborn patience had taken hold of them; as long as there was a coin or two in the kitty, they would keep going, and perhaps – the unspoken thought was loud in the air between them – Dic Sharp would crack first.

At five minutes to ten that evening, Roger came out of Mario's pub, buttoning his donkey-jacket rapidly against the freezing air. The night was windless, clear, and intensely cold. The lights of Caerfenai prevented the stars from being fully visible, but as Roger looked up into the black sky he knew that, once up in the mountains, he would see them sparkling and gleaming, exaggeratedly large in the unstained darkness. He hurried along to the square. The yellow bus was in its accustomed place, and already half full of passengers, but its interior lights had not been switched on and the passengers were sitting in such light as came from outside. That meant that Gareth was not there yet. It was unusual for him not to be at the bus before the passengers.

Roger went into the bus and switched on the lighting. The passengers looked pleased, the level of conversation rose, and several people who had been standing about in the square, perhaps half-hoping for the sudden appearance of the liver-coloured bus, now boarded Gareth's bus and took their seats. Roger picked up his leather bag: in a moment he would start collecting fares. Gareth would be along and they would go. Several town clocks began to chime ten. Even inside the bus, with conversations going on, he could hear them, so clearly did the sound cut through the frosty air. Ten o'clock, and no Gareth? He moved uneasily from one position to another, staring through the windows. The square was almost empty. A few General buses were standing with their lights on, ready to go, and here and there an overcoated figure would move quickly towards the promise of a fireside. One shop window showed an oblong of light; it would go out at eleven.

Then Roger saw a burly figure striding across the square towards the bus. It was not Gareth, yet because it was almost as thick-set and almost as familiar to him, for a split second he could have fancied that it was Gareth, walking somehow differently, carrying himself on stronger legs. Then he saw that it was Gito.

Gito came straight for the bus and up the steps. His face had a set expression. As a concession to the cold, he was wearing an old trilby hat, which, by concealing his baldness, made him look younger. Roger had seen Gito without Ivo, but never without his shiny bald pate. Gito bent his big head towards Roger. He looked round the bus, as if to see who might be listening, and then spoke in a quiet, serious voice.

'I've come to take the bus up.'

'Where's Gareth?' Roger asked.

'In the Cottage Hospital,' said Gito. He got into the driving seat and felt in his pocket. 'Gareth gave me the key,' he said. 'I've got a commercial licence, isn't it?'

'But,' said Roger. He swallowed. 'What's happened to Gareth? How d'you know he's in the hospital? Have you seen him there?'

'We took him. Me and Ivo.'

'But what's the *matter* with him?' Roger asked loudly. The passengers, except for a few at the back, stopped talking and looked over at the two of them. A ripple of awareness passed through the bus: something was happening.

'Broken wrist,' said Gito. 'And bruises. They'll examine him. We found him, me and Ivo. We took him straight there. He gave me the key and said the ten o'clock must come up.'

'Broken wrist? Bruises? In the hospit –'

'He got into a fight,' said Gito. 'Seemingly,' he added, to convey that he had not actually witnessed this occurrence. Then the lights dimmed for an instant as he started the engine. It began to drum rhythmically and the lights went back to their even radiance.

Gito was obviously not going to talk any more until they got to Llancrwys. If then. He eased the bus across the square and along the road out of town. Roger, dazed and with a heavy, dismayed feeling in his chest, went about the business of collecting fares. As he went down the bus, almost every passenger

267

asked him where Gareth was. In each case he took the fare without answering, gave the change where necessary, and then said, 'He's off duty.'

Mrs Pylon Jones was on the bus. She was one of the few who did not ask where Gareth was. She merely handed Roger her fare in silence, at the same time looking at him with a mixture of compassion and self-righteousness. Her expression told him that in her opinion he had, entirely through his own foolishness, blundered into a very bad situation and that she, for one, was not at all surprised that something dreadful had happened to Gareth.

By the time they were half-way to Llancrwys, Roger had finished collecting the fares and he had nothing to do but sink into a vacant seat near the front and stare past Gito's trilby into the dark mountain night. At once he became so anxious and depressed that he wished he had some more fares to collect. At the same time, irrational as it was, he felt an acute pang of envy for Gito. Gareth looked on Gito as a real friend, a man he could depend upon in an emergency. If it had been Roger who had found Gareth and taken him to the Cottage Hospital, would he have given the key of the bus to Roger and asked him to drive it up? Well, but Gito had a commercial vehicle licence. It was legal for him to drive the bus, and, environed by enemies as they were, it would never do for them to make a glaringly obvious false move by letting Roger drive the bus unlawfully. All this Roger knew. Yet he still envied Gito, who kept the bus moving smoothly and skilfully, up and up and up, round the endless curves, stopping every few minutes to let people off and starting without juddering even on the steepest incline, so that one remembered that he and Ivo had run a bus service themselves. Yes, till Dic Sharp had got the better of them. They had gone under, leaving Gareth to face Dic Sharp's malice alone. Whereas he, Roger, had taken the quarrel on himself, had been loyal to Gareth, had served Gareth, had put himself entirely at the disposal of Gareth. But it could never be that he would get as close to Gareth, would achieve the unquestioned, easy closeness of relationship with him, that came unsought to such a man as Gito. That Christmas Day had been an exception, a wild ebullience of the spirits.

These thoughts clanked slowly through his head like prisoners in chains. And now they were at Llancrwys, had stopped two or three times in the length of the village, and had halted at the top, the end of the run, beside Gareth's corrugated iron garage. It was time for the bus to rest. Without speaking to Gito, Roger got out and opened the garage doors, then waited while Gito drove the bus carefully in, stopped the engine, fastened the garage doors on one side, came out, fastened the door on the other, and then at last stood facing him in the star-pierced darkness.

'Well?' said Roger. 'Who was it attacked Gareth?'

'I didn't see,' said Gito. 'We found him in the passage outside the pub. Somebody heard a noise and went out and found him lying there. He fetched me and Ivo because they all knew we were friends of Gareth's, isn't it? We went out right away. He wasn't unconscious, he was just getting to his feet, but he was a bit slow because they'd winded him and that. His right wrist was broken. He couldn't do nothing with that hand.'

'But who was it?'

'I don't know that,' said Gito. 'But I know who was behind it, and you do too.'

'Yes,' said Roger.

There was a silence. Far away in some fold of the mountains, a dog barked; or perhaps a fox.

'Well, the bus won't come to no harm now,' said Gito in a matter-of-fact voice. 'That'll be Ivo,' he added. Below them, the labouring of a well-worn lorry engine could be heard, coming up towards Llancrwys. 'He said he'd pick me up at the top.'

'You'll be off then,' said Roger.

'Somebody'll need to tell Mrs Jones,' said Gito thoughtfully.

'I'll do that.'

'Tell her not to worry,' said Gito. 'He'll be back up tomorrow or the next day. And the bus won't come to no harm.' He spoke as if assuming that Gareth's mother would be likely to worry primarily about the bus.

'I'll tell her,' said Roger.

Ivo swung the lorry up the village street and stopped with the engine running. He waved to Roger through the cab window, but made no attempt to lean out and say anything to him. Gito went over and got up beside Ivo and the lorry drove off.

After it was gone, the silence on the mountainside seemed like that of an uninhabited planet. Roger had never in his life felt so alone. But there was no need to dwell on the thought. Out there on the mountain, at the foot of the towering black quarry-tip, Gareth's mother was waiting in the double darkness of her dead sight and her unlit room. She, at any rate, needed him. He began to walk briskly up the narrow road, which, he now saw, sparkled with frost.

The night was moonless. The clarity and stillness of the air made it possible to see one's way by the faint, chill light of the stars and the thin mirror-strewing of the frost. But on a larger scale the darkness was huge, oppressive, waiting. The mountains were black humps of silence.

As Roger walked up through the uppermost streets of the village, he felt his mind slow down and come more soberly to grips with the situation. There was no comfort in this sobriety. Gareth had been attacked, severely enough to be 'found' by Ivo and Gito (dazed? unconscious?), and taken away to hospital. And the attackers had got away, unidentified, and probably flushed with triumph. If they had been bold enough to tackle Gareth, it would cost them no effort to move on to him. He was less physically strong than Gareth, less rooted in the goodwill and protectiveness of the community, altogether more vulnerable.

Roger walked quickly. At the top of the village, a last street-light threw its pale circle on the ground. After that, the dark path, the silent mountains, and the black cliff of slate hanging over the cottage.

He moved on, no longer knowing whether he was hurrying to Gareth's lair to succour the old woman or to find strength and protection in her presence. One thing he knew for certain. He was not going back to the chapel tonight. Perhaps he would never go there again.

The gate clanged, and he was walking across the field towards the cottage. He could just make out the glimmer of its low whitewashed walls, at the foot of that dark man-made cliff. If only there were a light in the window, a welcoming square of yellow that spoke of home and warmth and safety! But the old woman sat in her darkness, in the dark cottage, on the dark mountain, facing the dark flatness of the sea. He was going from one blackness to another.

Roger tried to muster all the courage still left in his blood. But the fear that came down on him was irresistible, numinous, total. Half-way across the field, his feet seemed to root themselves to the ground. The slate-tip reared up between him and the stars, the slope of the ground tried to force him back, the cold and darkness and loneliness went spreading out in great concentric circles until they covered the whole earth. It was all useless, he had failed, the mountains did not want him, the rock rejected him, the slate roof shut him out, and all around him the blind black slopes were covered with murderers.

With one last convulsive effort, he covered the thirty yards to the door of the cottage, and knocked on it several times. He had just enough self-control left to keep himself from beating on the door in a frenzy. Even so his knocks were loud and rapid, and to the old woman sitting in her imprisoned calm it must have been clear that there was something badly wrong. But her voice was strong and even as she called out from the fireside:

'Dowch i mewn.'

He turned the handle and the door opened effortlessly. That was how vulnerable she was, how alone, as unprotected as a moorhen on the nest. Mrs Jones, he said, shutting the door quietly behind him.

Is Gareth with you? she asked.

No, he said. Gareth is staying down in Caerfenai tonight.

Put the light on, and come and sit by me, she said, and tell me what happened.

He obeyed. She was sitting, as she always did, by the electric fire, with the coal fire in the grate ready to be lit when Gareth came home. Roger sat down and spread his hands to the warmth. It calmed him; made him feel less like a hunted wild creature of the night.

First of all, Gareth's all right, he said.

But he's hurt, she said softly. He's hurt in some way.

His wrist is broken, Roger said.

Did he have an accident?

No. Not an accident.

She waited in silence, but her clasped hands moved with an intolerable nervousness.

I won't lie to you, he said. Somebody attacked him.

Where is he? she said, her voice louder and higher than before.

Resting, said Roger, in the hospital.

She caught at her throat, then slowly lowered her hands.

In the hospital?

Just to rest, Roger said. And to have his wrist bound up.

Who did it? she asked.

They got away. But of course everyone knows who's really behind it.

That Dic Sharp, she said. He came to tea here one Saturday, when they were both little boys at Llancrwys school. I didn't trust him then. One of the hens had laid away, and when he and Gareth were playing after tea they found the nest. He said nothing about it, but before he left he stole the eggs and took them away in his cap and sold them in the village.

Roger made some appropriate noise, but he could see that Mam was not heeding him. Her face was puckered with remembrance, her mind was turned inward. Physically she was sitting opposite him in the unwavering glow of the electric stove, but mentally she was standing at the open door, forty years earlier, seeing her Gareth, the lopsided being she loved so fiercely, walk down the hill towards the school where he would jostle all day with thoughtless and cruel normality.

She rocked gently back and forth in her chair, her face clenched in its pain. Gareth bach, Gareth bach, she said softly.

Roger waited for her to come back to him, and when he judged that she had, he said softly, I shall stay here tonight.

Stay here tonight? she said. Why?

So as not to leave you alone, he said firmly. It's what Gareth would want.

Did Gareth say anything about it?

I didn't see him. It was Ivo and Gito who . . . found him. Gito drove the bus up. But I know Gareth wouldn't want you left alone.

I can manage, she said. Everything's to my hand.

Do you mean you don't want me?

No, she said and paused for a moment. No, I don't mean that.

I'd feel happier, staying, he said. And I'm sure Gareth would want me to.

Well, she said. You can sleep on the sofa.

Roger relaxed. All at once he knew the extent of the fear he had been holding back. He would have died sooner than go out into that dark night again, to meet whatever it was that might be waiting for him there.

May I draw the curtains, he said to Mam, and light the fire?

Yes, she said. And you can make us both a cup of tea.

He lit the fire, watched it begin to draw up, and then went through into the kitchen, Gareth's kitchen, as neat and contained as a ship's galley.

Tea, kettle, milk and sugar were all at the ready. In a few minutes they each had a steaming cup.

What about some supper? he asked Mam.

You have some, she said. There's bread and some fresh cheese, if you don't want to bother with cooking.

The thought of cheese made him suddenly hungry, and he got up to go to the kitchen again. What about you? he said.

I shan't have anything, she replied.

Not a nice bit of bread and cheese?

Nothing.

Her voice was so decisive that he knew she must be revolted at the thought of food. Her anxiety would choke her if she tried to eat. He marvelled at the control that kept it from appearing in any other way.

He took a chunk of bread and butter and some cheese to the fireside.

Forgive my eating when you're not, he said.

You've got to work, she said simply. Behind the remark lay years of a hard, outdoor life in which the men had to be fed, whatever happened: stoked up for the unending labour by which they were kept alive. But work? What kind of work lay ahead for them now?

Gareth won't be able to drive the bus for a bit, he said.

Which wrist is broken? Mam asked.

I don't know. But that bus takes a bit of holding with both hands, never mind with one.

Is it the end? she asked gently. Has Dic Sharp won now?

Roger chewed his bread and cheese. I simply don't know, he said. For the moment, the bus is safe in its garage. But there'll be no service till Gareth can drive again, and I don't know when that'll be.

You can't drive it? she pursued.

I might, he said, remembering a certain evening of swirling rain and hissing fat tyres. I might, but I haven't got a commercial licence and it takes time to get one.

I see, she said, turning inward again to her memories.

Roger was silent. To himself he frankly admitted that his chief object, at that moment, was to stay where he was safe. No, that was putting it too strongly. If safety were all he wanted, all he need do was go down to Caerfenai station the next morning at daylight, and wait for a train to carry him out of the district, and beyond the reach of Dic Sharp's myrmidons, for ever. But he had never considered such a thing, and was not considering it now. As long as there was anything to do in the cause of Gareth *versus* Dic Sharp, he would stay on the scene and do it. That, however, was not the same thing as offering himself up on a plate to be carved. Probably the men who had attacked Gareth (he felt sure it must be more than one) were even now looking for him at the chapel, peering in at the windows, feeling the door-handles ... his inside felt cold at the thought. And when they realized he was not there, what then? Would they come on here?

Perhaps so, perhaps not. The only thing to hope was that they would decide not to attack him while he was with Mam. Not that a blind woman could act as witness! But, old as she was, she might offer some resistance, and have to be quietened, and then, if they were ever caught, they could expect little sympathy from the law. He wished he could convey these cool, sober considerations to their minds, whoever they were.

Roger was afraid, that was the fact of the matter, hideously afraid. His bladder was distended, but he was unwilling to go outside to the *tŷ bach*. His imagination peopled the darkness with horrible bone-splitting sadists, and the darkness began at the back door.

What then? Was he to lie on the sofa in torment till dawn came?

Perhaps so. Better that, than . . .

But Mam was getting up out of her chair with slow but assured movements.

It's time to go to bed, she said. I'll leave you alone in here, Mr Furnivall. You'll find the sofa quite comfortable, I think. And you know where everything is.

Yes, Mrs Jones. Thank you.

She picked up a light cane that lay beside her chair, and, as he watched, moved towards the kitchen, tap-tapping as she went with firm, practised strokes. Sitting still, he heard her open the back door and go out. Ought he to go with her? To stand guard? No, surely, because if they were hanging about outside it would not be Mam they would be waiting for, but him.

Springing up with sudden decision, Roger hurried over to the front door and opened it. Then, standing just inside the doorway, inside the warmth and light that protected him, he unzipped his trousers and began to urinate into the darkness, a long curving jet that started in the electric light and lost itself in the blackness. He could hear it pouring on to the grass. Ah, relief, relief.

He zipped up and came back to the fireside. Would it seem true, when he recalled all this one day, in some new and unimaginable setting – in some centrally-heated apartment in Uppsala, with black leather furniture, an abstract on the wall, a case of Scotch in the kitchen and a blonde on the divan – would it seem credible that he had been afraid to go outside to piss? That he, a sedentary urban man, had been as beleaguered as that, as afraid of the silent night of the mountains?

All too credible, he reflected. In the world as it was becoming, violence of any kind was one of the commonplaces. Already, people in half of the cities of the world were afraid to go out at night. Ah, Furnivall, ah, humanity!

Mam came tapping back, put her sightless head in at the parlour door, and said, Goodnight.

Goodnight, he said, and thank you for letting me stay.

It's I who should thank you, she said. Get some sleep now.

Once he heard Mam go into her bedroom, Roger went to the front door and locked it. Then he went through and did the same for the back door. The kitchen light was on; he left it on. The same with the parlour light. Mam, with a blind person's acute hearing, might wonder why she didn't hear the click of the switch as he settled down for the night. Well, she would have to wonder. He was too nervous to put the light out.

He made up the fire, so that it would burn for another three or four hours at least, even if he fell asleep. As he did so he thought suddenly of his stove back in the chapel, thought of it with a little sting of pity. It would be just about going out now, the last warmth and colour dying in it, the cold dark night settling down . . . He felt as a man would feel who had to leave a faithful donkey unfed and unwatered in its stall. Well, he would go back and relight it in the daytime. And meanwhile he had done everything possible, here at Gareth's cottage. If he and Mam did not have a peaceful night, it would not be his fault. He untied his shoelaces and loosened his shoes so that they did not feel tight on his feet, but he did not take them off. He would have felt very vulnerable in stockinged feet. Then he lay down on the sofa and covered himself with his coat and a blanket.

Now to sleep. Or should he look about for a weapon? By the fire was a short, thick poker. He laid it carefully on the floor beside his head. Now let them come, if they dared.

In Gareth's cottage. Let them come and attack him, while he slept, if they dared. If they cared. If they came. While he slept. While Mam lay blind and sleepless, weeping for her Gareth. Let them come to Gareth's lair. Let them dare. To the lair. Sleep, weep. In from the dark mountain. The anger of the wet rocks. Let Dic Sharp count his money: Christmas was over. Sleep, Jenny, sleep. I need your tongue. Hidden from me, all hidden. Gently, gently, sleep, till Christmas comes again to the mountain, my lonely darling, sleep.

Next morning, strong sunlight flooded the world, and he and Mam were like friendly strangers. She encouraged him to fry eggs, and even allowed him to nag her into eating some bread and butter with her tea. But there was a gulf between them. She was still enclosed in the situation of last night, while he was roused to a new day. The sunlight flooded his blood cells: there was work to be done, a new beginning. He had slept, fitfully at first and then deeply, and the assassins had not come for him. The mountain was safe again, the sea was radiant.

He promised to keep in constant touch with Mam.

I'll be able to give you some news of Gareth very soon, he said. I'm not sure when, because with no bus service I don't know how quickly I'll be able to get down there and back up again.

(No bus service? The liver-coloured bus would be exultantly there, would it not?)

I'll be glad of anything you can let me know, she said.

I'll make it my business, he promised her. And now, will you be all right?

Yes, she said. Maldwyn comes this afternoon. He'll take me down to the shop and he'll brew tea.

Right then, Roger said, getting into his coat. And now I'll be off. I must be there if it's only to tell people why the bus isn't running.

Of course, Mam said.

Roger closed the cottage door behind him. He felt he was leaving the old sybil shut up in her own mysterious square of space, in the darkness of her suffering. He pitied her. Yet at the same time he felt that pity was not the only emotion she aroused. There was something enviable about her as well. Her darkness was tragic, but it was immensely strong, being so completely permeated with the uniqueness of her being. She was like something formed by time and nature, not by any example of man. Like mother, like son.

Meanwhile, it was essential for him to get down to the garage. He hurried down the road. The sun was well aloft by now and the mountainside was bathed in an entirely clear, steady light. Except for a few piled-up masses of dazzling white cloud, the sky was blue. Everything looked very cold and very beautiful. Amid all his preoccupations, Roger could not help noticing, as he strode rapidly along, that the colours were stronger than he had ever seen them before. Even the stone walls, which he had always registered merely as grey, were not uniformly grey at all but an endless variety of grey and green, with dark patches of moss in green and brown, and large circular spots of lichen which stood out in a much lighter shade, almost a Chinese white.

The sun shone brilliantly on the corrugated iron of Gareth's garage. But, as he hurried up, Roger noticed something else.

The door was ajar. It was a double door, opening in two halves from the centre, and when Gareth put the bus away for the night he always bolted one side at the top and bottom and secured the other side to it by means of a lock and a large stone. Gito had done the same last night. Now the lock was hanging from its metal loop and the stone had been moved aside. The bolted side was still shut but the unbolted side was ajar. Some-one had gone into the garage, and then, not to make the fact too obvious, had drawn the door more or less closed, without troubling to shut it completely. Perhaps whoever it was did not expect to stay long. Certainly, anyone looking from a dis-tance would hardly have noticed that everything was not as usual.

Roger's heart beat savagely. He took hold of the half of the door that was not secured and pulled it wide open. There was a scurrying sound, like the noise of rats, and in the gloom of the garage he saw two men straighten up from the off-side back wheel of the bus. His eyes were adjusted to the crystalline light of the mountainside, while theirs were accustomed to the dim-mer light in which they had been tampering with the bus, so that as he confronted them Roger had the sense of being watched by baleful little eyes that missed nothing, while his vision of them was hardly more than an outline. But he saw two pale, vicious faces, and one of them was the dough-face of the driver of the liver-coloured bus. The other man had a long spanner in his hand. It looked more like a weapon than a tool, and he was holding it like a weapon.

Roger tried to get back through the door and shut it on them. He could hardly succeed in holding the door shut against two men if they both put their shoulders to it at once, but at this time of the morning there were often people about, even up here at the top of the village, and he might get some help. He felt that the garage contained some evil, secret form of life that ought to be trapped, without ceremony, like a swarm of blackbeetles. He stepped back quickly and reached for the handle of the door, but he was not quick enough. They were two small, nimble men and they moved like lightning. Roger snatched at the jacket of the second man as they brushed past him, but the rough cloth tore in his hand. He turned to see both figures running down the road that led out of the village.

There were five or six houses on the other side of the garage and then the road took a sharp turn between high banks. The men were out of sight in a moment. Without pausing to think, Roger set off after them. His fear had gone, dissolved in the sharp sunlight. More than he had ever wanted anything, he wanted to lay hold on one of them at least, and drag him to justice. Then the whole miserable story would come out, and Dic Sharp would be finally shown up and everyone would be safe from him for the rest of time. Roger ran fiercely round the bend, away from the houses. Then he stopped.

The two men were waiting for him. All at once he knew that these must be the two who had beaten up Gareth, and who would have done the same for him last night if they had got hold of him. They had run away from him not because they were afraid but because they wanted him to follow them to a spot where there would be no interference and no witnesses. Where they were standing now was barely a hundred yards from the garage, but there was no one about. The road took a dip, following a fold in the hillside, and the three of them stood there, between the high banks and the stone walls, in a quiet cup of sunlight.

As he faced the two men, the words suddenly formed in Roger's mind, 'it was all over in a moment'. He visualized these words as if he were reading them in a newspaper. It was one of those moments of horror when the mind sometimes draws aside, looking at the situation as if it were a picture in a frame. Because Roger's fear was so great he observed the scene almost dispassionately. He noticed, for instance, that both the men were considerably younger than he was. They were in their twenties, while he suddenly felt every month of his forty years. But they had nothing juvenile about them. They were not childish offenders, to be led away and reasoned with by a hefty policewoman, but hard adult criminals. He wondered, still in the same dispassionate way, where Dic Sharp had got them from.

Without speaking and therefore giving Roger no chance to locate his accent, the man with the spanner moved forward and swung the weapon at Roger's ribs. Roger jumped back, causing the spanner to miss by perhaps half an inch. The man came after him, swinging viciously, and meanwhile his companion ran round behind him in a fast circle, backing Roger against the wall. There was no escape route that was not blocked by the menacing arabesque of the spanner as it whirled like a gnat in the sunlit air.

Roger was in a state of sheer terror. Yet, inside him, there was the dispassionate thing that observed and meditated. *Is this death?* it asked. *Will they kill me now? If so, I am glad to have lived to see the start of this beautiful day in the mountains.*

The man who had driven the bus now stopped and picked up a stone that had fallen from the wall. He moved in to smash this into Roger's ribs. Activated purely by fear, Roger stepped out to meet him, caught his throat in both hands, and squeezed hard. The man swung the stone, but it fell harmlessly behind Roger's back, and, using his superior weight, Roger managed to wheel him round so that he formed a shield against the man with the spanner. They swayed desperately. The bus driver was flailing his fists, but wildly, and a lot of the blows were not landing. Roger hoped that by hanging on to his throat he might manage to throttle him to death, and then the other man might be frightened at the sight of a dead body and run away. He was too afraid to feel any compunction at the thought of killing the man; he saw death simply as a thing that might not happen to him if he first caused it to happen to someone else.

The man with the spanner now moved round and hit Roger on the right shoulder. He was probably trying to break his collar-bone and so render that arm useless. But the blow fell awkwardly, on the padded part of the jacket, and though it frightened Roger it did not cause him to let go of the driver's throat, which by now must have been getting very painful. Roger could not tell whether or not he was squeezing hard enough to cut off the air supply to the man's lungs altogether. It felt like it, but perhaps the man was able to get some breath by wheezing very hard. Otherwise, why did he not lose consciousness?

The man with the spanner lifted it again, aiming at Roger's skull. Roger sank his head down between his shoulders and pushed very hard at the driver's throat, forcing him back into the other man, so that the three of them reeled in a grotesque embrace. The driver tried to bring up his knee into Roger's groin. Roger swayed aside and kicked him hard on the shins, without letting go of his throat. *How bright the sunlight is,* he thought.

The rock, with which the driver had tried to stave in Roger's ribs, was lying by his feet. Despairing of cutting off his breath supply, Roger suddenly let go of the driver's throat, bent and picked up the rock. As the driver staggered backwards, his hands moving up to his throat, Roger threw the rock at him with all his might. He wanted to smash that pale, evil face.

His muscles must have been fluttering with fatigue, because, even at that distance of three or four feet, he somehow contrived to miss, and the rock flew harmlessly over the man's shoulder. In the silence, Roger heard it hit the wall on the other side, and roll down the bank to lie innocently in the roadway once more. That sound told him that he had lost the fight. He had made his effort, and his adversaries were still alive, not even seriously damaged. Now they would get him. *Do the sheep hear us?* mused the voice inside him. *Do they care about a fight among men?*

The sheep, Roger decided, would look on. They would not stop chewing their cud while he got the beating that would put him into a wheelchair for life, or damage his brain and turn him into an idiot, drooling in some forgotten corner of an institution. Geoffrey, here I come to join you. Or perhaps death. Much better death. Death, come and take me, come before the spanner.

The two men moved forward at a leisurely pace. They seemed to know quite well that Roger's resistance was over. Roger glanced down at his hands. How could he have thought that those hands would be strong enough to choke a man's life out? They were nervous, elongated hands. If he had been a manual worker, his hands would have been stronger. But even Gareth's huge, gnarled hands had gone down last night on the pavement. The sun still shone brightly, and it was very quiet. In the silence, Roger plainly heard the men's feet scrape slightly on the road as they came for him. He also heard another sound. Not far away, round the bend that led across the mountain, a metal gate clanged. Someone was coming.

The two men also heard the gate. They exchanged a quick, expressionless glance with their baked-currant eyes, then moved quickly towards Roger. A few seconds, three or four crippling blows, a few kicks as he lay on the road, and they could melt away. Probably it was just a woman or a child who was coming. Some farmer's wife going into Llancrwys to buy groceries. All they had to do was to keep their backs to that side and not let her see their faces, and they could finish the job even after she got there.

But the clang of the gate had woken Roger from the lethargy of despair. It meant humanity. The world did not, after all, consist of himself and two murderous assailants, alone in a world of silence, sunlight and sheep. These mountains were inhabited, there were people here who had names and faces, who could smile, and help one another, and feel human emotions. If he could stay alive and unharmed for just a few seconds longer, till whoever it was came round the bend in the road ... Gathering every ounce of his strength, he suddenly leapt on to the man with the spanner and tried to snatch the weapon away from him. It was useless; the man was stronger than he was, particularly about the arms and wrists. But the sudden counter-attack had taken him by surprise, and Roger clung desperately to the spanner, at the same time dragging him half to the ground. The man who had driven the bus was trying to get at Roger, but for an instant he was baulked by the struggling figure of his companion. He punched at Roger, but missed. Then the person who had clanged the gate came round the corner. It was Iorwerth.

For one black, terrible instant, Roger sank into a despair worse than anything that had gone before. Iorwerth, who had never greeted him with anything but a scowl, who cared nothing for Gareth or their bus and regarded Roger himself as a contemptible intruder : Iorwerth, who was probably sadistic enough to enjoy standing by while these two slaughtered him !

But Iorwerth surprised Roger. Surprised him, and filled him with remorse (at having misjudged Iorwerth) and joy (that the earth was not, after all, a basically hostile place, but a place where great, flamboyant pieces of good fortune came flaring out of the winter sunshine); the surprise and joy never afterwards wholly left him.

The man who was wrestling with Roger for the spanner suddenly let go his hold. Roger, taken by surprise, slackened his grip, whereupon the man made a lightning grab and took the spanner away from him. Such an old trick, such a simple trick, remembered by everyone from his infant-school playground! But it worked. And immediately the man clouted Roger in the ribs with the spanner. Roger doubled up, feeling that his rib-cage must have given way under the impact, and in an instant the two of them were on him, punching and kicking. He went down. The air roared in his ears. Then, as suddenly as it had begun, the attack stopped. He opened his eyes. He was alive. Still lying down, he looked round, and what he saw made him forget his aching ribs and sit up.

Iorwerth had the bus driver's head under his arm and was punching him rhythmically in the face. At each impact of his huge fist, the man gave a high, choking cry. After the fourth or fifth blow, the other man came up behind Iorwerth and raised the spanner to club him on the skull. Iowerth, whose head was continually moving on his massive neck, must have been keeping watch at all points of the compass. As the spanner rose into the air, he backed heavily into the man, trampling his shins. Then, without letting go of the bus driver, he gripped the other man by the back of the neck, stepped back to get a firm footing, and swung the two heads together.

Roger would have thought it impossible for bone on bone to meet with such an impact without breaking. In the utterly quiet air, the collision sounded inhumanly loud. Iorwerth released the bus driver, who fell to his knees. Then he seized the man who had tried to club him with the spanner and began to beat him about the face and body with his huge, stony fists. After a while, Roger turned his eyes away. He did not care if Iorwerth killed the man, but he did not feel called upon to watch it happen. It was like being fond of bacon without wanting to stand and watch a pig being killed. At the moment that he ceased to watch, Iorwerth had the man up against the wall and was punching him rhythmically in the mouth. At each blow the man's head was driven back against the stones.

Roger shut his eyes. Everything looked red as the bright sun beat down on his closed eyelids. His ribs hurt: worse than hurt: they sent waves of intolerable pain through his body every time he breathed. He fingered them, still sitting in the middle of the road with his eyes closed. They did not feel broken; perhaps they were only cracked. He bent over as if trying to be sick.

Then Iorwerth was with him, helping him to his feet, and Iorwerth's dark strong voice was saying in Welsh:

Are you hurt? Do you need a doctor?

Roger opened his eyes. Not badly hurt, he said. You came in time.

Try to stand up, said Iorwerth.

Roger got to his feet. His breathing seemed easier now. Perhaps his ribs were not even cracked, just bruised. His donkey-jacket, which he had been wearing at his work the day before and was therefore still wearing, had been thick enough to muffle the blow a good deal.

I think I shall be all right, he said.

Behind Iorwerth, the man who had taken the worst beating was climbing to his feet. There was blood on the road. The bus driver had already begun to stumble away in retreat, without waiting for his companion. He had left the road and was moving downwards, in the general direction of Caerfenai and the sea, over the open hillside. The other man, swaying and holding his face, now began to follow him.

Oughtn't we to hold them? said Roger feebly. The police . . .

Never mind the police, said Iorwerth. I taught them their lesson. Let them go and show themselves to Dic Sharp looking the way they look now.

Yes, said Roger, that would be best.

Iorwerth looked closely at Roger's face. You need a bit of a rest, he said. You're dead white.

I expect so, said Roger. He passed a hand over his forehead: it was clammy and chill.

There'll be no bus service this morning, said Iorwerth. I heard about Gareth. You'd better rest. There's nothing for you to do.

Roger felt drowsy. The shock of being attacked was causing his mind to work very slowly. At the moment, the chief feeling he had was one of guilt that the residents of Llancrwys would have to walk to work.

I'm sorry there's no service, he said. The bus itself is all right. I stopped them before they did much damage to it, I expect. But there's no one to drive it.

I'll get a lift, said Iorwerth.

If you see anybody waiting for the bus, said Roger, faintly, you might tell them what's happened ... or at any rate, tell them that ...

Go and get some rest, said Iorwerth. If you want a doctor I'll telephone for one.

No, thanks, said Roger. He could not bear the thought of being thumped and tapped and questioned by a doctor.

I'll get on, said Iorwerth. You won't be seeing those two again.

He glanced down with pride at his knuckles.

Skinned, he said.

I'm sorry, Roger murmured.

Iorwerth grinned, thrust his hands into his coat pockets, and began to walk away down the road. Roger sat down on the grass verge and watched him go. It occurred to him that he had not thanked Iorwerth. He drew in his breath to shout *Thank you*! after Iorwerth's receding figure, but the expansion of his ribs gave him another stab of pain, and he let the breath out again, gradually and silently.

Well, Iorwerth had been right. There was no work for him to do that day. Rest was the thing. He stood up and began to walk, through the bright, still morning, towards the chapel.

When he got there, and let himself in, the first thing he registered was that it was cold, though the brilliant shafts of sunlight that came in through the windows made it look warm. The stove had gone out, of course. He went straight across to it, knelt, opened it, and began to clear it out for re-lighting. It was good to have something mechanical to do. Lighting a fire was a humble Martha-task, yet it was cheerful, with a bright little core of creativity. Keeping his mind a blank, avoiding all thoughts of what had happened that morning, Roger moved purposefully about with firelighters, scraps of coal, matches. He shut the doors of the stove and opened it at the bottom to roar it up into a bright flame. There. He gave it a few minutes to catch. Now for a good bellyfull of stove nuts. Carefully, he shook these on, then shut the doors and sat down to wait. Heat, lovely welcoming heat, would spread slowly outwards until the chapel was warm. Then, when it was warm, his mind would relax, and he would be able to take some cognizance of what had happened to him.

He sat, waiting, in the wooden armchair. It was very quiet: he listened to find out if he could hear a single sound, but he could not. The world seemed entirely given over to silence and light.

He sat quite still, but his eyes moved here and there, taking stock of the place. He would be safe here. Iorwerth had frightened off those two men for good, and surely Dic Sharp would find it very difficult to hire others to renew the attack, after such a defeat. This was Roger's den, his refuge, and he was safe here. But he had been neglecting it. The sunlight lay accusingly on a film of grey dust on floorboards and furnishings. He could spend today sweeping and polishing. He need not concern himself with anything else. There was nothing else in his life to claim his attention: nobody and nothing. Roger sat utterly still, listening again to the windless winter silence. Then, uncomprehendingly, his mind registered that the silence was being broken. A bee-like drone, a changing note, lower, then higher, all the time louder. Then slowing. A car. Outside his chapel, drawing up, stopping, a car with a small engine: the engine stopping, one door opening, then another, voices in the dazzling air.

He knew it was Jenny before he identified her voice. Perhaps, in the marrow of his bones, he had been expecting to hear her mini-car drive up and halt outside his chapel. Or, more accurately, he had been expecting to dream that he heard it. Perhaps that was what he was doing now: sitting in his armchair, dreaming among the sunlit dust.

She knocked on the door, and in the same instant he opened it. Her back was towards the all-powerful sun: he could not see the expression on her face. Beside her, Mary and Robin clustered, one holding a doll, the other a small paper-backed book.

'We didn't know whether we'd find you in,' she said.

'Come in,' he said. 'I've got the day off.'

He opened the door wider and they entered. 'I was thinking of doing a bit of spring cleaning,' he said. 'But I don't think it's too dusty to sit down.'

He motioned Jenny to the armchair, and she sat in it. Mary held up her doll to him.

'This is my chief doll. She'd be the queen only I don't have queens. She's the duchess. You can see she's dressed like a duchess, can't you? I'm taking her to show my grandpa and Nana.'

'She's lovely,' he said. 'Can you find somewhere for her to sit?'

'She'll sit by the fire. She's cold.'

Robin was wordlessly holding out his book.

'What's that, Robin?'

'Puzzles,' he said.

Roger bent to look. 'Here, sit with me.' He sat down on the bed and lifted Robin on to his knee, careful to keep him on the side away from his hurt ribs.

'You have to finish them,' Robin explained. Roger looked through a few pages; each one had a drawing either incomplete or scrambled. Some were a jumble of lines which, if shaded in specified areas, revealed a picture: others required a line to be drawn through numbered dots: in one, four faces had been depicted, each face broken into two halves and the halves mismated.

'I've done some of them,' said Robin. 'I got one wrong but it was only in pencil. You can get a rubber and rub it out.'

'Yes.'

'Here's one I'd like to do,' said Robin. He showed Roger a picture of a small boy smiling complacently and holding his hands as if carrying something. Round the hands was a beeswarm of numbered dots.

'Yes, do that one,' said Roger. 'Join the dots together. I'll find you a pencil if you haven't got one.'

'I have got one. Look.'

'Right, let's see you do that one. Join the dots up, starting from 1, then 2, you see here, and then 3 . . .'

'I can't see how to do it,' said Robin.

'He doesn't know his numbers yet,' Jenny put in from her place by the stove.

'The duchess'll teach him,' said Mary. 'She knows her numbers. She knows everything.'

'He can do it if he has a list of numbers,' said Jenny. 'He follows the list and gets it right.'

'Good,' said Roger. 'Here. These numbers go from one to twenty-three. Now, I'll put down all the numbers in order.' He picked up a copy of the local paper from the floor, and in a margin made a column of figures. 'Now, that's one to twenty-three. You follow those and join them up and we'll see what the boy in the picture's carrying.'

'All right,' said Robin. 'I had this for Christmas. I had some big presents and some little presents. This is one of the little presents, but I like it very much.'

'Anyway the big presents are all packed,' said Mary. 'These are just for the journey.'

Robin took himself off to a corner of the bed, using it as a work-bench, and began slowly hunting for one figure after another, following Roger's list. Mary was arranging the duchess's hair. Now Roger could give his attention to Jenny.

'Well?' he said, sitting on the part of the bed nearest her chair.

'Well, what?'

'You're on the way somewhere. I hear talk of packing, and a journey. Going on holiday?'

'You could call it that.' Her voice was drained of expression, almost sullen. And he saw now that her face was pale, her eyes dark-ringed.

'What would you call it?' he asked.

'Oh, I'd call it a holiday. Defeat's a kind of holiday, isn't it? Final defeat. Going on holiday for ever. If only one could.'

'Tell me what's defeated you,' he said.

She looked away. 'Can't you really guess?'

'Of course I can guess. Your marriage.'

She nodded: 'I'm on the run from it. I'm never going back.'

'Good for you.'

She turned quickly to face him, with a flash of something like anger. 'You say that. But you don't have to face the problems.'

'Wrong. What you mean is, I'm not allowed to face them. You know I'd willingly share the whole situation with you.'

She was silent for a moment, then, 'Do you mean that?'

'You had my letter, didn't you?'

She nodded. 'That's why I'm here, I suppose.'

'Well, then.'

'I thought,' she said carefully, 'your letter might have been just a mood. One of those moods that come at three in the morning.'

'There's no difference, as far as my feelings for you are concerned, between three in the morning and three in the afternoon.'

'Right, Roger Furnivall,' she said. 'You've spoken, and you're going to be taken up on what you've said, for once.'

'That *for once* is unfair. I'm always taken up on what I say.'

'Not always as promptly as this,' she said, 'or as thoroughly.'

'Are you sure of that?' For an instant, Roger saw the lonely twist in the mountain road, the two hate-hungry faces, the whirling spanner.

'No, of course I'm not sure. I don't know anything about your life, except what you've told me. But I'm in a desperate corner, and I'm going to throw myself on to you.'

'Throw away,' he said.

'I can't stand another hour with Gerald. There isn't time to go into it now, and perhaps I never shall go into it. All I know is, I've had one of those glimpses into the pit. Last night he brought that worm, Donald Fisher, back for dinner, and after an evening of misery and boredom, we started quarrelling after Fisher had gone home, then patched it up, then started again, and in the end I had to admit that there was no way of making things any better because I hated him and hated the life he'd brought me into. Oh, I don't know that I'm expressing myself properly. What I hate isn't so much Gerald himself as what he does to me.'

'It's generally that way,' he said, 'as far as I can gather.'

'Well, I'm frightened. I've done it and now I'm frightened. Gerald went out after breakfast, without speaking to me, and straight away, before I had time to go back on it, I told the children we were going over to see my parents and they were going to stay there for a few days. I rang my mother and she said yes, bring them over. She could probably tell from my voice that I was in some sort of desperate need, not that I told her anything. I just said we needed to dump the kids for a few days, that something had come up. I tried to make it sound as if Gerald had suddenly been invited to a conference in the Bahamas or something, and wanted to take me. But I couldn't make up any cock-and-bull story. It'd have died on my lips. Anyway, I packed their stuff at once and I'm driving them over now.'

'And you?'

'I'm coming to you,' she said.

Roger's heart rattled against his battered ribs. For a moment he thought he would not be able to breathe again. Then his lungs began to fill and empty as before. He said, 'You're welcome.'

'I shall move in with you for a week,' she said in a dry, level tone, behind which he could feel her fear and trouble. 'Gerald won't know where I am. A week should be long enough for us to tell whether we can get on all right together. It's as long as I can give it, anyway.'

'A week will do to start with,' said Roger. He got up briskly from the bed. 'Where do your parents live?'

'Near Nantwich.'

'That's a good day's drive, there and back. It might be awkward if you ran into bad weather. And you're tired to start with. I'd better come with you and co-drive.'

'Oh, but —'

'Don't start thwarting me already.'

She smiled. And now the deadness had lifted from her face, and her smile revealed gratitude, with a crumbling edge of helplessness. He loved her for everything she was, and most of all for being vulnerable.

'Well, it's a long way to Nantwich,' he said. 'We'd better get on the move. But first, a cup of something hot.'

He bustled about and made coffee. Jenny had a bottle of milk in the car, and he warmed it for the children, saw that everybody had something inside them, Roger the provider. The children were talked to a little more, Robin's attempt to draw what the boy in the picture was carrying was duly recognized (it was an aeroplane), and then they were almost ready.

'Come here, loves, and have your coats on.'

'I'd better show you where the plumbing is. They'll need to go.'

'Oh, yes. Oh, how funny. This must have been the vestry.'

'Do you want to go, Mary?'

Etc., etc.

Before leaving the chapel, Roger filled the stove with special care. It had to stand guard over the place, to represent life and warmth during the long cold hours they would be away. Because, because, because he was bringing Jenny back with him tonight. He knew the fact with his brain, but it would not penetrate to his bones. Never mind, there would be time for that. In any case, his function was a restricted one for the first few days. First-aid, wound-bandaging. The first thing was to get the two solemn little shock-headed ones off to a kindly, accustomed sanctuary.

'Do you like going to stay with your mother's ... with Grandpa and Nana?'

'Yes,' said Mary decidedly. 'We have lovely things to eat. And we go to see the trains.'

'You make it sound as if I half-starved you,' Jenny said, comically petulant.

'Nana gives us chips whenever we ask for them.'

'Nana's got plenty of time to cook chips.'

'Grandpa's made a model train,' said Robin. 'It's as big as that.' He spread his arms wide. 'And there's a pond with ducks on it right behind his house. Their necks are all different colours.'

'He means they change colours,' Mary explained.

'When they bend their necks they go different colours. Then they stand up in the water and their tails point right up.'

'Come on,' said Jenny, buttoning Robin's coat.

Outside, the blue mini-car stood waiting. Luggage was strapped to a rack on the roof.

'They always need such a lot of stuff. Like going to China for a year.'

'Would you like to go to China, Mummy?' Mary asked.

'Yes,' she said.

'How about my driving the first half and you the second?' said Roger. 'That'll put you in charge when we get to the part you know best.'

'Fine.' She handed him the keys.

They piled in, the children hugging a litter of toys and books.

'Can I sit on your knee, Mummy?'

'No. Later perhaps. You can't start off on my knee.'

Roger started the willing little engine and swung the matchbox-shaped car out on to the road. 'Nantwich, here we come,' he said.

Jenny was silent, huddled in her seat. For an hour and more he drove steadily without disturbing her. Then he began to wonder whether he ought not to interrupt her train of thought, move her gently out of her silence.

'What does your father do?' he asked.

'He's retired.'

'What did he do?'

'Surveyor,' she replied.

This seemed to close up one conversational avenue. Roger shot a glance across at Jenny. Her face was dark, indrawn, troubled.

'Is anything wrong? Apart, I mean, from just about everything?'

She gave him a quick smile. 'I wouldn't say everything was wrong, Roger. Far from it. I'll come out of this bed of glue I'm stuck in and you'll see I'm grateful.'

'Never mind about that,' he said. 'You can't surface all at once, after a disaster, even one that's a blessing in disguise.'

'What I'm waiting for,' she said doggedly, 'is a blessing that *isn't* in disguise.'

'Oh,' he said, keeping his voice light, 'they happen along.'

After another silence, she forced herself into speech again. 'Roger, there is something specially worrying me. I mean something in the foreground.'

'Well, let's hear it,' he said, expertly guiding the Mini round a long, fast curve.

'I don't want you there when I'm with my parents.'

'All right,' he said.

'You see, I've got to be bright. And that means being false. And I'm going to make up a pack of lies about why I need to drop the children on them.'

'Why not take them on one side and just shoot them the whole works?'

'I couldn't, that's why not. I've got to get a bit of energy and a bit of courage together before I can calmly tell them I'm leaving Gerald. It'll mean a first-class inquest, and if I had to go over it now I'd just come to pieces.'

'I see. I was a fool to suggest it. You can't take all your hurdles at once.'

'You do see, don't you?'

'Yes, my darling.'

'And I'm going to be so *false*,' she said. 'It'd kill me to have you there, listening. Quite apart from the little problem of explaining your presence.'

'That would be easy enough.'

'Yes, it would but it'd be another pack of lies. I want to get by with as little lying as I can manage.'

'Yes, it's a good thing to economize on.' He changed gear; they were going up a short hill.

'But I was afraid to say that to you,' she said. 'I knew I ought to say it, before we left your place, but I was afraid that if I told you I didn't want you to come to the house, you might not have wanted to come at all, and I needed you and I couldn't bear that . . .'

'Oh, Jenny,' he said, and put his arm round her trembling shoulders. 'I'm here and I'll always be here whenever you want me.'

'Is Mummy cold?' said Mary from the back seat.

'Yes,' said Roger. 'She's cold and I'm warming her.'

'The duchess is cold, too.'

'The duchess has got you to warm her.'

'But I'm cold,' Mary piped.

'I want to sit on your knee, Mummy,' said Robin, beginning determinedly to wriggle his way forward between the front seats.

Roger drew up at the roadside while this *imbroglio* was sorted out. In the end it was decided that they should drive on for a certain distance with both the children crushed together in Jenny's lap, and that the grown-ups would then change places, Jenny would drive, and Mary and Robin would go back to their places.

The rest of the journey was smooth and uneventful, and they rolled into Nantwich towards lunch-time.

'Put me down anywhere,' said Roger.

'But Roger . . . what will you *do*?'

'Tell me what time to be on what street-corner, and you worry about the rest. There's plenty I can do. I shall walk about the town and get to know it. I like these little Cheshire towns, always have.'

They settled on a suitable point for Roger to be dropped and picked up, and he agreed to be there at six o'clock to begin the journey back. She stopped the car, and he got out.

'Good luck,' he said.

'Oh, God,' she said. 'What a mess it all is.'

'Aren't there any bright spots?' he asked, leaning in through the door.

'You're the only bright spot,' she said. 'I'm learning to trust you already. But I don't want to go too fast.'

Roger nodded to show that he understood. Then he straightened up, and patted the roof of the little car in salute as it slid from under him. Now, suddenly, he was alone. Sleet was driving hard down the street. He had to get into shelter. Looking round, he saw a big, busy pub, bright with lights and people, on the opposite corner of the street, and suddenly he knew that, more than anything else, he needed a drink.

'Did you have an interesting walk round the town?' Jenny asked.

'I stayed in the pub till they threw me out. That left me three hours. It had stopped sleeting by then, so I walked round breathing in and out until I'd got rid of some of the alcohol.'

'It sounds quite a cheerful day.'

'Very cheerful. And you.'

'Oh, I managed.'

They were moving down the dark main road. Settled in the passenger's seat, his legs comfortably crossed, safety-belt clipped on, the road flowing beneath their wheels, Roger felt once again the power of physical circumstances to dictate the flow of his thoughts. On the way there, with the children chattering and the luggage strapped to the roof-rack, his face towards Jenny's family home, it had seemed natural to think chiefly of her life; now, facing back towards Caerfenai, his internal radio picked up the signals that had become familiar to him during these past three months. He found it natural, now, to think and speak of Gareth, of Dic Sharp, of Mrs Pylon Jones, of Ivo and Gito. These things were, as yet, unknown territory to Jenny. Other parts of his life were already open to her. She knew Madog, for instance; and she had, from years of living there, an instinctive knowledge of the places and people among whom he had blundered, that autumn, like a greenhorn. She would have understood Rhiannon, for instance, at first glance. And, for that matter, Mario. And Mrs Cledwyn Jones. And the two women who refused to give evidence.

'I'm going to talk,' he said, 'In a steady, uninterrupted stream.'

'About yourself, I hope,' she answered, looking straight ahead, through her black-framed glasses, at the flowing road.

'About myself, and what's been happening to me since I came up here last autumn. My life's been tangling with the lives of people who would ordinarily be a long way from me. It's all been very educative, and sometimes a bit painful. You'll meet most of the principals in the next few days – in the next few hours, some of them – so I'm going to tell you who they are.'

She listened, and he talked. It was an enormous release and satisfaction. Words, sentences – they had so much healing and controlling power. Happily giving his mind to the talk, Roger made a good story of it, shaping the narrative, introducing the main characters one by one, describing them, bringing them to life. As he talked on, he stood outside himself and recognized what he was doing. Language distanced experience, put it into a frame for contemplation. How rough the animals must find their wordless existence, having to swallow experience just as it came!

He talked until everything was explained. By the time he fell silent, she was guiding the car over the bridge into Llangollen, and he was able to draw a neat line under his story with, 'Time to change over. I know a good pub here. We'll have a whisky and then I'll take the wheel.'

The halt over, the whisky warming his inside, Roger felt confident and relaxed. The wheel was comfortable in his hands, the little car happy with its light load, the roads familiar and, on that raw night, almost empty. He and Jenny were enclosed in their shared situation as they were enclosed in the metal of the car. The darkness on either side, the speeding headlight-beams fingering out in front, the hot air that flowed from somewhere about their ankles, the sense that one set of problems had been laid to rest while another waited to be faced, all contributed to a keying-up, a heightened sense of his own personality, a feeling that what they were doing was urgent and important.

Oddly enough, the question of his relationship with Jenny, its larger dimensions, the problems of its future or non-future, did not press very strongly on him. What they were doing, from one hour to the next, was enough.

'We shall have to call in at Gareth's,' he said. 'We'll get that done right away, before we go to my place.'

'All right,' she said easily.

Roger drove on, enjoying his own skill and sense of purpose, sweeping the car round curves, changing gear and braking with the precision of a thoroughbred machine. He could do anything, he was King Roger. Only once, when a traffic-light halted them in the empty street of some anonymous little town, did his vitality flicker out for a second: staring out into the pallid street-lighting, he knew, suddenly, that he was in that state of fatigue which is no longer felt as fatigue, that his euphoria was based on a tension that had not relaxed since that morning, that somewhere inside him he was still carrying the fear and desperation, the silent rat-like men, the lungeing spanner. Iorwerth's great square fists, like swinging bricks, had ransomed him, but nothing had unscrewed his tension, and he was ready to snap. But the light changed from red through yellow to green, he let the car surge forward, his hands lay lightly on the wheel, and Jenny sat beside him: he could go on, and if he could, he would.

Five miles from Caerfenai he turned off the main road and took to little, twisting lanes that lay like loops of string across the dark mountains. This saved them some distance, and also gave him a sense of authority: his local knowledge, in this immediate area, was greater than Jenny's.

Coming this way, they dropped downhill into Llancrwys.

'Shall we go straight to Gareth's now?' she asked.

'I must call in at the chapel first,' he said, 'and see to the stove.' He had been about to call it 'home', but 'the chapel' came to his tongue more easily. It wasn't, quite, home yet; a day or two ago, before all these sudden changes, it had been, but now it would have to alter and enlarge its nature, becoming a home to both of them.

Jenny waited in the car, with the engine running and the heater on, while he hurriedly let himself in to the chapel and made up the stove. It had been on the point of going out. He gave it light scattering of stove-nuts and three parquet blocks. That would make a hot fire within an hour.

'Now,' he said, getting back into the driving seat, 'to Gareth's.' It was almost ten o'clock; there was no time to waste.

They drove through the village, up the steep road beyond the last house, and stopped at the point where the metalled surface ended. Roger cut out the engine, and the silence of the mountain night rang in their ears.

'Where is it?' Jenny asked, opening her door.

'We walk a little way,' he said.

They locked the car and walked along the rough track. Near Gareth's field Roger noticed a dark shape, visible as a stationery patch of deeper blackness in the blackness of the night. It was a vehicle of some kind, and for an instant he had a fancy that it was a shape familiar to him. But he had no attention to spare for it: they were on an errand of high concern; two important segments of his life were about to be joined together.

He led Jenny through the field gate, and pointed. 'That's the cottage. At the foot of the big slate-tip.'

'Well, Gareth's in,' she said in her most matter-of-fact, Northern-homely voice. 'The light's on in the front room.' He realized that she must be covering up strain, and for a moment let his arm go protectively round her shoulders.

'Will they accept me?' she half-whispered.

Roger decided that an echo of her downrightness would be the tone most likely to reassure and encourage. 'They'll accept you to the exact extent that they've accepted me. Just how far that is, I can't tell you with any precision. But at any rate they won't put pepper and salt on you and eat you.'

'I'd taste bitter, if they did,' she said. 'Rancid and black and bitter inside, full of the mess of the last few weeks.'

He let this go in silence. They reached the door and he knocked, the noise clapping out into the still air like a gunshot.

Gareth opened the door. He was in his shirt-sleeves, one bandaged arm in a sling, and from behind him an enticing warmth and light spilt out. The sling and bandage made his right forearm seem enormous, like Popeye's.

'Roger,' he said. 'I'm glad you came. You've saved somebody a journey.'

'I have a friend here,' said Roger.

Gareth stood back from the door. 'Come in, both.'

They entered. Mam was sitting in her accustomed place. Next to her, on a wooden chair from the kitchen, sat Ivo, his woollen cap stuffed into his pocket. In the worn armchair that was Gareth's usual seat, Gito's heavy frame stiffened to attention as he looked up at the newcomers.

'It's Roger Furnivall, Mam,' said Gareth. 'He's brought a young lady with him.'

With everyone's eyes on her, even the blind old woman's face turned expectantly in her direction, Jenny walked sedately across and, reaching down, took up Mam's right hand.

'Jenny Grayfield,' she said. 'I'm glad to meet you, Mrs Jones.'

It stirred Roger's emotions to hear her call herself by what must be her maiden name instead of Twyford. Her renunciation of Gerald, her refusal to belong to him or his world any longer, were suddenly vivid to him.

'Welcome,' said the old woman. 'A long way up the mountain you coming, and late on a cold night.'

'Oh,' said the girl lightly, 'Roger's looking after me.'

For an instant, the eyes of the other three men flickered in Roger's direction. He felt like a dog with a bone in his jaws, walking past three other dogs. Then the iron shutter of decorum fell and all their faces became expressionless again.

Ivo's eyes had flickered with the most intensity. Roger had never given the subject any thought before, but now it flashed on him that Ivo, with his quick nervousness and intensity, was probably a sexually voracious man.

The thought swept through his mind and became history. Things were moving too fast for reflection.

'It's good to see you at home, Gareth,' he said. 'I was afraid they might have kept you at the hospital.'

'I was there long enough,' said Gareth. 'They put this stuff on me –' he looked down at the plaster, 'as soon as I got there, and the rest was just waiting about. They wouldn't give me my trousers and let me out till the doctor came round, and that wasn't till eleven o'clock this morning. So I was in over twelve hours.'

'I'm glad they took good care of you.'

Gareth pulled down the corners of his mouth. 'If somebody'd

only been there to shout *Look behind you*! at a certain moment last night, we'd have seen who would take care of who.'

'Meanwhile,' said Roger musingly, 'they've got their come-uppance. But they're still ahead, on balance.' His hand went tenderly to his bruised ribs as he spoke.

'Ahead?' said Ivo, his voice sharp and enquiring.

'Well, the bus will have to stay in the garage till Gareth can drive again, and how long will that be?'

'Four weeks,' said Gareth, 'at least.' His eyes had almost disappeared into their deep sockets: his face was a mask of strain and fatigue.

'Well, then.'

'Why not make yourselves comfortable, you and the lady,' said Ivo. He was brisk and authoritative, unmistakably in the chair for the evening. 'We haven't been wasting our time, and we've got one or two notions it might concern you to hear.'

'I'm concerned all right,' said Roger drily.

'We met Iorwerth,' said Gito. 'That was a lucky thing for you. Perhaps the turning-point of luck for all of us.'

'We could do with it,' said Roger, thinking of Jenny.

'We've been having a council of war,' Gito went on. He spoke gently, almost apologetically, perhaps trying to soften Ivo's acerbity. He had edged forward in his seat as if uneasy about sitting down in Jenny's presence but self-conscious about making the courtly gesture of standing up, and now sat balanced on the edge of it. His big face and wide, gleaming bald head turned from Roger to Jenny and back again as if asking for reassurance.

'I can't find any more beer,' said Gareth, groping behind chairs. 'We were just about finishing, so of course we drank it up.'

'Don't give it a thought,' said Roger. He and Jenny had found themselves somewhere to perch, and all he wanted now was information. 'I've been away all day. How has the situation developed?'

'We've got the situation mapped out,' Ivo said crisply, 'and we've made our plans. The main thing is, matters have taken a turn that ought to favour us, right? When Dic Sharp sent those men up to tamper with the bus and attack you, and they must have been the same ones he'd already set on to Gareth the night before, well, when he did that he crossed a line. And if we can nab him before he gets back across it, we've got him.'

'On toast,' said Gito in his high, husky voice. Roger could not help noticing, as so often before, that the big man with the deep chest had the high voice, and the small nervously active man had the resonant voice that could fill a room without being raised.

'He's moved definitely out of legality,' said Ivo, bringing out the big words with a flourish. 'He's made himself a criminal. As long as he was only snapping up Gareth's trade, he was within his rights as far as the law went. There's no monopoly on bus routes, isn't it? As long as a bus has the proper licensing and insurance, it can go anywhere where there are passengers for it. But that didn't work. Gareth hung on too well.'

Mam suddenly stirred in her chair and said in a firm voice, 'And we know who that was thanks to.'

'We know who that was thanks to,' Ivo caught her up. 'That's why if we miss this chance, if we don't all work together and catch him now we've got him red-handed, we'll be letting Roger down as well as Gareth.'

'And ourselves,' said Gito, drinking.

'Those bright boyos this morning,' Ivo continued, 'got away. It doesn't seem to have occurred to anybody to hold them so as they could be taken to the police.'

'I thought of it,' said Roger, 'but I was too . . .'

'And of course Iorwerth wouldn': bother,' said Ivo. 'He's the type who thinks a good clout on the jaw's a better answer to any problem than policemen and magistrates and courts. If they were going to be prosecuted, he'd have had to show up and be a witness, and I can't see our Iorwerth wanting to bother with anything of that.'

He looked round at the circle of faces. How he delights in this, Roger thought. The summing up of evidence, the use of his clear mind. He should have been a lawyer. Then the thought came: there are many lawyers, but so few Ivos.

'We met Iorwerth in the town,' said Ivo. 'He told us the story. And one important thing, isn't it? – the bus driver was one of the two. That means he's out of the picture. He won't show up again. Partly because he'll be too banged up to work for a day or two, but much more because he'll be afraid to show his ugly mug. He's been caught out, and his best chance is to get out of the district.'

'He was an outsider anyway,' said Gareth musingly. 'Dic Sharp can get them from all over.'

'So at first,' Ivo continued, 'we half thought there might be no more visits from the bus. If he's got to find another driver, and not everybody'd be too keen on it . . .'

He looked round again, enjoying the suspense of his narrative.

'Only we heard the lad,' Gito prompted him unnecessarily.

'Yes,' said Ivo. 'We went to the Fisherman's for a drink at dinner-time, not to Mario's like we usually do, and we heard from the saloon bar. You could hear him all over the pub. That son of Dic Sharp's, the warty little snot-nosed bugger.'

'I'm here, Ivo,' said Mam.

'A lapse of the ling, Mrs Jones. A slip of the tongue. I'm sorry for it. Anyway, that little Prince Charming was in the saloon bar, and a good skinful in him. He was, saving everybody's presence, inebriated out of his maggoty little mind. Some of the stuff he was coming out with, well, it didn't concern us at all, but some of it did. And one thing in particular he kept saying. They were coming up to finish us.'

'You mean finish me,' said Gareth.

'No, Gareth, us. Everybody's in this together, boy.' Ivo picked up his empty glass, looked at it, set it down. 'He said that pirate bus would be on the run tomorrow morning and every morning. That Gareth wouldn't be able to drive for a month, and that was the month when they were going to finish it once and for all – clear it off the books, he kept saying.'

Roger could hear the fair-haired young man's voice saying the words, over and over again, with his thick, creamy, sneering intonation. *Clear it off the books, clear it off the books.* 'We'll see about that,' he said.

'You're right we'll see about it,' said Ivo. 'Now, here's what we're going to do. We've got a little two-stage surprise for whoever drives the bus, isn't it?'

'A little two-stage heart failure,' said Gito delightedly. He thumped the arm of the worn chair with his fist.

'Number one,' said Ivo, grinning sharply from face to face, 'we're going to travel with him.'

'Travel with him?' Roger echoed.

'As passengers,' Ivo grinned.

'But he'll never stop for you. As soon as he sees you waiting, he'll –'

'That's where we need a little help,' said Ivo. With conscious dramatic suddenness, he switched his full attention to Jenny. 'Miss – I didn't quite hear your name –'

'Jenny,' she said. She knew this was a test for her, and Roger, watching, had no doubt that her North-country streak of combativeness would make her relish it.

'Jenny,' said Ivo. His voice had softened; it was almost caressing, yet with a velvet undertone of mockery. 'It's a piece of luck for all of us here that Roger brought you along tonight. I might go further. Not just luck. Almost like – well, something *meant*.'

His eyes held Jenny's. Roger leaned forward to watch. Ivo's technique with women was worth studying closely.

'Meant?' she said coolly.

'The answer to our special problem,' he said. 'Now the main thing is, can we persuade you to turn out at eight in the morning?'

'If it's important,' she said.

'It's important all right. But we don't want to ask the impossible. Will you be anywhere near here, tomorrow morning at eight?'

'I shall be at Roger's place,' she said. Her glance, as she spoke, met Ivo's with a bland, unconcerned matter-of-factness. Roger wanted to applaud. She had outmanoeuvred Ivo, making it impossible for him to load the situation with innuendo, simply by laying the whole matter on the table and forcing him to go on from there.

Ivo was too clever not to realize this, and his next move was into straight, military exposition.

'Good. Then I'll come for you with the lorry about ten to eight. You too, Roger.'

Roger nodded.

'I hope you'll be wide awake,' Ivo could not resist saying.

'I'll be awake, Ivo. I've given three months to this exercise, you don't think I'd want to spoil it now?'

Ivo took the slight defeat gracefully. He had distrusted Roger at the beginning, warned him off: Roger had the right to his one crack of the whip now.

'Right. So the plan is this. We shall pick you all up, in the lorry, before eight, and go down in good time, so that we don't run any risk of meeting the bastard coming up, I beg pardon Mrs Jones, meeting the pirate bus coming up, and then take up a position at a certain point about one-third of the way down, where there is a bus stop.'

He paused and Jenny said into the silence, 'I'm waiting to hear why it's a special Providence that I'm here.'

'I was coming to that,' said Ivo. 'When I say a bus stop, I mean of course a point at which passengers gather from habit. There aren't any official stops on a country run like this. The spot we have in mind is a small junction. A lane, with five or six cottages in it, runs into the road there. The banks are high. We can get behind them and not be seen. Those of us, I mean, whose appearance would be likely to frighten the driver away if it was anybody who happened to know the set-up.'

'I see. So I stand out in front and flag the bus down, and when it's safely stopped –'

'When it's safely stopped,' said Ivo, pursing his lips with satisfaction at the thought, 'the rest of us come out and get on with you. Me, Gareth, Roger. We do nothing: we state our destination; we pay our fare if he asks us for one. Already the man is rattled, but there's nothing he can do.'

'You and I and Gareth,' said Roger. 'What about Gito? Where will he be?'

'Where Gito will be,' said Ivo, 'is the second stage of our little two-stage surprise for the bus driver. I think it would be better if I left it at that.'

'Why should it be better?' Jenny asked flatly.

'Because,' Ivo's manner was unruffled, 'surprises are more fun to watch when they're real surprises. And you and Roger, if you're going to be up and dressed and fed and watered by eight o'clock, deserve a little fun.'

Roger was content to leave the last word, the last tying-up of the arrangements, with Ivo. Ivo had so much invested in this evening, while his own main effort lay elsewhere. 'Well,' he said, 'if we've got to be in action early, it's time to be getting some rest.'

Gito heaved his square frame out of the armchair, and Ivo got to his feet at the same time.

Gareth, who had been so quiet, seemed to feel the need for one assertion of his hostly role before they all went. 'Wait for a hot cup of tea,' he said, moving on quick stumpy legs to the kitchen door. 'The kettle's warm. It'll boil in a minute.'

Roger and Jenny were beginning to demur, to make excuses, but Gareth cried almost fiercely, 'It's not a night to go out without anything,' and Mam added her gentler voice. 'Come and sit over against me, young woman. Near the fire, and talking to me a minute.'

'Gladly,' said Jenny at once. She went and sat beside Mam's chair, on a low stool, and in the desultory conversation that broke out Roger could hear their two female voices, low and confiding, busily weaving a sheltered corner where men's clumsiness could not break in.

Gareth, as good as his word, came back with mugs of strong tea in a very short time. He was just in the act of distributing them when the old woman lifted up her blind face and cried in Welsh.

Gareth! I smell violets!

Are you sure? he asked, pausing.

Sure as I sit here, she said.

What does she mean, said Roger, violets?

It was Gito who answered. Some of the old people, with the old ways, he said, they can smell snow in the wind. It comes to them like the scent of violets.

I did have the back door open, said Gareth, for a moment.

They had all resumed speaking in Welsh in their excitement; but Ivo, who had not relaxed his watchfulness, spoke in his usual English, that English which, Madog had said, carried no smell of the Cambrian soil, and kept his eyes on Jenny. 'If there's heavy snow, Miss Grayfield, the bus might not be able to get up. If that happens, we transfer the arrangement from day to day, complete. Until we strike a day when the bus *is* there.'

'I understand,' she said.

Meanwhile Gareth had gone quickly to the front door and was staring out.

The first flakes, he said.

Roger looked past him into the night. Already, the dark grass was beginning to glimmer with grey.

Will it be heavy? he asked.

If Mam smells violets it will, said Gareth. He closed the door again. 'I should drink up that tea, Miss,' he said to Jenny. 'You'll need to be on your way. The snow could trap you on the mountain. Yes,' he insisted in the face of her half-smile of incredulity, 'even between here and Roger's chapel.'

'Roger's chapel,' she said. 'That's a good one.'

Suddenly everyone was laughing, relaxed and comradely, their serious business done.

'Well,' said Ivo, 'it's right for Roger to live in a chapel, after all. I don't know anyone who needs it more.'

'Wait till you hear my sermons,' said Roger. 'I'll invite you to a preach-in as soon as we've got rid of Dic Sharp.'

Joking, they put on their coats, wished Gareth and Mam a good night, and went out into the night of crowding flakes.

'This is the real thing,' said Ivo. 'A mountain snowstorm. Better get moving, Roger, while you can.'

Roger, Roger. He never remembered their bandying his name about so much before. It seemed as if, always till now, they had been shy of it, drawing back from the familiarity implied, the welcome, the acceptance.

'All right, Ivo,' he said. 'See you at a ten to eight, if you can get through.'

'That's as may be,' said Ivo, disappearing among the white flakes. 'But the first morning it's possible I'll be there.'

He and Gito waved and they were gone. Roger's last impression of them was of the whiteness of their shoulders, and the way their feet slipped on the thickening snow.

'Come,' he said to Jenny. They clanged the gate, walked down the path, which was already invisible and had to be guessed at, and found the mini-car, patient under its crest of drifting snow.

'God,' Jenny said suddenly. 'After a day like this, to be stuck out on the mountain – I'd *die*, just thinking about warmth and comfort and bed.'

'You won't be stuck,' he said. 'And you won't die. You'll live.'

She unlocked the door, then handed him the keys. It was

understood, without discussion, that he was to drive. She was in his hands now.

He started the motor, got into gear, and cautiously let in the clutch. At once the fat little wheels started to spin and slither.

'We may not make it,' he said to Jenny.

'Never mind. Let's take her as far as she'll go.'

The world was wet and white. Snowflakes crowded one another so thickly that there seemed to be hardly any distinction between the earth, piled with soft, uncompacted snow, and the sky, crammed with big, eddying particles.

'There go your friends,' said Jenny. Away to their left, a lit-up, roaring shape lowered itself down the mountain, taking the other fork.

'I hope they get there,' he said briefly and then gave all his energy to ploughing and sluicing along the lane. It was more like piloting a boat than a car: they moved, but heavily, as if in fluid, and the steering was slow and approximate.

'Are there any deep ditches here?' Jenny asked, peering into the swirling blankness.

'I don't think so. Or we'd have been in them by now.'

Several times they nearly swam to a halt, but in the end the chapel loomed up to one side of them and Roger slewed the little car off the road.

'It'll be all right here,' he said. 'There won't be any traffic, in any case, till this lot clears away.'

They got out. The snowflakes, waltzing down, muffled the slam of the doors, one on each side. Then they were together at the chapel door, and Roger was feeling for his key.

'Here it is. Go in first.'

She entered obediently. Now she was his, safe in his den. But he couldn't feel it: too much had happened, too much was getting ready to happen. This was an interlude, only an interlude.

'Wait.' He switched the light on. 'Now make yourself comfortable. I'll get the stove going.'

He felt glad of this prosaic duty. When he had riddled and replenished the stove, he stood back, grave with satisfaction.

'I'll let it burn up,' he said, shutting the doors and leaving the bottom open, 'in five minutes that'll be lovely.'

'I know. My mother's got one.'

'Now,' he said, unbuttoning his coat. 'Some tea?'

She shook her head. 'One lot's enough, at this time of night. I'd never sleep –'

She caught herself up. For a second her expression was almost sheepish; then, quickly, they both laughed. In Roger's case, and doubtless in hers, the amusement was genuine. The unguarded remark had so perfectly revealed her attitude. About to go to bed for the first time with a man who might – just might – be all-important to her future, she was thinking primarily of sleep. They had travelled so far, thought and spoken of so many things, seen and heard and felt so much, that she had forgotten all about love. Or, rather, she was conscious of love chiefly as meaning that they were together and could help and comfort each other. Passion – that was in another country.

'I'm glad you feel like that,' said Roger.

'Feel like what?'

'Unemotional. Routine. Thinking about this night as being like any other night when you've had a long day and look forward to sleep. Because that's how I feel too.'

She mistook his tone, thought he was being ironic. 'I'm sorry,' she said.

'Don't be.'

She sat down on the Fräulein's divan and looked at him through her glasses. 'I'm tired, Roger. I can hardly stand up any more.'

'Well, don't stand up,' he said. 'If you need rest, then rest.'

'Are you disappointed?'

For one horrible moment, it crossed Roger's mind that she was going to ask him to spend the night in the armchair, or on the floor, and leave her alone in the bed. His anxiety must have shown in his face, because she suddenly burst into laughter, throwing her head back.

What nice teeth she has, he thought.

Still laughing, Jenny got up and came across to where he stood. 'Your face!' she said, between little exploding puffs. 'If I'd told you I wanted you to sleep outside in the snow, it couldn't have been more – the corners of your mouth went right down, you should have seen it!'

He joined in her laughter. She put her arms confidingly round him, lacing her fingers at the small of his back.

'This is your place, Roger,' she said simply. 'The snug little hideout you found for yourself on the cold mountain. You've made room in it, and perhaps in your life, for a woman who's going to be a damn nuisance to you –'

'No.'

'Yes,' she corrected gently. 'A woman with a slab of lived life behind her that she can't help bringing along. Problems, kids, a divorce, troubles – perhaps you'd have done better to find a young girl with no history, nothing to weigh her down.'

'I like history,' he said. 'I'm a professional scholar.'

Outside the snow fell steadily, anonymously, hiding their traces, building them a defence against the world.

'You know, I say all that,' she said, leaning against him, 'but I'm not really feeling it. My history isn't here, nor is yours. There's nothing with us – it's just now, and the snow, and your lovely bright stove, and bed.'

'Yes,' he said. 'The stove and bed.' He stooped, opened the stove doors, and let out a flood of cherry-coloured warmth.

'How lovely!' She clapped her hands like a child, then, as simply as a child, began to unbutton her dress.

'I'm so tired, Roger.' She yawned, then smiled. 'Are you warm in bed?'

'Like a horse. Many's the stranded wayfarer I've saved from freezing to death.'

She took a nightdress out of her bag. 'I ought to clean my teeth, but I'm too tired for that, even. I'll just put this on.' She shook it out. 'Roger, come to bed.'

'Ready,' he said.

'Where are your pyjamas?'

'In there,' he said, nodding towards the bed, 'but I shan't be needing them.' He went over to the switch and turned out the light. Now they were standing in the glow of the stove, all outlines soft and kindly, all shadows velvet.

'Get into bed,' she said gently. He finished undressing and slipped in between the cool flannel sheets.

'See,' he said, 'how I do everything you tell me.'

Calmly, she undressed, hesitated for a moment over the nightdress, then threw it aside and slid in beside him naked. For a long moment they were silent.

'You,' she murmured at last.

'Yes.'

'All this is you.'

'And all this is you?'

They were silent again.

'It's like meeting for the first time,' she said.

'It *is* meeting for the first time.'

Her breasts were heavier than he had expected. They contrasted with the slightness of her body. His bruised ribs hurt when she pressed against him, but he did not care.

'Roger.'

'Yes, darling.'

'Now that you've met me, do you like me?'

His answer was wordless.

Her breath came quickly. 'What shall I do to please you?'

'You're doing it.'

Outside, the snowflakes went on with their secret dance: and the appeased ghost of Geoffrey, moving away, left no footprints on the white skin of the mountain.

Next morning, the drifts lay high and creamy, hiding the walls, filling the hollows in the ground, smoothing the outlines of the harsh boulders. Roger went to the window, took in the scene, and shivered with sudden pleasure.

'A day's holiday,' he said, turning to speak over his shoulder to the softly moulded Jenny-shape under the blankets.

'What did you say?' she asked, moving her face out into the morning air. Her eyes, naked without their glasses, explored the room as if she were coming back by slow stages to the knowledge of where she was.

He went back and disappeared into the bed with her, covering up her face.

'I said, a day's holiday. The snow's too thick for anything to use the roads. We stay here.'

They stayed there.

The snow insulated them, not only by cutting them off from normal contact with the outside world, but by making that world so new, so unfamiliar, so magical, when they looked out at it through the windows. All that day, and all the next, they took a holiday from reality, or at least from any reality alien to themselves. The chapel was an island in the uncharted sea of

309

whiteness that lay across the contours of the everyday world, effacing landmarks, roads, barriers, responsibilities. Roger had expected Jenny to talk exhaustively about her troubles, and had been ready to listen, to enter into the experiences she would recount, to help her to live through them again and surmount them, so that she could feel that she had indeed come out on the other side. In fact, she never mentioned them. For two days they were absorbed in one another, in the discovery of each other's bodies and minds, and also in the small, shared problems of emergency housekeeping. There was plenty of fuel, and though some foods ran out almost at once (they had no bread from the very beginning, and no sugar after about half-way point) others held out well, so that by the evening of the second day they still found themselves able to sit down to a hearty, if slightly bizarre meal: sardines, mashed potatoes, tinned butter beans, with cornflakes and sliced bananas as a second course, and mugs of black coffee to finish with. The snow lay over the mountains like a clean starched coverlet, and they went to bed utterly happy. But they agreed that their strict isolation was now at an end: the next morning, shortage of nearly all necessities would enforce an expedition to the village shops.

When they woke (late) and got up (later), and when they had breakfasted somehow on whatever scraps were left, Roger began to hunt for his stoutest shoes and most waterproof coat.

'D'you want to come?' he asked.

'No, thanks. The clothes I've got with me just aren't made for deep snow. They'd get soaked and I'd be all day trying to dry them. Besides, I'm going to give this place a good sweep out while you're away.'

'Wait till I come back,' he said, lacing up his boots, 'and we'll do it together.'

'Nothing doing. I want the sensation of being a squaw. I'm going to slave for you. On the other hand I want to do it when you're not looking. I don't want you helping and I don't want you sitting like a pasha and watching while I toil. So go. And take your time about getting back.'

'I can guarantee that, squaw,' he said. 'The snow must be three or four feet deep all the way into the village. And goodness knows how many times I'll fall into drifts up to my neck.'

'If you're not back in three hours,' she said, 'I'll send the St Bernards out. And now give me a kiss, and go.'

Roger kissed her and went out. The snow was deep, but not sticky. He found he could get along quite well, though it was very deep in places. His chief difficulty lay in telling where the edge of the road would be; several times he slithered into the ditch, but the powdery snow soon brushed off his clothes, and in his present mood of gaiety these comic little disasters were nothing but delightful jokes, part of a playfulness in which all creation was free to share.

In Llancrwys itself, men using shovels, or perhaps a small petrol-driven snow-plough, had made narrow paths which had been trodden yellow amid the dazzling white of the roofs and gardens, and down the middle of each street was a cautious ribbon of tyre-tracks. Roger stepped more briskly, swinging his basket. It was then that he caught sight of Rhiannon. She was walking from the centre of the village towards her parents' house. The lovely marionette! He adored her more than ever, now that he no longer needed her.

Rhiannon moved slowly, but with a country-bred sureness of foot, among the deep snow-ruts. She was wearing her green suède coat, and boots that laced elaborately all the way up the front, like skating boots. She was bareheaded, but her ears were protected by two delicious little woollen muffs, joined by a stiff arch which went across her neatly casual coiffure. The sight of her coming towards him gave Roger acute enjoyment. She was lovely to behold, and he was free to savour the sight of her without painful longings and shattering disturbance of his care-fully gathered tranquillity. Jenny had made him happy, his wants were satisfied, his flesh no longer scolded and nagged at him. So Rhiannon could come close to him, could cause him a delicious tremor, and the tremor would stay delicious, without modulating into bitterness and pain.

He stationed himself in her path, and waited. She smiled at him before she drew near enough to speak; evidently they were friends, he was in good standing.

'Hello, Roger.'

'Hello, Rhiannon. How beautiful you look.'

'Flattery won't get you anywhere,' she said, 'but it's nice. Give me some more.'

'It's just a spontaneous observation. I'm surrounded by beautiful things this morning. The sea, the sky, the whiteness on the hills. The way the mountains seem to hang in the sky, like a vision, because there's a mist on the lower slopes and the peaks are clear. The clouds! And then *you* walk on to the scene! It's all too much.'

'It only needs Dilwyn's aeroplane,' she said, her face straight.

'Don't,' he winced. 'Let me cut my losses.'

'Talking of losses,' she said, 'the bus business can't be very healthy just now.'

'Too much snow,' he said noncommittally.

'Yes, snow,' said Rhiannon. 'And not only that. Listen, I heard about the goings-on. How they attacked Gareth.'

'And me.'

'No, did they attack you too?'

'They tried to, but I got help and drove them off.'

'Well,' she said, 'I'm glad I ran into you. I was thinking of trying to get a message to you, only I hadn't got time to struggle out to the chapel.'

Roger had a quick vision of Rhiannon knocking on the chapel door and Jenny opening it. In a way, he was sorry it was not going to happen. It would enhance his sexual status.

'What was the message,?' he asked.

'Tomorrow,' she said, 'everything'll be back to normal. The snow-ploughs are out, and they're due up here this afternoon about tea-time. I heard the Borough Surveyor talking in the bar. So you know what that means.'

'It means,' he said slowly, 'that Gareth's bus would be able to run, only it won't be able to because they broke his wrist.'

'It won't be Gareth's bus that'll be running tomorrow. It'll be Dic Sharp's outfit. He knows the roads'll be clear and his bus will run at eight tomorrow.'

'But the driver,' said Roger. 'The chap who's been driving for him up to now. He won't be there, I know that.'

'No, he won't. The other one's going to drive, the one who was doing the conducting.'

'How do you know that?'

'Never mind how I know. I know everything, you should realize that by now.'

'Darling Rhiannon,' he said, 'I think you do know everything.'

'What I don't know,' she said, 'is how you're managing, all by yourself in that chapel.'

Was it a probe? Had she heard rumours of Jenny's presence? Or did she really feel for what she took to be his lonely, snow-bound plight?

'You're kind,' he said, 'to spare me a thought. Everything that happens to me I've brought on myself.'

'I'm sure of it,' she said lightly.

'If you're concerned about me,' he said, 'come and visit me. Bring me the sunshine of your smiles.'

'There's enough sunshine going about,' said Rhiannon tartly, 'without any more. But I just thought I'd warn you. Dic Sharp's bus'll be up here tomorrow, and he plans to keep it on the road so that by the time Gareth's ready to drive again, his service will just look unnecessary.'

'I see.'

'I don't know whether there's anything you can do about it, but –'

'Yes, there is. Rhiannon, tell me this. Are you planning to travel down tomorrow at eight-fifteen?'

'Me? No. I shall be down in Caerfenai tonight. I've just come up to get a few things from home. I had the chance of a lift, so I came. Strictly speaking I should be at the hotel now, but –'

'Good,' he said. 'If you had been intending to ride tomorrow morning, I'd have warned you to keep clear.'

'Why? Is something going to – ?'

'I've said enough. To anyone else, it would already have been too much. But I know you'll keep silent as the tomb.'

'Yes, but I'm curious.'

'There's nothing I can tell you, really. It's just that we've got a plan and we're going to put it into operation tomorrow morning.'

'We? You and Gareth?'

'Gareth and I and two others. Our team, you might call it. You see, even we,' he finished proudly, 'have friends.'

'Of course. I'm one. I've just given you a valuable tip-off.'

'So you have, my love,' he said. 'It makes me love you even

more, if that were possible. I only wish there were something I could do for you.'

Rhiannon interpreted this last remark as Roger evidently intended her to interpret it, and with a reproving wag of the finger she went on her way. Roger, his mood suddenly serious, decided to leave the shopping until he had taken this news to Gareth. Hurrying, floundering and slipping, he made all haste up to the cottage at the foot of the slate-tip, where he found Gareth sitting aimlessly by a slack fire, while Mam in her accustomed place bent patiently over the quietly talking radio. Gareth seemed depressed, beginning already to be rotted by inactivity and boredom, but the news about the snow-plough gave him back his animation.

We must tell Ivo and Gito, he said. I'll get down to the phone.

I'm going back to the village. I'll ring them.

No, I need to speak to them. Wait, I'll get my boots on and come with you.

They hurried down the white, heaped slope. At times the snow was up to Gareth's thighs.

They'll have a job, he said, clearing this lot, snow-plough or no snow-plough. But they'll get through, I know that.

In the telephone box, Gareth's forehead was flushed with excitement. He could not hold the receiver in his right hand because the plaster extended down to the palm and interfered with his grip. Roger watched from outside as he laid the receiver carefully on one side, put the coins in the slot with eager precision, then lifted it to his ear. He motioned Roger to come in and listen to the conversation, but Roger smiled and shook his head. There was no room for two people to stand comfortably in the box, and he was afraid of crowding Gareth's broken wrist. Waiting outside, he picked up a few words through the glass.

I'll tell him.

Bring the girl, yes.

This should do the trick.

When Gareth came out, the door of the glass booth swinging ebulliently behind him, Roger saw real elation in his face.

The lads are ready, he said. Quarter to eight tomorrow.

And, said Roger carefully, Jenny and I?

Ivo will come for you. With the lorry. Exactly as we planned before.

Suppose the lorry can't get through as far as the chapel?

It'll get through. Gito knows the man in charge of the snow-plough. He'll get him to take it down that far.

Gareth gave a slow, delighted grin as he said this.

Well, said Roger. Good luck be with our efforts.

Amen to that, said Gareth. He turned and began to walk back towards his house.

Be ready in the morning, he called back, and leave the rest to the lads.

Roger made some appropriate noise of assent, then went into the village shop. He wanted to make his purchases and get back. It seemed to him, suddenly, a long time since he had seen Jenny.

The next morning Roger's alarm clock, which like its owner had been off duty for some days, was back in full peevish voice, and in the darkness of seven o'clock Roger was moving about, rattling the stove, brewing strong tea. Jenny blinked like an owl in the softness of the bed, but after a mug of Roger's dark tea she got up willingly enough, dressing in the cerise glow of the stove.

'Better eat something,' Roger said sagely.

She accepted a buttered crust and chewed. 'What do they want me to do?'

'Act as decoy duck.'

'Well, I've done some funny things in my time.'

They finished dressing and were ready to go. Some minutes went by.

'It seems very dark outside,' said Jenny restively. 'Are you sure it's morning?'

'Both my watch and the alarm clock say it's a quarter to eight.'

'Perhaps the lorry can't get through.'

At that moment they heard the whine of the old Dodge's engine, cautiously slowing down, levelling out to a steady drumming. Then Ivo's voice came through the darkness: 'Roger! We're here!'

'Come on,' he said to Jenny. 'This is it. Action at last.'

'You've waited a long time for this, haven't you?' she said as they hurried across to the door.

'Yes,' he said, 'a long time,' and snapped off the lights.

Outside, the first cold light was creeping over the white slopes. Gito was alone in the cab of the lorry; in the back, looking down at them over the high wooden sides, were Ivo and Gareth. Ivo, his woollen cap jammed down on his head, was wrapped in an old sheepskin coat; Gareth was wearing his leather jerkin, and had a scarf wound round his head to keep his ears warm.

'Get up in front,' said Ivo, motioning.

Roger and Jenny obeyed. Gito welcomed them with a nod, and, without attempting to speak over the drumming of the engine, at once put the lorry into reverse gear and started to move backwards. The snow-plough had cleared a track just wide enough for them to move, but not to turn round. Using his rear-view mirror, and occasionally warned by a sharp cry from Ivo or Gareth, he gently moved the cumbrous bulk of the lorry back down the lane for three or four hundred yards. There, at the entrance to a smallholding, enough snow had been cleared away to allow him, cautiously, to ease round and face in the right direction.

They moved more quickly, after that, over the frozen, rutted snow, towards the centre of Llancrwys. Roger and Jenny, huddled together, held hands and stared through the windscreen at the familiar landscape seen, now, from an unfamiliar elevation and in the strange, sharp light of dawn. Gito, intent and calm as he guided the big lorry between the high white banks, was separated from them by the metal housing of the gearbox. They went past Gareth's corrugated-iron garage, where the yellow bus waited in its enforced hibernation; they turned downhill at the crossroads in the centre of the village; they went past Mrs Pylon Jones's, the green and brown of its two front doors just coming up into visibility as the dawn advanced; they cleared the last few straggling houses of Llancrwys, and then Gito was throttling down, braking carefully, stopping by the entrance to a tiny lane.

'This is where you get down,' he said to Roger and Jenny.

'Right.'

They opened the door and swung down over the big front wheel. Ivo and Gareth had already scrambled down from the rear, and Gareth was putting the tailgate back in position.

'O.K., Gito,' he called.

Gito accelerated gently and the Dodge moved away, down the road towards the coast.

'Now,' said Ivo commandingly, 'we wait here.' He led the way to a place in the lee of the wall where they could stand without being seen. The snow-plough had not cleared this little lane, but there was a path along the centre of it, beaten by the feet of the villagers and their animals. In addition, close under the wall, someone had shovelled away a patch about six feet square, intended for people waiting for transport, or possibly for milk-churns.

'What about me?' said Jenny, her voice, in that conspiratorial setting, hardly rising above a whisper, 'Don't I stand out in full view?'

'Not yet,' said Gareth. 'He's got to come up first. Better not give him anything to notice.'

They stood in a knot, backs against the snow-packed wall. After a few minutes Roger stiffened and said, 'I hear something.'

They all listened. It was a bus engine, climbing towards them.

'He's coming up,' said Gareth, with suppressed delight. 'He'll find some passengers at the top, and he'll turn straight round and come down.'

They all stood well back, where a mound of drifted snow could mask them from the road. As the bus roared past them, Ivo quickly moved his head out and back.

'It's him all right,' he said.

'Who's driving?' asked Gareth.

'Didn't get a chance to see.'

'We'll know soon enough,' said Roger. He felt fierce excitement rising in him. Ah, this was life at last.

After what seemed too short a time for the bus to have climbed to the centre of Llancrwys and turned round, they heard it again on its way down. Something as tangible as an electric current ran through them all: a wave of determination, of preparedness.

'Now, Jenny,' Roger prompted her.

Jenny detached herself from the group and walked out into full view, looking steadily up the road toward Llancrwys. *How resolute she is*, Roger thought. *How naturally she takes her place in all this, sharing our early-morning adventure*. He felt absurdly proud of Jenny, not so much of anything she was doing, but simply of her being there, participating.

The noise of the bus was loud now.

'Keep your heads down,' said Ivo in a low, tense voice. 'don't make him suspect anything and drive on.'

The bus was roaringly there, upon them, slowing down in answer to Jenny's lifted hand. It was a shuddering oblong of light, with a presence like that of some large animal: it was a moored ship of the mountainside, it was Dic Sharp's moving lair, it was the enemy.

'Come on,' said Gareth abruptly. This was his moment: he assumed full command. Both Roger and Ivo stood back to let him pass. His broad, humped buffalo-shape moved on suddenly nimble legs across the intervening five yards of snow and he was up the steps, into the bus, and Ivo behind him, and Roger.

Rhiannon's information had been right. The young man with the ferret-face, who had often travelled as a conductor, was now at the wheel. He was, of course, taking no fares. He had never taken any fares, even when he had been conductor and worn a shiny peaked cap. His function then had obviously been merely to give moral support to the driver. Now the driver was beyond the reach of moral support. He had been thumped away from it by Iorwerth's fists. Instinctively Roger glanced down the bus: yes, Iorwerth was there, sitting at the back. His face was as expressionless as ever; the other morning might have been all a dream. No, he was grinning. He was watching Gareth and grinning.

Jenny had passed down the bus and taken a seat at about mid-point. There were about a dozen people on board, all watching eagerly and silently. His eye flickering over the scene, Roger noticed Mr Cledwyn Jones and one or two other stalwarts. Mrs Arkwright, he was glad to see, was absent.

Then he looked rapidly back to the driver. Gareth was standing over him. There was a handrail running along the top of the engine cover, designed for passengers to be able to steady themselves in the moving bus. Gareth was gripping this rail with his good hand, and leaning over until his face almost touched the ferrety young man's. The scarf was still wrapped round his head, giving him a nightmarish appearance.

'What . . .' said the ferrety youth. Then his voice died away.

'What, what?' Gareth asked in a low, murderous voice. The passengers leaned forward in their seats.

'What – yer doing?' the ferret managed to jerk out through his panic-rigid jaws.

'Getting a good look at you,' said Gareth. He smiled almost sweetly. 'I've been wanting to get to know you.'

'Drive on, man,' said Ivo from behind the hill of Gareth's shoulders. 'If you're running a bus service, run one.'

There was a murmur of agreement from the passengers, and Mr Cledwyn Jones cried out, 'Some of us have work to go to.'

Ivo and Roger sank down into seats near the front of the bus. Roger looked back over his shoulder at Jenny: she smiled at him in sudden, flashing triumph. Gareth continued to stand beside the driver, holding firmly on to the rail. The driver, his face paper-white, started the bus moving again.

'Gareth,' said Ivo, leaning forward, 'you'd be safer sitting down.'

Gareth looked down at Ivo as if he had never seen him before. Then he shook his head and grinned, 'I'll hang on,' he said.

'Better,' said Ivo. And as he spoke, it happened.

The bus was moving at about twenty-five miles an hour, on a comparatively easy section of the slope, between high, snow-packed banks. A few yards ahead was the outlet of another side lane, but there was no need to look out for traffic emerging from it; in this weather, it would be certain to be blocked. Certain? As certain as anything in this world. But suddenly the driver was snatching at the wheel with his ferret-claws, his face grimacing in quick terror. Out of the lane, immediately in front of them, too close to be avoided, like a grey battleship sliding determinedly into their path, came the high bonnet of the Canadian Dodge. Gito's set face. The lorry's steep, battered sides.

The ferret-driver lost control immediately. One wild swing to the right, on the slippery surface, and the bus was slewing sideways, all adhesion gone from the wheels. Several of the passengers cried out: the driver dragged the wheel the other way, and the bus shuddered as if trying vainly to straighten itself. There was a high metallic *bang*!, followed immediately by a roaring, scraping crunch. Then silence, as the bus settled at an angle of forty degrees. Its near-side front wheel was in a ditch of soft snow; its engine spluttered and died out.

Gareth straightened up and called down the length of the bus, 'Open the emergency door.'

A woman was crying loudly. But the rest of the passengers, now that they realized that the bus had stopped and they were unhurt, seemed calm enough. They were almost ready to begin enjoying the drama of the situation. Roger's feelings, however, were the other way round. He had been keyed up for action while these people had been sitting somnolently on the bus going to work, and now he felt nervous and shaken. The bus seemed to him to be canting at an alarming angle; the door was jammed hopelessly against the bank, and the only way out was at the back where Iorwerth was even now struggling with the handle of the emergency exit. The handle was stiff: it had not been maintained in proper condition. What if the engine were to leak fuel and burst into flames? It must certainly have suffered some damage in the impact. If so, he would not get out in time. A light sweat suddenly bedewed his skin; the steepness of the road, as well as the crazy angle of the bus, obtruded on his attention. The passengers had left their seats and were jammed in the aisle: Jenny was three or four places up from him, too far away to be touched. She seemed calm, thank God. She even turned and smiled at him again; and in the same instant, Iorwerth forced open the emergency door.

They were safe. The first passengers emerged into the open air, and as one followed another the bus became less claustrophobic. Roger's attack of nerves wore off. He even lost his desire to get out of the bus. He wanted, instead, to see what was happening behind him, between Gareth and the ferret.

Turning, he saw that Gareth had shot out a hand and hauled the ferret half-upright. Ivo, standing with his back to Roger, was saying loudly, 'Unqualified. Unfit to take responsibility for people's safety.'

'He came out at me,' the ferret squealed. 'I never had a chance. He was out to get me. You saw it.'

'We saw nothing,' said Gareth. He gave the ferret a mighty shake. 'Stop your rattle. Wait till you get up in court.'

'He crashed us on purpose,' said the ferret again. Gareth swung his free left hand and smacked his face contemptuously.

'Assault . . .' he whimpered, then subsided into the driving-seat.

Roger looked past him, through the windscreen. The Dodge was standing still about twelve feet away from them. It had a crumpled mudguard and a smashed lamp, but its wheels were firmly on the road and it was obviously fit to be driven away. Gito had got down and was standing impassively by the bus, watching the scene through the window.

'You'll answer for this, my lad,' said Ivo to the ferret. He turned to Roger. 'Is somebody telephoning for a policeman?'

'I got witnesses,' said the ferret, looking quickly from one face to another. 'All those people back there.'

'That's right,' said Roger cheerfully. 'I was a passenger and I'll be a witness. I saw you handling the bus incorrectly, going down the hill much too fast for the prevailing conditions. When the lorry came slowly out of a turning, you panicked because you knew your brakes wouldn't hold you. It's a mercy no one was injured.'

'What about that lady with the nervous upset?' Ivo asked. 'She's still crying out there. She won't be normal for years. Your employer'll have a heavy bill for damages.'

'My employer . . .' the ferret said, and stopped.

'Yes, it'll all come out now,' said Gareth. 'You go and ring for the police, Roger. I'll see he doesn't leave the bus.'

'Listen,' said the ferret quickly. 'My boss won't want no trouble. Never mind bothering the police. He'll pay for the damage to the lorry. And he'll get the bus moved at his own expense. No fuss, no bother, see?'

'But we want fuss and bother,' said Gareth.

'My boss'll make it worth your while to let it all drop,' said the ferret. 'He'll give everybody five nicker all round not to give no evidence.'

Gareth looked at him stonily.

'Ten,' said the ferret.

Gareth slapped his face again.

'Go and telephone, Roger,' he said.

Roger went.

The police sergeant was a dry, sandy man. His hair was sandy and his voice was scratchy as if filtered through sand. He had spatulate fingers and a hard, appraising eye. With him was a big heavy young constable who looked about eighteen, and who

321

undertook the humbler duties: driving the car, taking down things in his notebook, and measuring skidmarks by pacing them out. This last was impossible on the hard-packed snow of the mountain road, but he made an intelligent guess and wrote it down in his notebook.

The police sergeant began by telling all the passengers that they would be free to go about their business as soon as their evidence was collected. After that, only the principals would be required: the two drivers, and anyone who wanted to claim shock or damage.

'Now, all those of you who witnessed the accident,' he said. 'Give your name and address to the constable and tell me in your own words what you saw.'

He was like an army instructor with a platoon of awkward recruits.

Roger half expected the ferret-driver to launch a passionate appeal to the passengers to support him. But the youth seemed paralysed, like a sand-grub after being stung by a wasp. His fear at finding himself in close proximity with two dark-blue uniforms had robbed him of the power to act, to think, almost of consciousness itself.

There was a brief silence in which it became apparent that none of the passengers properly so called, those who had been on the bus before Gareth's party boarded it, was going to volunteer any information. Either they had genuinely seen nothing – and the event had come suddenly out of nowhere and had been over within five seconds – or they had no wish to be drawn into time-wasting and possibly embarrassing police-court inquiries.

Before any of them could change their minds, Roger said decisively, 'I witnessed it.'

'Name and address, sir,' said the constable.

Roger gave them and proceeded. 'It was my impression that the driver was taking the bus down the hill too fast. Having regard to the conditions.' He liked that touch: *having regard to* was real police-court English. 'Then the lorry came out of the side turning ahead of us –'

'How far ahead?' the sergeant cut in.

'I wasn't noticing exactly.'

'But you said you witnessed the occurrence.'

'I did, but I still couldn't swear to the exact distance at which the driver of the bus must have become aware of the presence of the lorry.'

'Could you make a guess?'

Roger considered. 'Not in exact figures.'

'Did it appear suddenly?'

'No more suddenly than would be considered usual round here. With all these sharp intersections and the road running between high banks, everybody develops a sixth sense. Of course that wouldn't apply to someone from outside the district.'

The sandy sergeant eyed Roger sceptically and said, 'That's what I'd call an evasive answer, sir.'

'I saw it,' said Gareth suddenly. He had moved determinedly through the press until he was standing at the front, challenging the policeman to take notice of him.

'You did?' said the sergeant, conveying a maximum of polite scepticism. It is the business of the police to know what goes on in their locality.

'You know my name and address,' said Gareth to the constable. 'I was watching. The lorry came out of that turning well ahead. There was plenty of time for him to avoid it, if he'd been fit to have charge of a bus at all.'

'How far ahead was it?' asked the sergeant, looking Gareth straight in the eyes.

Without hesitation Gareth said, 'Seventy-five yards.'

'Seventy-five?' said the sergeant drily. 'Not eighty?'

'Seventy-five,' said Gareth.

The constable wrote down the figure.

The sergeant calmly turned his back on them all and walked over to the intersection at which the Dodge had appeared. He stood for a moment looking down at the snow-packed lane. The sun had come up and there were long blue shadows on the hard whiteness.

'Strange,' he said to himself. Then he walked back and said to Gito, 'That side road is closed. There's nothing there but a small cleared space. You couldn't have been *coming* that way. You must have gone in there deliberately.'

'Yes,' said Gito. 'I went in to reverse.'

'You needed to reverse? You came up here as early as that in the morning and you needed to turn round and go back?'

'Yes. I'd forgotten something.'

'What had you forgotten?'

'My sandwiches,' said Gito.

The sergeant turned abruptly to the waiting passengers. 'You good people are free to go on your way,' he said. 'We have enough evidence and we shan't need to detain you any longer.'

'What about transport?' called Mr Idris Jones.

'The General buses are running, when you get to the bottom of the hill,' said the sergeant. 'And it's an easy walk.'

'It's highly inconvenient,' said Mr Idris Jones. 'Some of us have responsible work to do. And we've been kept hanging about.'

'If the police,' said the sergeant, 'were to assume responsibility, every time there's an accident, for getting everybody to wherever they happened to be going, there'd be nothing for it but to give up police work and go into the taxi business.'

'And a lot more use to the community they'd be,' said Mr Cledwyn Jones, quietly but audibly, as he moved off.

'When you make that kind of remark, Mr Jones,' said the sergeant, 'have the goodness to make it in Welsh. Then I can pretend I wasn't meant to hear it. Remarks passed in English are official and they go on the record.'

'While you're standing here,' said Mr Cledwyn Jones bitterly, 'probably half-a-dozen water pipelines have been blown up and two or three people murdered in their beds.'

He led his mutinous band of voyagers away down the hill.

'Right,' said the sergeant. 'I shall need you and you,' he indicated Gito and the ferret, 'at the station. For statements. No one else.'

'I saw the accident too,' Jenny put in.

'And I saw it from first to last,' said Ivo.

'Enough evidence is enough,' said the sergeant. 'If we decide to bring a charge for dangerous driving, we might call you. But in view of the weather conditions the magistrate probably wouldn't find him guilty. There'll be minor collisions like this one all over North Wales this morning. No,' he went on thoughtfully, 'I've an idea the charge will be something more serious.' He turned suddenly to the ferret. 'Got your licence?'

For a moment the ferret stood quite still. Then, his limbs moving with painful slowness, he took out a small red-covered document and handed it over. The sergeant barely glanced at it before handing it back.

'Don't waste my time, lad,' he said. 'This is a Group G licence. It entitles you to drive a motor-cycle.'

Weakly, the ferret feigned surprise. 'I must have brought it out instead of me proper one,' he said in a scarcely audible voice.

'You'll have an opportunity to produce your proper commercial vehicle licence if you have one,' said the sergeant. 'in which case the charge would be the much lighter one of failing to carry it with you while in charge of the vehicle. Insurance?'

'Ins . . . ?'

'Have you got your insurance cover note on you?'

The ferret's arms fell down by his sides as if the muscles had turned to water.

'No,' he said.

'He'll produce it at the same time as he produces his commercial licence,' said Ivo. 'And bring out the Crown Jewels at the same time.'

The sergeant nodded towards the waiting police car. 'We'd be serving the interests of the taxpayer better if we got on our way to the station. Though,' he made Ivo a small, stiff bow, 'it would be more pleasant to stand here in the snow, cracking jokes.'

Ivo smiled courteously. 'If you're going down to the police station,' he said, 'perhaps I could come along. I'm part owner of the lorry, and I'm concerned in the matter.'

The sergeant gave him a long, steady look. Then he said, 'You're part owner?'

'Yes.'

'But you weren't riding in the lorry?'

'No.'

'You were riding in the bus?'

'Yes.'

'You had to go down to town,' said the sergeant slowly, 'so you took the bus.'

'Yes.'

'I suppose,' said the sergeant, 'you'd forgotten your sandwiches too.'

Ivo said nothing.

The sergeant nodded towards the waiting car. Ivo, Gito and the ferret-driver went over and took their seats in the back. The two policemen sat in the front, with the constable in the driving seat. The sound of the doors shutting sounded loud in the crisp air. Then the car moved away, round the next bend in the road and out of sight.

At once, a primeval peace descended on the mountainside. The slopes of snow, marked only by the light feet of birds, lay silent in the pale sunshine: the liver-coloured bus leaned stiffly into the ditch like a dead dinosaur. Only the old Dodge, wheels firmly planted on the road, bearing its ruined mudguard and smashed headlight like honourable scars, still spoke of the skirmish that was over.

Gareth walked across to it. 'I expect she's still running,' he said. Swinging himself up into the high cab, he began fiddling with switches and pulling knobs. In a moment the engine began its steady, slightly asthmatic breathing. He grinned down at Roger and Jenny. 'Come up,' he called above the engine note. 'We'll drive into town in style.'

Roger helped Jenny up on the side opposite Gareth's, then had to help her down again when Gareth pointed out that he, Roger, must sit in the middle. He did not mind this: it gave him pleasure to swing her fine-boned body up and down, supporting her now round the waist, now by the wrists. When they were settled, Gareth took the wheel firmly with his left hand, holding the bulky sling-and-plaster mould of his right arm close to his belly. 'Now, Roger,' he said. 'We'll drive together.'

'The gears?' Roger asked, staring down at the stubby lever.

'Yes. I can do everything else.'

'What about the handbrake?'

'All right. Take it off.'

Roger released the handbrake and the big lorry began to roll forward over the shining snow. Once again, as so often before on this mountainside, he felt the sense of adventure leap in his pulse. And Jenny beside him, as pleased as a child.

'First gear,' said Gareth. He pressed down the clutch and Roger eased the lever home. 'Fine. Now second.' He spoke in the tone of a surgeon saying 'Sponge ... forceps ... clamps.' Roger wanted to giggle.

With one great hand easing the wheel back and forth in slow, assured movements, Gareth piloted the lorry down to the main road. Then Roger came into action again, easing the motor back through third gear, into second, first, neutral; then back again into top for the easy run along the cleared highway into Caerfenai. They parked the Dodge under the snow-crowned walls of the castle and went into the café in the square to wait for Ivo and Gito.

'Will the police keep them long?' Jenny asked.

'Not more than a few minutes, I should think,' said Roger. 'They've only got to take statements from them and turn them loose.'

'What about the boy and his licence and insurance and all that?'

'He'll be given twenty-four hours to produce them and if he can't he'll be charged.'

Gareth, blowing on his tea, was silent. Roger sensed a withdrawal; Gareth was shrinking back, inch by inch, into his carapace. When they had driven the Dodge down the hill, moving in co-ordination, controlling the big beast together, he had felt very close to Gareth. Now, Gareth was alone; his thoughts enveloped him. Was this because they were three? Would he have stayed open to Roger's presence if there had been just the two of them, sitting round the chipped formica table-top as they had sat so many times? Or was it the intensity of the conflict they were engaged in, forcing Gareth into a commander's loneliness?

There was no knowing. But probably it was Jenny's presence that was isolating Gareth. The whole woman-and-marriage side of Roger's life, after all, represented an area into which Gareth could not follow him even if he had wished their lives to run parallel. Suddenly, for the first time, Roger found himself wondering about Gareth's sexual emotions. Had he somehow managed to get rid of them? To blow them out harmlessly in the discharge of other emotions? Or was there, in some fold of the mountains, an unguessable she whom Gareth, when the rutting moon was at full, walked over to visit? Or was the whole pent-up force still there, like a boiling underground lake, ready one day to erupt as a scalding geyser?

Jenny was asking him something.

'Is there a very heavy fine for driving a bus without a proper licence?'

'Yes. It isn't so much the licence as the insurance. If you haven't got a proper licence you can't get proper insurance, and that's a serious crime.'

'So Dic Sharp's going to get into a lot of trouble because of this morning.'

'It depends on how much of the blame he wants to take. It's his bus and he's hired somebody to drive it who doesn't have the right insurance. On the other hand, the crime is actually committed by the person who takes the bus out.'

Gareth, who had not seemed to be listening, stirred in his chair and said, 'Dic Sharp can keep his nose clean if he wants to. But he'll never get anyone to do his dirty work for him again if he just lets them go to prison when things go wrong.'

'D'you think that's what'll happen to him?' Jenny asked Gareth, her eyes dark and wide. 'Prison?'

Gareth shrugged with huge indifference.

At that moment, Roger, who happened to be looking out through the plate-glass window into the square, saw a cluster of cars go by, slowly because they were getting in one another's way. One of them was a long grey car with a high gloss on its bodywork. This car cruised gently by, close to the kerb, and behind the wheel Roger saw, briefly but unmistakeably, the elongated rooster-face of Dic Sharp.

'Look!' he said quickly. The others looked up in time to see the car and its occupant.

'Going to the police station, eh?' said Gareth softly.

Roger went to the door and looked cautiously out. The police station was only a hundred yards further on. The grey car nosed about hesitantly, looking for a parking space, then came to rest and Dic Sharp got out. Without looking to either side, he walked up the steps of the police station.

'Yes,' said Roger, rejoining Jenny and Gareth. 'He's gone in.'

'There must be some action going on,' said Gareth. He spoke with studied calm, but Roger could feel the stretched impatience of his tight muscles under the old leather jerkin. More than anything else in the world, Gareth needed to *know*.

They waited again, and now their waiting was openly painful. Roger felt unable to say anything to Gareth, to break in on his titanic, lonely vigil; on the other hand it seemed unthinkable to chatter about this and that with Jenny. If he and Jenny spoke at all, it must be about the action in hand, and about that they had, and could have, nothing to say.

Jenny evidently picked up this feeling intuitively from him. She sat with downcast eyes, keeping very still, only occasionally opening her handbag and rummaging aimlessly in its depths. The minutes went by slowly. To create a diversion, Roger went and got three more thick white cups of tea. The morning was beginning to slant towards lunch-time. One or two customers had already come in and ordered sausage-and-mash, or egg, gammon and chips.

Roger was just coming to the conclusion that he could stand it no longer when they at last appeared on the pavement outside. Ivo came through the door first. His face was thin and grim. Behind him, Gito's dome hovered uneasily. There was no triumph or happiness in the lines of either man's face or body.

Gareth sat as still as a rock as they walked across to him. His eyes were fixed on Ivo's, and they changed focus as Ivo approached, but nothing else moved. Without speaking, Ivo halted and looked down at him.

'Well?' said Gareth. His voice was hardly above a whisper. 'What's the bad news?'

'No bad news,' said Ivo.

'What went wrong?'

'Nothing went wrong.'

There was a short silence. Roger looked quickly from face to face. Ivo's was closed. Gito's large and sorrowful. Gareth's was merely expressionless, like a lump of rock on the mountain.

Finally Gareth spoke again. 'Are we in the clear or not?'

'We're in the clear,' said Ivo.

'Then what's the matter?' Gareth demanded. 'From your faces I thought Dic Sharp must have got him off the hook or something.'

'No,' said Ivo. 'Dic Sharp didn't get him off the hook. He left him on the hook.'

'Look,' said Jenny suddenly, pointing through the window into the square. The long grey car was moving back the way it had come.

'Ay, cruise on, shark,' Gito muttered.

'I need a drink,' said Ivo abruptly. 'Let's get out of here and go back to Mario's. He'll be open.'

'All right, we'll go,' said Gareth. He pushed his chair and stood up. 'But tell me one thing first. Whose story did the police believe? Ours or whatever Dic Sharp told them?'

'Dic Sharp didn't tell them anything,' said Ivo. 'He didn't have any story. The young chap said again that the accident was our fault, and we said it was his fault. The police accepted our story because we're experienced heavy vehicle drivers, because we've driven in this neighbourhood for twenty years and never had an accident, and he was just a kid from nowhere who was driving a bus without a licence. And now let's get that drink and I'll tell you a bit more, if I can bring myself to talk about it.'

He turned and started towards the door. Before following, Gareth swung round to face Gito with a look of mute inquiry. Gito moved his head slowly from side to side. Whatever it was that had happened at the police station, he did not feel like putting it into words any more than Ivo did.

They all left the café and walked silently along the pavement. Jenny and Roger brought up the rear, and as they hurried along she took his arm and said in an undertone, 'They're both terribly fed up, aren't they?'

'They seem displeased or deflated, it's hard to say which.'

'Are they turning against Gareth?'

'I don't see why they should,' he replied.

Mario's pub had only just opened when they got there; it had that pristine atmosphere that bars have before their day has begun, before anyone has breathed their fresh new air or used their bottles and glasses or spoken any words into their clean, expectant silence. With Ivo ahead, they swept up to the bar in a tight knot.

'Buon giorno,' said Mario, his eyes and teeth all congratulations. 'Great goings on this morning.'

'You've heard all about it already, then,' said Ivo rather sourly.

'Not all,' said Mario. 'The inside story I wait from you. I only hear about the accident to Dic Sharp's bus.'

It struck Roger with a tiny *frisson* that this was the first time Mario had ever introduced the name of Dic Sharp into a conversation of his own accord. Even in an empty bar. Some kind of spell had been broken, then, by that impact on the white, slithering mountain road.

'A pint of bitter,' said Ivo.

In silence, Mario drew the first pint of the day and pushed it across to him. He took it in an unnaturally steady hand, raised it to his lips with unnecessary care, then suddenly threw two thirds of it down his gullet in a wild tide of amber and froth.

They all watched him as he carefully put his glass down again on the clean, shiny bar.

'It wasn't only Dic Sharp's bus that suffered an accident this morning,' he said. 'It was Dic Sharp's driver.'

'Yes?' said Mario.

'Yes,' said Ivo. 'He got pushed down the pan and had the chain pulled on him. Now he's down in the sewage system somewhere and there's nobody cares or wants to care.'

He turned and looked quickly round at the ring of faces staring into his face. Then his expression changed to one of exaggerated gaiety.

'Drinks all round!' he called loudly. 'This is celebration day. Let the town flow with beer and wine. Let children paddle in it, let old grandmas sail in it in their opened-out brollies.'

Mario, his face thoughtful, began drawing pints. Gareth moved up close to Ivo. His eyes bored into Ivo's as if trying to read his innermost thoughts.

'Is that why you both came in with such long faces?' he asked roughly. 'Because that young fly-by-night is going to be prosecuted?'

'Yes,' said Ivo. He picked up his mug and drank the last of his beer. 'Same again, Mario.'

'Well,' said Gareth, 'your kind feelings are a credit to you. As for me, I'd break his neck between my fingers.'

'If you did,' Gito suddenly put in, looking over Ivo's shoulder, 'that'd be a lot cleaner than what has happened to him.'

'I don't care what's happened to him,' said Gareth. His face had gone back to being a mask of straight lines. 'If you're sorry for him, start a silver collection.'

'You don't know what we're talking about,' said Gito, warningly.

'Damnation,' Gareth suddenly roared. 'I've just won the first battle for years and I want to be *told* I've won.'

'All right,' said Ivo. His voice was dancing and light, only delicately streaked with irony. 'You deserve it, Gareth. Don't think we're not on your side, boy. We're your soldiers, remember? The battle's won and we're having our beer-up and we'll go on having it this livelong day. It's just that –' he passed his hand briefly across his eyes, as if in a sudden spasm of a weariness too great to be borne – 'Gito and I have just seen a snake swallowing a rabbit, close up, and it's not a pretty sight.'

By this time they all had drinks in their hands. Ivo was back in his familiar role of *jongleur*: he was going to make a story of it: the shock, the disgust, the recoil, would be transcended, distanced, lifted up by the power of art. Roger, watching and listening, knew this and knew, too, that he understood at last the reason for that stubborn misgiving about art which appears in every human generation, that icy fear that its power may be, after all, the power of the devil. For does it not build a leaning tower of joy on a quicksand of suffering, often the suffering of the forgotten and nameless who are beyond its help and who ought to be remembered in silence and prayer?

He drank, and looked quickly at Jenny as she sat hunched at the bar, her eyes heavy with concern under her thick dark fringe. Love, rescue, conflict, suffering, art, pleasure and oblivion. So much was happening so quickly.

'At first,' Ivo was beginning, 'the poor little mucker was too frightened to say anything except *Are y' goin' te lock me up?*' With perfect instinctive mimicry he caught the exact Birmingham intonation of the ferret's voice, and also its fear-loaded whine. 'He couldn't think about anything but the cells. He nearly fainted when they took him up the steps of the cop-shop. He didn't believe he'd ever get out. *Are y' goin' te lock me up?* The policemen kept telling him he was there to make a statement and he'd be free to go and they'd charge him later. But he was too frightened to understand what they were saying. Sweat was pouring off him.' As Ivo remembered, his body hunched over with fear, and his sharp face seemed to grow wan and starved. He huddled into himself as if trying to disappear. 'My boss,' he said in the ferret's voice. 'My boss'll need to look into this. I've got his number, his telephone number.'

Agonizingly, he fumbled with imaginary scraps of paper. 'I know I've got it ... the number ...' 'If it's Mr Jones you want,' he straightened up and his voice became that of the dispassionate, sandy police sergeant, 'we can telephone him for you.' On and on Ivo mimed and impersonated: he was the ferret, sweating and whining; he was the Olympian sergeant; he was the young constable taking down the statements, dipping his pen fastidiously into the ink-bottle and each time, before he dipped, jerking his arm out to its full length with a quick, dapper movement to get the hand entirely free of the shirt-cuff; he was himself, he was Gito, he was the whole police-station, the snow outside, the damaged lorry and the liver-coloured bus abandoned up on the mountain road. The entire episode flowed through his tense, wiry body and his mobile face. Gradually he became manic, possessed by the narrative. But to Roger, sitting on the fringe of the circle, the story came across in all its pitiable starkness.

It was nothing very much, as stories go; neither elaborate nor unpredictable. Dic Sharp, as the owner of the liver-coloured bus, had been telephoned by the police and asked whether he would mind being present at the exchange of statement and counter-statement. Bland, forewarned (for surely the news had travelled to him, by one route or another, within a short time, and even if it had not, he must have been in a constant state of preparedness for *something* of this kind to happen), he had obligingly presented himself. His mind was made up, his expression of polite inflexibility soldered into place. As Ivo told the story, it was obvious from Dic Sharp's first entrance that the ferret was to be sacrificed. Ivo became Dic Sharp entering the police station; he took a few steps in Dic Sharp's walk, holding his body like Dic Sharp's, talking with his intonations. *He was acting contrary to my instructions. I'm very shocked to find that this could go on. The regular driver was off sick, and I left instructions that the bus wasn't to be taken out.* Then Ivo became the ferret. Tiny spurts of incredulity, then of resentment, finally of rage and hate, pierced the veil of his fear like a needle jabbing through heavy cloth. Everybody knows you told me t' take the bus out. *Who knows it?* Why, everybody. Everybody knows it.

'You deny that you gave him instructions to take the bus out?' Ivo-sergeant asked in his sand-dried voice.

'Certainly I deny it,' replied Ivo-Dic Sharp, his tone and expression conveying amazement that anyone should find the question worth asking.

'He told me – he told me I'd have to drive it till Bert came back and I could have his wages. Bert's wages,' the Ivo-ferret spluttered.

'What kind of a service was this bus on?' Ivo-sergeant asked.

'An emergency service,' Ivo-Dic Sharp replied. 'Serving an area where the ordinary transport arrangements had broken down.'

'You mean Gareth Jones's wrist had broken down when somebody hit it with a piece of lead pipe,' Ivo interrupted in Gito's soft, high voice.

'Will you kindly answer when spoken to,' Ivo-sergeant admonished him, while the real Gito hugged himself with joy but could not resist whispering to Roger, 'I didn't put it that neatly. That's what I *would* have said, if I'd had Ivo's head.'

'Silence in court,' said Ivo. 'More drinks all round.' His replenished glass was handed to him.

Ivo-ferret now began to shrink into himself. His pasty skin glistened with terror. After an entire adolescence of being conditioned to hate and fear 'the fuzz', he was now firmly in the grip of the police, and the one man who could have helped him had chosen instead to give him the push that sent him finally over the edge. He twitched and looked beadily from face to face; his eyes flickered towards the door as if meditating a desperate dash for freedom.

Behind Ivo, the door opened and shut several times a minute, as the pub slowly filled up. But the performance never faltered. Dic Sharp was smoothly self-protective; the ferret became more incoherent and more pitiable; Ivo and Gito faded out altogether; the sergeant and the cuff-shooting constable continued to play their expressionless roles. Finally the sergeant said, 'That's all for now, lad. You'll be hearing from us.' At first, Ivo-ferret could not believe his ears; he had not thought it possible that they would ever let him walk out under the sky again; but when Ivo-sergeant said, 'We'll let you know when we want you. Quarter Sessions, I expect,' and nodded dismissively, Ivo-ferret, with one burning look of hate at Ivo-Dic Sharp, scurried for the door.

Applause and laughter broke out. Everyone felt relieved. The cruelty, the meanness of that scene at the police station, the naked ugly betrayal of a powerless human being by a relatively powerful one, which had nauseated Ivo and Gito, setting their faces into grim lines and turning them momentarily into mourners for themselves and for the whole human condition – all this melted under the bright sunlight of Ivo's talent. Mario was laughing and talking excitedly, Jenny wore a broad smile, even Gareth's face had relaxed. Glasses were emptied and jokes cracked as at a successful party.

An hour and more went by. It seemed to Roger that he had never been with a gayer company. Problems remained, but they had suddenly become soluble: the power of Dic Sharp had been broken at a blow. And everybody was discussing it openly. The name 'Dic Sharp' fairly rang through the multiple conversations that went on all round the bar.

At last, tired out with rejoicing, Roger bought a couple of meat pies and found a quiet corner for himself and Jenny. They had eaten nothing since that incredibly distant dawn, when the lorry had come for them and Ivo had called through the darkness. He settled her comfortably, with her pie and a fresh drink, and they began to eat. But almost at once he knew that something was wrong; some cloud had come over her. She nibbled a little, frowned, pushed her plate away, and fell into a brooding silence. As he watched, she took her glasses from her handbag, put them on, took them off again. Then she took a sip at her drink, but without enjoyment.

'Are you all right?' he murmured, putting his mouth close to her ear.

'Mm?'

'I just said – are you all right?'

Instead of answering, she stood up and pushed the table a little way back.

'I must just . . . I shan't be a minute.'

Assuming that she needed to go to the lavatory, Roger moved his legs aside to let her pass. Was she distressed? Should he follow her? No, let her sort it out. It would only embarrass her to have him fussing, drawing attention to her change of mood. Perhaps the elastic of her knickers had broken or something.

He waited, chatting to Gito, but the minutes went slowly. In spite of the tension that gripped his inside, he forced himself to swallow several mouthfuls of pie; if something had indeed gone wrong, there was no sense in trying to cope with it on an empty stomach. He finished the pie, slowly, but Jenny did not reappear. At last he stood up to go and find her, but at that moment she was there in the doorway.

He saw at once that whatever had been troubling her was now much worse. Was she ill? In pain? Her face was tight closed, her mouth a thin pen-stroke in its whiteness.

Excusing himself, Roger pushed past Gareth and Gito and went over to her. 'What is it, my darling?' he asked.

'I want to go home,' she said.

Home? To the chapel on the mountain, the divan and the pot-bellied stove? Or did she mean something darker, colder: home to her prison without bars, her loveless marital stall?

Suddenly, as the chill ran through his bones, Roger felt the dreadful precariousness of their relationship. He loved her so much. But life had not yet brought any substance to their love: it was like straw that flared up in a grate.

'Come along,' he said, 'I'll take you.' Inwardly he determined to assume, unless and until contradicted, that by 'home' she meant the chapel.

Ivo, seeing the two of them going through the door, interrupted himself in surprise. 'Going?' he asked.

'Yes,' said Roger. He tried to smile pleasantly. 'Don't let us spoil the celebration. It's just that we have something to attend to.'

'Keep in touch, Roger,' said Gareth. 'I'll let you know how things develop. We may have the bus back on the road sooner than we expected.'

'All right,' said Roger. He tried once more to give a comradely smile, but he felt it emerge as a mirthless grimace. What was the bus to him, compared with this black cloud that had suddenly come over on the wind? He glanced at Jenny: her eyes were still downcast, her face was a mask of pain. Some dreadful inner collapse had happened to her.

Outside, on the pavement, he could not keep himself from asking abruptly, 'What's suddenly the matter?' But she walked on as if he had not spoken. Perhaps she really had not heard.

With the Mini still in its snowdrift on the mountain, a taxi had to be found and its driver coaxed into taking them up to Llancrwys. The ride was a dismal one. Roger didn't dare break the silence. Jenny sat beside him as if they were two strangers in a train. Whenever he glanced at her, he saw that same dead, numbed look in her eyes.

Just before they drew up at the chapel she put her head quietly down on her hands and began to weep: a silent, agonized gasping as if her grief were being drawn out of her with fish-hooks. When the taxi stopped, Roger tried to put his arm round her shoulders and draw her to him. But still weeping silently, still hiding her face, she pushed open the door and got slowly out. He followed her; she walked to the chapel door and stood, in mute patience, waiting for him to come and unlock it.

Inside, she went over to the armchair and sat down. Her weeping had stopped now and she was staring ahead with a hard, intent expression, making no attempt to wipe away the tears that glistened on her cheeks.

Roger suddenly felt hungry. It struck him as grotesque, perverse, that at a moment of such misery, hers and his own, the emptiness of his stomach should choose to make itself felt. But so it was. The unpredictable, paradoxical nature of the human machine decreed it, and it came about. Faced with the leaden spectacle of Jenny's suffering, knowing that she had retreated into a hinterland of pain where she would not hear him if he called to her, Roger had a sudden vision of crusty bread, butter thickly applied, and a wedge of sharp, full-flavoured cheese. His mouth flooded with saliva.

'Would you like something to eat?' he asked her timidly.

She shook her head, a slight, impatient movement that hardly constituted an acknowledgement that he had spoken.

'Jenny, can you tell me what's the matter? You went out of the pub in the middle of our celebration, to go to the lavatory I thought, and you came back – well,' he gestured, 'as you are now. May I know what happened in those few minutes?'

She turned and focused those dull, pain-blurred eyes on him. 'Yes, of course you may. You've a right.' She spoke slowly, painfully. A long silence, then her voice began again : harsh, flat, monotonous. 'I didn't go only to the Ladies. I went to the telephone.'

'Oh.'

'And spoke to my mother.'

'I see.'

'You don't see,' she said, suddenly fierce. 'You haven't any children, Roger.'

'No. That makes me like Macbeth, doesn't it?'

'You can't possibly know the pain ...' her face crumpled, then straightened into rigid lines. 'Gerald hasn't lost any time.'

'What has he done?'

'He went over there yesterday. He told my mother, *in front of Mary and Robin*, that I'd run away and he didn't know where I was. He took an axe to my carefully built-up story about our being away at a conference together. And it worked. He got what he wanted. Mary and Robin started crying and then they got more and more upset until they were hysterical. And they kept bringing your name into it – Mr Furnivall this and Mr Furnivall that, and Mother had taken them to see Mr Furnivall and he'd driven to Nantwich with them, and they were sure he was being kind to Mummy and why wasn't Daddy with Mr Furnivall too ... It seems Gerald made very little effort to reassure them, or my parents for that matter. He just got what he wanted and then he made a cold, formal statement to the children. Stood them up in front of him on the hearthrug and told them their mother had run away and if she didn't come back they would have a housekeeper and a nanny to look after them till he could find them a new mother. And they both howled like dervishes and he left them howling.'

'My God.' Roger's teeth were clenched. 'Couldn't he stay at least and comfort them?'

'My mother says he was "upset",' said Jenny. She carefully, and with distaste, indicated quotation marks round the word. 'As far as I can gather, he was in an ice-cold fury. I can't see further into it than that. I've been drifting further and further away from him for years, and I just don't know him all that well. Perhaps it was just a colossal sense of affront. His dignity had been upset, I'd interfered with his plans – it must have been like having a piece of furniture suddenly turn round and defy you. Or perhaps I'm wrong. Perhaps he really has some love for me left, deep down under the crust – his own kind of love, whatever that is.'

'An extension, if that, of his self-love,' said Roger coolly.

'How can either of us tell? What I do know is that the children still look up to him and depend on him. I know they're suffering now and I long for them with an ache, a deep animal ache. I can't stand it. As I put the telephone down I knew I would never be able to rest for a second, to think of anything else for a second, till I'd comforted them and made everything all right for them.'

'Your mother'll comfort them.'

'No, she won't. She's knocked off her balance by this. It's been too sudden for her and she's old, she can't cope with anything that comes without warning. As for my father, he needs six months' notice before he can tell you whether he'll have one lump of sugar in his tea or two. They'll be dithering, and their dithering'll make the children even more agonized. Oh,' she wept openly now, her voice rising to a wail of hopelessness, 'the mites, the poor little mites!' Sobs drowned whatever words she had intended to speak next.

'Well, said Roger, fighting to stave off ultimate disaster, 'if you feel you must be with them, go and fetch them.'

'*Fetch them?*' she shot the words at him with a terrific intensity of contempt. 'To this place?'

'Well,' he said again, his voice trailing off into uncertainty. 'They could manage for the time being, till we . . .'

'No, they couldn't *manage*,' said Jenny. Her tears had ceased abruptly, halted by the sudden heat of her contempt. She spoke quickly, fiercely. 'I was a silly irresponsible fool ever to dump them and come here.'

'No, you weren't. You were getting away from a –'

'I was getting away from my duty to – no, never mind duties now, my *need* to make a home for my children. A home that would be secure and adequate. When I choose a man, I have to choose an environment as well. For a childless girl, it's all right. She can lie down with the man she wants on a bed of straw in a barn. Or on some other woman's studio couch in a hovel like this. Making a home can come later. But how could I bring Mary and Robin here? Where would they sleep? What should I do with them all day? You just haven't *thought*.'

'Yes, I have. I –'

'It's not that I blame you,' she said, but she looked at him as if she blamed him very much. 'You don't know what it feels like. Nobody does, who hasn't had children.'

'Gerald's had children and he doesn't seem to have much idea of how to –'

'Gerald's probably mad with pain, just as I'm mad with pain at this moment,' she said. 'Don't bring Gerald into it when you can't possibly understand what he must be feeling.'

'Oh, all you can tell me is how I can't *understand*. How are you so sure of that? How do you know I haven't longed for marriage and children, ached for children that don't exist, just as deeply as your bones are aching for your children that do exist . . . how do you know what I understand and don't understand?' Roger was shouting now, beside himself with anxiety and rage. 'How dare you go on casting me in that one role, *the person who doesn't understand?*'

'Don't get so angry. I'm not trying to insult you – it's just an objective fact. You *don't* understand.'

Helpless, Roger stood beside her chair. At last he said, 'Well, Jenny, what is there I can do?'

'I don't know,' she said. 'I don't suppose there is anything we can do, either of us. Not tonight, anyway. When daylight comes, I suppose I can drive over to Nantwich and get the children and take them back home.'

'Back to Gerald?'

She raised her eyes to his with that dead, blank, beaten look. 'Where else?'

'But you can't –' He stopped. She all too obviously could.

'The children are upset, Roger. They're suffering, and they're without their father *and* their mother. The first thing to do is to get them where they're close to me and reassured by my presence. I'm sorry to go away from you, because it was all flowering very nicely, but it hurts too much to be away from the children at a time like this. I just can't stand it, that's all. And I haven't any money to take them anywhere. It means going back to the family home, however much I hate it.'

'You don't deny, then,' he said wearily, 'that you hate it?'

'Of course I do. And it'll be even worse when I have to go back to Gerald defeated, humiliated, the errant wife who didn't get any further than round the first corner before she found she couldn't manage things on her own and came back.'

Roger thought desperately. 'I've got a small flat in London. It's been shut up since I've been here, but I paid my cleaning woman a lump sum to go in once a month and dust round. It should be habitable. Take them down there.'

She shook her head. 'The runaway wife in the boy-friend's London flat, with the kids frightened and bewildered. And living on what?'

'Well, I could scrape up a few pounds –'

'Roger, it won't work.'

He was silent for a moment. 'So we're beaten, are we? When we had a vision opening out in front of us, a chance of happiness –'

'Oh, you can go on having your vision,' she said, utter exhaustion in her voice. 'You'll find some other girl. You'll be happy if you want to be happy. But don't choose one with children next time.'

'But I could so easily love your children, Jenny. Already I'm fond of them.'

She lay down on the Fräulein's divan and covered her face with her hands. 'Roger, go out. Take the car and go down to Caerfenai and have a drink. It'll make you feel better.'

'If I do,' he said, 'promise you'll still be here when I come back.'

'You're taking the car,' she said flatly.

Roger walked out into the chill, dark evening. It was thawing faster now, and ribbons of slush were laid along the road with long streaks of dirty water beside them. Jenny's voice sounded in his head with the sullenness of despair. *It'll make you feel better.*

'Nothing will make me feel better,' he said aloud, speaking to the darkness and the cold, melting snow on the mountain. 'Ever again.' Then he got into the blue Mini and started the engine.

Conditions were difficult, and often the little front wheels spun crazily as he applied the power, but he got the car down to the coast road, and from then on it was easy because the traffic had already splashed and scrubbed the snow away from the road, leaving it merely greasy and unpleasant. In a few minutes he was driving into town, seeing the lamplight in the square and the overcoated figures walking about. But now his spirits sank even lower, as he tried to decide where to go for the drink that was going to pick him up, give him courage to face the next round of difficulties and disasters. Mario's pub, his usual haunt, seemed impossible: he had so recently been there in high feather, celebrating the great victory, and that celebration had been so unhappily cut short: he could not pick up the threads there, certainly not this evening, perhaps never again.

Where else? He drove aimlessly along the street. Most of the pubs were depressing in themselves, doubly so if one were alone and miserable. That dreadful little box of smoke that Gareth frequented from choice ... Roger shuddered. Such habits must have their origin in masochism. That was all; he had wasted all these months on a gang of masochists.

Still driving without any idea of where to go, he saw the Palace Hotel loom up, scene of his first frustration of this season of frustrations, Rhiannon-haunted, Dic Sharp-infested hutch of stale lusts. Why not? His thoughts would at least be tinged with a sharp irony as he held his glass in a drooping hand and looked round at the room where he had first set eyes on Jenny, where he had treated Beverley to what the girl herself would doubtless have described in her impoverished jargon as 'a snow job', where he had cruised like a shark in the lobby in the hope of biting a chunk out of Rhiannon.

Ah, Rhiannon, city of flesh. Perhaps in the end his emotions would settle back on her and he would spend the rest of his life lurking behind walls to get a glimpse of her, or shinning up drainpipes to try to catch her in the bath. Ah, that vision of ultimate bliss, Rhiannon, model-aeroplane-encircled Circe.

He swung the little car adroitly into the Palace Hotel car park and slithered to a stop in the thin slush. Smiling frostily at nothing, he opened the door, and was just about to get out when his attention was caught by something that caused him to draw his leg back and sit, staring hard, with the door open.

Drawn up a few yards away was a long, black, opulent car. Its smoothly arrogant lines proclaimed it as a Rolls-Royce or possibly a Bentley. At the moment Roger drew up in the Mini, a uniformed chauffeur came down the steps of the hotel and opened a rear door, causing a light to spring into brightness on the ceiling of the passenger compartment. A few yards behind him, swathed in a thick overcoat, waddled a man in spectacles and a black hat of the kind Roger vaguely identified as a homburg. With him, bending courteously, walked Madog, bareheaded and wearing a mackintosh.

They moved to the other side of the Rolls-Royce, and their voices were masked from Roger's hearing by the bulk of the car. But he caught a fragment or two: 'I wish you every success with it,' from the homburg man, and from Madog. 'It'll bear fruit for twenty years, I can promise you that.'

They spoke another two or three times each and then shook hands, and the chauffeur closed the door and went round to the driving seat. Roger, watching shamelessly, enjoyed the way the chauffeur eased the smooth length of the car out into the centre of the car park and then, silently except for the splash of the tyres in the pulpy slush, into the traffic stream. Madog, who had not noticed Roger, stood looking after the big black car for a moment like a man who has seen a vision; then, clasping his plump hands above his head, he swayed his body to and fro as if acknowledging tumultuous applause. Unconscious of Roger's eyes on him, he bowed to invisible crowds, then lowered his arms and executed a rapid hornpipe. Finally, out of breath, he halted with his eyes staring straight into Roger's. Gradually, recognition appeared in them, and he walked up to the Mini and rested his arm on the roof.

'Greetings, Hiawatha,' he said.

'Your birthday?' Roger asked carelessly.

'In a sense,' said Madog. He walked, a trifle breathlessly, round to the other side of the Mini, opened the door and got in beside Roger. 'Nice of you to offer me a lift,' he said.

'Don't mention it.'

'Let's go into Mario's. I'll buy you a drink. A big one. The biggest one you ever saw.'

'Right,' said Roger. All of a sudden, Madog's mysterious gaiety sparked to him in turn. 'This calls for a celebration,' he said.

'What does?' Madog said craftily.

'Your Order of Merit,' said Roger.

Madog chuckled cagily. They manoeuvred out of the car park and drove through the wintry streets to Mario's.

Once there, Madog, without hesitation, went to the bar and said to Mario, in Welsh:

Fetch it out, boy.

He came? said Mario, his eyes bright with curiosity.

He came, Madog answered.

And it's all arranged?'

It is arranged, said Madog in a suddenly full, ringing voice, down to the last detail. And now, bring out the bottle.

I have it, said Mario eagerly, at the exactly right temperature. I have examined it every four hours.

He hurried down the cellar steps and reappeared after a moment with a bottle of champagne.

How many glasses? he asked Madog.

One for you, said Madog gravely, because you are the physical symbol of our aspirations. The Mediterranean *genius loci* who has come to preside over our struggle for Cambrian fulfilment.

A stout and mild, cried a man in a cloth cap indignantly, rapping on the counter with his glass.

Wait, said Madog imperiously. A glass for me, because I am a bard and follow the craft of the bards.

Mario put two wide, shallow glasses on the bar.

And a glass for Roger Furnivall, said Madog, courteously making a half-turn towards Roger, because he is a scholar and wishes well to all civilizations.

Accept my thanks, said Roger.

Give me a pint of bloody stout and mild or I'll go to the next pub, cried the man in the cap. I'll get your licence taken off you.

Have it on the house, said Mario. He poured the man's drink and handed it to him with a flourish. 'Anybody else want serving?' he called out in English.

Say that in Welsh, shouted the man in the cap. He was shushed by the assembled company and led away to his corner. Nobody else did want serving: all were watching the champagne ceremony.

Mario produced a napkin, undid the wire fastening, and skilfully thumbed off the cork with a satisfying *pop*! Cheers broke out at the far end of the bar. Mario quickly poured three glasses of the champagne and raised one to his lips.

Madog! he cried, throwing a challenging look round the room. Madog the king!

Hardly that, Madog smiled. He took a glass and handed one to Roger. But I accept your good wishes.

Roger drank a gulp of his champagne. It was dry, slightly chilled, of superb quality.

Am I the only person here, he asked, who has no idea what's going on?

On the contrary, said Madog. Mario and I are the only ones who have.

Mario produced a swizzle stick and stirred up the bubbles in his glass.

A wine for the great celebration, he said.

Like a soap-bubble lasting for ten or fifteen seconds, the mood held, iridescent and fragile. Then the door opened and three men in wet raincoats came in, one of them pulling a small dog on a leather lead.

Come on, come on, Meic, he said crossly. It was not clear whether Meic was the name of the dog or one of his companions. But the entry of this trio, and the blast of dank air that accompanied them through the door, acted as the rough touch of quotidien reality that broke the bubble of celebration and lowered the mood of the pub on to its usual plateau. Roger and Madog, after topping up their glasses of champagne and giving them a stir with Mario's swizzle stick, went over to a quiet corner to drink at their leisure.

Madog, sinking into his seat, looked expectantly at Roger, obviously waiting to be questioned. Roger would willingly have avoided disappointing him, but the words would not frame themselves. His momentary lifting of the spirits, caught from Madog, had passed already. The champagne, which ought to have exhilarated him, suddenly made him feel suicidal. It was Jenny who ought to have been sitting where Madog sat, holding a glass of champagne and smiling at him. He should never have left her, up there on the dark hillside, marinating in her misery. He was a coward. And if her despair proved final, if she never came out of it, if their vision of a life together had been only a bright dream lasting a few days and nights, that was all the more reason why, in the last few hours before they parted, he should be at her side, steadying and consoling her.

These thoughts racing through his head, he put down his glass of champagne and threw Madog a despairing look.

'I'm sorry,' he said. His mind was too darkened even to allow him to find words in Welsh. He tried to think of something to tell Madog by way of explanation and excuse for not sharing his mood of exultation, but all that came out was 'I'm sorry,' again.

'My God,' said Madog. He, too, put down his glass. 'Forgive me, Roger. It's the first time I've looked at you closely . . . forgive me, I was absorbed in myself . . . you're ill, aren't you?'

'No,' said Roger, 'not ill.' He swallowed a little more champagne, as if to prove that his stomach was not upset. 'I'm well in health, Madog. It's my happiness that's not well.'

'Do you want to talk about it?' Madog asked. 'I'm ready to listen, if you do.'

'It's a shame to spoil your celebration, whatever it's about.'

'Oh, never mind that,' said Madog. 'It's true that my affairs are prospering for the moment, but we can talk about that later. Or not talk about it at all . . . But I'm sorry to see you so low.'

'I love Jenny Grayfield,' Roger said. He had been about to say 'Jenny Twyford,' but at the last second his tongue had refused the name. Madog, who knew the girl only by her married name, looked puzzled. 'The wife of that excrescence Gerald Twyford,' Roger clarified.

'Is he an excrescence?'

'I've always found him one.'

'I don't care for his friends, certainly,' said Madog. 'But I've always found her very intelligent and sympathetic.'

'She is both.'

'And you love her,' said Madog carefully.

'I love her, and I thought until tonight that she loved me. It may be that she does. She was going to leave her husband, who's absolutely no use to her. She'd even got as far as walking out on him, taking the kids to her mother's to give herself a bit of a breathing-space, and moving into my place. But suddenly she's been hit by panic. Not just cold feet, real panic that's frozen her in her tracks. All she can think of is that she must get the children back to their father and a normal home life as soon as possible. And that she, for her part, must give up all

346

fancy ideas about being happy, and slink back into the kitchen where she belongs, with a halter round her neck.'

Madog studied the stem of his wineglass. 'Why does she feel like that?'

'I don't know. My inadequacy, probably. I just don't give her enough confidence to make her feel that she can face the hell of a divorce and the day-to-day difficulty of explaining to the children that they've got a new father. That smooth swine has got all the cards in his hand and he'll play them. Not because he really cares whether he gets her back. But because he doesn't like to lose.'

'So he'll get her back?'

'He'll get her back unless I can get her over this hump. And I've no chance at all of doing it. You see, I'm at such a crippling disadvantage when it comes to anything like that. This Twyford has his warm, comfortable house, waiting to receive the poor neglected children and the errant wife. I've got nothing except a draughty converted chapel on the mountainside. Very amusing. And if Jenny were a girl of eighteen, in revolt against a respectable home and eager for freedom and *la vie de Bohème*, it would probably put me at an actual advantage. But this is a woman with *children*, Madog. She's built one nest and started to rear her chicks in it. And I can't get her away without offering her an alternative nest. The chapel just isn't good enough, and it'll be months before I can get anything else really set up, even if I drop everything I'm doing here, walk out on Gareth tomorrow, and give my whole time to working on it. That's what she feels, and that's what upsets her. It's something deep and dumb, a part of her animal life as a breeding mammal, and I can't win against it ... But what's the matter, for God's sake?'

Madog had begun to sway about on his chair. His face had reassumed the expression it wore when he was dancing the hornpipe outside the Palace Hotel.

'Speak, can't you?' Roger ordered brusquely.

Madog stood up, went to the bar, and grabbed the champagne bottle. He poured some into Mario's glass, then carried the bottle over and filled Roger's glass and his own. That emptied the bottle, and he set it down reverently.

'Drink,' he said. 'Your troubles are over.'

'What on earth is the good of –'

'*Drink*,' said Madog sharply.

Something in his voice made Roger obey, and with a faint fluttering of hope in his heart he drank off the rest of the champagne. They put down their empty glasses and looked at each other.

'Well?' said Roger.

'Simply,' said Madog, 'that I have the answer to your problem.'

He flickered an imaginary speck of dust from the sleeve of his crumpled blue suit.

'It's time for me to tell you,' he went on, 'that in the spring I'm acting as host and organizer to a gathering of Celtic poets who will read their work aloud to an enraptured audience. Nothing on this scale has ever been seen before. Welsh, Breton, Cornish and Irish poets, yes, and a Gaelic-speaking Scot or two, if we can find any.'

'Very interesting,' said Roger. 'But my mind happens to be running on Jenny.'

'So does mine. This reading is going to be big. It'll start on the Friday afternoon and go on without stopping till the Sunday night. Poets, critics, scholars, with a following of journalists and media men on the look-out for something newsworthy. Now. Here's where Jenny comes in. I know her quite well, and I know she's an efficient, capable, educated girl with a knowledge of these matters. I don't think she knows any of the Celtic languages, but she knows what the whole thing's about. If she were my assistant, I shouldn't have to stop every five minutes to spell out to her what we're doing it in aid of.'

'Your assistant?'

'Secretary to the whole event,' said Madog. 'With the title of,' he thought for a moment, 'Co-ordinator.'

'And will you kindly tell me how being Co-ordinator would help her out of the hole she's in?'

'With pleasure,' said Madog. 'To begin with, there's a fat salary attached to it.'

'Oh. Now you're talking.'

'Of course I'm talking. There's a thundering grant from UNESCO to get the whole thing mounted, and then there are very useful contributions from the Welsh Arts Council and the equivalent thing in Dublin. The French haven't actually made a direct contribution yet but they're sending all these Breton poets over at Government expense.'

'Oh.'

'I believe I mentioned to you some time ago,' said Madog loftily, 'that the time had gone by when these things had to be done on a shoe-string and a couple of fag-ends.'

'Yes. It was when you were sitting with that chap, what was his name . . .'

'André,' said Madog. 'There's another good case in point. He'll be here to make recordings for Radio Canada and we'll be able to cane them up for another fat sum. You see, the world's woken up to the importance of minority cultures now. It's partly a sense of guilt –'

'Yes, yes, I see all that. But Jenny?'

'As soon as Jenny accepts the post of Co-ordinator of the Colloquium of Celtic Poets,' said Madog, 'she can move into the Palace Hotel and have a suite of rooms. There'll be plenty of room for her children to be with her, and if they're old enough to go to school she can drive them there every morning so they won't have the change in their habits. All they'll do is live with their mother in the hotel instead of being at home. A change, I grant you, but not a catastrophic change.'

'How long would this go on?'

'The event is to take place on St David's Day, the first of March. On the second of March, her employment would terminate and she would receive her last instalment of salary.'

'The second of March, eh?' said Roger. It sounded right; it could be made to fit in well enough with his own plans. 'It might work, it just might,' he said, trying to fight down a mounting excitement, an impulse to hug Madog, to slap him on the back, to start dancing round the bar and leaping over the furniture. Was it the champagne? Or Madog's news?

'Of course it'll work,' said Madog. 'Why don't you go and offer her the job now?'

'I will,' said Roger, standing up. 'But you can start assuming straight away that she's on the strength. I believe it now. You have the answer. And Madog . . . I'm grateful.'

'Poetry saves lives,' said Madog. 'It's the great humanizing force. It's saved more people than diseases have killed.'

'Well, it's certainly saving me.'

'So be it,' said Madog. 'Get the child to move into the Palace Hotel tomorrow and be ready to start work the next day.'

Roger went back to where he had parked Jenny's little car. All the way up the mountain he kept his foot hard down, continually shifting between third and second gear, sliding a little on the corners, singing a Welsh song into the darkness outside the windows.

Part Four

Jenny was still lying on the divan, fully dressed, as if she had not moved during all the time Roger had been away. Exuberantly, he woke her and told her of Madog's offer. Her mood of despair was unbreakable, for the time being at any rate, and she listened as if what he was saying hardly concerned her. Fortunately he knew just enough about women not to try to argue the case frontally: having fed the information into her mind, he concentrated on comforting and soothing her, getting her to take some food, to sit by the stove, finally to undress and come with him to bed. Once there, he was prepared to let her sleep, but almost at once she turned on him, provoking him, with a dumb ferocity of lust that he was at a loss to interpret. Either she thought of herself as saying goodbye to him, claiming his powers for the last time, or it was the first flicker of a new hope, an affirmation of their need and their rightness for each other.

Later, lying awake, they talked.

'But it's a silly idea. What have I to do with all that?'

'It gives you a breathing-space. You can move out of here and have the kids with you.'

'In an hotel?'

'Children like hotels, as long as they don't have to live in them for ever.'

'But what shall I do with them all day?'

'They'll go to school.'

'There won't be room. We'll be all on top of one another.'

'You'll have a suite.'

'I can't cope with a lot of Celtic poets.'

'Madog will cope. Your work will just be office work and you'll be paid enough for it to make you independent of Gerald.'

'And of you,' she said thoughtfully.

'And of me, if that's what you want.'

'Oh, Roger. Oh, God knows what I want.'

'And God has begun by sending you this opportunity. I shall tell Madog you'll report for work immediately.'

'Well, God knows. Well, I suppose I might as well. But I must fetch Mary and Robin first. Poor little homeless dabs.'

'They're not homeless. They have the Palace Hotel to live in.'

Once Jenny was installed with Mary and Robin in the hotel, a new rhythm took possession of Roger's life. It became more relaxed and diffused. There was no longer any need for his energies to be concentrated on the long, cold vigil against Dic Sharp, or for the chapel on the mountain to be his lonely bolt-hole. He still travelled with Gareth's bus, very seldom missing a run, but there was an unspoken agreement between them that this was the final phase of their partnership. As a bus operator, Dic Sharp was probably finished; but they wanted him to declare plainly that he was finished, to give some concrete sign that the struggle was over. Once that happened, Roger would feel he had his *congé*. And since Jenny was committed to working for Madog until the first of March, it was easiest to jog on, until that date, with things as they were.

But of course there were changes. Roger spent far less time at the chapel. He called there, between runs, to keep the stove alight, and he slept there at nights. He had, once, tentatively brought up the suggestion that he might move into Jenny's suite at the Palace Hotel and begin living with her openly and fully, but she had vetoed this. It would be too disturbing for the children; it would conflict with the story she had concocted for them. When they were tucked up in bed, she would often get a good-natured chambermaid to listen out in case they woke up, and then she would drive up to the mountain to join Roger in his fastness for two or three hours. He had to be content with this; and, in addition, they saw each other several times each day. He always had lunch with her at the hotel, and joined her for a drink and dinner after the seven o'clock run down. She usually had the children in bed by that time, so that their longest uninterrupted period together was from seven-fifteen to ten. Then, if Mary and Robin were asleep and Jenny did not feel tired after a day's work for Madog. she would get into her Mini, follow the bus up to Llancrwys, and stay with Roger till about midnight. It was a scrappy life, but they both enjoyed it. They knew it was no more than a prelude to their serious life together, and it had an atmosphere of improvisation which was delightful to them after the years of routine they had both lived through.

Altogether, it was a pleasant, dream-like period. Roger sometimes woke in the night and worried about the slight tinge of unreality that seemed to have spread to everything, but for the most part he was content to go along from day to day. After all, there was not much they could do except wait. They were waiting for Dic Sharp to reveal his hand, waiting for Gerald Twyford to begin legal hostilities, waiting for March the first to arrive and bring with it the consummation of Madog's efforts.

Madog worked Jenny hard, but not as hard as he worked himself. There were innumerable letters to be written, accommodation to be booked, representatives of this and that organization to be lunched and dined, journalists to be talked to. The Celtic Poets' Colloquium grew bigger, and drew nearer, and took on firmer and firmer outlines. The Town Hall was booked, letters for and against were published in the local paper, and Madog put in so little time at the estate agent's office that he seemed to be challenging his employer to give him the sack. He was perpetually running in and out of the hotel, his pockets full of telegrams and letters. The hotel staff, who at first had been inclined to cool scepticism, became gradually impressed with the importance of what was happening. They took their cue from the manager, who had seen the colour of Madog's UNESCO money and was also watching with approval the steady stream of expense-account lunches and dinners that were going down the throats of assorted *literati*, bureaucrats, and men from the media.

Even Rhiannon, though her eye took on a sardonic gleam when it rested on Roger, showed signs of being gathered up into the excitement. Roger liked her for that, and for the fact that she did not, as an English girl would, regard a gathering of poets as something half-way between a basket of cobras and a nurseryful of governesses.

So the weeks went by. Roger's relations with Gareth were excellent; he even spent a couple of Sunday afternoons at Gareth's cottage with Jenny and the children. It was all good. That was the trouble. It was too good to be true. Something must be wrong.

One day this feeling became so insistent that Roger told Gareth he would like to take the next three days off.

'Business?' Gareth asked, wiping the windscreen of the bus with a chamois leather.

'Yes. I've decided I ought to bite the bullet and go down to London to see if my flat's still there. You see, I shall be needing somewhere . . .'

'To take Jenny and the children,' he had intended to say, but he let his voice die into silence. It was, for some reason, impossible to discuss that side of his life with Gareth. His relationship with Gareth was real and deep, but its reality was enclosed in a magic circle, and it faded when it left that circle. He left the sentence unfinished; and Gareth's acquiescence was a silent nod.

That night, Roger conferred with Jenny. The flat in London would be no use as a permanent home; on the other hand, it had two good-sized bedrooms, and they could hole up there while Roger found something bigger. He would look for a better job; perhaps they would travel, work abroad for a few years; London, as a place to bring children up in, did not appeal to them, and in any case the world was before them: Europe, America, Africa.

'But we'll come back here in the end.'

'Before the end, Jenny. I promise you.'

'Even if Gerald's still here?' she asked.

'He won't be. His sights are on money and power. North Wales won't hold him.'

'No. But it'll hold us, won't it, when we want to settle down?'

'It'll be perfect.' He kissed her.

The next day, Roger took the train to London and a taxi to his flat. It was cold, meaningless, too long uninhabited, but it would do. Looking round it for the first time with the eye of a family man, he saw its deficiencies, but also its possibilities. They would manage, easily enough.

For the rest, what struck him about London was its unreality. The ugly streets, the pale crowds scurrying about like harried ghosts, the bad food, the all-pervading *Ersatz* and falsity, were like some transient monochrome image flashed on a screen. Often, in the hurrying street, he stood still and thought of the mountains, the glistening plain of the sea, the smoke rising from the chimney of Gareth's cottage under the steep tip. That was a language; this, a demented babble.

Still, he had his bargain to strike with this unreal world, his little term to serve yet before he could get release from it. He went to see the university authorities and confirmed that he would be resuming his duties in the summer term; privately, he resolved to start applying for other jobs at once. Uppsala? Why not? – but the blondes, he thought with a warm glow of security, would be superfluous now.

In the afternoon of the third day after his departure from Llancrwys, Roger decided that he had completed his business, and went to the station to get the train back to Wales. Settling happily into his seat, he opened a book. The cushions were soft underneath him, he had ample leg-room, and he looked forward luxuriously to a few hours in which he could rest his bones and have no demands to meet. But he had hardly begun to read when he felt the unmistakeable sensation of being looked at. He raised his eyes. The train was just beginning to move out of the station, and the usual file of late-comers was moving down the corridor, peering into each compartment in search of a seat. One figure in this procession, however, was doing more than look for a seat : it had halted and was staring fixedly down at him, and it was Donald Fisher.

With an inward groan, Roger dropped his eyes to the page and went on reading intently. By rights, Fisher ought to avoid him. He belonged to the opposite camp; he was a Twyford man, and for that matter, at heart, a Dic Sharp man. They could have nothing to say to each other. On the other hand, he was not so *naïf* as to suppose that Donald Fisher would be capable of neglecting any chance to initiate a conversation, to worm his way into some kind of talk, merely in the hope of gleaning some fragment of information that could be useful. He was a man who lived by contacts. What he lacked in talent, and it was everything, he made up by 'knowing everybody'. His gift was for being in the right place at the right time, whether he was wanted there or not.

Roger read on, fiercely, and after a moment Donald Fisher passed on. There were, mercifully, no empty seats in Roger's compartment. He was safe, and this safety lasted until, about two hours later, thirst drove him from sanctuary and he went along to the buffet car. Business was slack, and after he had bought himself a beer at the counter he had a table to himself where he might sit and drink it. A cautious glance round showed no detectable Fisher-figure: but the man must have been lurking behind a newspaper somewhere along the route, for in a moment or two he was there at the bar, outfitting himself with a drink, then advancing on Roger with a false grin of *bonhomie*. Roger looked round for escape, but every other table had two or three people sitting at it and there was no chance of changing tables silently and unobserved. In any case, it hardly mattered: the journey would not last much longer. Already, they had left behind the mud-flats of the Dee estuary and the mountains were coming into view.

Fisher began at once to exude an uneasy, over-hearty affability. He evidently wished to fend off any latent hostility that might arise from the fact that he was a sycophant of the man whose wife had left him in favour of Roger.

'Well, back to the wild wet woods,' he said, glancing with distaste at the rural scene sliding by the windows. 'I've just managed three days in town, thank goodness. Saved my sanity for a while. Last night was particularly amusing. The American cultural attaché gave a party for Diethof Backwax.' (Or some such name.) 'You've heard of the *Paleface Review*, I suppose. Well, in addition to running it, Backwax has the chief post in the Brandingiron University Press. I expect you know Brandingiron run the *Paleface* as one of their subsidiaries.'

'I didn't, as it happens.'

'Oh. Well, they do. Remarkably well-heeled that lot. The rumours that were flying about, concerning Backwax's salary! And he's only been there five or six years, you know. He worked in Munich before that, running the literary section of *Kunst*.'

Donald Fisher's eyes gleamed with covetousness. His shiny

bald head, like an ignoble version of Gito's stately dome, moved up and down nervously.

'Everybody was there,' he said. 'It was pretty much an open secret that Backwax had asked for a full parade. I believe he's on the look-out for staff.'

Roger began to understand. Fisher had been arse-licking again. He wanted to do what this Backwax had done – get where the money and the sinecures were, and consolidate his position with the best people, which nowadays meant not the impoverished aristocracy but the rich institutions.

'It's a job that would suit me down to the ground,' Fisher went on. 'Helping to edit the *Paleface*, with a chance of getting in at the Brandingiron Press. Publishing's a lot more interesting than teaching, and if it's publishing against an academic background with all your losses guaranteed, you simply haven't any worries.'

'So you went up and asked him for a job,' said Roger.

Donald Fisher grinned. 'Well, not as directly as that. I'm not in a hurry. There were one or two people there, I needn't name names, who seemed to me to be getting Backwax into a corner a lot too fast, and arousing his resistance. Naturally, I let him see I was interested, though.'

Why are you telling me all this, you loathsome crawling milli-pede? Roger wondered.

There was a silence and then Fisher said, 'I believe you know that chap Madog pretty well.'

'Yes, I know him.'

Fisher leaned forward and said confidentially, his voice only just audible over the rattle of the train, 'Is there anything really in this jamboree of his?'

'His Celtic Poets' Colloquium, you mean?'

'Yes,' said Fisher. He grinned spitefully. 'Sounds to me like a lot of smug little nationalists feathering their nests.'

'That's not how I'd describe it.'

'How would you describe it?' Fisher pressed.

'Oh,' Roger yawned. 'I've had a long day and I'm tired. If you're interested, why don't you ask Madog? He'll tell you all about it.'

'Ask Madog, h'm,' said Donald Fisher. 'Well, that's just the trouble. You see, Madog and I haven't always hit it off all that well.'

'You adopted patronizing airs toward him, didn't you?'

'I hadn't much faith in the things he stood for, if that's what you mean.'

'No that isn't what I mean. What I mean is that you thought he was a funny little Welshman in a blue suit, and he wrote poems in a language that nobody in the *New Statesman* office could understand, and he and his crowd were despised by Gerald Twyford and *his* crowd. So for you that settled it.'

'I say, you're taking his part rather vehemently, aren't you?' said Donald Fisher. His defensiveness caused him to drawl more heavily than usual, but the vowels of South-East London came through more strongly than ever.

'Oh, get off it,' said Roger. 'You never wanted to come up here in the first place, you came because it was the only place where you could get a job, and right from the start you weren't interested in anything you found going on up here. Well, that's fine with me, but for God's sake be consistent. If you haven't been interested up to now, just go on not being interested.'

'Well, but the trouble is,' said Donald Fisher, his eyes moving from side to side rapidly and occasionally flickering towards Roger's, 'the trouble is, I've told Backwax . . .'

'Oh, no!' Roger interrupted. He felt like shouting with laughter. 'You've told Backwax you're an authority on present-day Celtic culture, and now he wants you to write an article about it or something, and you're done for unless you can pick Madog's brains.'

'Well, it's not as simple as that,' said Donald Fisher. 'But the fact is, I could do with a conversation with Madog. Just to find out whether there's anything really in this business he's running.'

'Why d'you want to know? You might as well come clean.'

'There's nothing to come clean about,' said Donald Fisher with what he imagined to be dignity. 'Backwax runs a series of Despatches in the *Paleface Review*. Reports on the literary and artistic scene from all over. He was setting a few of them up at this party. Naturally I'd have liked to write about the set-up in town, which I know like the back of my hand . . .'

Or like the back of other people's bums, Roger thought. Outwardly he said, 'But when Beeswax heard that you lived up here he asked you to do a Despatch from North Wales, and you thought to yourself that that would be a toe in the door, and said yes, and now you're desperate to get to talk to Madog.'

'I've told you, it would be a help to have a talk with him. After all, he ought to welcome the publicity, if I write him up in the *Paleface*.'

'I don't see why. If Madog wants publicity he can get it from people a lot better qualified than you. And there's another thing. Now that he's in a position to hand out favours, why should he hand them out to people who've been sneering at him for years?'

'He could let bygones be bygones.'

'If you mean he could refrain from actually kicking you in the teeth when he happens to meet you, I agree. But I don't see why he should start spooning out gravy.'

Fisher scowled. 'All right, if he wants hostility he can have it. I'm in a position to do him a lot of harm.'

'No, you're not. You can write a few snide little pieces in the London papers, sneering at him and his Celtic poets. But nobody's being taken in by that line of talk any more. If anything, they're too credulous on the other side now. After years of taking no notice of people like Madog, the cultural establishment is falling over itself to compensate them. It's Madog who'll get the big grants and hand-outs from governments and foundations from now on. It's Madog who could have a job with Bugjaw any time he wanted one. The Brandingiron University Press have probably got a multi-million-dollar project for printing the complete works of every one of these Celtic poets, together with photostats of all their work and notebooks since they started writing. You might as well face it, Madog's waste-paper basket will be worth more in cool cash than all the clever little reviews you can write for the rest of your life.'

'Interesting,' said Donald Fisher. 'That's only one assessment of the situation, of course. But I'm interested to know that's how you view it. It certainly sheds light on your motives.'

'What sort of light?'

'Well,' said Donald Fisher carefully, 'it explains the way you've been behaving lately. If you've decided that this Celtic stuff is the new growth industry, I can see why you came up here to learn Welsh. And I can see why you talked Gerald Twyford's wife into coming over to your side of the fence.'

Roger stood up to go. He did not want to become involved in a brawl, and he knew for certain that if he had to sit and listen to Fisher expounding his view of the world, and assigning Jenny, of all people, to her niche in that world, he would lose control of himself, and treat Fisher to a thump on the jaw.

'I see I'm right,' said Fisher, grinning up at Roger. 'Well, don't think I blame you. Everyone has a right to paddle his own boat.'

'I shouldn't bother to paddle yours any more,' said Roger, departing. 'It's too leaky.'

He was on his way out, but Fisher caught his sleeve as he walked by. 'You're very satisfied with yourself. But you wouldn't be so smug if you knew a few things I know.'

'I dare say not. Let go of my sleeve or I'll –'

'Your boat will be a lot worse than leaky,' said Fisher, 'when Gerald Twyford's finished with you. It'll be sunk right to the bottom.'

Roger stopped tugging. He bent down till his face was close to Fisher's.

'If you're threatening me on his behalf,' he said, 'save your breath. I'm ready for the worst he can throw at me.'

'You may think you are,' Fisher grinned. 'But wait till you see what he's lining up. He can afford to get good lawyers, you know. These big corporations he works for –'

'Listen, Fisher,' said Roger. 'There was a time when I'd have been scared stiff at the thought of somebody setting a pack of clever lawyers on me. But I don't scare so easily now. In the last few months I've got a lot stronger.'

'Oh?' Fisher sneered. 'Been on a weight-lifting course?'

'Something like that,' said Roger. He pulled his sleeve free and went back to his own compartment.

He reported back to Jenny that same evening, as she soaped the children in their bath.

'I've felt for some time, in my bones,' she said. 'He's going to set the lawyers on to me. I've been getting vibrations.'

'Mummy, it's going in my eyes,' said Robin.

'Keep still – let me sponge it.'

'I'm ready to come out, Mummy,' said Mary.

'Wait a minute, love. Sit there and soak for a while. I'll take you out.'

She went from the bathroom to her bedroom, beckoning Roger to follow. 'I don't want to talk about it in front of them. Robin just thinks his father's away on a journey and we're living here while I help Madog. But Mary's damn' certain I'm up to something with you. She keeps asking if I like you. And today she asked the question I've been waiting for and dreading, rather.'

'Let me guess,' said Roger. 'She asked if you liked me better than you liked Daddy.'

'Correct,' said Jenny. She took a bottle of gin out of the wardrobe and poured herself a drink. 'Will you have one? There's tonic on that window-sill.'

They opened tonic-bottles, poured, and drank.

'Yes, the crunch is coming,' Jenny sighed. 'And yesterday something happened that nearly stopped my heart beating. I was bringing them back from school in the car and we were a bit earlier than usual. I got there in good time and either the teacher's watch was fast or something, because the bell went and they came out and it was still only twenty-five past three, and half-past is the official time. Anyway, I scooped them up and started to drive off, and I hadn't gone fifty yards before I saw Gerald walking along the pavement.'

'Towards the school?'

'Towards the school. It doesn't look like coincidence. My guess is that he's going to turn up, as if casually, and confront me and the children **at** the school gates, just where my hands will be tied. Their friends, the other mums, a teacher or two thrown in for good measure – if he manages to make them hysterical in front of that lot, it'll be a good stick to beat me with. I'm the one who's walked out, anything the children might suffer is my fault.' She drank rapidly, nervously. 'Not that I care a damn whose fault it is. I just don't want them to suffer, any more than they're absolutely bound to, that is.'

Roger was about to make some reply when Mary, her hair clinging to her scalp, came into the room. She had wrapped a towel round herself, and only her wet little head and feet protruded.

'I know what you're talking about, Mummy,' she said calmly.

'Oh,' said Jenny.

'Yes,' said Mary. 'You want Roger to be our new Daddy. But Daddy was always very clever and earned lots of money so we could live in a nice house.' She turned to Roger. 'You don't earn lots of money, do you?'

'I could do,' Roger said.

'But you work on the bus. That's not a job for a clever person. My Daddy wouldn't work on the bus.'

'No, he wouldn't.'

'But you do and you don't live in a nice house. I've seen where you live and it's quite sweet but it isn't a nice house for a family.'

'It's true that I've been working on the bus lately,' said Roger. 'But it isn't the only thing I know how to do.' He sat Mary, unresisting, on his knee. 'I know how to make lots of money and have a nice house for you to live in. If I did that, would you like to live with me?'

'Yes,' said Mary. 'If you did it.'

'I'll do it. Just you wait and see.'

'What about Daddy?' asked Jenny, splashing a little more gin into her glass.

'I've thought of that,' said Mary. 'He can come on Sundays. I like him best on Sundays anyway. That's when he wears his lovely fur hat and we go for walks.'

She slid off Roger's knee, but not impatiently. 'I've got to go and see Robin now,' she said. 'He's playing with his plastic boat.' She went back into the bathroom.

Roger looked at Jenny across the room. Jenny took a drink, then set the glass down with a large sniff, and Roger realized that she was crying.

'Don't cry, sweetheart,' he said, going over to her. 'The signs are good.'

'Yes,' she said, her face pushed into his chest, 'that's why I'm crying. We just could get away with it, Roger, we just *could*.'

'And if we did . . .?'

'I'd die of happiness,' she said, 'and be born again straight away and go on living for ever.'

January went out, February sloshed in. The sea glistened like lead foil, the stones of the castle wall streamed with boisterous rain that seemed to dance in the spring light. The weather was still hostile, but the year was unmistakeably opening out. Roger's heart was like a bowl of crocuses on a sunny window-sill.

But disagreeable shocks were still in the air. Gerald Twyford had not reappeared, at the school gates or anywhere else, but his aggrieved spirit was hovering about the *ménage* in the hotel. Jenny drove off one morning, and went to Nantwich for the long-dreaded scene in which she talked the situation out with her parents. It was after midnight when she got back, and Roger, who had waited in the suite, had to put her to bed in a state of exhaustion that almost qualified as nervous collapse. Fortunately it was a Friday, so she was able to get up late on the following day. Slowly, that week-end, she surfaced and regained some cheerfulness. Roger forbore to question her, and she never told him anything about the ordeal except that it had been in every way as bad as she had feared. 'But it's over,' she added. 'I drove it into their heads.'

'Do they want to meet me?' Roger asked, steeling himself.

'In due course,' she said. 'When we're man and wife will be time enough.'

There, matters rested. And as St David's day cast its approaching shadow and Madog bounded up the hotel steps a dozen times a day with some urgent behest, Jenny thankfully gave herself up to the bustle of the Colloquium.

'After all,' she said to Roger, 'Celtic poets *matter*. If it wasn't for them, we shouldn't be together now.'

Roger responded by inventing a fanciful visiting-card for himself:

> Mr Roger Furnivall,
> Ungovernable seer,
> 9, Bean-Rows,
> Innisllancrwys.

But the excitement had caught him up, too; he felt it in his blood. St David's day, this year, was certainly going to be a memorable date in their lives. He said as much, one evening, to Rhiannon, who was sitting idly behind the reception desk during a slack time, lacquering her nails and in a mood to gossip.

'It'll be a date to remember all right,' she said. 'You don't know the half of it.'

'What don't I know?' he asked.

'It isn't only Madog who's got plans for that day,' she said. 'Dic Sharp has them too.'

'Well,' Roger said impatiently.

'You'll find out soon enough,' she teased. 'But I'll tell you. He's having the big sale that morning.'

'The big . . . ?'

'Selling back the buses. Every single one. He's getting out of the business.'

'Are you sure?'

Her eyes met his. 'Am I ever wrong?'

'No, Rhiannon,' he said, 'you're never anything but right, and wise, and good, and beautiful.'

'I wouldn't say that,' she said, and went back to her lacquering. 'But I get to know things.'

It was, of course, true. Rhiannon's information never lied. Within a day or two, notices were pasted up all over Caerfenai and in every surrounding village. Roger tried to discover whether there was any significance in the choice of a date. Was Dic Sharp, in some obscure way, trying to compete with Madog? But Ivo ran into the auctioneer who was to be in charge of the sale, and was assured that the explanation was entirely prosaic. St David's day was a Saturday; these auctions were always held on Saturday mornings, when the greatest number of buyers were free to attend; this particular Saturday was the first on which the sale-room would be free.

'It'll bring everybody into town, just when there's no room for them,' Roger commented to Ivo.

'There'll be room, man. This is an expanding town. It'll open up – the buildings are mounted on wheels. And it's just been discovered that the castle's made of cardboard. It's a stage castle left over from a royal pantomime staged by Hereward the Wake. They're going to put a match to it. There'll be plenty of room, plenty of room.'

Everyone in Caerfenai was now openly living for March the first. Or nearly everybody. One gusty evening, Roger was in the narrow street that ran along the side of the Palace Hotel. One of the hotel's three bars had an entrance on this lane, and he was about to go in and have a drink when his attention was caught by a copy of the ubiquitous notice. 'SALE OF PUBLIC TRANSPORT VEHICLES.' 'Comprising omnibuses and equipment.' He stopped, as he always did, to read the notice and enjoy the slight flicker of triumph at seeing it in black and white, Dic Sharp's armistice. The typography of the notice was old-fashioned and comfortable; it looked like a Victorian playbill; the same printing press must have clattered out notices announcing the sale of horse-drawn carriages. 'At eleven o'clock promptly.' 'In the auction rooms, Castle Square, Caerfenai.' He read, and glowed.

Then the door of the bar opened, and quick, scuffing footsteps sounded. Roger glanced up, then stayed alert. It was Dic Sharp's son, swaying down the steps with that characteristic bustling movement of the shoulders and arrogant toss of the fair mane. He saw Roger, hesitated a second or two, then came over, staring with pale hate.

'Hope you're satisfied with yourself,' he said.

'I'm not dissatisfied,' said Roger. He raised himself slightly on his toes, shifting his weight cautiously from foot to foot. If it came to a punch-up, he wanted to be light and fast in his movements.

Dic Sharp's son looked quickly up and down the lane, as if to make sure there were no witnesses before launching an attack on Roger. But instead of lashing out, he leaned towards him confidentially and said, 'Tell me one thing. Just one thing I want to know.'

'Yes?'

'When you going back where you came from? Get off our backs round here.'

'It isn't me,' said Roger levelly, 'that's been on people's backs round here.'

Dic Sharp's son shook his head several times, as if to clear it. Roger realized the lad was drunk. He began to feel protective.

'Been a right mess for me,' said Dic Sharp's son. 'Those buses. We'd have sold to General by now and it was going to be my twenty-first birthday present.' The corners of his mouth travelled downwards. 'You done me out of my twenty-first.'

'You'll live,' said Roger kindly. 'Not everybody gets a fleet of buses for their twenty-first birthday. I tell you what, get your father to buy you a watch and chain instead. I promise not to do you out of that.'

The youth stood blinking under the rain-smeared street lamp, as if he had not understood Roger's words. Then, suddenly, he swung round and walked away, banging one shoulder several times against the wall. Roger hoped he would not fall under a bus before getting home; or that, if he did, it would at least be a General bus.

He went on into the bar, treated himself to a celebratory drink, and then peered through into the lobby of the hotel. Jenny would be putting the children to bed, and he had formed the habit of looking in at this time and saying goodnight to them. But this evening, which had started differently, continued differently. Emerging into the lobby, Roger saw that Rhiannon was at her desk and that she was being confronted, and perhaps questioned, by a man whose back, neatly clothed in a grey business suit, Roger thought he had seen before. He moved up discreetly behind the man, in time to hear him say, 'What number is she in? I'll go up.'

'I'll ring through, sir,' said Rhiannon with frosty politeness. 'Then if she wants you to go up, she can tell me. That's our custom.'

'You might as well tell me the number and save everybody that much trouble. I'll be going up anyway.'

So Twyford had finally got to the point of invading Jenny's fastness. Roger was just about to intervene when Rhiannon got up from her stool, turned and walked through a doorway behind her. Roger understood why she had done this. Normally she would have picked up the telephone on her desk and asked the switchboard girl for the number of Jenny's suite. But with Twyford bending over her, listening for the number, to do so would have been to give away Jenny's position. So Rhiannon went back to telephone from the switchboard herself. She knew, of course, because she knew everything, that Jenny was escaping from her husband, and she was obviously not going to let Gerald Twyford stampede his way in to see her and tread flat an inviolable hotel regulation at the same time.

Twyford, with a click of impatience, straightened up, turned, and found himself looking straight into Roger's eyes. The surprise must have been an unpleasant one, but he contrived to mask it under his usual silkiness.

'Ah, Furnivall,' he said. 'I have expected to run into you somewhere in these purlieus.'

'If it's Jenny you want,' said Roger, 'why not just leave a message? If it's me you want, here I am.'

'It certainly isn't you I want,' said Twyford with bland disdain. 'I intend to pay a short social call on my wife and children.'

'That's out of the question,' said Roger brusquely. 'Now that she's finally decided to leave you and take the children with her, she doesn't want you popping in and out of their lives. It unsettles them.'

'They happen to be my children, you know.'

'That doesn't give you the right to inflict suffering on them. Till they can get into a stable routine and accept a new pattern of life, you should leave them alone.'

'Have the goodness to mind your own business,' Twyford snapped.

'It is my business. Jenny's going to marry me as soon as she gets free from you.'

'Yes, that's the rumour you've been busily putting out,' said Twyford. A dangerous flush was spreading over his smooth, spectacled features. 'But I think I'm entitled to hear it from Jenny herself.'

'Then telephone her. Communicate with her through a lawyer. Do anything you like. But don't come muscling in here and throw the children into hysterics.'

'Why should I make everything nice and smooth for you? You've stolen my wife, and you can damned well take the consequences.'

'Your marriage was a failure, Twyford, why not face it? With me, she has a chance of happiness.'

'Very noble of you.'

'It's not in the least noble. I'm doing it for my own sake and I don't mind admitting it. But the fact remains that I can make Jenny happy and you couldn't.'

'I'm not convinced of that.'

'No, but she is, and that's the important thing.'

'Tell me this, Furnivall,' said Gerald Twyford, leaning forward keenly as if engaging in a debate on television, 'are you proud of what you've done?'

'Pride doesn't come into it. Some people suit one another and some don't.'

'And you took it upon yourself to decide that I didn't suit Jenny.'

'From what I can gather, neither of you had much enthusiasm for the marriage.'

Twyford drew in his breath sharply. 'I find your hypocrisy very distasteful, Furnivall. Why not simply admit that you met Jenny, decided you'd like to marry her, and don't care a damn about anything else?'

'All right,' said Roger. 'I met Jenny, decided I'd like to marry her, and don't care a damn about anything else. Now what will you do?'

At that moment Rhiannon returned, and Twyford turned expectantly towards her. 'I shall go up to see her, to begin with,' he said to Roger.

'She says she'll come down in a few minutes, if you'd care to wait,' said Rhiannon correctly.

'You'll have to be satisfied with that, Twyford,' said Roger.

Gerald Twyford's mask of Olympian calm was clearly beginning to split down the middle. 'Don't start telling me what I'll have to be satisfied with. I'm going up to find my wife and my children. I'll knock on every door in this damned hotel till I find them.' His voice was suddenly shrill and loud.

'You'll be thrown out if you do.'

'Oh? Who's going to throw me out?'

'If no one else does it,' said Roger easily, 'I will.'

'If you lay a finger on me, I'll call a policeman.'

'In that case the policeman will throw you out of the hotel. You must know the legal position. Since your wife has left the marital dwelling, you can sue for divorce and the law will, in its own good time, annul your marriage. It may give you certain rights over the children's upbringing. That is as much rope as you'll get. By leaving you, Jenny has put herself in the wrong matrimonially, but she still has her other rights under the law, and one of them is the right not to be pestered by you if she doesn't feel like it.'

'She has no right to abduct my children,' said Twyford stonily.

'Show me anything in the law,' said Roger, 'that calls it abduction when a mother's looking after her own children, feeding and clothing and caring for them, and even taking them every day to their accustomed school. And that's another thing. If you're thinking of turning up there and making the school impossible for the children to go to, by disturbing their tranquillity there, Jenny can get an injunction to restrain you.'

Twyford's eyes moved from Roger to Rhiannon, and back again. For the first time, he seemed irresolute.

'Well, anyway,' he said at last, 'when my wife comes down, at least have the decency to leave us alone. I don't want to talk to her in front of you.'

'I'd like to oblige you, but I can't. Anything you have to say to Jenny concerns me. If you want to get her on her own, the reason can only be that you want to play on her feelings and upset her. I'm going to be on hand to prevent that.'

'Oh, take your shining armour off, Furnivall. Ever since you came into the district you've had a Messiah-complex.'

'Well put,' said Roger.

'Quite apart from grabbing someone else's perfectly contented wife, and don't think I've finished with you for *that*, you engage in this ridiculous pseudo-activity with the local transport people. All deception and delusion. A complete non-event. You make a fool of yourself for months on end and finally achieve nothing.'

'We have achieved something. The man who was victimizing the local bus operators has called off the campaign and isn't victimizing them any more.'

Twyford smiled: he had recovered his self-possession. 'Oh you poor innocent. How can a man live to your ripe years and be so blazingly simple.'

'Easily. Just breathe in and out and don't think in terms of economic jargon.'

'You realize, don't you,' said Twyford almost tenderly, 'that your supreme efforts have won these small bus operators at most a respite of – what shall we say? Eighteen months? Two years at the most? –before they're swallowed by a far bigger fish than the one that was chasing them?'

'Meaning the government, I suppose,' said Roger. 'Yes, surprisingly enough, I'm not a fool. I know the whole shooting-match is going to be nationalized.'

'And you actually thought it was worth going in for these silly capers, wasting your time and making yourself look silly for a whole winter, just to gain that end? To have them sell directly to the government rather than to the bigger company first?'

'A minnow,' said Roger, 'would presumably rather be caught in a net and taken off to an aquarium, then be swallowed by a pike five minutes before the pike is caught and taken to the same aquarium.'

'A picturesque image,' Twyford sneered.

'I think in picturesque images. They lead me to the truth.'

The lift doors opened and Jenny came out. She had her glasses on and looked set and determined. Roger and Twyford stood absolutely still as she walked towards them: Rhiannon frankly watched, leaning her elbows on the desk.

'Gerald,' she said, 'I haven't anything to say to you and I don't want to talk to you alone, ever again.'

Twyford's face was sick and pale, but he stood his ground. 'It was Mary and Robin I wanted to talk about,' he said.

'Well, talk about them,' said Jenny.

'In front of these people?'

'There's nothing to hide any more. For years I've had to hide everything. All my real thoughts and feelings. Now, I'm never going to hide anything again. You didn't know it, Gerald, but what you were forcing on me was concealment. Well, I've finished with concealment for the rest of my life – finished with lying, finished with evasion. What I am, I'll be, in front of all the world.'

'What were you lying to me about?' Twyford asked.

'Every breath I drew was a lie,' she said. 'It was all part of the big lie that I was a living woman, when actually I was a corpse. Now, whether I stay with Roger or not, I'm going to be alive, for the rest of my time on this earth.'

Twyford opened his mouth to speak, but closed it again and merely nodded his head. They waited, but he did nothing except nod, three or four times. Then he turned and walked heavily to the door, picking up his overcoat, on the way, from the back of a chair.

When he had safely gone, Jenny slumped a little with exhaustion. She took off her glasses; her face was soft and tired.

'Roger,' she said, 'buy me a drink. And buy Rhiannon one, too. She must need it as much as I do after listening to all that.'

'I'm on duty,' said Rhiannon, smiling.

'Oh, come on,' Jenny urged. 'It isn't part of your duty to listen to people's sordid matrimonial break-ups. You need some recompense.'

'I can't leave the desk, honest. It's more than my job's worth.'

'Then I'll fetch you a drink,' said Roger. He piloted Jenny off to the bar, set her up with a whisky, and took another to Rhiannon. 'There,' he said, setting it firmly on the desk. 'Drink it.'

'I'd better, before someone comes along and reports me for drinking on duty.'

Rhiannon picked up the glass and drank. As she did so, Roger thought how much he loved her. She was so unbelievably beautiful, so challenging to every male drop in his body, that he had no hesitation in admitting to himself that she possessed his imagination. And yet he also knew that he did not love her as he loved Jenny: that, offered freely the choice of either one of them, he would still take Jenny. She was nothing like as beautiful, but she was more real. Rhiannon's beauty made her seem like a mirage: furthermore, it gave her a nimbus of luxury, a lushness of outline. Though she came from steep stony Llancrwys, she represented the valleys of plenty: and Jenny, cradled on the level Cheshire plain, was mountain-natured. Suddenly, Peacock's jingle came into his mind:

> The valley sheep are fatter
> But the mountain sheep are sweeter.

'I love you, Rhiannon,' he said. 'But I'm glad I'm going to marry Jenny.'

'Hush,' she commanded. 'Nobody loves me till I'm off duty.' She handed him back the empty glass. 'But about Jenny,' she said. 'I'm sure you're right for each other.'

Roger nodded. Suddenly, he felt too emotional to speak. He trusted Rhiannon's judgement; he felt that she had, in these matters, a deep intuitive wisdom.

Clutching the empty whisky-glass, he hurried back to his

love, his warmth, his future. She had blown her nose, put her glasses back on, and was ready for another drink.

The encounter with Gerald had shaken them up, and they talked for some hours: talked hard, realistically, facing their situation. In the end they decided to move away from Caerfenai immediately after the all-important St David's day. Their business in the district would be over; the stronger threads of attachment, through feeling and habit, could be taken up again at a later and easier time. From a distance, they could deal more effectively with Twyford's hostility, and also plan their next move while Roger earned a salary.

From that evening on, their lives were aimed, like two arrows, at St David's day.

The Day began with Mrs Arkwright. That is, it began effectively with her: she provided the first memorable incident in what was to be an unbroken chain of memorable incidents extending over twelve hours.

The eight-fifteen run down, blinking away sleep and watching in bemused delight as the hard spring sunshine came flooding over the mountains and every colour sprang to life; the quick visit to Jenny at the hotel, finding her nervous, preoccupied, but gay, the burden of waiting at last about to slip from her shoulders; the ten-thirty run up, carrying a few early shoppers – all this was routine. But when Roger, after a brief visit to the chapel to put fuel on the stove, reported for the eleven o'clock run down, he found Gareth standing beside the bus and staring fixedly along the street.

Can I believe my eyes? he said.

Roger followed the direction of his gaze. In the distance, slowly approaching, came the figure of Mrs Arkwright. She was bending over at some forty degrees, presenting her profile to them, and moving sideways. This was because she was laboriously rolling along an object too big and heavy for her to lift.

A dustbin, by God, said Gareth between his teeth.

As he spoke, the metallic drumming of the metal on the hard surface of the road reached their ears.

Does she want to leave it in the main street? Roger asked. For the men to pick up?

It's not their day, said Gareth.

Suddenly he bounded up the steps of the bus and got into the driving seat.

Let's go, he called to Roger.

It isn't eleven, said Roger, leaning in and peering up at him. And there are some people still coming. Look.

He pointed to where a number of deliberately moving figures, some in clumps, some alone, were converging without haste on the main street, with the evident intention of taking the bus.

Gareth started the engine.

Never mind, he shouted above the noise. We'll go without them. I'm not taking that thing.

What thing? Roger shouted.

Mrs Arkwright's dustbin.

Hearing the engine start, the approaching passengers quickened their pace, and one or two of them waved imploringly. One old lady waved her umbrella above her head as in semaphore, and Mrs Arkwright allowed the dustbin to settle for a moment on to its base while she shook her fists in the air.

Roger went up the steps and put his head close to Gareth's.

We'd better wait for her, he said. Or we'll never hear the last of it.

Gareth groaned and put his face in his hands. The passengers, expostulating freely, arrived at the bus and took their places. Then everybody settled back to watch Mrs Arkwright trundle the dustbin the last fifty yards.

Some man should help her, said the old lady who had waved her umbrella.

The cry was taken up by female voices on all sides. The only male passenger, as it happened, was the little wizened shepherd with the big boots. He looked round defensively and said in his big resonant voice:

It's a young man's office.

There's no young man present, said Roger quickly.

You're the youngest man here, said the shepherd sternly. And you work for the company, don't you? On a voluntary basis, he added kindly. But still.

Mrs Arkwright, her face shiny, had now almost gained the bus. Roger felt the collective will of the passengers lift him forward. He left the shelter of the bus and went toward her.

'Good morning, Mrs Arkwright,' he began.

'What's good about it?' she snapped. 'Help me with this bin. It wants lifting up the steps.'

'The steps,' he faltered.

'The steps of the bus. Come on, hurry up, else he'll have an excuse to leave me behind and I know it's all he's waiting for. I can see it in his eye.' She glared through the windscreen at Gareth, who sank his face once more into his hands.

'But you can't take a dustbin on the bus.'

'Don't stand there arguing. I've been very patient with them for years. But I've always said I'd do it one of these days, if they went on the way they did.'

'Do what? Went on what way?'

'They won't collect my rubbish,' she cried. 'I've argued till I'm blue in the face but they won't do it. Say I've got to take it down to the collection point. A lone widow-woman. My Hubert told me how it'd be. But I shan't be beaten.'

'But what –'

'I'm taking it down,' she said, glaring at him triumphantly. 'I shall trundle this bin into the Public Health Department and leave it right in the middle of their office.'

'But it's Saturday. They won't be there.'

'All the better. Let them find it when they come to work on the Monday. It'll have a good strong smell by then, I shouldn't wonder.'

'Mrs Arkwright, you must see that –'

'It'll focus attention on my problem,' she said. She had lowered her voice and now spoke quite reasonably, but she gave Roger a peculiar sidelong glance, and he had the feeling that she was not telling him the whole truth. He hesitated, with one hand already on the dustbin.

'Couldn't you put it off till next week? When they'll be there?'

'No time like the present,' she said. 'I can't take it all the way back now. Lift it up the steps for me, there's a good lad.'

His resistance at an end, Roger bent and picked up the dustbin. 'It's heavy,' he panted.

'There's no ashes in it. Just kitchen refuse,' said Mrs Arkwright. She marched ahead of Roger, up the steps and into the bus.

A short wrangle with Gareth followed, but Mrs Arkwright

had the feminist sentiment of the meeting behind her, and finally it was settled that a space should be cleared at the front of the bus and that the shepherd should move forward and keep his hand on the dustbin to steady it on the corners, while everyone else rode in the back half of the bus, and Roger collected their fares. It was further negotiated, as a concession, that the shepherd should travel free of charge.

And in this fashion they made the eleven o'clock run down to Caerfenai.

When they arrived, and pulled up in the square, Mrs Arkwright once more dug in her heels and refused to leave the bus until Roger had agreed to carry the dustbin to the exact spot she indicated. This proved to be a corner of the pavement outside the porticoed entrance to the Town Hall. She wanted the dustbin left in the lee of the steps, unobtrusively wedged into the corner.

'It won't be in anybody's way there,' she said, giving Roger that crafty look again.

'But the Health Department isn't in this part of the building. It's round the other side.'

'Never mind that,' she said placidly.

Roger shrugged and set down the dustbin. He was wondering whether to reason any further with Mrs Arkwright, when his attention was caught by the sudden appearance of Madog, hurrying out of the Town Hall and down the steps.

At the sight of Roger, he stopped dead, stared hard at him for a moment as if determined to sort out reality from fantasy, and said, 'Thank God you're there at least.'

'Why shouldn't I be?'

'Well,' said Madog, 'no one else is.'

Roger looked closely at Madog. The bard had exchanged his blue suit for a similar but obviously new suit of chocolate-brown, with almost imperceptible stripes running longitudinally through the cloth. This suit, however, was crumpled and Madog's hair was dishevelled. His eyes were wild. Early in the day though it was, Roger divined that Madog had already had much to endure.

'I have two problems,' said Madog, still staring at Roger. 'Number one, the Irish aren't here. Number two and more serious, the Scotch are here.'

'The Scotch? I thought there was only one poet from Scotland.'

'There is only one. If that. I'm not even sure whether they've brought the poet with them. What I do know is that a bus-load of Scotch patriots have arrived, all of them wearing kilts and most of them already drunk.'

'Drunk?'

'Either with alcohol,' said Madog, 'or with nationalistic fervour. I can't tell the difference.'

'Where's Jenny?'

'Calming the Bretons,' said Madog heavily. 'They're camera-shy.'

'Camera-shy . . .?'

'My God,' said Madog. 'Don't say you're another who hasn't heard about our welcoming ceremony?'

'I'm afraid not.'

'We only fixed it up at the last minute. It was the idea of the television people. They want to get a shot of the Mayor of Caerfenai welcoming all the poets, on the steps of the Town Hall. On these steps here, where I'm standing.'

'Oh.'

'He's going to welcome them, in Welsh of course, and declare the event open.'

'It was in the paper,' said Mrs Arkwright at Roger's elbow. 'Yesterday evening's paper.'

Roger, who had forgotten Mrs Arkwright, now turned and looked at her with a wild surmise.

'Mrs Arkwright – you're not –'

'Jenny!' Madog cried suddenly.

Jenny had come hurriedly along the pavement and up the steps. 'The Bretons won't appear with the Scots,' she said. 'They say they're insulted with them.'

Madog clutched his temples. 'My God? How?'

'Their poet can't speak Gaelic. None of them can, in fact. And when the Bretons greeted them in their language, they made ribald remarks and one of them started singing "I Belong to Glasgow".'

Madog passed the tip of his tongue over his lips. 'What have you done?' he asked faintly.

'Put them in separate rooms,' she said.

'That's my girl,' said Roger encouragingly.

'Oh, you're there, Roger. That's good. Listen, the bus auction has started.'

'No, really?'

'Yes, they're all in there already.' She pointed to a building on the other side of the square.

'How's it going?' Roger asked.

'Very fast, I believe. The auctioneer's been told to unload the buses for what they'll fetch. Nobody's in the mood to hang about.'

'Do you realize,' said Madog, 'that in half-an-hour we've got to parade all these poets on top of these steps, and they're quarrelling already?'

'It's not the poets who are quarrelling, to be fair,' said Jenny reasonably. 'Most of these Scots are just hangers-on. They've come to have a booze-up and shout against England.'

'Oh, God,' said Madog. 'That's all it took. Well, they're not coming to the Mayor's reception ceremony.'

'But the television man wants them. He says the kilts will make it.'

'Well, he's not having them,' said Madog wildly. 'I'm not going to stand by and see the whole thing ruined for the sake of plaids and bare knees. If any more of this mountebanking element creeps in, we might as well stage the whole thing on ice.'

Muttering, he hurried away.

'Hello, darling,' Roger murmured to Jenny. 'I haven't told you I love you yet today.'

'Well, save it till I've got time to listen,' she said, kissing him lightly. 'I told Mary and Robin I'd be back in a few minutes.'

'Where are they? At the hotel?'

'Yes. Looking after the folk-dancers.'

Roger remembered now that the festival was to start with a manic burst of folk-dancing on the lawn inside the castle walls. 'Why do they need looking after?'

'They need somewhere to change.'

'Change?'

'Into national dress, of course,' she said impatiently. 'I've told you enough times. The whole thing fascinates Mary – she'll probably insist on appearing with them . . .'

At that moment, a large green van drew up alongside the

Town Hall steps, and a thin-faced man with greying side-whiskers jumped out and ran up the steps. 'Right, let's get started,' he said to Roger. 'Are you organizing these poets?'

'No,' said Jenny, interposing herself determinedly. 'I am.'

'Good.' The thin-faced man produced a piece of chalk from his pocket, stooped down and began rapidly to chalk large X's on the plateau at the top of the steps. 'Let's suppose the Mayor comes out through those corridors and stands *here* – then we can have the frogs here, the micks there, one or two of these nuts in kilts at the front. Terry!' he called. 'Peter.'

Two young men, festooned with cables, hurried to join him. Roger turned away, thankful to leave Jenny to cope with these communicators and thus build a bridge between Madog and the great Saturday-afternoon public who would in any case be watching football on the other channel. Coverage, he realized, was the important thing, whether or not anybody saw the coverage. Madog would be able to report back to UNESCO that the event had been seen on television, and his next grant would be that much easier to get.

As Roger walked across the square, the heavy doors of the sale-room opened and Gareth came out. He looked flushed and concerned.

'How's it going?' Roger asked.

'Fast,' said Gareth. 'There's fifteen buses to sell, each one with a backing of spares and equipment and in most cases, a garage.' He spoke in English, and was presumably quoting some of the auctioneer's own patter. 'The sale's only been on an hour, and already he's sold five. All to their original owners. And now Ivo and Gito are bidding. There's a bit of counter-bidding, but it's not heavy, and I think they'll get their bus back. But I got worried and came out. I can't stand the excitement.'

Roger, devoured by curiosity, pushed open the big doors and slipped quietly inside, as one might into church. The sale-room was full of men. Nearly all of them belonged to the same type: work-hardened, weather-beaten. The occasional business suit and office-pale face stood out as a rarity. The auctioneer, a sweating, thick-set man in glasses, was driving the sale rapidly along.

'Spare-parts-including-tyres-valued-at-two-hundred-pounds,' he was droning, 'vehicle-itself-in-excellent-condition-carefully-maintained.'

'Seven-fifty for the lot,' said Ivo, on his feet and tense with concentration.

'Eight,' said a man in the far corner.

'Contractor from Portmadoc,' Gito whispered to Roger. 'Wants it to take his workmen to sites. He's tried for two or three buses and missed them all so far. Eight's his limit.'

Ivo, his face set into an expressionless mask, said loudly and with great precision, 'Eight twenty-five.'

'Eight-thirty,' said the man in the far corner.

'Am-I-bid-anything-further-to-eight-thirty, come-along-gentlemen,' the auctioneer snuffled.

'Can you go any higher?' Roger whispered to Ivo.

Ivo shook his head.

'Going,' said the auctioneer indifferently.

'Go a bit higher,' Roger urged in a whisper. 'I can lend you up to fifty.'

'Going,' said the auctioneer. He raised his hammer.

'Eight-fifty,' said Ivo into the stillness.

The auctioneer looked at the Portmadoc man, who shook his head.

'Gone,' he said. 'Eight hundred and fifty pounds –' he brought down his hammer smartly – 'for this excellent working vehicle, thirty-two seater, all spares, extra wheels, two new tyres and four re-treads. Next : lot number so-and-so,' after the flicker of excitement involved in ringing up a sale, he went back to his bored routine.

Gito turned to Roger with a grin so broad that there was hardly room for it on his ample face.

'Come and have a drink,' said Roger, slapping him on the shoulder.

'As soon as we've signed the papers,' said Gito. 'See you in Mario's.'

Roger went out and told Gareth that Ivo and Gito had got their bus back. The news, he could see, affected Gareth powerfully. It was as if this morning's sale gave him, at last, concrete evidence that the fight against Dic Sharp had been won. It was understandable that he had found the tension too great and had left the sale-room.

It's all coming back into shape, Roger said to him gently. All those chaps are getting their buses back.

Gareth leaned against the radiator and looked round the square as if seeing it for the first time.

I never knew till this moment, he said, how alone I've been feeling for the past year.

You must have done, said Roger, still gently.

Utterly alone, said Gareth. Except for the old lady and you.

For a moment, Roger thought that Gareth was going to embrace him, gather him into a rib-crushing bear-hug. But the impulse, if there had been one, passed, and Gareth turned and went up the steps into the bus. After a moment or two he poked his head out and said:

No twelve o'clock up today.

You're cancelling it? Roger asked.

Nobody'd want to go, said Gareth. There's too much going on down here. If anybody makes a fuss, I'll give 'em the price of a taxi, out of my own pocket.

He thought for another moment and then asked:

Have you seen Dic Sharp?

No, is he about?

He was earlier on, said Gareth. He went into the sale-room for the first few minutes, just to see them start off. But he's taken himself off somewhere.

Roger was about to say something in reply when a twelve-seater transporter rolled into the square, and, after hesitantly circling it once, pulled up beside him. A number of tired-looking men, some of them in green jackets, began to get down from it.

'That'll be the Town Hall over there?' one of them, who seemed to be in charge, asked Roger.

His accent revealed to Roger that this was the missing Irish contingent. 'Yes, welcome,' he said excitedly. 'Here, let me introduce you . . . Jenny! Jenny!'

Buffeting through the thickening crowd, they slowly forced their way across the square to the Town Hall, whose steps were now festooned with thick cables. Strong arc lamps competed with the bright sunlight. Jenny, summoned by Roger's repeated cries, gathered up the Irish poets and took them off to the hotel to wash and get their breath before the ceremony. As they disappeared, they were explaining to her that they had been on the night boat to Holyhead, that the sea had been rough and the bar open to all hours.

It was almost twelve o'clock. Madog appeared, surrounded by a knot of men in kilts. 'Only the poet,' he was saying. 'There isn't room for anyone else.'

'But we're his guard of honour,' replied a huge, black-bearded man who had to lean down to make his voice audible to Madog. 'Jock never goes anywhere withoot his guard of honour. It wadnae be deegnified.'

'Yes, yes, we must have a few kilts,' the man with greying side-whiskers said irritably to Madog. 'It's a visual medium, a visual medium, remember.'

Roger wondered which of the Scotsmen was the poet. They all looked about equally likely or unlikely. A number of Bretons now emerged from the interior of the Town Hall, where they seemed to have been hiding. The crush at the top of the steps was intensified, and the television crew had to fight gallantly to keep clear a small chalked circle for the Mayor of Caerfenai.

'Where are the Irish?' Madog was asking unsteadily. Roger tried to get near him to pass on the glad news that Jenny would soon join them with this contingent, but before he could squeeze his way through, the press was made suddenly worse by the arrival of a large party of folk-dancers in Welsh national costume, who came hurrying along the pavement and infiltrated among the crowd.

'Get them near the front!' the side-whiskered man was shouting. 'We must have them among the kilts. But pointed hats to the side, please. They'll mask the Mayor's face.'

In the distance, Roger saw Gareth, Ivo and Gito walking toward Mario's pub. He decided it was time for him to join them. As he turned, however, the Irish poets, led by Jenny, came along the pavement in a determined scrum and began to force their way up the steps. A number of voices, in a number of languages, began trying to make themselves heard at once.

Watch who ye're shoving, me fine friend. – Keep back, ye clumsy mick. Peidiwch a sathru fy nhraed! – Camera! Don't mask the Mayor's face! – Which of you is McAlister? – Well, I'm nae McAlister's brither. – 'r esgob mawr! – Who's ready for a ball of malt? – Give the Mayor a chance.

As Roger lingered, wishing to be in saner surroundings and yet unable quite to tear himself away, the Mayor came out through the doors of the Town Hall and advanced to the microphone. Smiling confidently at the TV cameras, the poets and the assembled populace, in that order, he began a resounding speech of welcome in careful academic Welsh. At that moment, Mrs Arkwright suddenly appeared staggering up the steps with the loaded dustbin in her arms. With a supreme effort, she carried it to the top step, set it down, and violently pushed it over, sending a swirl of cabbage-stalks, tea-leaves, tins, bottles, plastic containers, eggshells and fruit-rinds about the ankles of all present. A multilingual farrago of curses assaulted the sky.

'That's my protest!' Mrs Arkwright shouted above the pandemonium. 'A widow-woman! It's a danger to health! All the way from Bolton to settle in Llancrwys! Honour the stranger that is within thy gates!'

Still shouting, she was led away by a sympathetic policeman. The Mayor, scuffing his feet to remove some bacon-rind from the soles of his shoes, went on with his speech, starting again at the first sentence as if what had gone before must now be regarded as a rehearsal.

Roger had seen enough, and took himself unobtrusively off to Mario's pub. There, all was Gargantuan rejoicing. Within a few minutes he had downed more than his usual lunch-time ration of beer, and had learnt that not only had Ivo and Gito bought their bus back, but Ieuan had bought his bus back, and Ceredig and Twm, and that Twm had also gone into partnership with his cousin Cedric and bought not only his own bus but Elfed's, because Elfed had left the district in the meantime. The whole place seemed to be full of grinning, pint-lifting, square-cut men. They transformed the atmosphere of the pub; they brought with them the smell of oil and the clatter of engines, but also the wind of country roads and the long habit of neighbourliness formed among people who crouch against walls together in a mountain rainstorm, waiting for the bus that will heave into sight through the squall like a pitching lifeboat.

Roger was enjoying the spectacle so much that Madog, who now entered, had to pluck at his sleeve three or four times before attracting his attention. Turning, Roger saw that Madog's suit was more crumpled than before, his hair and eyes wilder, and that he was surrounded by Scotchmen.

'Roger,' said Madog out of the corner of his mouth. 'Help me with this lot.'

The Scots were for the moment absorbed in ranging themselves along the bar and getting fitted out with drinks.

'What d'you need?' Roger asked.

'To get shut of them,' said Madog. 'If not for good, at least for a while. Fortunately there's a good way of doing it. They didn't book accommodation. We've got a room for McAlister, of course, but the rest didn't make any provision and left to themselves they'll probably sleep in the gutter. So Jenny rang round the hotels and she's found that the nearest place with room for them is Beddgelert.'

'Good. That's too far for them to walk back, once we've got them there.'

'Precisely. So I thought, could you and Gareth take them over in the bus?'

'Gareth,' Roger called over. 'We've got a charter job. UNESCO wants to hire us to go to Beddgelert.'

'With this lot?' Gareth asked cagily, jerking his thumb toward the broad kilted rumps ranged at the bar.

'If we can carry dustbins, we can carry them,' Roger urged.

For God's sake, said Madog in quick, imploring Welsh, take them to Beddgelert and leave them. St David's day is no time to have this lot wandering about here.

'Laddie,' said the immense bearded Scot, turning from the bar and scooping up Madog in a brotherly embrace, 'what are ye talking aboot in that sonsie wee language o' yours?'

'Just arranging accommodation,' said Madog, one eye pleadingly fixed on Gareth.

'We're going to run your party over to where you can get nice rooms,' said Gareth.

'Not yet awhile, ye're not,' said the Scot. 'We're just getting comfortable in here.'

That's what I'm afraid of, said Madog aside.

'Speak English, I'm warnin' ye,' said the bearded man.

Mario, who during the lull in the uproar had caught these words, leaned over the bar and said in a silky, dangerous voice, 'Mister, is Santo Davido's day today. Anybody wants to speak Welsh in my pub any time, he speaks Welsh, but on Santo Davido *nobody speaks English!* He thumped the bar. 'Here, we not a colony. We get ready for the day when we shake off the English.'

Roger stood well back, fearing an outburst of mayhem, but to his surprise the bearded man broke into a smile and took Mario's hand in his vast paw.

'Puit it there, ma little man,' he said affably. 'Up with Saint David and awa' wi' the English!'

A speech was now made by McAlister, the Scotch poet in whose ostensible support this meinie was assembled. Roger could not make out much of it, owing to the refusal of Mario's Welsh customers to intermit their conversation, but McAlister's peroration, which he read from a well-creased piece of paper, was uttered in a loud, sonorous voice which managed to be audible throughout the building.

'To transmute the anti-English passion,' McAlister trumpeted, 'into a passion of hatred against the vulgarity and materialism' (cheers) 'whereon England has founded her worst life' (cries of 'All of it!' 'Och aye!') 'and the whole life that she sends us –' His concluding words were lost in gales of applause, and he stood down well content.

This speech delighted Mario. '*Risorgimento!*' he cried. 'To the day of *liberazione!*'

Through the crush Roger recognized the crew-cut and horn-rims of André, Madog's Canadian collaborator. He had set up a small portable tape-recorder on top of the bar, and was watching with satisfaction as its diminutive drums revolved, storing all this high rhetoric for posterity. Pushing his way towards it, Roger shouted into the microphone, 'Dominion status for Liverpool! Anglophiles go home!' André frowned and switched off the machine.

By this time Madog and Gareth had made serious progress towards corralling the Scotch satellites and moving them towards the bus. 'Free whisky at the other end,' Gareth kept saying in a loud, grating voice. 'At the other end of the rainbow,' he added in an undertone as he passed Roger. Little by little they eased the gaily bedizened warriors out of the pub and into the bus. A tumult of protests broke out when they discovered that McAlister was not coming with them, but Madog explained soothingly that it was necessary for all the poets to attend a rehearsal for that evening's reading, and McAlister himself ordered his henchmen to leave him in peace for an hour or two.

Once they were all installed in Gareth's bus, the journey to Beddgelert was smooth and uneventful. Having disgorged the swarm at the door of the hotel which had accepted them, and watched them file into the bar, Roger and Gareth got quickly into the bus and drove back to Caerfenai. It was not yet two o'clock when Roger went into the Palace Hotel, in the dual hope of getting some late lunch and having a few quiet minutes with Jenny.

She greeted him cheerfully, though she had no leisure to spare for talk. 'Things are better now, thank God. The folk-dancing went well. It was a gamble to have it in the open but the sun obliged. Everyone's in a better mood now.'

'Good. Have you got time to rest a bit? Where are Mary and Robin?'

'I bribed a girl to take them for a long walk and to a café for tea. That's question two. Question one: no, I haven't. There's going to be a big buffet supper here after the final reading tonight. Everybody's coming. We're spending everything that's left in the kitty. Booze and sandwiches. I expect you'll be along?'

'Yes.'

'Better get some solid food inside you before you come,' she said. 'The drink's going to flow like water ... but I'll see you before that.'

'Of course. We're going to listen to Madog.'

They kissed and she hurried away. As it was now the slack period when Gareth had no need of him on the bus, and there seemed to be nothing he could do to help Jenny, Roger took the opportunity to borrow the blue Mini and drive up to the chapel. He was going there for the last time, to close it and pull out. As he drove up the mountain he turned over in his mind the question of how seriously he ought to try to remove all traces of his occupancy, to give Fräulein Inge, when she came back, the impression that the place had not been touched. He decided, turning at the cross-roads in Llancrwys, that this would be impossible. After spending so much time there, he would inevitably have left small marks of his presence here and there, and it would be the work of weeks to efface every one systematically. For that matter, the window-pane he had broken, in order to get access to the place that first time, with Rhiannon, had never been mended. He lacked the skill to put in a new pane himself, and he had shrunk from getting a local craftsman to do it, because that would have been to admit another person into the secret.

Not that they did not all know, in any case, that he was squatting in the chapel. But there was a difference between knowing it as a matter of village gossip and knowing it, so to speak, officially because one had been invited in.

For the same reason, Roger had never tried to get his refuse collected by the Corporation wagon. In that respect, he had lived these months as a male, stoical Mrs Arkwright. His policy had been to make huge bonfires on the mountainside on lonely winter afternoons, sending his rubbish billowing up to the sky in dark, quickly-rolling smoke. The unburnable material, such as plastic containers, he had buried in a patch of swampy earth, material for post-historic archaeologists. As for the broken window, he had mended it with a neat square of thick white cardboard, firmly held in place with Scotch tape.

Arriving now at the chapel for the last time, he took out his final load of refuse, arranged it skilfully on the improvised hearth he had made from three rocks, poured a little petrol on it, and stood back to watch it burn. The sun was shining from a pale, inciting spring sky. Even in those Alpine days of midwinter, when the snow threw back the hard stellar glare of the sun, he did not remember the light's being as bright as it was now. This was spring light, filling the sky, soaking the earth in luminous waves that seemed to penetrate beneath the topsoil; the sea lay laughing at a distance; the air above Roger's bonfire quivered with pale, daemonic heat.

Going back into the chapel, Roger tried to look round at his habitat with the eyes of Fräulein Inge. Well, obviously, she would see that someone had been there. But he had damaged nothing. What would she check first? Her canvases? Perhaps, perhaps not. Roger found it difficult to imagine that Fräulein

Inge took her art very seriously. It was, he suspected, more in the nature of an act, something she performed to give herself a personality and to earn the right to 'an artist's way of life', whatever that might be. Anyway, she need have no fear for her canvases. After his first perfunctory investigation, he had never laid a finger on them; they stood exactly where she had left them, stacked against the dryest wall. And it was arguable that, by keeping the chapel heated, Roger had taken better care of Fräulein Inge's masterworks than the Fräulein herself had.

He stripped the bed in which he and Jenny had first lain together, and immediately the shadowy presence of Fräulein Inge faded like the smoke from his bonfire. This place was his, and it would remain his if he never again set eyes on it, no matter what happened to it and who used it. He had lived such a crucial passage of his life within these walls that his thoughts and emotions had soaked into the plaster, the beams, the stones, the very rocks under the foundations. It had been the witness of his final, long-delayed coming of age; it had seen his liberation; here, he had begun the story of his life with Jenny, and here he had parted, in mutual love and kindness, from the pacified ghost of Geoffrey.

Roger gathered the last of his belongings and stowed them in the Mini. There was just about room for everything. Then he went in for the last time, hung the spare key on the nail where Rhiannon had found it on that Sunday morning, and was ready to go. As a last benediction to the place, he knelt and fuelled the little stove so that it would burn for eight hours after he had gone. He put on a few stove-nuts and the last three of the oak parquet blocks. Gito's blocks. They had lasted all the winter.

When he was sure the stove was burning efficiently, Roger closed it, stood up, and walked briskly over to the door, which he pulled shut behind him. Then he went round the side of the building and through the wrought-iron gate, which he carefully closed. Before getting into the Mini and driving off, he took one final look back to see that there was nothing he had forgotten. Except for the neat square of white cardboard taped into place in the glassless window-pane, and the smoke busily rising from the chimney, the chapel looked exactly as it had done when he first set eyes on it. Only the mountains behind it, shining in the livery of the year's renewal, spoke to him of the new life that had come to him there.

He started the engine and drove to the Palace Hotel, Caerfenai.

The Colloquium had now definitely settled on an even keel. It was as if the Scotchmen, like some collective bekilted scapegoat, had carried Madog's entire ration of bad luck away into the desert. From the moment of their departure, it was a feast of sweetness and light: attentive audiences, poets in good voice, an atmosphere of tranquil corporate homage to the Muses. André's little tape-recorder worked unceasingly, UNESCO officials smiled in corners and cuddled their briefcases of moulded plastic, and the hunted look in Madog's eyes was replaced by a gleam compounded of visionary ardour and administrative complacency. Even Jenny, though she was running faster and faster between the Town Hall (to soothe poets) and the hotel (to galvanize an army of minions who were preparing that night's gigantic buffet supper), was looking more relaxed.

Roger joined Gareth's bus for the four-fifteen up, the five o'clock down, and the five-forty-five up. On every run, passengers questioned him eagerly about the outcome of that morning's sale. Was it true that all the buses had gone back to their original owners? Most of them, Roger was able to reply. The situation had levelled itself out. No more take-overs.

'So Gareth won't be the only one standing out on his own any more?'

'No,' Roger smiled. 'The whale's jaws have opened and all the Jonahs have stepped out.'

Mrs Arkwright, flushed and triumphant, travelled up on the 5.45. The Mayor had personally requested the police to take no action, and she had been let off with a caution. The dustbin had been confiscated, but this did not discompose her.

'We'll see a change in the collections now,' she was prophesying to her fellow-passengers in the back of the bus. 'Action always pays. It's the only thing these people understand. Send a gunboat.'

The light was fading when they reached the top of the village. The last passengers moved away in the violet-tinted silence that was spreading across the mountainside, to their homes. Roger and Gareth stood beside the bus.

Are you doing anything till we go down in an hour's time? Gareth asked.

No.

Not going to the chapel?

No. I've closed it up. I'm staying in the hotel tonight.

And in the morning?

Going, I expect.

Gareth stood motionless. In the sunset a dark, humped cloud, parodying his shape, slowly disintegrated against the dying brightness.

Well, he said at last. Come and have a cup of tea at the house.

In silence, but not sadly, they walked along the stony track to the cottage. Lights were burning; two women from the village were visiting Mam, and they were settling down for the evening, with a great rattling of tea-cups and poking of coals. Gareth arranged to see them off when he came back after the ten o'clock run up. Roger was glad that the women were there; they absorbed Mam into their own world of gossip and cosiness, and though she knew he was there, and addressed one or two remarks to him, she evidently did not realize that this would be his last visit, and so he escaped without farewells.

As they walked back to the bus, for the seven o'clock run down, Gareth broke his silence.

I shan't forget the pouring wet night I came walking down here and found the bus gone.

Roger chuckled. Last autumn you mean?

Yes, of course.

Well, said Roger. I've tried to make amends for that.

You've succeeded, said Gareth. If I could have looked ahead and seen the way things would turn out, I'd have been a happy man that night.

I reckon things have gone well for both of us, said Roger. We both needed a change of luck, and we've both had one.

They had reached the bus; the first passengers were already assembling. Gareth switched on the lights, and the bus became what it had been on that first rainy evening: a haven of light and cheerfulness on the dark hillside.

They were absorbed in their duties, and neither of them spoke again.

Some three hours later, Jenny and Roger sat side by side in Caerfenai Town Hall. The main event of the Colloquium was nearing its end. For Jenny, this was the reward of a long, anxious haul. She had only joined Roger in the last twenty minutes or so; till then, he had been sitting beside an empty seat, shooing away anyone who showed signs of wanting to sit in it, while Jenny flitted about backstage, carrying messages, lining up contributors in the right order. It had all gone smoothly: Breton, Irish, Welsh poets had paraded in the announced sequence and read their work; even the Scot, shorn of his claque, had delivered himself of no more pawky near-English than was set down in his agreement. And now, Madog was onstage, and he was reading from 'Gwilym Cherokee', and all the poets who had already read had come round into the auditorium and were looking up and listening, and Madog was still Madog but he was also someone else, Madog the scholar and lover of language whom Roger had glimpsed at their first meeting; but over and above that, he was Madog the bard, the rapt singer with a flame in his tongue, the poet of the sorrows of his people, Madog the Cherokee, Madog the poet of Gwynedd who worked in an estate agent's office and wove his bower of words by instinct, like a bird, and also from memory, like an elephant, and also from love and joy and trouble, like a man, and as Roger sat beside Jenny and looked at Madog, his Welsh, now easy enough to carry him forward on the tide of Madog's dark and surging images, he knew at last that Madog's poem was Gareth's yellow bus, and that he, Roger Furnivall, had ridden up into the mountains now in one, now in the other, and that they had taken him to where he had found himself.

Madog read for twenty minutes, growing in stature all the time, justifying minute by minute all those uneventful years passed in the humdrum triangle between his place of work, Mario's pub, and his semi-detached roost in the featureless outskirts of Caerfenai, the town he loved most in the world, his home and the centre of his being. When he rose to his crescendo, on a tall wave of epic narrative that hung for twenty breathless lines and then broke in thunder and foam, Roger sat for a moment in silence, then, coming to himself amid the applause, looked about him in surprise at finding the Town Hall still unchanged, the rows of wooden chairs as prim as ever, the timbered ceiling above him rather than the star-pierced blanket of the sky.

Then it was over. The chairman of the evening, a prognathous caryatid from the local university college, uttered the closing banalities and everyone filed out. Roger and Jenny, by a prior arrangement, went to look for Madog in Mario's pub.

The choice of this *venue* had not been accidental. The bus operators, spear-headed by Ivo and Gito, had already put in a couple of hours' brisk celebration after the auction; then, when Mario closed the place for the afternoon just in time to send them back to the auctioneer's office sober enough to tie up the details of their business, had gone through the various rituals involved in becoming once again the owners of their buses. That evening when he opened again, they were back : the same men, but changed, enlarged, their pulses beating to a new rhythm. The gloriously impossible had happened; they were their own masters again.

Roger and Jenny, entering, stood for a moment inside the door, taking in the scene. It was warm, smoky, noisily tuneful, thick with Welsh talk. Everywhere, pint mugs were tilted, broad grins grew broader. Mario, his face gleaming with sweat, dispensed beer and pies, moving faster and faster, shouting in Welsh and Italian.

'Ah, there you are, you two,' said Madog, striding in through the door behind them. 'I've got one tiny bit of business here and then the evening can really get started.'

'It looks pretty well started already,' said Roger. 'Madog, you were magnificent just now. Your poem will win a world audience.'

'My poem?' said Madog. 'It's just breath on a pane of glass. The condensation from my life, and the lives of these men here. That's what I've come for.'

'What is ?'

'To summon the Cherokees to a feast,' said Madog. 'Listen.' Abruptly leaving them, he pushed his way to the bar and spoke into Mario's ear. Mario listened, nodded. Madog climbed on to a chair, thence to the bar.

Gentlemen! he cried. I have a word to say to you!

From the understanding in the faces that were turned up to him, it was obvious that everyone there spoke Welsh.

This is a night of triumph, said Madog, for me, for you, for all of us. And I have the honour to invite you all, without further ceremony, to join me and certain friends of mine at the Palace Hotel, where food and drink will be available free of charge and in unlimited quantities.

When? cried several voices.

Immediately, Madog smiled. He got down from the bar amid a swelling wave of applause.

Now hear me! Mario shouted. This public house is closed. The law requires everybody out of here within five minutes. Well, I require you out faster than that. I don't even give you the five minutes. I want to get to that party. Empty your glasses and come with me!

We're allowed time to drink up, cried a watery old man in the corner.

I allow you nothing, Mario shouted. Outside on the pavement. Go where the drink is free!

He disappeared into the fastness at the rear of the pub, and emerged a moment later wearing a loud check overcoat and a Tyrolean hat with a shaving brush stuck into it. Without further ado, he abruptly switched off all the lights expect for one low-powered bulb over the bar, which gave just enough light for the company to find their way to the door and out.

'Come on, boys, we can take a subtle hint,' Ivo's voice, falling back on his comedian's English, sounded the bugle-call. 'It's time to be getting along to the hotel. We'll all make a night of it. Free caviar and raisins in brandy. Throw away your troubles.'

Perhaps feeling that when it came to responding to a gesture, no true Celt would let himself be outdone by a Latin, virtually the whole party formed up on the pavement behind Madog and Mario, who linked arms and led the way toward the hotel. Roger and Jenny, holding tight to each other, allowed themselves to be carried along in the swaying, voluble, laughing and singing phalanx. They reached the Palace Hotel without incident; as they surged in a tight mass up the steps and through the revolving doors, Roger had a quick vision of the appalled face of the head porter before the man was annihilated by a glance from Madog.

'Where's the party, my man?' Madog paused long enough to ask.

'Party?' the head porter began stammeringly.

'The reception,' said Mario politely, 'which I have spent the last six weeks, among other things, in organizing.'

The head porter shook his head in despair. Speech had deserted him.

'It's upstairs,' Jenny called from the body of the crowd. 'In the Main Banqueting Room.'

'Very well,' said Madog. Turning to the assembly (and Roger could tell that he visualized them, at that moment, as magnificently feathered Redskins), he pointed, using the full length of his arm, to the main staircase, and cried in ringing tones, 'Gentlemen, you are invited to the Main Banqueting Room!'

The head porter put a hand to his forehead and leaned against a pillar. 'The Main Banqueting Room,' Roger heard him moan, 'and not a necktie between the lot of them.'

The man's pitiable distress was disregarded as the company, laughing and joking loudly, made their way up the main staircase. When they emptied into the banqueting room, Roger saw at once how much the head porter must be suffering. After twenty years of protecting the formal respectability of the hotel, screening out those who tried to sully its bourgeois purity by wearing jeans or leaving off ties, and generally ensuring that its dust-free corridors and discreetly-lighted rooms were patrolled exclusively by men in well-cut lounge suits (at the very least), and their women in twin-sets and pearls or whatever was the equivalent that year of twin-sets and pearls, he had already reeled back from the influx of the Celtic Poets' Colloquium, whose participants – Welsh, Breton, Irish, one loud solitary Scot – had poured in from the Town Hall, led by their grimly-smiling zombie of a chairman, less than ten minutes previously. He had no authority to keep out this horde, whose sartorial tastes violated every principle he had spent his life in upholding, and this new onrush merely trampled down a man already pushed to his knees. Even now he might have rallied if he had been given determined support by the manager, but the manager, seeing what was coming, had decided to treat himself to a twelve-hour nervous breakdown and was now locked in his private quarters, watching television while he waited for the sleeping-pill he had taken to club him into merciful oblivion.

In the Main Banqueting Room, all was gaiety, noise, laughter and international amity. Long tables were set out, and food and drink stood invitingly on the snowy cloths. No one lacked thirst or appetite; if the hubbub of talk and laughter had not been so colossal, it would surely have been drowned in the roar of Gargantuan chewing and guzzling.

Roger and Jenny were engaged in conversation, immediately on entering, by a Cornish participant in the Colloquium, who began to outline to them his scheme for a Celtic free trade area, economically sealed off from the rest of the world. Until tankers could be built, the poet explained, the Breton fishing fleet could be put into transport service, refuelling at Tintagel for the journey up to Wales and across to Ireland. When Roger was foolish enough to point out some practical difficulties, the poet assumed that he had not made himself sufficiently clear.

'It's this wretched ambiguous English language,' he said with an irritable shrug. 'Here, I'll outline it again, in Cornish.' He passed, without jolt, into this ancient language. Roger found the slight but continual effort of transposition required to understand Cornish through Welsh an excellent means of putting on philological muscle, but on the other hand it had been a long day, the room was hot and noisy, and he had to fight against successive waves of drowsiness as the Cornishman explained the economic advantages of supplying the citizens of Cork with oysters in bulk from Locmariaquer. Jenny slipped away on some pretext or other. Nearby, Madog was explaining to two Irishmen the ground-plan of his epic, while simultaneously they were explaining to Madog and to one another the ground-plan of their epics. Gareth, on the other side of Madog, was eating sandwiches and grinning to himself. A sudden uproar near the entrance signalized the return of the Scotch contingent, who had walked most of the way from Beddgelert and worked up an excellent thirst in the process.

'Roger,' said Jenny, suddenly appearing at his elbow, 'did you know Dic Sharp was here?'

'Dic Sharp?' the name jerked Roger awake, and he looked round the room. In the wake of the Scotsmen, a new knot of people had entered, one of them carrying a large cardboard box. And it was true, at the centre of this group was Dic Sharp.

'I thought I'd never see him again,' said Roger.

'I beg your pardon?' said the Cornish poet in English. 'I take it you see the advantages more clearly now.'

'It's an excellent scheme,' said Roger, wringing his hand enthusiastically, 'and I hope you'll get sound political backing for it . . . and now if you'll excuse me . . . urgent business . . .'

He moved toward Madog, succeeded in prying him away from the Irishmen, and asked, 'Does it matter that Dic Sharp's here?'

'Why should it matter?' said Madog. 'Tonight, what *could* matter?'

Roger gestured. 'But he has – so many enemies here –'

'The men of Gwynedd,' said Madog, 'are not bearers of grudges. They'll fight if they have to, like wild cats. But they would always rather drink with a man than fight with him.' To illustrate his point, he tossed back a glass of wine. 'Even Dic Sharp is welcome here tonight. All grudges are buried. The auction room was the conference-table. There, the chiefs held their last palaver.' He slipped back into Cherokee imagery. 'The tasselled pipe of peace went from hand to hand. The paleface marvelled . . .'

Roger saw that there was nothing for it but to leave Madog to his high rhapsodic thoughts. He turned away, and as he did so he realized that Dic Sharp had seen him and was making his way slowly but determinedly through the crowded room toward him. His muscles stiffened involuntarily. Was the man coming to attack him? As he came closer, Roger saw that he held a bottle of champagne in one hand and a glass in the other. Champagne, eh? Was he going to perform the time-honoured gesture of throwing his glassful in Roger's face?

But Dic Sharp was smiling shyly. 'Have a glass of champagne,' he said to Roger. 'Go on, there's some clean glasses on that table there.'

Roger picked up one and held it out to be filled. 'I didn't know there was any champagne going,' he said.

'There wasn't,' said Dic Sharp. 'Till I arrived with a dozen bottles. It's my contribution to the party.'

Roger drank deeply. 'It's good,' he said.

'Bollinger, Special Cuvée,' said Dic Sharp. 'It's not the best in the world, but it's the best you can get in this town.'

Roger drank off the rest of his glass, and his eye met Dic Sharp's. 'All right,' he said. 'Now tell me why you felt the impulse to come to the celebration and bring a dozen bottles of Bollinger as a contribution to it. You must know what they're celebrating.'

Dic Sharp turned his head this way and that, casting an eye round the room. Everywhere, people were laughing, joking, emptying glasses. The quick, jerky movements of his head made him look more than ever like a rooster, but the expression in his eyes, as he turned them back to Roger, was not a hard, empty cock-stare. It was grave, compassionate, ironic.

'I'll tell you why,' he said. 'I feel so sorry for the poor devils.'

'Sorry for them?'

'Aye, man,' cried Dic Sharp. 'They're such pitiful bloody fools. They don't know enough to wipe their own noses. And after all they are my own fellow-townsmen. I've known them all my life. When I see them being so helpless and bloody silly, I could weep over them.'

The effrontery of this, even coming from a man from whom he expected nothing but effrontery, set Roger back on his heels. He rapidly poured himself another glass of Bollinger, Special Cuvée.

'You feel an urge to look after them?' he asked.

'I wouldn't go that far,' said Dic Sharp. 'But it makes me sad to see how incapable they are of looking after themselves.'

'So that's the line you've decided to take. You did all you could to be a wise shepherd, but the flock insisted on straying.'

'A goat got in among them,' said Dic Sharp, eyeing Roger sadly.

'Well,' said Roger grimly, 'you certainly did everything you could to get rid of the goat, I'll say that for you.'

'Pity it didn't work,' said Dic Sharp gently. 'If those boys could have taught you the lesson you needed, up there on the mountain –'

'Or if I'd broken my neck when the wheel flew off that hired car,' Roger put in, his voice bitter in spite of his effort to keep it light.

'Yes, if any of those little measures had succeeded, everybody round here'd be in a much better position tonight. And all this –' Dic Sharp waved in the direction of the guffawing, chattering throng –'would be unnecessary.'

'Why the hell shouldn't they enjoy themselves a bit ?'

'Because it's all an illusion, that's why. They'd be better off facing facts. Look, Mr Englishman, do you know why I sold those buses back today? Eleven thousand pounds I cleared, what with the buses and the stock and the garage leases. That eleven thousand goes back into my business to work for me, rather than being tied up by obstinate one-eyed little people who won't budge an inch. Now get this straight. I'd soon have made them budge. The fight was only just beginning. I'd have had you and Gareth Jones out of here like a couple of magpies out of a nest. But I got certain information,' Dic Sharp leaned forward and put his face close to Roger's, at the same time glancing to right and left out of the corners of his eyes, 'certain information that showed me in a flash that I'd be wasting my money and time putting them into buses anyway.'

'Don't tell me, let me guess. The whole shebang is going to be taken over by the government, the managing director of the General Bus Company has defenestrated himself from the fifteenth floor of the office building, state permits to ride on buses will be sold only at Post Offices, and anyone trying to run a bus for private profit will be sent to a penal settlement in the Hebrides.'

'Very clever,' said Dic Sharp, nodding contemptuously. 'Very clever, and just about bloody right. You see all these chaps here ? Cock-a-hoop because they've got their funny little buses back? Well, in less than twelve months' time they'll be bought out whether they like it or not. Nationalized. It'll all come under one board and any idea of competition'll be dead.'

'I thought everybody knew that already.'

'It's been in the air for years,' said Dic Sharp. 'But there's so much government interference in everything now, stopping and starting and bloody well backfiring, that nobody believes anything till it happens. Well, I've seen the details. I'm in the know. I see to that, with my contacts.'

'Of course,' said Roger. 'Your contacts. Mustn't forget those.'

'It'd surprise you to know who some of my contacts are,' said Dic Sharp. 'I pay them good money to keep me informed.

There's more than one chap drawing a nice little salary from me, as a consultant. Just pin money, isn't it? A hundred, two hundred pounds a quarter. But it stops if any quarter goes by when I don't get an inside tip from them on the way things are going.'

Roger realized for the first time that Dic Sharp was slightly drunk. He had reached the stage in which a man's wishes and his reality become subtly interlaced by alcohol. This business of retaining consultants – was it pure fantasy? Something he had always planned to do when he got big enough?'

'You don't seem to believe me,' said Dic Sharp. An aggrieved look, of the kind so frequent among men who have drunk rather too much, came into his face. 'I suppose you want to go on thinking you've scored a great victory. Thinking you've pushed me over. Well, I don't let people push me over. I'll prove it now, right away.' He took Roger's sleeve between thumb and forefinger. 'Come over this side of the room. There's someone you know. You can ask *him*.'

'Someone I know?' said Roger. He looked toward the door, where the party which had come in with Dic Sharp was still mainly concentrated. A small table had been set up, and the dozen bottles of champagne set out on it. Bending over the bottles, examining their labels, was the youth Cedric, whom Roger had seen before in Dic Sharp's company. In profile, tilting her head back as she drank off a glass, was Dic Sharp's heavily handsome blonde wife. A little beyond them, Roger saw the sweaty face of Donald Fisher. He had cornered the Canadian André, and was obviously giving him a good working-over. *Vive l'opportunisme!* Standing near Donald Fisher, facing him and with his back to Roger, stood another man who had something familiar about his shoulders, the back of his neck, the carriage of his head. Yes, it was Gerald Twyford.

What was he doing here? Had he come to persecute Jenny? To try to ruin Roger's moment of triumph? Roger's eyes searched the room. Jenny was safely away in a far corner, being talked to in a whirlwind of affirmatory gestures by Mario. She did not seem to have noticed Twyford; her attention was wholly taken up by Mario. Perhaps all would yet be well. As for himself, Roger cared nothing for the presence of Twyford. He felt large, generous, a giant in the moment of his victory.

Dic Sharp pulled Roger steadily across the room towards Twyford. They passed Mrs Dic Sharp, who ignored Roger entirely, and Cedric, who gave him a quick, interested glance and quickly turned away.

'Here's somebody I think you know, Mr Twyford,' said Dic Sharp, indicating Roger. His tone was neutral, his face expressionless, but Roger saw at once that his motive in bringing the two of them together was malicious. Naturally he would have heard the gossip. Perhaps he was hoping to involve the two of them in a brawl that would wreck the evening.

Twyford, however, looked at Roger indifferently, almost sleepily. All he said was, 'Yes, I know him.'

'You can confirm what I've just been telling him,' said Dic Sharp with slightly drunken insistence. 'He doesn't believe it from me. He still thinks these chaps have got something to celebrate about.'

'Celebrate?' said Twyford with a shrug. 'They're toads under a harrow. The harrow's been lifted for a moment, before it starts going in a new direction. That's all they've got to celebrate.'

'I was never so bethumped with rural metaphors,' said Roger. 'In this very hotel, when I first met Dic – our friend here,' he realized that he did not know Dic Sharp's real name. Was his surname actually Sharp? No, surely that must be a cognomen, an attribute-name. His surname must surely be Jones, like everybody else's. 'When we first talked together, he told me that Gareth was like a hedgehog that's run over by a car. Now you tell me that all these people are like toads under a harrow, I suppose one could go on: they're birds poisoned by chemical spray on the hedges, they're trout dying in a polluted river, they're seagulls with oiled wings after a leaky tanker has passed that way.'

'And you're a gallant conservationist,' said Twyford, his spectacles flashing pure scorn, 'fighting a rear-guard action for them.'

'Tell him,' said Dic Sharp eagerly. 'Tell him what you told me about the new government plan.'

'It's simply that all this clutter's going to be swept away,' said Twyford. 'Some economic sense is going to be brought into the mess and muddle. Of course there'll be the usual fandango from the nationalists if the regional authority is sited in England, so it's just possible they'll make that much concession and site it in Wrexham or somewhere. But within a year, all these chaps will have been bought up, so they might as well have sat on their hands now.'

'I don't agree with you,' said Roger, 'but I hardly expect you to care whether I agree with you or not.'

'Frankly,' said Twyford, 'for me you don't exist. You're just a hole into which my wife and family have fallen. I'm arranging a rig to pull them out.'

'All right, go ahead and salve your pride. Get what the law allows you in the way of access to your children, and what harm you do them I'll try to remedy, with their mother's help. And now let's drop that subject.'

'Willingly.'

Donald Fisher now approached them. He had an air of lip-licking inquisitiveness, which gave place to one of disappointment when he saw that Roger and Twyford were not at each other's throats.

'Well, you must admit, Gerald,' he said. 'I wasn't exaggerating when I told you everyone would be here.'

'I wouldn't have let you drag me here,' said Twyford, 'if I'd had anything better to do, but that much at least I can grant you. Everybody's here.' He looked round with weary distaste. 'Thank God I'll be in New York next week.'

'Don't forget to give my messages,' said Fisher quickly.

'Furnivall here was just telling me,' said Twyford, 'that he doesn't agree with my reading of the local economic situation.'

'I said nothing of the kind.'

'I said these men had nothing to celebrate about and you said you didn't agree with that.'

'Economic factors aren't the only things people can celebrate about,' said Roger.

'Here we go again,' Twyford sighed.

'No,' said Roger, looking at him attentively for perhaps the first, certainly the last, time. 'We don't go again. I've nothing to say. I'm not going to bore you.'

'Meaning, of course, that I wouldn't understand?'

'Oh, I don't underestimate you. I know a clever man when I see one. But Twyford, we all die. And death alters everything.'

'How apocalyptic,' Donald Fisher chortled, glancing sideways at Twyford to make sure that he was earning his approval. 'We don't keep company with poets for nothing.'

Roger moved away. As he did so, a young woman passed close by him – almost, in her single-mindedness, pushed past him – on her way to the table where the dwindling stock of champagne was still laid out. Roger's eyes rested on this person for a second or two, without really registering her. He had never seen her before, but then in the large crowd there were a number of people he had never seen before. She was short, with red hair and pouting, almost bee-stung lips. She might have been the girl-friend of one of the foreign poets. Or just a local girl who had found out that there was some champagne to be had for nothing. She flickered into Roger's field of vision and out again, leaving no impression.

Roger was moving toward Jenny. He could see her, in the distance, being plied with drink by Mario. He could see that Mario was interested in her; perhaps he was about to take this opportunity of inviting her to go for a walk with him round the battlements, or come for a drive up into the mountains in his car. Mario was well looked after by a shapely black-haired wife, but every man liked an occasional change from meat and potatoes. Except me, Roger thought. I shan't ever want a change. He felt sympathetic towards Mario, but moved across the room to break it up before he started pinching Jenny's behind. He was halted after a few paces, however, by the immovable bulk of Gareth.

Gareth wore his shiny old leather jerkin. His face was flushed, and his eyes in their shadowy sockets seemed to absorb light and hold it in deep, still pools. He was very happy.

Gareth, said Roger. He put his hand on one of Gareth's great shoulders. It felt as hard as a rock of the mountains. It's after ten o'clock, he said.

Extension tonight, said Gareth. We're not going up till ten-thirty. I announced it on the bus going down. And I'm paying a lad five shillings to sit in the bus and tell any strays that come along. They can wait a few minutes on this night of all nights. The pubs are only just closing, and if they're women and don't want to go in the pub they can sit in the nice warm bus and do some knitting.

This, for Gareth, was a long speech. It was the measure of his expansiveness.

Well, said Roger, looking at his watch, it's half-past ten now, gaffer.

That's all over now, Roger, said Gareth softly. He put out his big leathery hand.

Roger put his own hand into the crushing grip.

It's never over, Gareth, he said. You'll always be my gaffer.

As Gareth's hand closed, the agony in Roger's fingers swamped every other thought. It seemed like five minutes before Gareth slowly relaxed the pressure, nodded slowly, and turned. Roger stood for a moment watching his great misshapen back, cased in that familiar jerkin, moving away toward the door. The bus would be waiting, out in the windy square.

Then Gareth was gone and a great chunk of Roger's life was over.

He moved to where Jenny stood, close up against the endlessly rolling gin-mill of Mario's conversation. She was smiling, but edging slowly away, and she caught sight of him with well-suppressed relief. 'Ah, there you are, Roger,' she said. 'Mario's been explaining to me about the new order that's coming in Wales.'

'Tonight is the beginning,' said Mario, beaming. It was impossible not to like him. 'Back to the Wales of the bards. The courts of the princes. The wheel turns, it comes round again. Madog is the new Dafydd ap Gwilym.'

'I'll go along with that,' said Roger. He took Jenny's arm and deftly guided her away. 'Excuse me a minute, Mario bach. There's something I need to tell Jenny.'

He moved her a little way off among the joking, jostling mob. 'This is what I need to tell you,' he said. 'First, that I love you. Second, that your husband's here.'

She looked about quickly. 'Where? Do I have to talk to him?'

'Of course not. As far as I can tell, he hasn't even come with that in mind. My guess is that Donald Fisher, who's also here, wanted to crash the party so that he could scrape acquaintance with anyone who might be useful, and he lacked the nerve to do it on his own so he got Gerald to come along for moral support.'

'Of course,' she said, 'Fisher would change overnight. He's been sneering at people like Madog for years, but when they finally get recognition and money on their side, he comes flapping in like a carrion crow.'

'Another rural metaphor,' said Roger.

'I don't know what you mean about that, but never mind. Listen, have you talked to Gerald?'

'Yes.'

'What did he say?'

'He talked economics at me. Dic Sharp style.'

She tossed her head impatiently. 'What do you mean? How could he have done?'

'Just like that. Dic Sharp took me up to talk to him with a kind of ambiguous half-hint that he employed Gerald, or at any rate chaps as big as Gerald, to give him inside dope from the board-rooms and the corridors of Westminster. I don't know whether I believe him and I'm not interested enough to check on it. Anyway. Up we march to Gerald. Go on, tell him, Mr Twyford, says Dic Sharp, tell him all these chaps are sitting on a branch that's half sawn through. They're all glad to see their buses again and in another few months they'll be bought out compulsorily and that's why I'm too fly to invest any capital in buses. Quite right, says Gerald, it's all over with them and it's nothing but what they deserve.'

'And what did you say?'

'I?' said Roger. 'I just told him that death changes all.'

'I see,' said Jenny. 'Give me a drink and tell me what you meant exactly.'

He found her a glass of white wine. 'I couldn't spell it out to him, but I can spell it out to you easily enough. You see, it's a question of the gulf between people like Gerald and Dic Sharp, on the one hand, and people like these on the other.' He indicated the party in general.

'Who, the bus men or the poets?'

'Both. There's no essential difference because they're all men who do their own work. They don't manipulate, blueprint, sit at the top and arrange for the people underneath them to do the job. They do it themselves, they sweat and get their hands dirty.'

'Yes; and so?'

'And so, they don't see things impersonally. To them, the struggle of life is a series of contests which they personally fight, and which they personally win or lose. It's a struggle for the Dic Sharps and the Geralds, too, but they have a different attitude. They're like statesmen whose country is at war. Or like field-marshals who work with statesmen. Their attitude is that the individual battle doesn't matter – only the final result of the war, and the settlement round the table at the peace conference.'

'And death,' she said. 'How does that come in?'

'Because if there were no death, if that last personal defeat weren't waiting for each one of us, the field-marshal view would be a possible one. But since death does exist, it's the other type who have the wisdom. The type whose attitude isn't that of a field-marshal but of a soldier of the line. Every battle, every skirmish in every battle, every hand-to-hand struggle round a slit trench, is a separate episode. A separate victory for one, a separate defeat for another. They're not tempted to add it up. They live from day to day, from one clash with the enemy to the next. That's why they're rejoicing now. They're not fools – they don't think their troubles are over. They know their lives will be one struggle after another, and at the end of it, every one of them will lose, because death will cut him down. There'll always be that one last fight that no created being can win. So when they've had a hard day's fight and won some ground that they can see, they rejoice and enjoy themselves and take a drink when it's offered them. Look at them, girl, and tell me if they aren't right.'

'Yes,' she said. 'They're right.'

Gito, his bald head gleaming like a dome of Italian marble, passed by them with an empty glass in his hand.

Enjoy yourself, Roger, he called. No sad thoughts on St David's day, man.

'Was I thinking sad thoughts?' Roger asked Jenny.

'No, funny darling old you. Just serious ones.'

Jenny had been wearing her glasses. She now took them off and put them in her handbag. Roger was beginning to recognize this as a sign that she felt herself relaxing, going off duty, ready to turn to thoughts of recreation and happiness. She looked up, now, and caught Roger watching her.

'What are you thinking?' she asked, laying a hand gently on his lapel.

'You'd slap my face if I told you.'

She smiled. 'And when the party's over, what are you planning to do, Mr Furnivall?'

He answered the question quite straight. 'I shall stay here. The chapel's all closed up. My Llancrwys *villeggiatura* is over. I tried to get a room in the hotel, but Rhiannon told me there wasn't even a bathroom to sleep in. It's bursting at the seams. So I shall flop down in an armchair in the lounge or something. Unless, of course . . .'

'Unless?'

'Unless I know a kind person with a suite who'll give me a corner of the carpet to sleep on.'

'Try asking me when the time comes,' she said. 'I might be able to do better than a corner of the carpet.'

When the time came, Roger asked her. And later, when they were drifting to sleep in one another's arms, he murmured into her ear, 'What about the kids?'

'What about them?' she said into her pillow.

'They'll come in and find us in the morning.'

'Well,' she said, gently yawning and wrapping herself more closely round him, 'they'll just have to get used to that. From now on, they'll be finding us *every* morning.'

After breakfast the next day, Roger came out of the lift at the Palace Hotel, carrying two suitcases. They were moving out. Jenny was gathering up the children's odds and ends and he had gone ahead to get these two suitcases strapped on to the luggage rack of the Mini.

He went out of the back door of the hotel and carried the suitcases over to where the car waited under cover of a corrugated iron roof. As he did so, his mind went back to his first evening here. He had stood, disconsolate and lonely, looking out through that door into the rainy yard, wondering if he would be able to stand the boredom. He heard again the pop-pop of Beverley's motor-scooter, turning in to the hotel yard in the curving rain. Bless the girl, after all; without her, he might never have met Gareth.

He fixed the cases securely on to the roof-rack and turned to go back to Jenny and the children. At that moment, the short young woman with red hair, whom he had glimpsed at the party last night, came briskly out of the hotel and unlocked the door of a Porsche that stood near Jenny's little car. She pushed in a suitcase, walked round to the door on the driver's side, unlocked that and got in. Roger, his attention caught by a stylish car, watched as the girl reversed smartly into the middle of the yard, turned in a tight half-circle, and drove out. The car was new and shiny. Its exhaust gave a series of rasping snorts as the red-haired girl changed gear and disappeared among the traffic.

The red-haired girl was Fräulein Inge. Roger could not be blamed for not recognizing her, since he had always imagined Fräulein Inge as a tall, willowy blonde, with a thin mouth and a bad-tempered expression. The real Fräulein Inge had none of these attributes except the last. And even this faded from her face as she drove the Porsche out of the town and up the mountain road towards Llancrwys.

Fräulein Inge was in a good mood. Things had been going well for her of late. She had quarrelled with Mr Robertson in Morocco, and though she had given him the impression that things had been patched up, she had decided privately that she would leave him. She had met, that winter in sun-dried North Africa, a much more satisfactory man. This citizen had a small but respectable private income, and contributed small but respectable art criticism to several small but respectable papers. He had, for whatever reason, bestowed some praise on Fräulein Inge's gifts as a painter, and their acquaintanceship had flowered rapidly. This man lived in London: to be precise, in Baron's Court, where he had a small but not irksomely respectable maisonette. In this maisonette Fräulein Inge was preparing to join him, at his pressing invitation. The invitation had not been for a stated period, and she felt she would not mind if it turned out to be for life. However, like a sensible Northern European, she was prepared to cross that bridge when she came to it.

Fräulein Inge was a good driver, and the Porsche hugged the road as it rounded the tight curves round which Gareth's bus was accustomed to crawl in first gear. The road vanished under its eager, shark-like snout, and Fräulein Inge rested one elbow on the window-sill and hummed a little song. The Porsche was a present from Mr Robertson. It had been waiting for her when she got back to England, and one of her reasons for keeping Mr Robertson in the dark about her intentions had been a very natural wish to say nothing to upset him until she had taken delivery of the Porsche. It would make a nice going-away present. Altogether, the spring sunshine shone brightly on Fräulein Inge. The winter had been very satisfactory; the new season was opening out. She would stay at the chapel for a few days, or a week at the most, putting her belongings in order, packing up her canvases, leaving a short note of dismissal for Mr Robertson, and then hey for the glittering cosmopolitan world of Baron's Court.

As Fräulein Inge reached the cross-roads in the middle of Llancrwys, Roger was just coming out of the suite which Madog had hired for Jenny. Mary and Robin were hopping about, carrving some of their toys in gaily-coloured paper bags, and Jenny, her arms barely meeting round a stack of paraphernalia, brought up the rear.

'Are we going on a big train?' Robin was asking.

'Of course we are, silly,' said Mary. 'Little trains don't go to London.'

'But we shan't have any lunch,' said Robin. His underlip began to turn outward. 'I'll be hungry. We'll be in the train all day. You said.'

'I've got good news about that,' said Roger. 'On these big trains, there's a special car where you can go and have lunch. There are tables and tablecloths and knives and forks and glasses and nice waiters who come and ask you what you want.'

Robin thought. 'Is it hot or cold? The food they give you?'

'Both, but mostly hot.'

'Where do they keep it hot? In the engine?'

'No,' said Roger. He pressed the button to summon the lift. 'They have a stove, yes, actually a kitchen on the train. I'll show you. They cook the meals as the train goes along, and when it's ready they ring a bell and you go and have it. You'll see. It's marvellous fun.'

'Can you have pie?' asked Robin.

'Yes.'

'And cheese? And fish cakes? And potatoes and . . .'

Both children began, in high, sing-song voices, to enumerate every comestible they had ever heard of. Roger kept nodding and saying 'Yes.'

Jenny, clutching her great armful of impedimenta, came and stood close to him. 'Think you'll be good at this?'

'I'll be marvellous at it. I want to add to the team. At least another six.'

'After last night,' she said, nuzzling him, 'you'll probably get them all at once.'

'Will there be cherries? And dripping? And fish fingers? And doughnuts?' (Yes, yes.) 'Will there be Christmas pudding?' (Yes, at Christmas.) 'Will there be . . .' They went on and on.

The lift arrived. Roger suddenly had a powerful feeling that something was turning over in the pit of his stomach. He knew that once the doors of the lift opened and they all got in, a new life would begin for every one of them.

'You can have anything,' he said to the children.

'Can we have ice cream?'

'You can if you start out by eating plenty of things that are good for you.' Swiftly, he bent and kissed them. 'When you live with me,' he said, 'I'll see that you get lots of everything that's good for you.'

'Me too?' Jenny asked.

'You too,' he promised.

The doors of the lift were open. They all got in and Roger pressed the button.

Up on the mountain, Fräulein Inge unlocked the door of the empty chapel.

More about Penguins
and Pelicans

A Kind of Loving

Stan Barstow

The magnificent first novel by a Yorkshire miner's son ...

A young man is physically infatuated with a girl he
doesn't love. Inevitably he gets caught, for miracles only
happen in fairy tales. His struggles to find a solution to a
classic problem are told by Stan Barstow with a realism
and honesty that put his first novel into a class of its own.

About a Marriage

Giles Gordon

About a Marriage tells of the very basic emotions which afflict
a young husband as he struggles to understand the
incomprehensible : the needs of the girl he married, her urge
to bear children, the frightening range of her happiness and
despair. It is the story of a young man in a permissive
age, trying to justify his belief in marriage – an everyday
occurrence, endlessly fascinating, endlessly changeable.
Strindberg was obsessed by it, Albee probed it, Penelope
Mortimor mourned it. Now, in Giles Gordon's novel comes
a fresh masculine viewpoint which makes an original
contribution to an explosive subject.

Hurry on Down

John Wain

The book that was the pioneer of the new kind of
English novel which appeared in the fifties, linking the
names of John Wain, Kingsley Amis, Iris Murdoch, and
later John Braine.

'*Hurry On Down*, a young man's first novel, is a
bustling kaleidoscope of a book, by an author fertile
in expedient, keenly observant and occasionally probing
the heart of darkness' – *Sunday Times*

Not for sale in the U.S.A.

The Contenders

John Wain

Robert Lamb and Ned Roper lived to outdo one another.
It had been friendly rivalry at school in the Potteries,
but age gave an edge to the competition between the
passionate artist and the calculating businessman.
Dead-heating in the success stakes, the two fought it out
over a woman. And amiable Joe Shaw was left to pick
up the bits.

Not for sale in the U.S.A.

The Smaller Sky

John Wain

Arthur Geary left his wife and two children and went to
live on Paddington Station. It was the only place he could
get away from the sounds of the terrible drums; where he
could feel comfortably anonymous, safe and calm under
a smaller sky. But they had to hound him out. They had
to know why. They had to prove him mad; friends,
family, psychiatrist, even a TV journalist after the
ultimate tragic scoop.

Not for sale in the U.S.A.

Death of the Hind Legs
and other stories

John Wain

In John Wain's stories the characters inhabit worlds of
sadness, loss and disappointment. Sometimes they win.
They always get wiser.

What would they have thought if they'd seen Williams
talking out loud to a tree that wasn't there? But there
was now something else in that garden even more
compelling than the tree that was planted the day he
was born.

Dannie couldn't start looking for a new pair of hind
legs at this stage of the game. They were demolishing
the theatre straight after the last performance, so the
fact that the back end of the pantomime horse had a
heart attack in the middle of the show didn't add all
that much to his worries.

Fred was strong but dim. If he set himself up as an
all-in wrestler fighting in rigged bouts he could get
eighty quid a week to stop Doreen nagging him. So enter
King Caliban and a new Fred who stopped everyone in
their tracks.

Not for sale in the U.S.A.